P9-CDE-723

THE JEWELED SPUR

GILBERT MORRIS

CARMEL • NEW YORK 10512

Cover by Dan Thornberg

This Guideposts edition published by special
arrangement with Bethany House Publishers.

Printed in the United States of America

Library of Congress Cataloging-in-Publication Data

Morris, Gilbert.
   The jeweled spur / Gilbert Morris.
      p. cm. — (The House of Winslow ; bk. 16)

    1. Frontier and pioneer life—West (U.S.)—Fiction. 2. Man-
woman relationships—West (U.S.)—Fiction. 3. Young women—
West (U.S.)—Fiction. I. Title. II. Series: Morris, Gilbert. House of
Winslow ; bk. 16.
PS3563.08742J48   1994
813'.54—dc20   94–27179
ISBN 1–55661–392–X   CIP

This book is dedicated to Paul and Mary Root.

A man loses many things as time washes away the years—
but the memories of the fine times
we've had together are safe—
locked up in my heart along with all the other good things!

THE HOUSE OF WINSLOW SERIES

★ ★ ★ ★

1. *The Honorable Imposter*
2. *The Captive Bride*
3. *The Indentured Heart*
4. *The Gentle Rebel*
5. *The Saintly Buccaneer*
6. *The Holy Warrior*
7. *The Reluctant Bridegroom*
8. *The Last Confederate*
9. *The Dixie Widow*
10. *The Wounded Yankee*
11. *The Union Belle*
12. *The Final Adversary*
13. *The Crossed Sabres*
14. *The Valiant Gunman*
15. *The Gallant Outlaw*
16. *The Jeweled Spur*

GILBERT MORRIS spent ten years as a pastor before becoming Professor of English at Ouachita Baptist University in Arkansas and earning a Ph.D. at the University of Arkansas. During the summers of 1984 and 1985 he did postgraduate work at the University of London and is presently the Chairman of General Education at a Christian college in Louisiana. A prolific writer, he has had over 25 scholarly articles and 200 poems published in various periodicals, and over the past years has had more than 20 novels published. His family includes three grown children, and he and his wife live in Baton Rouge, Louisiana.

CONTENTS

PART ONE
LAURIE

1. Apaches 17
2. Visit to Wyoming 29
3. The Legacy 41
4. Journey to Omaha 53
5. Laurie Finds a Teacher 65
6. The Desire of the Heart 77

PART TWO
CODY ROGERS

7. The Way of a Woman 93
8. No Quarter Given 105
9. Cody Loses Out 115
10. Cody's Day in Court 129
11. Behind the Wall 139
12. Race With Death 149

PART THREE
THE FUGITIVE

13. A New Friend..163
14. Buffalo Bill Takes a Fall............................173
15. The Net Closes......................................185
16. End of the *Dixie Queen* 199
17. Cody Finds a Place 211

PART FOUR
BUFFALO BILL'S WILD WEST SHOW

18. Sitting Bull..225
19. Little Sure Shot....................................237
20. "You Listen to Me Preach—
    And I'll Watch You Shoot!" 247
21. Cody Goes to Church 257
22. All Kinds of Love..................................267
23. "I Can't Do It!"...................................279
24. A Matter of Faith 289

THE HOUSE OF WINSLOW

★ ★ ★ ★

THE HOUSE OF WINSLOW

★ ★ ★ ★

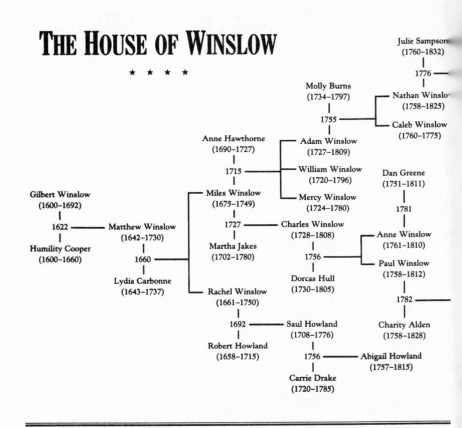

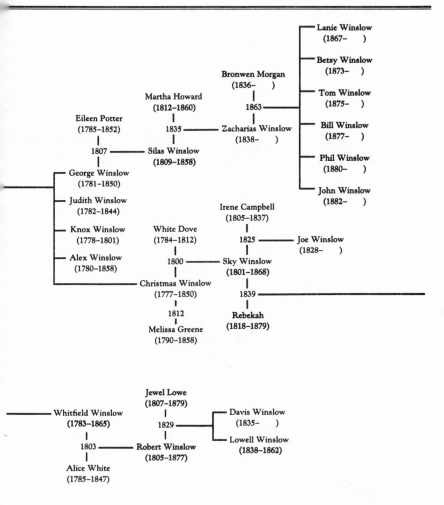

Lanie Winslow
(1867–   )

Betsy Winslow
(1873–   )

Bronwen Morgan
(1836–   )

Tom Winslow
(1875–   )

Martha Howard
(1812–1860)

1863 ─────────

Bill Winslow
(1877–   )

1835 ───────── Zacharias Winslow
(1838–   )

Eileen Potter
(1785–1852)

Phil Winslow
(1880–   )

1807 ───────── Silas Winslow
(1809–1858)

John Winslow
(1882–   )

George Winslow
(1781–1850)

Irene Campbell
(1805–1837)

Judith Winslow
(1782–1844)

White Dove
(1784–1812)

1825 ───────── Joe Winslow
(1828–   )

Knox Winslow
(1778–1801)

1800 ───────── Sky Winslow
(1801–1868)

Alex Winslow
(1780–1858)

Christmas Winslow
(1777–1850)

1839 ─────────────────────────

1812

Rebekah
(1818–1879)

Melissa Greene
(1790–1858)

Jewel Lowe
(1807–1879)

Davis Winslow
(1835–   )

Whitfield Winslow
(1783–1865)

1829 ─────────

Lowell Winslow
(1838–1862)

1803 ───────── Robert Winslow
(1805–1877)

Alice White
(1785–1847)

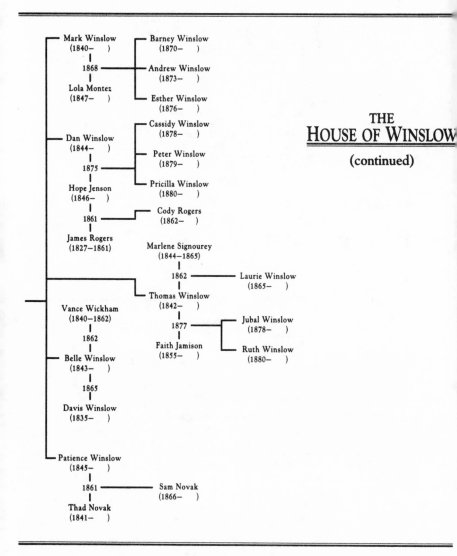

Mark Winslow
(1840–)

1868

Lola Montez
(1847–)

Barney Winslow
(1870–)

Andrew Winslow
(1873–)

Esther Winslow
(1876–)

Dan Winslow
(1844–)

1875

Hope Jenson
(1846–)

1861

James Rogers
(1827–1861)

Cassidy Winslow
(1878–)

Peter Winslow
(1879–)

Pricilla Winslow
(1880–)

Cody Rogers
(1862–)

Marlene Signourey
(1844–1865)

1862

Thomas Winslow
(1842–)

1877

Faith Jamison
(1855–)

Laurie Winslow
(1865–)

Jubal Winslow
(1878–)

Ruth Winslow
(1880–)

Vance Wickham
(1840–1862)

1862

Belle Winslow
(1843–)

1865

Davis Winslow
(1835–)

Patience Winslow
(1845–)

1861

Thad Novak
(1841–)

Sam Novak
(1866–)

PART ONE

LAURIE

★ ★ ★ ★

CHAPTER ONE

APACHES!

★ ★ ★ ★

The Apache made no more noise than the white cloud that drifted across the hard, blue Arizona sky.

Only the sound of the gelding's steel-clad hooves—a sharp clicking on the feldspar floor of the desert—disturbed the silence of the land. The rhythm of the horse's gait had made Laurie Winslow sleepy, and her eyes were half-shut against the rays of the burning yellow sun.

There was no warning—except for a jackrabbit that popped up suddenly, his ridiculously long ears flopping wildly as he zigzagged around rocks and disappeared into a small patch of yucca cactus.

One moment Laurie had been smiling, thinking of something her father had said; the next, the sudden appearance of the rabbit jerked her out of her somnambulant doze—which may have saved her life. She had been taught better. Her father had warned her many times: *Don't take it for granted that there's nothing behind that innocent-looking rock. It may hide a Chiricahua Apache.*

Just as Laurie's head snapped up to catch sight of the vanishing rabbit, a flash of movement drew her eyes to the left. There had been only a stone formation, gray and rounded by a hundred years of weather, but just as Laurie whirled around, an Indian erupted from behind it!

He was small and wiry, as were most Apaches, dressed in a shirt, breechclout, and moccasins with leggings folded down. A headband rested on jet black hair, and his eyes glittered as he threw himself at the horse. He moved faster than a striking snake, closing the distance between him and the startled girl in two bounds. His hand grabbed for the bridle even as Laurie drove her spurs into Star's flanks.

The powerful black horse let out a shrill cry, lunging forward with a force that snapped Laurie's neck—but the Indian was too quick. His fingers just missing the bridle, he caught the saddle horn with his left hand as his right clamped down like a vise on Laurie's arm. The force of his grip pulled the girl half out of the saddle, but she was a strong-nerved young woman. Knowing what would happen to her if she lost her saddle, she reacted by grabbing the small .38 her father insisted she carry.

Even as she drew the pistol, the strength of the Indian's grip pulled her off balance. Looking down, she saw the evil leer on his broad lips. He cried something in Apache she didn't understand, but the cruel, metallic glint in his black eyes left no doubt of his intentions.

She was falling as she lifted the pistol, swung it over, and pulled the trigger. At once the smashing sound of the explosion was followed by a cry of pain and rage. Star gave a tremendous bound, almost causing Laurie to fall the rest of the way, but then she grabbed the saddle horn and pulled herself back into the saddle. Twisting around, she saw the Indian scrambling to his feet and felt a rush of relief that she hadn't killed him.

But as she watched, another Apache stepped from behind a cactus, lifted a rifle, and fired. Instantly Laurie felt a white-hot burning high on her right side and knew that she'd been hit. Ignoring the pain, she managed to turn and fire three shots at the pair. She must have come close, for the Indian with the rifle dodged to one side and did no more shooting.

As Star pounded across the desert at a dead run, Laurie looked back and saw that the two had mounted their ponies and were in pursuit. "Come on, Star!" she shouted to the gelding, leaning low over the saddle and moving in rhythm with the animal. She was four miles from the fort, but she knew that the Indians would not follow close enough to chance an encounter with a patrol of troopers. She also knew that the scrubby Indian ponies could never catch her—not when she was mounted on a horse like Star.

By the time she crested a low hill and the walls of the stockade came into view, she saw no more of the Apaches when she looked back over her shoulder. Slowing Star to a trot, then a walk, she took a shaky breath. The suddenness of the attack and the short, vicious struggle had left her no time to be afraid; but now that the danger was over, the reaction set in. Her stomach wanted to erupt and a sense of nausea swept over her as Star champed at the bit, ready to run for the fort and his dinner. Looking down, Laurie saw that her hands were trembling violently. A light-headed sensation made her reel slightly in the saddle, but she fought against it.

A streak of pain from her right side made her grimace, and she stopped Star and pulled her shirt up. The bullet had raked across her side, gouging out a small track that was bleeding. Pulling out her handkerchief, she pressed it against the wound, then pulled her shirt down, clamping her arm tightly against it.

Holding Star back to a walk to give herself more time before entering the fort, she took a deep breath and expelled it slowly, feeling the trembling and the nausea pass away. *Better!* she thought with relief. But as she approached the gate, one question loomed before her: *What will I tell Dad?*

As the guards swung open the gate and she rode inside, Laurie knew she had to tell him the truth about what happened. *He's trusted me enough to let me ride, so I'll have to be honest with him, even if it means no more riding alone.* She rode across the parade ground, and even troubled as she was over speaking with her father, she glanced around with distaste at Fort Grant.

It was only a shabby collection of buildings, made of warping cottonwood lumber and closely surrounded by a stockade of logs set upright in the ground. Each corner was capped by a small bastion from which sentries might view the surrounding countryside at night. The ground was worn smooth of vegetation, all the living quarters were paintless, their walls pulling apart from the effects of the relentless sun and rain. Fort Grant commanded no more than a wide expanse of desert and broken rock formations, exposed to the full rigors of winter's harsh winds and summer's brutal heat. The walls of the fort were formed by back edges of barracks, storehouses, officers' quarters, and stables, all facing a parade ground where sweating troopers drilled under a blazing summer sun.

As Laurie dismounted in front of headquarters, a wave of despair welled up in her. It was such a forlorn place! There were no diversions, no entertainments, no breaks from her dull and confined life. To the east and west stretched an empty land. Forty miles to the south lay the Indian agency, and much farther to the north lay Phoenix and Prescott—much too far for a casual ride.

Entering her father's office, she was greeted by Corporal Ned Randall. "Well, now, howdy, Miss Laurie." Randall was a skinny man of twenty with rusty hair and light blue eyes. "Enlisted man's dance next month," he said abruptly, adjusting his left arm, which was in a sling. "I'm puttin' my bid in early."

"You're too late, Corporal," Laurie smiled. She was feeling the effects of the bullet wound in her side now, but she clamped her jaw tightly, determined not to show her pain. Laurie was thankful that Ned was too taken with her to notice her injury. "Sergeant Reinman asked me a month ago."

"Aw—!" Randall groaned, letting his thin shoulders slump. Then he brightened up. "How about the Christmas dance? I ain't too late for that, am I?"

"No. I'd be glad to go with you, Ned." Her words pleased the young man, and Laurie was glad. She knew how lonesome it was for the young troopers, and tried to play no favorites. "I need to see my father if he's not too busy."

"Oh, go on in, Miss Laurie—"

Laurie took him at his word, knocked on the door, and entered when she heard, "Come in." Major Tom Winslow was bent over some papers on the battered desk, but when he looked up and saw her, his dark face brightened. "Well, you're back early. Have a good time?" He was a big man with heavy shoulders and the slim flanks of a horseman. At forty-one, his dark hair had no trace of gray, and his blue eyes were alert as he looked at her.

Laurie said at once, "Dad, two Apaches jumped me about four miles from the fort."

Instantly Winslow's pleasant expression grew watchful. "Tell me about it," he said, coming to his feet. He listened intently to her story, then walked to the door and said, "Corporal, have Sergeant Morgan assemble a detail. As soon as they're mounted, I'll give them their orders."

"Yes, sir!"

Turning back to his daughter, Winslow said, "I was afraid of this, Laurie."

"But the Indians have been so peaceful, Dad!"

She made a pretty picture to him as she stood before him. *Got the same black eyes and hair as her mother*, he thought as she spoke. He thought then of Marlene Signourey, his first wife. She'd died at Laurie's birth, and her last words to him had been, "I never loved you, Tom—it was always Spence." But as Winslow looked at Laurie, he realized that somehow he loved her more because her mother had not cared for him. He was not a man who analyzed his own emotions, but he sensed that this young woman would always have some part of his love that he couldn't give to the children he had by his second wife—as much as he adored them.

Suddenly he realized that she was keeping something from him. They'd been closer than other fathers and daughters—mostly because of the demands of his job. He'd been with the Department of Indian Affairs for years after the war and had always taken her with him. Then he'd joined the army, and he'd married Faith and they'd had their own children. But he and Laurie had stayed close, and now he asked directly, "Don't think you can hide anything from your old man! What is it?"

Laurie said weakly, "Well—it's not *serious*, Dad—"

"Suppose you just tell me, and I'll make up my own mind as to how serious it is."

Desperately, Laurie blurted out, "He—he shot at me, and it just scratched—"

"You've been *shot!*"

"Daddy, it's not bad!"

"Where did it get you?"

"Right here—" She lifted her arm to show the shirt, which was caked with blood.

"Come along!"

"Come where?" Laurie gasped as he took her other arm and guided her toward the door.

"To the infirmary, of course!" He gave her a look that was an odd mixture of concern and irritation. Ignoring her protests, he led her toward the infirmary and marched her inside. The surgeon was dozing over a book, but he came to his feet with a bewildered stare as the two entered the office.

"Why, Major Winslow—!"

"Major Stevens, Laurie's been shot," said Winslow.

"What—!" Winslow's words shocked the older man, and his face turned pale. Stevens was in his early sixties and had never been a quick thinker. However, he stiffened and nodded. "Let's have a look, Miss Winslow. Sit up on this table."

Laurie glanced at her father, pleading, "Daddy, it's just a scratch!"

"I'll just have a look at it," Major Stevens said. "Where is it?"

"Here—on my side." Laurie lifted her right arm, and as soon as Stevens saw the blood, his face grew serious. "All right, just slip out of that shirt, Miss Laurie."

Laurie gave the two men an agonized look, her face burning. She saw, however, that there was no escape, so she whispered, "Daddy, will you wait outside—please?"

Tom Winslow stared at her. "As many of your diapers as I've changed—"

"Daddy—*please!*"

"Oh, all right." Winslow wheeled and left the room, realizing that at the age of eighteen Laurie could no longer be handled the same as when she was six. It wasn't the first time it had occurred to him, but somehow it troubled him. *Wish all kids would stay five years old forever,* he thought gravely. *A man can handle them at that age!*

Hearing the sound of horses approach, he stepped outside and shouted out, "Sergeant Morgan—Miss Winslow was jumped by two Indians." He gave the assembled detail the information, then said to the guide, "Luis, try to run them down. I want to make an example of them."

Luis Montoya was a lean, brown man with a sliver of a mustache. "Sí, Major—but you and I, we both know that trying to catch an Apache is like trying to catch yesterday's breeze. But we will try."

After the patrol had ridden out, Winslow returned to the office and paced the floor nervously for five minutes, trying to figure out how to handle the situation. The Indians had been quiet, very quiet indeed—or he would not have allowed Laurie to go to the Masters' ranch on a visit. But he knew Indians and thought, *This might be the beginning of trouble—have to stop it dead in its tracks!* Just then the door opened and Major Stevens nodded. "Not serious, but if it had been an inch or so to the right, it might have been."

A wave of relief swept through Tom Winslow, and he said gustily, "Thank God for that!" Then he straightened his shoulders and took his daughter's arm. "Thanks, Major. Come along, Laurie."

"Will you have to tell Mother?" Laurie asked as they stepped outside.

"Of course!"

When her father spoke that firmly, Laurie knew there was no hope of changing his mind, but she tried anyway. "It'll just worry her, Dad."

Tom Winslow was grateful for Laurie's concern. Faith had been a wonderful mother for the child—had given her the sweetness and gentleness that he could not. He knew that Laurie—except for some natural curiosity about her own mother—had accepted Faith totally. She had begun calling her "Mother" as soon as he and Faith were married, which had pleased his wife very much.

"She'll be worried—but she's got a right to know."

"Yes, sir."

Her tone was so forlorn that Tom abruptly put his arm around her shoulders, squeezing her gently to avoid hurting her. "I was so busy bawling you out that I forgot to say one thing."

Laurie looked up at him, her dark eyes even lovelier for being sad. "One thing? What was that, Daddy?"

"I forgot to say, 'Your dad is very proud of you!' " He smiled as her cheeks colored, adding, "Not one girl in a thousand could have done what you did." They walked along toward the house set apart for the commanding officer. "You've got two things every woman would like to have, Laurie." He paused, and when she looked up at him, her lips parted in expectation, he said fondly, "Beauty and courage."

Laurie was surprised, for her father was not usually so vocal with his praise. She had been told often enough that she was pretty—but since she was the only young woman among two hundred young men, she took all their praise with reserve. "These lonesome soldiers would think any girl who isn't cross-eyed and toothless is pretty," she'd laughed when telling her mother of how one youthful private had finally gotten up enough courage to tell her she looked "pretty fair."

And as for courage? She smiled up at this tall father of hers and said ruefully, "I think it was fear, not courage."

"They go together most of the time," he returned. "Some men—women, too, I guess—seem to be born without a sense of danger. I saw some like that in the war. Walked around with bullets flying everywhere." He grinned, adding, "I always thought trees were meant to hide behind, but those fellows didn't seem to know they could get killed." They had nearly reached the front steps of their house, and the children were running to greet them, so he said quickly, "It's the ones who are afraid but keep on going that I admire."

And then he was assaulted by Jubal, age five, and Ruth, three. Picking them both up, he said, "You two come with me. Your sister's got to have a talk with her mother."

As he walked away, bouncing the children in his arms until they squealed, Laurie realized that he was giving her a chance to tell Faith of the incident in private, knowing that she'd be embarrassed by his presence. *He's so thoughtful!* A warmth rose in her as she entered the house, and she thought, not for the first time, *I hope I get a man like him—but I don't think there are any more!*

★ ★ ★ ★

"Look at that, Tom!" Faith had been bringing the coffeepot to refill her husband's cup. When she stopped abruptly in front of the kitchen window, Winslow rose and came to look over her shoulder. He smiled at the sight of Laurie standing upright on Star's back, arms held up over her head, her long raven hair fluttering back in the breeze. They could hear her clear voice as she called to the children.

Placing his big hands on Faith's shoulders, Tom gently pulled her against him. The clean smell of her hair and the firm pressure of her body pleased him, and he whispered in her ear, "Mrs. Winslow, you're tempting me beyond that which I am able!"

Faith turned and put her arms around his neck. She was, to him, as lovely at twenty-eight as she'd been when he had married her. "You look about sixteen years old," he murmured, bending to kiss her. She clung to him, pleased with the strength of his arms and the ardor of his caress. Then she pushed him back, a glint of humor in her gray eyes. "You get to your soldiering, Major Winslow!" She nodded, then smiled. "We'll continue this conversation at a more suitable time."

Tom continued looking out the window at Laurie. A troubled light touched his dark eyes, and he sighed. He sat back down at the table as Faith first filled his coffee cup, then her own. "You're worried about her, aren't you, Tom?"

He didn't answer at once, but he moved the white coffee mug around in his bronzed hands. The sound of the children's voices floated to him from outside, and his brow creased as he nodded. "Yes," he said slowly, "I am."

"About the Indians who attacked her?"

"Not so much that—though it's serious enough. No more riding without an escort, I've made that plain." He lifted his eyes, studying her thoughtfully, then shrugged his heavy shoulders. "She's not happy here, Faith."

"She doesn't complain."

"We know it's true though."

Faith stirred her coffee with a spoon, thinking of Laurie. She loved Laurie as if she were her own, and for some time had been aware that the girl was going through a rough time. But there had been no remedy, for it was their way of life itself that made Laurie unhappy.

"Do you think this writing thing is good for her?" Tom spoke suddenly, and Faith realized he was not entirely pleased with Laurie's burning desire to become a writer. He saw writing as something that people did who had nothing important to do. He admired Laurie's expert horsemanship more than the pieces she wrote. "What could come of a thing like that?"

"I don't know, Tom." Faith glanced out the window and wondered how much she dared say to this husband of hers. She was a strong-willed woman, but she respected his judgment. He'd given his life to raising Laurie, but now he was troubled and confused by this side of her. *He's afraid for her,* Faith thought, and abruptly she knew she had to speak her own thoughts. "I think it might turn out very well, her writing."

"But—it's not much of a life for a woman, is it?"

"It wouldn't have to be her whole life. She'll meet someone and marry—but this thing is in her, Tom. I've been thinking and praying about it a great deal." Leaning across the table, she put her hand on his arm and squeezed it. "It's a gift from God, I think. And any gift from God can be used to bless others, can't it?"

Tom nodded slowly, absorbing her words. He trusted her judgment, and now recalled the first time he'd met her. She'd been on her way to serve as a missionary to the Indians—with no training at all. But he'd watched her win the respect of the Apaches, and any person who could do that deserved to be heard!

"What should we do?" he asked bluntly.

"She wants to go to school, someplace where she can learn to write," Faith said without hesitation. She had known this for a long time, but there had been no money—and there was none now.

"Wish I were a general," Tom said ruefully. "A major's pay doesn't stretch very far."

Faith was very much aware of this, for she'd learned to get by on the meager earnings of an army officer. She hated to see him depressed, so she said briskly, "Well, God owns everything. If He intends for Laurie to go to school, He can afford it!"

Tom smiled, his teeth very white against his bronzed skin. "Pretty free with the Lord's money, I'm thinking." Then he grew serious. "I'll talk to her about it."

And he did, three days later. Tom was a slow-moving man—except when the situation demanded otherwise, and he'd formed the habit of praying and waiting over important things—something he'd learned from Faith. But late on Friday afternoon, he saw Laurie practicing her trick riding and decided to voice his concern. "You aiming to join a circus?" he grinned.

Laurie touched Star's right foreleg, and the gelding immediately made a one-legged bow to Tom. "I might just do that," she said, sliding to the ground. "Are we going to Prescott soon?"

"Did you forget we're going to visit your Uncle Dan in Wyoming?"

"No! I haven't forgotten!" There was no chance of her forgetting, for the anticipation of going for a visit to Wyoming had been the brightest expectation of her life.

He smiled, adding, "Maybe Dan'll hire you to herd some of those cows of his."

"I could do it!" Laurie grinned impudently. "I can ride better than any old cowboy I ever saw!"

"Not very humble, are you? But I guess you can, at that." He walked beside her toward the corral where the mounts were kept. When she'd unsaddled Star and stepped outside the gate, he said, "Laurie, I've been worried about you." He saw surprise on her face and said quickly, "About this writing thing. You're pretty serious about it, I guess."

Laurie had known for a long time that her father was not convinced about this desire of hers, so she'd said little. But now her eyes flashed with excitement, and she nodded, "Yes, Daddy, I want it more than anything."

Tom Winslow was a determined man, and as he looked into the face of his daughter, so eager and so alive, he came to a decision. "Well, I don't know how—or when, Laurie—but you're going to get your chance at this thing."

"Oh, Daddy!" she squealed and threw her arms around Tom, holding to him almost desperately.

He knew he'd made the right choice and said, "Better start praying. As soon as we get back from Wyoming, we'll start looking around for a school—and the money to pay for it."

As they entered the house, Faith took one look at Laurie's excited face and said, "Well, now, I can see you two have been plotting something. Sit down and tell me all about it."

CHAPTER TWO

VISIT TO WYOMING

★ ★ ★ ★

Laurie stared out the open window of the train, blinking as tiny cinders flew against her face. "Look, there's a herd of antelope!"

At her words, a burly man sitting in the seat ahead of them lifted his head from the newspaper he was reading. Dropping the paper, he picked up a Henry rifle from under his feet, shoved it out the window, and emptied it. He missed with every shot, and the fleet, graceful animals bounded away and out of sight.

Tom Winslow hated to see game wasted and said loudly enough for the man to hear, "Good thing that fellow's such a rotten shot, Laurie. Hate to see meat go to waste."

The man with the rifle swung around, his face red with anger. He opened his lips to challenge the speaker, but one look into the somber eyes of the broad-shouldered officer made him pause. "Man's got a right to shoot wild antelope," he muttered, then turned and ignored Winslow.

Faith had watched the scene carefully, but without fear. She had seen her husband deal with many rough, violent men, and never once had he failed to handle the situation well. She shifted Ruth, who was sleeping on her lap, and asked, "How much longer will it be?"

"Almost there," Tom answered. He looked down at Jubal sitting beside him staring out the window. "Getting tired, son?" he asked, ruffling the boy's auburn hair.

"I wanna see the ranch, Dad." Jubal had watched with interest as the man had shot at the antelopes, and now asked, "Can I shoot your gun when we get there?"

Tom winked at Faith over the boy's head. "He never gives up, does he?"

"Like someone else sitting on this seat," Faith nodded emphatically. "Stubborn as a blue-nosed mule, just like his father!" She stretched her back, made a face, and rearranged the child's position. "It's a long trip—but it'll be good for us all."

"It was nice of Uncle Mark to get us free tickets, since he's a railroad official," Laurie observed. "We'd never have saved enough for all of us to come." She was accustomed, Tom realized, to the stringent economy necessary for a soldier's family. She would have said more, but the train whistle blew its hoarse bellow in the air, and she glanced out the window. "Maybe this is it," she murmured.

The conductor entered the car, calling out, "All out for War Paint—next stop!"

The Winslow family eagerly gathered their belongings, weary after the monotonous days of travel. As the train slowed to a stop, Tom stepped off first, gave Faith a hand with the children, then quickly piled all their luggage on the platform. Laurie kept a tight hold on Jubal's chubby hand while taking a good look at the shabby little town before them. It was just like all the other small towns they'd passed through on the trip. And as always, townspeople strolled up to break the day's tedium and to touch again for an instant the life they had left behind; to catch, in the train's steamy bustle, the feeling of excitement and freedom that had impelled most of them to come to the West, but which had died as soon as they had taken roots there. The railroad provided the town a single pulsebeat once a day—emerging as a black ribbon out of the emptiness, touching War Paint, then moving on toward the desolate horizon.

"Tom!" The man coming toward them was dressed in a pair of brown trousers, a blue shirt and vest, and a low-crowned black hat. Although Laurie had seen him only once when she was six, she knew at once this was her uncle, Dan Winslow. As he reached her father, gripping his hand and slapping his back, she saw he had the same build, tall and broad-shouldered, and the same dark hair and light blue eyes as her father. "And this is your crew, is it?" Dan Winslow said, turning from Tom. He removed his hat, took Faith's hand, and smiled. "I'm glad to meet you. My wife would have come, but she's home getting the house ready."

"We'll be trouble, I'm afraid," Faith said. "I know what it's like to have a bunch like this descend on you."

Dan laughed this off at once. "Hope's been looking forward to your visit more than anything I can remember. Gets lonesome out on a ranch." Then he turned to Laurie. "And this is Laurie—" Laurie put her hand out, but he smiled. "Nope, I have to have more than a handshake from my niece," whereupon he gave her a hug and a firm kiss on the cheek. He then stepped back and studied her with a twinkle in his eyes. "I think we better leave you in town, Laurie."

Laurie's eyes widened in surprise. "But—why, Uncle Dan?"

"You'll be too much trouble at the ranch." Dan winked broadly at Tom, adding, "You'll have every cowboy on the place fighting over you." He laughed at the sudden blush that touched her cheek. "Your father will have his hands full, I reckon."

"Already been through all that, Dan," Tom broke in. He put his hand on Laurie's shoulder and smiled. "You have to remember she's been the only girl on an army post with two hundred solders fighting over her. Spoiled rotten, that's Laurie."

"Oh, Daddy!" Laurie protested, but then the men turned and picked up the baggage. Dan Winslow led the way to a wagon fitted with a canvas to shield its passengers from the sun's rays. As they approached, a young man leaped from the seat and yanked his hat off.

"Want you to meet my boy Cody Rogers," Dan Winslow said. Laurie inspected the young man covertly, remembering that this was her uncle's stepson. His father had been killed at Bull Run before Cody was born. He was around twenty, she estimated, and a little under six feet tall. He was lean, but with the heavy shoulders and arms of a good roper, and there was a certain grace in the way he moved. He had a wide mouth, very dark blue eyes, and light blond hair that fell over his forehead. And then she heard Dan Winslow remark, "You don't have to worry about this one pestering you, Laurie. He's so much in love he gets on his horse backward."

Cody shook his head. "Don't mind what he says, Miss Laurie. I'll see to it that none of those bowlegged galoots on the ranch bother you."

"That's like putting the fox to guard the chickens!" Dan grinned. "Well, let's get started. I know you're worn out from that long ride." He helped Faith into the backseat of the wagon, then said, "Cody, you drive. Laurie, you take Jubal and keep an eye on Cody as well—he thinks he's the best driver in the county!"

Dan got into the back with Faith and Tom, who took Ruth onto his lap. As Cody pulled out with a sharp word to the horses, Dan said, "Now tell me about this Indian situation, Tom. Are they going to break out this year?"

As the wagon rolled along with the wheels lifting and dripping an acrid dust, Laurie tried to listen to the two men talk, but Jubal was full of questions and wiggled like a worm. She kept him pinned down with much effort, until about half an hour later, she'd had enough and said, "Go get in the back, Jubal," and the active five-year-old was passed back, her father depositing him in the open compartment of the wagon.

"Ever been in Wyoming, Miss Winslow?" Cody asked.

"Oh, just call me Laurie." She glanced at the bronzed features of the young man who sat loosely beside her, then went on. "No, but we lived in Dakota for a few years. My father was with the Seventh Cavalry when Custer died."

This caught Cody's attention, for everyone in the country had read of the tragedy she mentioned. The question as to who was responsible for the defeat was still being argued. "You ever meet General Custer?"

"Oh yes, many times." Laurie thought back to those early days, remembering the tawny-haired general and said, "He used to take me up in front of him on his horse after the drills, and he'd race around as fast as the horse would run!" She reminisced about her days at Fort Abraham Lincoln, then halted abruptly. Glancing at him, she said shyly, "I'm not usually given to so much talk."

"Well, you've got a lot to talk about," Cody answered. "Not many people had a chance to ride on General Custer's horse. How come your father didn't get killed with the rest of the men?"

"He was with the detachment Custer sent out under Reno. They were the only ones who didn't die that day." She hesitated, then said softly, "It's still sad to me—all those men dying. I knew some of them, just young boys no older than you, Cody."

The wagon swayed and shuddered as it struck a deep depression in the road, sending the impact through the passengers. The sharp scent of dust rose beneath their feet, mixed with the strong fragrance of the earth—the harsh and vigorous emanations of the earth itself. One of the jolts was so violent that it threw Laurie against Cody. "Oh—I'm sorry!" she exclaimed and quickly moved back to her own place.

Cody gave her a crooked smile, his eyes filling with humor. "Why, that's all right, Laurie. You can do that anytime." He was laughing at her, Laurie knew, and suddenly she felt that she could like this lean rider very much. *He might be courting some girl*, she thought, *but he's willing enough to flirt with me*. By the time they pulled up at the Circle W Ranch, the two were chatting freely, and as he helped her to the ground, she said, "Don't forget, Cody, you promised to take me riding."

"He might forget to work," Dan Winslow said, having overheard Laurie's words, "but Cody Rogers never forgets when it comes to taking a pretty girl for a ride!"

★ ★ ★ ★

Hope and Faith immediately took to each other, and the large dining room was soon filled with the smells of good food as the two women prepared the supper. It was a fun time, and when they all finally sat down, Dan looked around the table and shook his head. "What a bunch of Winslows!" The table was barely big enough for them. Hope held three-year-old Priscilla and five-year-old Cassidy, while four-year-old Pete sat squeezed up against her. Tom and his family occupied the other side. Dan and Cody sat at the ends.

"Wish Dad could have seen this, Tom," Dan said, regret shading his voice. "He loved kids so much."

Tom thought of their father, Sky Winslow, and said slowly, "He sure did, Dan. And Mother would have loved this bunch, wouldn't she?"

34

Dan said, "Let's have the blessing, and then we can light into this grub. My wife's a poor cook, but do the best you can."

The meal by the "poor cook" consisted of tender beef steaks, a bowl of thick gravy, hot potatoes boiled in their jackets, steaming beans liberally laced with onions and peppers, tender corn on the cob dripping with butter, and fluffy biscuits with golden brown tops. This was followed by apple and peach pies, which melted in their mouths.

Afterward, the children played noisily while the women washed the dishes. Finally, they put the children to bed, and just before Tom and Faith went to their own room, Dan said, "It's good to have you here—all of you. I miss having a big family like we had back in Virginia."

"So do I, Dan." Tom shook his head, adding regretfully, "Those days are gone, though. Can't go back."

Dan Winslow gave his brother a strange look, glanced at Hope, then said mildly, "Oh, I wouldn't be so sure about that, Tom."

Later, when Tom and Faith were in bed, Faith said, "They're so nice, aren't they? Hope is the finest woman!"

"Yes—but I know a finer one." He pulled her close and thought about Dan's words. "Wonder what Dan meant by that—what he said about the old days not being over? We're scattered all over the country." He named off the children of Sky and Rebekah Winslow—"We're in Arizona, Dan's here in Wyoming, Mark's in New York, Belle and Davis are in Washington. Only Pet and Thad are still living at Belle Maison—the old home place."

"He's probably thinking of a family reunion," Faith mumbled sleepily. "That would be nice." An idea came to her and she said, "Maybe Laurie could go live with one of them. She could find a school in one of those big cities—" Then she fell asleep, and Tom held her until sleep overtook him.

★ ★ ★ ★

Cody did not disappoint Laurie, and the next afternoon offered to take her for a ride. "Come on, and I'll pick you out a nice horse," he said. Laurie had raced around getting ready, and when she stepped out on the porch, Cody lifted his eyebrows.

"Hey, you sure look better than what the cows usually see around here."

Laurie was wearing her own riding outfit: a fawn-colored divided riding skirt, a brilliant scarlet blouse, a black vest, and a small, narrow low-crowned hat. Cody was surprised at how pretty she looked, noting the black hair that fell down her back and the large black eyes that sparkled with excitement. "Dance next Saturday night in town," he said. "You'll sure have to go and give the girls in this town something to get mad about."

"Will you be there—and your girl?"

"Oh, sure," he nodded, and as he turned to lead her to the corral, he added, "Want you to meet Susan Taylor. She's the prettiest girl in these parts, Laurie."

"Bet you have lots of competition courting her, don't you?"

Laurie had spoken in a jocular tone, but she noted that Cody hesitated, and a frown turned his wide mouth severe. "Yeah, I do," he said briefly. He said no more but led her to the corral where the riding stock stood in the sunshine. "Now there's a nice horse for you, Laurie," he said, indicating a small brown mare with fat bulging sides. "That's Nell. She's so gentle all the kids can ride her."

"Oh, I'd like something a little more spirited than that," Laurie said. Her eyes scanned the horses. "I'd like to ride that mare—the roan with the white feet."

"Why, you can't ride that one, Laurie!" Cody exclaimed. "She's pretty and fast, but downright tricky." He shook his head, adding, "Some good cowpokes have gotten throwed by that hoss."

"Oh, Cody, let me try!"

Cody was prepared to deny her request, for the horse was one of the most difficult on the ranch to ride. But when Laurie looked up at him, her face eager and alive, he finally gave in. "Well, I guess you can try her, but don't blame me if you get throwed and get that pretty outfit all dirty."

He took a rope from the corral fence and stepped inside. At once the horses began milling around, trying to avoid him. "Her name is Lady," he grinned, "which she *ain't*. Look how she's hiding behind them other hosses. Knows exactly what I'm up to."

Laurie had seen many men use a rope to capture a horse, but she'd never seen it done as neatly as Cody performed. Using only his wrist, he threw the rope between two horses Lady was using for a shield. The rope shot free, the end opening into a loop that Lady ran into despite all effort to escape. "Oh, what a fine throw!" Laurie cried. "I wish I could rope like that!"

"Maybe I'll give you a lesson or two," Cody grinned as he maneuvered the mare to the hitching post. Snubbing her tightly, he pulled a blanket from the fence and threw it over her back, followed by the saddle. Cinching it down securely, he put the bridle on. Turning to the girl, he said, "Laurie, this just isn't a good idea. Let me ride her, and you take my horse." But she pleaded so earnestly that he finally just shrugged. "Well, try not to break any bones when you hit the ground."

Laurie moved over to the side of the mare, stroked her sleek neck, and said quietly, "Lady, you and I are going to get along." Gathering the lines, she placed her foot in the stirrup, and with one smooth motion swung into the saddle.

"You got her?" Cody inquired. He'd been impressed at how easily she'd mounted but was still worried. *If she gets hurt, I'll get all the blame for it,* he thought, and almost decided to demand that she get down and ride his horse.

But he had no opportunity, for the mare took advantage of her rider by leaping forward and at the same time twisting to one side. She'd used this tactic often, and only the most alert and skilled riders had been able to keep their seat. But the light burden on her back had merely shifted, and abruptly Lady had felt a strong grip draw the bridle up, forcing her head high, thus preventing any more tricks.

"Now that you've got that out of your system," Laurie said firmly, "we understand each other." She looked back at Cody, who was staring at her incredulously. "Ready?"

Cody blinked, for he'd seen several good riders who'd been tossed trying that same maneuver. He shook his head in admiration. "Yeah, I guess I am." He moved to his own horse, swung into the saddle, and they left the corral.

Twenty minutes later, Cody reined his horse to rest. When Laurie pulled up beside him, he said, "Well, I guess you've got yourself a horse while you're here, Laurie. I never seen the beat of it, though." He shoved his hat back on his head and grinned at her. "I guess what Lady needed was another female just as stubborn as her. Where'd you learn to ride like that?"

"Don't forget, Cody, my father's a cavalry officer. I was riding when I was three years old." She was pleased by his compliment, much more than with his notice of her appearance. They took a long ride, and though Lady tried every mean trick in her repertoire, by the time they were back at the ranch, she was as docile as her name. "I can unsaddle her myself, Cody," Laurie said, and proved the truth of her claim. "Do you think Uncle Dan will let me ride her while I'm here?"

"Sure. He'll be real proud of you," Cody answered. "But you can't wear that outfit to the dance next Saturday. Did you bring a party dress?"

"No—I didn't think I'd be going to a party."

"Mom will have one you can wear. Save me a dance, because you'll be all booked up soon as you hit the floor!"

★   ★   ★   ★

By the end of the week, the two families had grown very close. They met Zane Jenson, Hope's younger brother, and his wife, Rosa, who lived on their own place only six miles to the east. "It's nice to have family near, isn't it?" Laurie had said to Cody.

The younger children of the two brothers were near enough in age to play well together, and the two women became fast friends. Hope had put her arm around Laurie, smiling, "I wish Cody would fall in love with you and marry you. Then I could keep you here."

"That's a good idea," Dan said, coming into the room. "I'm glad I thought of it. He doesn't look like much, but look at what a handsome father-in-law you'd have!"

"Oh, hush, Dan!" Hope said, putting on her bonnet. "Ready to leave for the dance?"

The dance was one of the best Laurie had ever attended. She was instantly besieged by numbers of young men, but her father used his rank to claim one waltz for himself, and then Dan Winslow took his turn. As they were swirling around the room, Laurie said, "Cody's girl is the most beautiful woman I've ever

38

seen, Uncle Dan." They both glanced over to where Cody was dancing with a young woman with blond hair and striking blue eyes.

"Yes . . . too beautiful, maybe," said Dan, keeping his eye on Cody and Susan Taylor. When he looked back at Laurie, he added, "She's a good girl, but I'm not sure she'll ever settle down to being the wife of a cowman. She likes the towns and the bright lights."

"Are they engaged?"

"No, not yet. Cody's tried everything to get her to take his ring, but Susan keeps putting him off." He changed the subject abruptly, and soon the number ended, and Dan took Laurie back to her seat.

Finally the hour grew late, though the time went fast, for Laurie had had a partner for every dance. It had been such a fun time, but now as she was on her way to the refreshment table, escorted by a soft-spoken cowboy, Smoky Jacks, she heard a disturbance at the other end of the room.

"Never mind that, Miss Laurie," Jacks shrugged. "We have a brawl or two at all these parties." Just at that moment Laurie saw Cody, his face stiff with anger, shove his way out of the crowd and walk toward the door. Susan Taylor called after him, but when he ignored her, she turned to a tall man in a beautifully tailored suit, who began to draw her to one side.

"Oh, it's just Cody and Harve Tippitt fighting over the Taylor girl. They're at each other all the time, but I guess Cody's had enough this time."

*   *   *   *

During the rest of their visit, the Tom Winslow family had very little communication with Cody, for he grew more and more withdrawn. Hope spoke of this to Laurie on the last day of the visit. "I wish Cody would forget Susan," she remarked as she helped with the packing. Looking up, her voice tinged with sadness, she added, "She's not the woman for him—but that's hard for a man to see when a girl's as attractive as Susan."

"I hear her family is well off, too," Laurie said.

"Two good reasons why she might not fit into ranch life," Hope said, then shook her head. "Dan and I have been concerned about it, but we know that Cody is stubborn. Gets it from me, I suppose."

Laurie smiled at this. "I guess all women have to make adjustments after they get married, don't they? But it'll work out, I'm sure."

In the living room, the two brothers were having a final talk. Tom said, "It's been a wonderful time for all of us, Dan. I hate to go back to that drab old army post—"

"Don't do it then, Tom," Dan said, giving his brother a sudden look. Seeing the surprise on Tom's face, Dan suggested, "Why don't you resign from the army, come here, and help me with this ranch?"

"Why—this is your place, not mine, Dan!"

"There are two ranches, really. Logan Mann and I bought one place, and Hope's first husband this one. After her husband and Logan died, we tried to make one ranch out of the two. But they're so spread out it's difficult to work together. Zane married Rosa and purchased a ranch not too far away. That way there'd be family close by." Dan came over and put his hand on Tom's shoulder. "It would be a good thing for all of you. This is a good place to raise kids—and I know you and Faith have been unhappy with the way officers are transferred from one post to another and how hard that is on kids."

Tom shrugged. "That's the army way, Dan."

"I won't press you. Why don't you just speak to Faith about it?" he said gently. "Remember when we talked about how it used to be—with all our kinfolks just down the road?"

"That was the best, but—"

"It could be like that again. Our kids could grow up together in this valley. They'd know their cousins and uncles and aunts. Our children's lives would be tied together like ours were."

Tom had never really given the thought much consideration, though he and Faith had wished for a more stable life. The army had become his home, but he'd been wondering if it was worth the sacrifices his family had to make.

"I'll talk to Faith, Dan."

"Fine!"

The two men said no more, but on the way back to Arizona, when all the children, including Laurie, were asleep, Tom told

Faith about Dan's proposal. She listened carefully, then said, "He's a generous man, your brother."

"Yes. What would you think of making the change?"

"I'll go where you go, Tom," she responded. She looked at Ruth sleeping on the seat, at Jubal across from them, and finally at Laurie. "It would be nice to be close to family," she finally said quietly. Then she took his hand and gave her ultimate answer— "We'll pray about it, Tom."

CHAPTER THREE

THE LEGACY

★　★　★　★

One of the "volunteers" of the cavalry troop commanded by Thomas Winslow was a huge dog, which had been named Ugly by the cook. He had suddenly appeared one day and had refused to move on. "Probably got away from an Indian camp," L.C. Holmes, the grizzled cook, had complained. "They eat all the good-looking dogs, but this one is too ugly to eat."

Laurie had never owned a dog, so she had immediately adopted him. Her parents had refused at first, but when Ugly wouldn't leave, they relented, with the stipulation that she couldn't have him near the house. She'd fed the hound by begging Holmes for scraps from the mess hall.

Late one afternoon two weeks after the family had returned from their trip to Wyoming, Laurie gathered up the remains of several meals and went to feed Ugly. She found him tied to a fence by a short rope. As she approached, Sergeant Hollis said in a disgruntled voice, "That blasted dog is a pest, Miss Laurie! I can't break a hoss for his meddling."

As the sergeant walked away, Laurie sat down and stared at the big dog. He was no beauty, being a multicolored mixture of red, brown, black, and gray, his coat resembling a patchwork quilt. His legs were too long for his body, and he had a blunt

head with cropped ears and a set of eyes that didn't match—
one blue and one brown.

"Why don't you act right, Ugly?" Laurie spoke sharply, and
Ugly gave her a disdainful look. He was not in the least affectionate, and when Laurie or the younger children tried to play
with him, he was known to give them a sharp nip—not enough
to harm them but enough to sting. Now, however, he was hungry and whined in his throat and pawed at her, signifying his
willingness to behave.

Laurie, disgusted with the dog's hypocrisy, took a bone with
a large chunk of meat clinging to it and extended it to the hungry
animal. Ugly snatched it from her hand and started to devour
it, but Laurie was feeling cranky and grabbed it from him.
"You're nothing but a greedy pig!" she exclaimed. "You never
appreciate a thing I do for you!"

When the girl held the bone toward him again, Ugly lunged
at it, but was stopped short by the rope around his neck. He was
a strong dog and the corral shook as he threw himself toward
the prize that Laurie held, but she tormented him by holding it
just beyond his reach. "Now, you ugly beast, will you be a little
bit grateful for what you get?"

"Don't reckon he will, Laurie."

Whirling at the sound of the unexpected voice, Laurie saw
her father standing behind her. He was watching her now with
a steady gaze, and Laurie flushed, embarrassed that he'd found
her tormenting Ugly. She had always wanted to please her father, and said, "Oh, Daddy, I don't know what's the matter with
me—being mean to poor old Ugly!"

Tom Winslow watched as she set the food on the ground,
then untied the dog. Ugly fell on the feast, the bones crunching
beneath his strong teeth, growling deep in his throat as Laurie
tried to pet him. She clenched her fists and put them on her
hips. "See if I bring you anything else, you sorry critter!" Then
she turned to her father, and he saw that this daughter of his
was close to tears—which pulled him up sharply.

Can't remember the last time I saw her cry, Tom thought. She
had been the pride of his life for a long time, and suddenly he
was aware that letting go of a child was a painful affair. *When
she was a little girl with a problem, she'd come to me, and I'd hold her*

on my lap and stroke her hair—but a man can't do that with a young woman like this. I've lost her somewhere along the way—that little girl with the trusting eyes and small hands that clung to me. A pang pierced Winslow's heart, and he realized it was the grief that all men and women suffer when time steals the gentle things from them, and when the young grow up so that all that's left of the past are the fleeting memories—*and even those slice at a man like a razor,* he thought.

"Old Ugly isn't the most affectionate dog I ever saw," he said, his voice soft on the August breeze. A smile turned the corners of his broad lips up, giving him a wry expression. "Reminds me of a friend I had back in Virginia when I was a kid. No matter how much anyone did for him, he snatched at it and never gave a word of thanks. Guess a dog as homely as Ugly just naturally gets fed up with people."

Laurie shot a startled glance at her father's tanned face. He had always taught her like this—finding something in his experience or in the surface of her own world to give her some guidance. But she was so unhappy that she shook her head, sending her train of glossy black hair swinging along her back. "I don't know what's wrong with me, Daddy."

"Why, I guess I do." Tom Winslow nodded toward the dog, who was finishing off the last of the meal. "You take a dog like Ugly, now. One sure way to make him cranky and mean is to tie him up and let him get bored and hungry. Then you offer him something he really wants, like some juicy bones." He paused, admiring the satin smoothness of her cheeks and the sweep of her clean-cut jaw, then shrugged, adding, "And then just when he's got it, why, you yank it back so he doesn't get it."

Laurie's eyes were fixed on her father's face, for she knew he was saying more than his lazy tones implied. She was a quick girl, especially with him, for the two had spent so much time together during the years on the plains, they could almost read each other's thoughts. As she pondered what he'd said, her eyes narrowed and her lips grew firm. Her father had always said that she was like a bulldog with a thought, that she'd never give up until she got the meaning of things.

"You mean that our trip to see Uncle Dan made me unhappy?"

Winslow nodded, then stepped closer and laid his hand on her shoulder. "You've been discontented here at the post for a long time, Laurie. Then you had a fine time when we went there. It wasn't just Wyoming, though," he said gently. "You're hungry to get away—just like Ugly was hungry for those bones. And just like him, when you got a taste of freedom from this life, and then it was snatched away from you—why, you have to get a little mean or you wouldn't be human. We're all like that when we don't get what we want."

"No, that's not right," Laurie answered swiftly. Looking up into his face, she looked very vulnerable, but there was a stubborn set to her lips and a directness in her dark eyes. "You're not like that, and Mother's not. Neither one of you likes this post, but you don't go around tormenting animals!"

Winslow suddenly laughed aloud, then put his arms around Laurie and squeezed her so hard she gasped. "You're a real desperado, you are!" She struggled to free herself, but he held her firmly for a moment. When she did look up, he said, "You're a fine girl, Laurie. No man ever had a better daughter."

"Oh, Daddy, I feel so—so *useless!*"

"Never think that, Laurie!" Winslow spoke almost sternly and released her. He started to say more, but glancing over at the drill field, he saw it was filling up with mounted men. "Time for retreat," he murmured. He wheeled, saying, "Wait until I come back."

Laurie nodded and moved over to stand in front of the feed barn. One of the things she did like about the post was the daily ritual that took place every evening as the sun went down. It was a splash of color and drama that bloomed in the midst of the gray monotony of the army post.

She watched as five cavalry companies filed out from the stables to the parade ground. The officers yelped sharply, like foxes, shrill in the air. "Column right! Left into line! Com-m-pany, halt!" The mounted men guided their horses expertly, the animals sending quick puffs of dust rising into the air. One by one, the five companies came into regimental front, each group mounted on horses of matched color, each company's guidon colorfully waving from the pole affixed in the stirrup socket of the guidon corporal's stirrup.

Then the moment came when the milling horses seemed to freeze into position, each trooper sitting with a grooved ease in his McClellan saddle, legs well down and back arched, sabre hanging on loosened sling to the left side, carbine suspended from belt swivel to right, dress helmet cowled down to the level of his eyes.

Laurie stared at the sunburned faces all pointed toward her father and to the adjutant now taking his report. She felt a quick glow of pride rush through her as her father took the report and answered the adjutant's salute. Always at a time like this, she was proud of him, for all these men were in her father's hands, and she knew how they trusted their commanding officer.

Then a word was spoken, and the band broke into a quick march. The officers of the regiment rode slowly front and center, formed a rank, and moved upon their commanding officer. Laurie watched them salute her father, and then they swung around and marched down the front of the regiment, in full tune, and wheeled and marched back. They halted, and at once the little brass cannon at the base of the flagpole boomed out, its echo filling the parade ground. The flag began to descend, and when a trooper received it, Major Winslow called out in a ringing voice, "Pass in review!"

The first sergeants barked their stiff calls as the companies wheeled around, and the band broke into a march tune. It turned the corners of the parade ground and passed before Winslow, and the horsemen moved toward the stables, each company pulling away toward its own area.

The ceremony was finished, and almost at once Winslow came to Laurie, saying, "Got time for a ride?"

"Yes!"

Winslow called out, "Sergeant, let my daughter have your horse."

"Yes, sir!"

The lean, sunburned sergeant stepped out of his saddle and held the reins while Laurie found the stirrup and swung into the saddle with a graceful motion. He grinned, saying, "Major, don't let her get thrown. This horse is disrespectful."

Laurie smiled down at him, her cheeks flushed with pleasure. "Don't worry, Sergeant. I'll make him mind." She took the reins and followed her father as he rode out of the stockade at a fast gallop, pulling the bay up to ride beside him as soon as they were clear of the gate.

For half an hour they rode toward the west where the sun's violent flame rolled back like sea waves across butte and ridge and far-scattered clumps of timber. The harsh sunlight that had burned the ground all day caught up the thin and bright flashes of mica particles in the soil, and the heat that had been piled layer on layer began to dissipate as the evening breeze started to stir.

The pair rode silently, soaking in the night air, now freighted with the scent of baked earth and a faint aroma of timber as they pulled their horses up at a small creek. The only sound was the huffing of the horses blowing into the water and the pleasant off-key tinkling of metal gear.

"I want to explain why we're not moving to Wyoming to take up ranching." Laurie turned in the saddle, startled by the sound of his voice slicking across the silence. Tom had his back to the sun, so she could not read his face, but his voice was serious. "Been meaning to talk to you about it, but your mother and I have had a difficult time coming to a decision."

"I know, Daddy."

"Do you? Well, I guess you can read your old man pretty well." He stroked the neck of his horse, then went on. "It wasn't easy, Laurie. The army is a tough life—more so on women and youngsters. Monotonous, nothing much to do. I've regretted that for you, most of all, I think."

Suddenly, Winslow heard a sound off to his left, and at once his hand went to the revolver in the holster at his side, his eyes peering at the clump of timber half-hidden in the dusky light. Then a deer leaped out, saw them, and veered sharply, disappearing into the growing darkness.

"Don't see them this close to the fort very often." Winslow relaxed slightly, but there was a vigilance in him that kept his eyes moving even as he continued. "You must have wondered why we've stayed in the army, haven't you?"

"I think a lot about the time when you and I followed the Indians, when you were an agent," she said thoughtfully. "That was better."

"It wasn't confining. If we got tired of one spot, we'd move on—but an officer can't do that." He sighed, regret edging his tone. "No life is more controlled than a soldier's, I guess."

"You could do well on a ranch. You'd do well at whatever you put your hand to, Daddy."

"Think so? Well, I doubt if I'm as good as you think I am, but I'm glad I've got you fooled." He arched his back, saying, "I've tried a hundred times to figure out what it is that keeps me in the army—and I've decided it's two things."

Waiting for him to go on, Laurie suddenly realized that not many men would go to the trouble of explaining their philosophy and their decisions to an eighteen-year-old daughter. *He's always talked to me like I was an adult—even when I was a little girl.* The thought pleased her, and she listened carefully as he spoke evenly, his voice a counterpoint to his thoughts.

"A man has to belong to something, Laurie. For a long time I floated around, not much in the way of ties. But as long as someone just does little chores that end with his hands and never reach his heart, he's no good to himself. Some things are real, and some are only illusionary, things that people wrap themselves in because they don't have anything real."

"Why—that's what I've thought for a long time!"

He twisted his head toward her, catching the classic profile of her face. "I know, Laurie. That's why I'm telling you how I feel. We're alike, you and me—got to have more to do than most."

"And the army does that for you?"

"The army is made up of good men—and some pretty bad ones, too. But when the trumpet sounds boots and saddles, they'll all swing up together; and when the bullets start flying, they'll all move forward. That's what men should do." Then he halted and shrugged his shoulders. "But I could find that in other ways and in other professions. It's more than that—and I don't even know how to say this to you."

"What is it, Daddy?"

"I believe," he said slowly, "that I'm in the army for a purpose. I think God puts people in certain places because sometime or other, there's a job that needs doing and they're the ones to do it."

"That's what Reverend Gliddings says."

"Yes, but I didn't need a preacher to tell me about it." He stopped his horse, and when she pulled up alongside, he said, "I'm no prophet, but somehow I know that down the line, I'll be doing something that God wants me to do."

Laurie had sensed this about her father, though he'd never spoken of it. Now she asked, "Does Mother feel that way?"

"Yes. As a matter of fact," he admitted wryly, "I was about ready to resign and move us all to that ranch for some easy living, but Faith came up with one of those flat statements that almost knock you down. She said, 'God has called you to be a soldier, not a rancher, Thomas Winslow, so be what He's made you!' "

They both laughed, for they had long delighted—and learned to trust—in Faith's sudden announcements about the will of God. "I guess that settled it," Winslow admitted. "But it makes things harder for you."

"Oh, I'm all right," Laurie said quickly. "The ranch was nice, but—"

"You wouldn't have been satisfied there, Laurie," Winslow interrupted. "It would have been more pleasant than this post, but in six months, you'd be miserable again." She started to protest, but he said, "Come on, let's get home." He spurred his horse forward and raised his voice. "Your mother has another one of her little 'announcements,' but I want you to get it straight from her."

Laurie was filled with curiosity, and as they rode back to the fort, she pondered over what her father had said. When they turned their horses over to the handlers and started toward the house, she asked, "What is it? Mother's announcement?"

"I'll tease you the same way you teased Ugly," Winslow grinned. "Let you wait on it. Maybe you'll be a little kinder to that poor dog next time."

When they entered the house, they found supper on the table; and her father whispered, "It'll have to wait until the kids go to bed."

For Laurie that was one of the longest evenings she could ever remember. She could hardly wait to get Jubal and Ruth into bed, but when she suggested that it was time for that, her father said blandly, "Oh, it's too early yet, Laurie. I want to read to them a little while."

Finally the last paragraph was read and the children plunged into bed ready for prayers. Laurie waited impatiently until her father came back into the room, then turned to her mother. "Daddy says you've got something to tell me."

Faith smiled at Tom. "How much did you tell her?"

"Nothing," he shrugged. "It's your idea."

A sudden gust of impatience burst from Faith. She gave her husband a disgusted look and shook her head. "No, it's not *my* idea! It's a word from God that both of us have prayed for."

Tom Winslow walked over and put his arm around Faith. He winked at Laurie, asking innocently, "I wonder why it is that God gives you all this information instead of me?"

"Oh, hush!" Faith turned to face Laurie, her gray eyes catching the reflection of the lamp's yellow flame. At twenty-eight she was as trim as she'd been when she'd come to the West to preach to the Indians and, according to Tom's testimony, even more attractive. She had been both mother and friend to Laurie, who'd never had either, and now a softness spread over her face as she said, "Laurie, did you know I was an heiress?"

"An heiress?" Laurie echoed blankly. "What kind of an heiress?"

"Are there two kinds?" Faith smiled. "I had an aunt who lived in Baltimore. I met her when I was six years old. My parents took me to her house for a visit, and we stayed three days." Her eyes grew thoughtful. "It was a wonderful time for me—and for her, too. She was very old, even then, but she was lively. My father's older sister, she was. She liked me very much—and when she died the next year, I cried an ocean!"

Laurie had never heard about this and asked with curiosity, "Did she have lots of money?"

"No, very little," Faith said. "She lived on a small pension and owned her tiny house. But when she died, my father was her only living relative, so she left everything to him. I asked him once what had happened to all her things, and he told me that she'd wanted them sold and the money to be given to me."

"If I'd known I was marrying an heiress," Tom grinned, "I might have shown more energy in my courtship."

Faith shot him an enigmatic look and murmured, "You were energetic enough—after you got started." She shook her head, adding, "It wasn't enough of a legacy to marry me for." But letting her gaze rest on Laurie, "It's enough to send you to school so you can study how to write."

The floor under Laurie's feet seemed to tilt, and there was a hollow ringing in her ears. She blinked and saw that her father was grinning broadly, and her mother was smiling too. "I've known all this time it wasn't for me, and now the Lord has made it plain that the money is for you."

"Oh, Mother—I couldn't take it!"

Faith tipped her head to one side and gave Laurie a penetrating look. "Are you telling me you don't want what God has sent to you?"

"Oh—no—!"

"Then are you saying that I'm mistaken and that I didn't hear from the Lord?"

Laurie flushed and ran to Faith, who caught her in her arms. "No! It's not that!" She clung to the older woman for a moment, then pulled away, her eyes brimming with tears. "It's just that—I feel so *selfish*! Your aunt didn't even *know* me!"

"But God knows you," Faith nodded firmly. "And that settles it. Now—let's talk about this school you're going to."

"The Lord didn't mention which particular school, I don't suppose?" Tom Winslow asked innocently.

"That will be what Laurie will have to seek God for," Faith answered instantly. "Unless," she said, turning to the girl, "you've already got some school in mind."

Laurie had always envied her mother's ability to find out what God wanted, and now she could only say, "There's one I've thought about, but I don't think God told me to go there."

"If it's in your mind, there might be a reason for it," Faith said. "I hope you don't expect a flaming angel to come and stand in front of you and bellow out the name of the school God wants you to attend."

Despite herself, Laurie laughed at the image. "No, I don't have to have that. But how can I know if what I think is what God is saying, or just what I'm thinking?"

"The scripture says, 'They that seek me early, will find me,' " Faith said quietly. "But God's not a servant you can summon up and demand things from." She hesitated, and her voice grew very soft indeed. "He will come—when you have waited until all other things are put out of your mind." It was her own method, and both her hearers knew well how at times this woman would separate herself from everything, go into seclusion, and would not be seen until she emerged with a peaceful look on her face.

"What school have you been thinking of?" asked her father.

"There's a school in Omaha, a new school. I read about it in the newspaper last year."

"Omaha? That's not as far away as I'd feared," Tom nodded. "What sort of a school is it? Can women attend?"

"Oh yes, they take women," Laurie nodded. "The president is a graduate of Oberlin College, and he's brought their methods to this new school." Laurie's face grew warm and her eyes sparkled as she explained the new venture. "It's going to be a school for artists, painters, and writers. And one of the teachers is going to be Barton Sturgis!"

"And who is he?" Faith asked.

"Why, he's a *writer*, Mother!" Laurie was shocked that neither of her parents had ever even heard of Sturgis. "He's written the two best novels ever published in America. All the critics say so!"

After thirty minutes of listening to Laurie talk excitedly about college and this Mr. Sturgis, Tom finally interrupted her and said, "Well, reveille comes early. Let's go to bed, Faith." He kissed Laurie and held her a moment, saying, "I'll miss you, you know."

Faith kissed the excited girl and gave one word of caution: "Be very careful about this, Laurie. I can't do it for you." She smiled. "God doesn't have grandchildren, you know—only children. So you must meet with God about this decision on your own. But you'll be guided, I know that very well."

When Laurie finally got into bed, she had never in all her life been less inclined to sleep. For what seemed like the entire night she lay there, trying to fall asleep, but the excitement was too much. Finally she drifted off—and dreamed of Ugly! But it was not the same—for in the dream, it was *she* who was tied by a rope around her neck! And it was Ugly who was sitting just out of reach—with a train ticket for Omaha in his enormous mouth!

Over and over he would come close, but when Laurie would reach out for the ticket, he would step back out of reach. Finally he *ate* the ticket—and Laurie found herself weeping bitterly into her pillow.

CHAPTER FOUR

JOURNEY TO OMAHA

★ ★ ★ ★

On the day Laurie received the letter of acceptance to Wilson College, she set a goal of taking Star with her. It would not be an easy battle, but she threw herself into convincing her parents that it *had* to be done. "I'll be gone for at least two years," she'd told them in her opening salvo. "It's too far to come home, and you can't visit me. I'll be lonesome for all of you—but if I just had Star with me, it'd be a little bit like being home. . . ."

She had lost the initial battles, but like a good general, she had not given up. Her mother was adamant, but Laurie quickly saw a chink in her father's armor. He himself loved horses, and she had used every tactic known to young women to convince her father to give her what she wanted most. She knew her father well enough not to try a direct assault, for he would have resisted that. Rather, she had done other things to win him, stopping to stroke his head as he worked over papers, just a light caress that would bring his head up so she could give him a warm smile.

In the days that followed, Laurie worked hard preparing his favorite dishes. She loved to bake, and got up early to prepare sweet breads and apple pies. And not a day went by but that she stopped by his office for a few minutes. Sometimes they would simply talk, but more than once she would wheedle him into taking a ride.

By the end of the first week, Tom Winslow had almost forgotten Laurie's request to take the horse to Omaha. The girl herself never mentioned it directly. Rather, she would sigh and run her fingers through his dark hair, saying, "I'll have lots of time at school. There won't be much to do there." Or perhaps, "Some girls have a hobby, like sewing—but I never did anything like that." Then as an afterthought, "—except ride, of course."

As the regular dropping of water in a cave can build up a large stalactite, so it was that Laurie slowly crafted the mind of Tom Winslow. Finally, when her departure was only a week away, the two of them were riding back to the fort from one of their outings to talk. They paused long enough for Winslow to dismount and look at his mount's front hoof, where he found a sharp rock. As he dug it out with his knife, Laurie slipped from her saddle and gave him a calculating look. When he straightened up, she said, "Daddy, I'm worried about Star."

"What's wrong with him?"

"Well, nothing now—but I won't see him for two years." Reaching up she stroked the smooth neck, and the horse bent down to get his muzzle stroked.

They made a pretty picture, Winslow thought, the sleek black gelding glowing with health serving as a perfect foil for the shining black hair of the young girl. Clicking his knife shut and slipping it into his pocket, he said gently, "Get fond of a horse, don't you? I remember my first horse, a jug-headed roan named Mike."

Laurie looked up at her father as he spoke, noting the fondness in his voice. Finally he said, "When he died, I just about wanted to die myself."

"I feel that way about Star," Laurie quickly said. "What if he should die while I'm in Omaha?" Her soft lips grew tense and she held to the horse's neck possessively. "I don't think I could stand it, Daddy! Being all alone and Star sick—maybe dying—!"

Winslow put his hand on her shoulder and pressed it gently. "Be pretty bad, wouldn't it?" *She hasn't had much*, he thought. *Don't see why she can't take the horse with her.*

"Well, I don't guess it'd cost too much to ship Star to Omaha—but it might be hard to find a place close enough to the college to board him."

"Oh, Daddy!" Laurie's squeal startled both horses, and she

dropped Star's lines and threw herself at her father.

"Hey now!" Winslow protested, almost knocked off balance by her sudden lunge. He held her with one arm, trying to control his own mount with the other, and when she looked up he saw such a light of joy on her face that he knew whatever the cost, it was worth it.

All the way home Laurie chattered about the arrangements, and when they got to the house, she ran inside, dragging her father by the hand, crying out, "Mother, Daddy says I can take Star to Omaha with me!"

Faith turned from the dishes she was washing to face the exuberant girl, a strange smile touching the woman's lips. "Oh? How did that get decided?"

Laurie hesitated, then blurted out, "Oh, it was Daddy's idea."

"Was it now?"

Tom Winslow gazed down at Laurie fondly. "I'm glad I thought of it."

Faith laughed aloud, but when Tom blinked and asked what was so funny, she shook her head. Later when she was alone with Laurie, she'd said, "Well, you got your way, didn't you?"

"*My* way?"

"Don't give me that innocent look, Laurie Winslow," Faith shot back. "You know what I'm talking about." Then seeing the apprehension in the girl's eyes, Faith laughed and gave her a hug. "It's fine with me, but it's no surprise."

"Why—"

"You could get that father of yours to cut off his foot if you set your mind to it!"

Laurie tried to look innocent, then giggled, and soon the two burst out laughing. " 'I'm glad I thought of it,' he said," Faith gasped. "Why, the poor man never knew what hit him!"

"Don't tell him," Laurie pleaded.

"I won't," Faith agreed. She touched Laurie's cheek lightly and turned her head to one side as she gazed fondly at her. "I've been doing that to your father for years. Do you think I'd give the secret away?"

★   ★   ★   ★

"I feel a little strange shipping my daughter off to school like this," Tom Winslow said. "Now that the time for you to leave has come, Laurie, I'm sure going to miss you." Trying to grin, he added, "I've always said you were a pretty little filly, but shipping you off in a railroad stock car—!"

Laurie was holding Star by the hackamore and stroking his neck, speaking in a soothing voice to the spirited gelding that disliked unusual settings. He snorted, tossed his head, and lashed out with his hooves, striking the sides of the car.

"Easy, Star—it's all right," Laurie whispered, holding his head down. Turning to give her father a quick smile, she said, "He'll be all right, Daddy. He just has to get used to it."

"Well, you can't stay in here petting him for three days." Winslow glanced at the horse, then shook his head. "Never heard of anyone taking their horse to school with them."

Just then the brakeman passed by on his way to the caboose. The loose-jointed redhead stopped long enough to look admiringly at Star. "Now that's one fine-looking hoss!" he remarked.

Winslow took a bill from his pocket and handed it to the young man. "Take care of that animal—and keep an eye on my daughter, too." He grinned at Laurie, adding, "I'm sending them both off to college."

The brakeman's grin broadened as he pocketed the bill and nodded. "My name's Monroe Whittaker, and I'll shore watch out for both of 'em, Major. Any hoss thieves or Romeos try anything, I'll bounce them right off the train!" The whistle uttered a shrill blast, and he said, "Guess you better get your goodbyes done, Major."

Laurie loosed her hand from the bridle and put her arms around her father, holding him close, and for one moment, she was afraid. But knowing he would be quick to recognize any signs of apprehension, she drew his head down and kissed him on the cheek. "Goodbye, Daddy. I'll write every week."

"It's hard to let you go, daughter!" Winslow's eyes were troubled, and he shook his head sadly. "First time we've ever been separated!" He stepped back, reached into the inner pocket of his coat, and pulled out a small package. "A going-away present for you—just from your old dad."

Laurie took the package and carefully removed the plain brown paper wrapping. A flash of brilliant red color caught her eye, and she blinked with surprise. What she held was a pair of beautifully wrought silver spurs—and in one of them was set a large brilliant ruby that winked as the sunlight touched it.

"Oh—Daddy!" Laurie whispered. "It's from your ring that Grandfather gave you!" Tears misted her eyes, and she shook her head. "I can't let you do it!"

"Too late now," her father grinned. "I've had it long enough. Time for another Winslow to wear it." He had gone to considerable trouble and expense to have the spurs made and the stone set in. But as he looked down at her and saw the pleasure on her face, he was glad. "Can't have you going off wearing those old rusty spurs you sport around here," he said. She threw her arms around him again and held him fiercely, her body trembling with suppressed sobs.

Suddenly another blast of the whistle broke the air. She lifted her face, kissed him, then, clutching the spurs, turned back to Star. The train lurched forward and gathered speed. Then Tom was gone. Laurie pressed her face against Star's smooth neck. "We're on our own now, Star," she whispered.

Whittaker came back through the car ten minutes later and noted that the girl was still holding tightly to the horse. "First time away from home, miss?" he asked.

"Yes, first time."

The brakeman took in the tense white line around the girl's mouth and the stiff set of her shoulders.

"Well, the good Lord will take care of you, so don't you fret." He wanted to pat her shoulder, but was too wise for that, so he nodded and moved to exit out of the car.

The brakeman's words were an encouragement to Laurie, and she pulled Star's head down and kissed his smooth muzzle. "Hear that? Even the brakemen are for us, Star! We're going to be all right!"

She moved to the slats that made up the side of the cattle car and watched the desert roll by, wondering what Omaha would look like. Even more than that, she wondered if she would be able to compete with the other students. Most of them had gone to fine schools, she suspected, while she'd learned on a dozen army posts under a rather eclectic set of teachers. But as the wheels clicked off the miles, she put her fears behind her.

"Like Monroe Whittaker says, Star—the good Lord is going to take care of us!"

★ ★ ★ ★

"Miss Laurie—we're comin' into Omaha."

Laurie awakened at the sound of Monroe's voice and opened her eyes to see the lanky redhead bent over her. She had fallen asleep on a pallet she'd made of blankets on a pile of straw in the cattle car, and as she sat up, she blinked at him. "How long, Monroe?"

"Oh, 'bout half an hour. Thought you might want to wash up a little." He grinned at her, adding, "Don't want to start college with straw all over your hair, I don't reckon."

"Thanks, Monroe." The brakeman had been exactly what Laurie had needed on the journey, and she'd become fond of him. He'd made it possible for her to stay with Star during the long trip instead of perching on one of the hard seats in the passenger coach. He had also seen to it that she'd gotten good meals at several stops. Twice he'd taken her to restaurants during long stops and entertained her with tall tales about his home state of Tennessee. Even more welcome had been his quick intervention when a man wearing fancy clothes had tried to force himself on her in the passenger car. The man had had glossy black hair and bold eyes, and had crowded against her in the seat. Laurie had tried to ignore him, but he had become more and more insolent, and Monroe had noted the situation in one glance.

"Laurie," he had said at once, "come along with me."

The black-haired man had turned to glare at the brakeman. "We're doing very well without you, Red. Move along or I'll have to move you." He was a big man, thick-shouldered and arrogant.

Monroe had been wearing a light jacket, and he pulled it back just enough so that both Laurie and the man could see the butt of a .44 shoved into his belt. Leaning forward, the Tennessean had murmured mildly, "I don't allow *nobody* to pester my sister, Jack. Now, you set."

Something in Monroe's pale blue eyes had caught the insolent man's complete attention. He sat back and weakly sputtered, "I was just trying to have a little conversation with the young lady."

"Come along, sis," Monroe said easily. When Laurie had slipped past, and Monroe had escorted her back to the cattle car, he said, "I shoulda plugged that sucker!"

Now as Laurie pulled the straw from her hair she laughed. "I guess they'll know I'm just a country girl even if I get this straw out."

"Naw, you just bust right into that ol' college and bat them big eyes of yours at them teachers. You'll win the whole shebang."

Laurie smiled at Monroe, then moved to the passenger car, where she washed her face and made herself as presentable as she could in the bathroom. She changed her wrinkled dress for her riding outfit, assuming she'd have to ride Star to the college, then find a place close by to board him.

Returning to the baggage car, she quickly saddled the horse, and as she was slipping the bit between Star's teeth, Monroe came in. Taking a look at her, he whistled. "Well, look at you, Miss Laurie Winslow!"

Laurie smiled at him. The riding outfit was new—a going-to-school gift from her uncle Mark. It was a fawn-colored divided skirt with silver conchos along the hem, a vest to match, and a pale blue silk blouse. The new boots were made of snake skin, and the hat that hung by a leather lanyard down her back was white with a low crown and a narrow brim. It also had silver conchos on a leather band around the base of the crown. She looked beautiful, and her eyes sparkled as she said, "Thanks, Monroe."

The whistle sounded twice, and he said, "Well, I pray the Lord will keep you safe, Miss Laurie."

Appreciative for all this fine young man had done for her, Laurie put her hand out suddenly. When he took it, she said, "I'll tell my father how well you took care of me, Monroe."

"Aw, I'd a done it anyhow, but thanks, Miss Laurie." Taking a sheet of paper from his pocket, he quickly scribbled a few lines, saying, "Take my address. I come through Omaha regular. If any of them scholars give you any trouble, jest drop me a line. I'll sidle in and give *them* a leetle education!"

Laurie's eyes squeezed together as she laughed. "Oh, I hope it won't come to that, Monroe—but I'll write to you." The motion

60

of the train altered, and she said, "We're slowing down. I'll get my things."

The train slowed to a crawl, then shuddered to a stop. Monroe shoved the sliding door open. "Here's the chute. Goodbye fer now!"

Laurie had tied her suitcase behind her saddle and now guided Star out the door. "Thanks for everything, Monroe!" she called as they moved down the chute. When the big horse reached the ground, she waved at the brakeman, and he waved back, a smile on his homely face.

When she was almost out of hearing distance, he yelled in a stentorian voice, "REMEMBER—DON'T SQUAT WITH YORE SPURS ON!"

The sun sat high in the sky, and the October wind was brisk as Laurie guided Star through the cattle loading pens and toward the station. Several men turned to stare at her with admiration, and one of them said loudly enough for her to hear, "Well, now, girlie, maybe I can get up on that black horse and we can have us a ride!"

Ignoring him, Laurie touched Star, and the gelding snorted and broke into a run. Laurie had been able to take him off the train for exercise only twice during layovers, and she was glad the trip was over. The station was some distance from the loading pens, which gave Star a chance to stretch his legs. As she pulled up in front of the red brick building, she held Star back. A fat man with a billed cap stood on the loading platform watching her, and she asked, "Can you tell me how to get to Wilson College?"

"Sure," the man nodded. "It's on the other side of town. You can either ride through town—or you can go around it." Eyeing her carefully, he spit an amber flow of tobacco juice on the cinders at his feet, then shook his head. "Was it me, I'd go right through."

"That sounds fine to me."

"Take that road over there. When you get to the Palace Hotel, turn right. That's Benton Street. Just stay right on it, miss. College is 'bout half a mile past the hotel."

"Thanks a lot."

Laurie turned Star's head toward the street that led to the

main part of town. The outskirts that lay beyond the railroad station were a jumble of poorly built shacks, almost all of them with garden spots turned brown by the autumn chill. An occasional cow nibbled at the dry grass. Small children, attracted by the sight of a girl on a fine black horse, came to the edge of the road. Many of them cried out, "Give me a ride!" but Laurie only smiled and rode by.

The town itself was bigger than any she'd ever seen. She passed a section composed of factories, and then rode into the main business district, taking in the shop windows filled with women's clothing that she'd seen only in advertisements. The streets themselves were broad and bustling with activity—congested with buggies, carriages, many horses, and large wagons loaded with freight.

Along this route, too, she attracted attention, for though she saw many women in the buggies, there were none on horseback. The stares of the people made her uncomfortable, and she began to wish she'd gone around the town.

Soon she arrived at the Palace Hotel, turned right, and almost at once found herself riding down a broad street shaded by huge elm trees. The houses were finer here, large Victorian style dwellings with gingerbread trim and high windows. Most of them had separate carriage houses and some had gazebos in the spacious front yards. The leaves were falling, carpeting the dry, brown grass with crisp layers, like a red and orange crust. Children played here, too, but were better dressed—though the smaller ones still came to the street to ask for rides.

Ten minutes later, she saw on her right a large two-story red brick structure set back at least a hundred feet from the street. It was not a house, for it was too plain and too large for that, and she saw numbers of young people walking along the pathways that crisscrossed under large oaks. "That must be it," she murmured, then seeing a small brass sign set back off the road, she rode closer until she could read the letters—WILSON COLLEGE.

Pulling the horse up sharply, she looked at the square building and noted that there were two frame structures, obviously housing for the students. Then she stooped and patted the neck of the horse. "Well, we're finally here, Star."

But she was uneasy, for this was another world. She had grown up in places where the land never seemed to meet the sky, but stretched out for enormous distances. This world was small, cut into sections and bordered by trees so that she could only see small parts of it. She felt it closing in on her and was filled with a sensation of being pushed into a tiny closet.

The people of this world would be different; she knew that instinctively. The denizens of her world had been hard-muscled, sunburned troopers, blowzy washwomen, seedy civilian clerks, and obsidian-eyed Apache. But somehow she sensed as she took in the well-dressed young people walking and laughing that even in this seemingly soft and gentle world there would be those who were not so tender.

Taking a deep breath, Laurie touched Star with her heels, whispering, "They'll just have to move over and make room for us, won't they, Star?"

A circular drive made of some sort of shells arched in front of the main building, and she stepped out of the saddle and tied Star to the hitching rail along with three other saddle horses. Moving resolutely, she mounted the three steps and reached out to open the polished oak door. It swung toward her even as her hand pulled the brass handle, and a small man with a pair of glasses perched on his nose almost fell flat on his face.

"What—!" Catching his balance, he straightened up and gave Laurie an indignant stare. He was a short man with a very rotund stomach, dressed in a gray flannel suit that made him look like a gray stork. He had a mouth like a purse and opened it now only slightly to demand in a nasal tone, "What's that you're wearing? Is the circus come to town?"

"Oh—no, sir," Laurie stammered. Behind him, in the entranceway, she noticed a covey of students watching her carefully; one of them—a girl with flaming red hair—was grinning at her. The redhead nodded toward the small man, made a circle with her finger to indicate he was crazy, then winked broadly. Laurie didn't know what in the world to make of that, but said quickly, "I'm here to enroll in college."

"Indeed? Well, *do* it then!" Without another word, the short man turned and stalked out the door, slamming it behind him.

The red-haired girl stepped up to say, "That was President

Huddleston. Looks like you've made quite an impression on him." She looked at Laurie's outfit and smiled. "You look good in that thing. All you need is a horse to go with it."

"He's outside."

"You're kidding—" The girl ran to the door, opened it, and having stared out, turned and said with awe, "You really *do* have a horse!"

"I'm afraid so."

The redhead laughed with delight, then came to stand beside Laurie. "I'm Maxine Phelps. Maybe I can help you get started."

The girl had a kind manner, and Laurie said gratefully, "I— I'd appreciate that. My name's Laurie Winslow. I hate to be a bother—"

But Maxine only laughed and waved her friends off, saying, "Tell Barton I'll be late, Betty," then proceeded to usher Laurie through the trials of registration. She even managed to get Laurie assigned as her roommate.

An hour later the two young women stepped outside of the building, and Maxine said, "Come on, I'll help you unpack." She watched with keen interest while Laurie untied Star's reins, and as they walked toward one of the two large homes Maxine asked, "Why'd you bring your horse to college?"

"I wanted to be sure of at least one friend," Laurie smiled, then added, "But now I see I'll have more. Thanks for all your help, Maxine."

Waving her hand, Maxine said, "Glad to have you. I was afraid I'd get a stick of a roommate. Nice to have a real cowgirl."

The two reached the two-story house, where Laurie untied the suitcase and Maxine took it from her over Laurie's protest. Then Laurie pulled the saddlebags free, putting them over her shoulder.

"What's in there?" Maxine asked curiously.

"Oh, just some books and my pistol."

Maxine had turned to mount the steps, but on hearing this, she stopped and faced her new roommate. "Your *what*?"

"Why, my .38," Laurie answered. "I've carried it since I was fourteen years old." Noting the strange look on Maxine's face, she explained, "The Apaches get pretty bold sometimes, so my dad bought it for me and taught me to shoot."

"I see. And did you ever shoot any?"

"Well—just one."

Laurie's simple reply delighted Maxine. Her broad mouth turned upward, and her bright blue eyes sparkled. "Come on, Laurie," she said. "I've got to make a list."

"What kind of a list, Maxine?"

"Why, a list of people you're going to shoot!" She ran into the house yelling, "Hey—come and meet my new roommate. But mind how you talk or she'll put a bullet in your leg!"

CHAPTER FIVE

LAURIE FINDS A TEACHER

★ ★ ★ ★

Finding a place to board Star had been a simple matter—but it had come about in a way that startled Laurie. She'd gotten permission to keep the gelding in the stable used for the horses belonging to the faculty for the first night, but the next morning, she awakened worrying about a permanent arrangement.

"I'll have to take care of Star before I start classes," she'd told Maxine. The pair were eating breakfast, and Laurie's head was swimming as she tried to remember the names of the students Maxine had introduced to her. Most of them seemed friendly, but some were obviously amused by the "cowgirl" who'd invaded the ivy-covered halls of learning. One of them, a sharp-featured student who was somewhat older than the others, had not bothered to lower her voice as she'd said, "Well, I hope she remembers to scrape the manure off her boots before she comes to class."

"That's Pearl DeLong," Maxine informed Laurie, seeing the shock on her new roommate's face. "Don't pay any attention to her, Laurie. Her old man's got all the money in Nebraska, and she expects everybody to kiss her foot."

Laurie shrugged the matter off, saying with a wry smile, "I don't guess you do much foot kissing, Maxine." Then she got up from the table, saying, "Well, I've got to go find a place for Star."

"You ought to get set with your classes first."

"I don't have any choice, Maxine."

She went straight to the stable and threw the saddle on Star. A wizened stablehand with gray hair and bright blue eyes was watching her, so she asked, "Do you have any idea where I can find a place to stable my horse—maybe a farm close by?"

"Don't rightly know of any, miss," the man shrugged. "There's a livery stable in town. Owner's name is Blakely."

"Thank you." Laurie swung into the saddle and rode out. For the rest of the morning, she moved along the main road, stopping at farmhouses but finding nothing. Finally she got a lead on a possibility and wound her way down a country lane until she came to a dilapidated house surrounded by fields and wandering pigs. The woman who came to the door had unfriendly eyes and snuff-stained lips. She listened to Laurie, then shook her head. "Ain't got time to take care of no stock," she said shortly.

Laurie thanked her, wondering what she could be so busy with, but in any case, she would not have liked to trust the care of Star to such people. By two o'clock she'd had no success at all, and in desperation rode back into town to check at the livery stable. The owner, a hearty man named Blakely, nodded at once when he heard her request. "Be glad to keep your animal." Laurie felt a wave of relief, but when he named the fee for boarding a horse, her spirit fell. "I'll see about it," she murmured.

There was nothing else to do but to board Star in Blakely's stable, but she knew it would take every penny she had—or would have. *I can't ask Daddy for more money. He and Mother have done enough.* Depressed, she rode back to the college, where she dismounted and pulled the saddle off Star. The small stablehand had been giving a fine buckskin a rubdown, but when he looked up from his task, he saw the discouragement written on the girl's face.

"No luck, miss?"

"No, I'm afraid not." She pulled the saddle blanket off, patted Star, and turned him into the corral. *I'll have to do something right away*, she thought, but as she turned to go to the office, her shoulders drooped. "I'll go ask if I can leave him here again tonight."

"Why, there'll be no trouble about that, I'm thinking." The man rose and moved across the floor with a strange jerking gait to stand beside her. "Michael McGonigal is me name, but it's Mac I answer to," he said in a speech thick with the flavor of Ireland. He had a squashed face like an old potato, a shock of iron gray hair, and a pair of sharp blue eyes. "That's a foine horse, miss. Ever race him?"

"Oh, just against other horses on the post."

"Post, is it? Why, you're an army girl, then!" His eyes lit up and he asked, "Which outfit?"

"The Fifth Cavalry. My father's the commanding officer at Fort Grant."

Mac McGonigal's face showed astonishment. "Do you tell me that? Why, I served a hitch with the old Fifth—under Major Reynolds, it was. What's your father's name?"

"Major Thomas Winslow."

"Don't know him, miss, but I've been out for a spell." Regret came to his eyes as he slapped his leg. "I'd be in the cavalry still, but my horse fell on me. Broke my leg so bad it couldn't be rightly fixed."

"I'm sorry, Mac," Laurie said. "I know how you must miss it all . . ." She stood there talking to the small man, and soon he had managed to find out most of her history. Finally she sighed, "Well, I'll have to go now." Biting her lip nervously, she said, "I don't know what to do about boarding Star."

McGonigal squeezed his eyes together, thinking hard, then asked abruptly, "Is it a Christian girl you are, Miss Laurie?"

"Why, yes, I am, Mac."

"Then ye'll be knowing that the Lord don't let us wander around down here like a bunch of blind moles! Me old mother taught me that—bless her memory!"

"She sounds like my own mother," Laurie nodded. "She hears from God all the time. But I don't seem to have the knack for it." A streak of impatience tightened her lips and she shook her head in frustration. "Why doesn't God tell *me* what to do? Where is He when I need Him?"

"Faith, girl!" Mac slapped his hard hands together sharply,

his blue eyes snapping. "Do ye expect the good Lord to come down and shout every little thing in your ear?"

"Well, no, but—"

"Before ye started out this morning to find a place for your horse, did ye ask God to help you?"

Laurie blinked, then answered feebly, "Well, no, but I didn't think I needed to pray over such a little thing."

"Oh, that's it? Ye'll handle your own business until you stub your toe, and it's then ye'll be goin' to God?" McGonigal shook his head and looked fierce. "Well, devil fly off, if that ain't a pitiful way of servin' the Lord!"

Laurie felt a flush of anger, primarily because she had been told essentially the same truth by her mother. "Well, I can't ask God for every little thing, Mac! And suppose I had asked—do you think He'd send a shining angel down to show me the way to a stable?"

"Well, He's got plenty of them, ain't He?—angels, that is! Don't the Word say, 'The chariots of God are twenty thousand, even thousands of angels'? It ain't my business—or yours—to figure out *how* God is going to lead us. It's ours to ask, and His to do!"

Laurie suddenly laughed and put her hand on the small man's arm. "When I write to my parents, I'll tell them they don't have to worry about me. I've got a fine Bible-believing trooper from the Fifth here to watch over me! " Her smile was warm and a happy light danced in her eyes as she added, "And I'll *ask* God about finding a place for Star. Does that satisfy you?"

McGonigal's rumpled face broke into a grin. "There's no need to ask now, because I can tell you where to keep your animal." Seeing the surprise on the girl's face, he swept the stable with a gesture of his arm. "Right here, it is."

"But—this is for the faculty and staff!"

"Go see President Huddleston," McGonigal said, smiling. "Tell him what you need."

Remembering her encounter with the short-spoken president the day before, she asked doubtfully, "Do you think so, Mac? He seems so *grumpy*."

"Now, Miss Laurie, here the Lord's given you what you want and you go doubting! Don't the Word say, 'Trust in the Lord with all thine heart'? You be goin' on now, and see the man!"

"All right, I will!"

Laurie left the stable and went at once to President Huddleston's office. By the time she got there, her confidence had eroded, so much that when she asked to see him, she half hoped he would be too busy to see her. But the middle-aged woman sitting at the desk nodded at once, "Go in, Miss Winslow. This is the hour that President Huddleston sets apart for talking with students."

Laurie knocked on the door timidly, then when a voice said "Come in," she entered and slowly approached the huge desk sitting squarely in front of the bay window that let the pale sunlight enter. President Huddleston lowered the heavy book he was reading and stared at her through the thick lenses of his glasses. Laurie had already heard his nickname, "The Snapping Turtle," and couldn't help thinking that he looked exactly like one!

"Miss Winslow, I think." Huddleston placed the book on the desk in front of him and motioned to a horsehide chair on the left of his desk. When she had perched on the very edge of it, as nervous as she'd ever been in her life, he said abruptly, "Tell me about yourself."

"Sir?"

"What kind of a young woman are you?"

Laurie could only stare in bewilderment at the small rumpled figure. Her simple request had been transformed into something quite different, and she stood there trying to collect her thoughts. She had always been a quiet girl, formed by the emptiness of the land she'd grown up in, and in no small measure, by the father she greatly admired. Faced with the blunt, unexpected question of President Huddleston, she was embarrassed and said so. "I—don't know how to answer that." But then she straightened her back and the inner core of independence that was part of her rose to the surface. "I'm a girl who wears funny clothes," she said evenly, thinking of his remarks of the previous day. She was afraid of the man and half expected that he might rebuke her for her impertinence—perhaps even send her back to Arizona.

But unexpectedly the president's thin lips curved slightly in what passed for a smile. Lowering his head, he peered at her over his glasses, and she saw that the brown eyes that appeared so formidable behind the thick lenses contained a surprising warmth. "So you do," he remarked, "but we're more than the clothes we wear. What do you want to do with your life? What have you done with your life up until now? Do you expect to go through the rest of your life riding a black horse?"

Laurie sat there as he peppered her with questions delivered in a shotgun fashion. When he finally paused, she was not quite as nervous and began to speak of her history. He sat there listening, his face impassive, but she had the impression that he was storing all she said in some sort of filing cabinet he kept in his small head. Finally she stopped, realizing that she'd talked for half an hour, more than she'd ever talked about herself in her entire life!

"I want to be a writer," she said finally.

"No, you want to *write*, perhaps," President Huddleston nodded abruptly, his voice crisp as dry leaves. "That's what you want to *do*." Leaning back in his chair, he clasped his hands and mused, "I ask people what they are, and they always tell me what it is they *do*. 'I'm a doctor—I'm a cleaning woman.' " Shaking his head, he stated firmly, "What do you want to *be*, Miss Winslow?"

Instantly Laurie shot back, "I want to be as good a woman as my father is a man!"

Her answer pleased the scholar, for he nodded sharply, "Now *that's* the sort of thing I like to hear! Tell me about your father. . . ."

An hour later, after Laurie had told President Asa Huddleston far more than she'd intended to, she was dismissed. "You're going to be an asset to our school," he'd said. "Now, you may leave and go to work."

Laurie blinked at such an abrupt dismissal, but didn't hesitate to obey his order. Crossing the room to the door, she realized that she'd discovered a man who was far more than just a college president. *I could tell him anything*, she thought, and then reaching at the door, she suddenly remembered her errand.

"Oh, President Huddleston," she said, turning to face him. "I can't find a place for my horse . . ."

He listened carefully, then waved his hand. "Tell McGonigal I said to take care of him. We'll find some way for you to work it out."

Laurie was stunned at the simplicity of the matter! Running back to the stable, she captured McGonigal and gave him the news with her eyes sparkling. ". . . and so he said to tell you to take care of Star right here in the stable!"

Mac looked at her, pleased with the whole thing. He'd liked this girl from the moment she'd ridden in, and now he'd had a hand in helping her. But he frowned, saying sternly, "Didn't I tell you? If you'd listen to me more, you'd know more!"

Laurie laughed, and suddenly threw her arms around the small ex-trooper, which almost shocked him out of his wits. Drawing back with a red face, he sputtered, "I'll be havin' a word with your father about this loose sort of manner you've picked up!" he threatened. Then to cover his emotion—for he was a lonely man—he said, "Now, can you ride this horse? I'll be giving you some special lessons. I'll not have one of the Fifth fallin' off her horse!"

He rambled on, but Laurie knew that whatever else came to her from this new life, she'd found two men she could trust!

★ ★ ★ ★

At the evening meal, after a rather hectic first day of classes, Maxine noted that Laurie had hardly eaten anything. When her new roommate excused herself and left the dining room, Maxine waited for five minutes, then rose and rushed upstairs to the room the two shared. When she pushed the door open and stepped inside, she saw Laurie lying across the bed, her face buried in a pillow. Maxine's first impulse was to go sit down and try to console the girl, but she wisely chose another course. "What's the matter?" she demanded.

Laurie hastily got up and tried to say cheerfully, "Oh, nothing, Maxine. Just too excited, I guess. My first day at Wilson College and all. Guess it wasn't as bad as I thought it might be."

Maxine stared at the tense lines of Laurie's pale face, noting the stiff lips and the false smile. "Liar," she remarked conversationally. "You look like you've been run over by a farm wagon." She moved to the huge walnut dresser the two girls shared, opened the bottom drawer, and fumbling around under the twisted nest of underwear, came up with a small cloth bag. Slamming the drawer shut, she produced a small rectangle of thin paper from inside the bag, then after deftly rolling it into a half-tunnel, she opened the bag and filled it with amber-colored tobacco. Expertly she licked the edge of the paper, finished rolling the paper into a tube, then twisted the ends. Taking it between her lips, she drew a match from her pocket, raked it across the top of the vanity and lit the cigarette. After drawing deeply, she expelled the blue smoke with satisfaction, then looked at Laurie and said, "You've been looking like a poisoned pup all day."

Laurie had watched with alarm as Maxine lit the cigarette. "Isn't that against the rules?" she asked cautiously.

"Sure it is." Maxine removed the cigarette from between her lips, rounded them, and blew a perfect smoke ring. It moved slowly through the still air, and she smiled, saying, "Takes a lot of practice to do that, kid." Then she waved the cigarette toward Laurie and said, "Listen to Mama and you'll learn something." She spoke in a mocking tone, but there was kindness in her eyes as she leaned back against the wall and began to lecture. "You found out that you're way behind some of the students here in the books, and that made you fold up. And you found out that Agnes Sipes is a pain, which everybody else *already* knew!"

At the mention of the Latin teacher's name, Laurie flushed. It had been one of the most humiliating moments of her life when the thin woman had exposed how little she knew, and she'd determined *never* to set foot in that class again!

"She's jealous of you, that's why she cut you to ribbons before the class." Maxine nodded when Laurie stared at her with doubt in her eyes. "Fact. She's scrawny and homely as a barn door, and not likely to get a husband. She hates all the pretty girls—and she'll do worse than she did today when she sees Barton Sturgis take after you."

"Barton Sturgis!" exclaimed Laurie.

"Yeah, Aggie Sipes swoons over him. I don't know why, but she does." Maxine took another draw on her cigarette, then nodded thoughtfully. "He gave her a little ride, I think, then dropped her. But she'd let him walk over her with hobnailed boots!"

"He won't pay any attention to me!"

"Honey, he'll try to hustle you—just like he did me and every other girl who's not cross-eyed." She laughed at the outraged expression on the girl's face, saying, "I know you've got some kind of crush on Sturgis, him being a big writer and all, but he's a *man*, so take Mama's advice, and watch yourself with him."

Laurie flushed, shaking her head stubbornly. "You make fun of everyone, Maxine. I don't believe any of that." She'd had time to pull herself together and said, "I know I'm dumb, but I'm going to show that woman! I'll make an A in Latin if I have to kill myself studying."

"You won't make more than a passing grade, 'cause Aggie won't give it to you," Maxine said matter-of-factly. She started to say more, but at that moment they both heard the sound of footsteps on the stairs.

"It's the matron!" Maxine dashed to the window, threw it open, and tossed the cigarette out. Grabbing a blanket off the bed, she began fanning wildly, whispering hoarsely, "Help me get this smoke out of here, Laurie! I've got eighteen demerits already!"

Laurie laughed suddenly, relieved somehow by what she'd heard from Maxine. "Maybe she'll think I did it. Everyone probably thinks I smoke and chew tobacco and swear like all wild west characters."

Maxine stopped fanning abruptly, surprise on her round face. Then she grinned broadly, and throwing the blanket down said, "It's my only hope. I thought you'd tell on me." She moved over and gave Laurie a hug, saying, "Don't worry, kid—you're going to do *great!*"

"Thanks for bucking me up, Maxine," Laurie smiled. "I needed someone to give me the spurs."

"Anytime you want somebody to peel your potato, kid, just give me a call!" Maxine moved to open the door, and as soon as Mrs. Reynolds entered and began her speech about smoking, she pointed at Laurie, saying anxiously, "I *told* her it was against the rules, Mrs. Reynolds, but you know how these wild west girls are!" As Mrs. Reynolds turned to lecture Laurie, Maxine winked broadly over her shoulder and carefully dropped the tobacco sack behind a chair. Laurie never said a word and silently endured the matron's warning about breaking school rules.

After Mrs. Reynolds left, the two girls fell into a fit of giggling, and even after they blew out the lamp and went to bed, Maxine said, "Don't worry about Latin, kid. Ella Barnhill is a whiz at it, and Miss Sipes really likes her. She promised to help me, and I'm sure she'll help you too."

The next morning at ten, Laurie entered the classroom where she would study literature under Professor Barton Sturgis. She was more nervous than she'd been in Aggie Sipes' class and had to fight to control the tremor in her fingers. The class was already filled, and several of the students she'd met smiled and spoke to her. Laurie envied the ease of their manner and felt out of place in the classroom.

When Professor Barton Sturgis entered, she was disappointed in his appearance, for he was neither large nor handsome. Not over five eight or nine, she guessed, and somewhat overweight. As he moved to stand in front of the class, she saw that he had ordinary brown hair that was beginning to recede, a pair of rather large brown eyes, and a round, florid face. Despite his unprepossessing looks, he had some sort of animation that some people have, so that whenever they enter a room, everyone stares at them.

His eyes lit on Laurie at once, and he said in a rather surly tone, "I suppose you must be Miss Winslow."

"Yes, sir."

Sturgis had heard of her, Laurie could tell, and feared he might make some mocking remark about her western roots. But he did not. Instead he asked, "Why are you taking this class, Miss Winslow?"

Laurie thought, *He's as abrupt as the president!* But aloud she said, "I'd like to learn how to write, Professor Sturgis."

Sturgis stared at her with impatience in his expression. He'd met too many aspiring young writers to get excited about one more. "I'll tell you what I tell everyone who gives me that answer—you don't want to *write*—you want to *have written!*" He made a slashing movement with his rather fat hand, adding, "*Everybody* would like to see their name on a book cover and make a lot of money writing, but precious few want to pay what it costs to get there." He stared at her for a moment, then said, "After class, Miss Winslow, you will stay, and I will read what you have written. It probably won't be much pleasure for either of us!"

Laurie had been terrified by his threat, and when the time came to hand him one of her writings, she was certain he would tear it to pieces.

Sturgis was pleased by the girl's manner when she handed him the paper. *Not giving a stack of apologies—and not using her looks to gain points,* he thought. Taking his seat and preparing to read, he thought sourly, *Probably can't write any better than the rest of them. . . !*

Since Sturgis had not told her to sit down, Laurie stood stiffly in front of his desk. She was too nervous to watch his face, but stared out the window and watched a red squirrel that was busy collecting nuts and carting them up to a hole in a huge oak. He was an industrious worker, and she fixed her mind on him, wondering how many pecans he had stashed in the crevice. She had that ability to focus on a thing until all other thoughts faded, so when Sturgis spoke, it startled her.

"Why did you write about this subject, Miss Winslow?"

"Why—I think because it made me feel very sad." Laurie had been fourteen when she'd seen a pack of wolves pull down a large doe and a helpless fawn. It had been a savage sight, and she'd never forgotten it. The incident had remained in her mind as clearly as a painting, and it had been both easy and painful to write about. Easy because she could almost literally *see* the details—and painful because she had never gotten over the grief she felt at seeing innocence suffer.

Sturgis stared at the girl, taking in the clean line of her jaw, the rich coloring that came from sun and wind—and not missing the clean rounded symmetry of her figure. He hated teaching, for most of it was a waste of time in his judgment. "You can't really teach people to write," he often said in private. "Aside from punctuation and spelling, there's nothing much one person can pass on to another." He had abundant proof of this theory, because none of his students had ever become successful writers.

But this one—she just might make it. Sturgis got to his feet, and walked around the desk. When he came to face her, he could smell a faint aroma of violets, and he liked the way she faced him squarely, though she was obviously nervous. *She's got nerve.*

Maybe that's the wild west part of her. "Most women don't write about violent death," he remarked. "They write about dances and flowers and beautiful houses."

"I don't know much about those things," Laurie answered evenly. "I can't write about things I don't know."

"Well, by heavens!" Sturgis exclaimed loudly. He stared at her with admiration, adding, "I'm glad to hear you've found out the one rule of good writing!"

Laurie flushed with pleasure but shook her head. "I don't really know much about writing, Professor Sturgis," she said. "I've always read a lot, and I like some writing and hate others. But I don't know *why*." Hesitating slightly, she said in a forthright manner, "I love your novels. That's why I came to Wilson—to see if you could help me become a writer."

"Why—"

Laurie interrupted him, saying, "I don't know if you can teach a person to make a story come to life, though. It may be something a person is born with—or born without."

Barton Sturgis was seldom at a loss for words—usually rather harsh words. But this young woman riding in out of the West had somehow shocked him into silence. She, without a doubt, had more raw talent than any young writer he'd ever encountered. And she seemed to be sensible in a way that very few amateurs were.

It had been his intention to steer clear of youthful writers— but as he stood there, he found himself fascinated by this almost unique combination of talent, beauty, and innocence. *I'm probably wrong*, he thought, *but even if she never learns to write, she's not a whiner—and she's pretty as a rose!*

"Miss Winslow," Barton Sturgis said slowly, "you and I are going to have to work very hard—very hard indeed!" He put his hand on her arm, squeezing it gently, and with excitement in his brown eyes he asked, "Are you willing to spend extra time on this work? I mean late hours and weekends, when the other students are having fun and relaxing?"

Laurie could not believe her good fortune. "Oh yes, Professor Sturgis," she whispered, her eyes bright with happiness. "I'll do anything to become a writer!"

"So," Sturgis murmured and released his grip on her arm. "We'll begin at once. Suppose we meet after supper tonight? We'll go over some of the things this paper needs . . ."

CHAPTER SIX

THE DESIRE OF THE HEART

★　★　★　★

After staring at the blank sheet of paper for twenty minutes, Laurie finally shook her head and almost desperately began to write:

Dear Mom and Dad,
    Please don't worry! When I got your letter, I wasn't disturbed by the fact that you won't be able to pay my tuition next year, but I could tell that both of you were terribly upset about it. And that makes me feel just awful! Please believe me when I say that leaving Wilson will not be a terrible blow. It's been an interesting year, and I've learned a lot—most of it not in books! I've made a few good friends, discovered some things about myself, and have learned a little about writing. That's a lot, isn't it? Some girls never have even one year like this. I'll always be grateful to you for making it possible.

I don't know how much of that they'll believe—but most of it's true enough. Laurie leaned back in her chair, letting memories of the past twelve months flow through her. *Seems like ten years since I got off the train with Star!* Suddenly she thought of her first day in class, how she'd been ready to quit until Maxine had talked her out of that! Then she thought of her first meeting with Barton Sturgis—and her lips tightened into a thin line. *He was going to "help" me so much! And I fell for the whole thing for so long, despite Maxine's warning!*

Bitterness welled up in her as she remembered those first months, especially those meetings with Sturgis. *I must have been the most naive girl who ever left home! And he took advantage of it!* But she had learned to let the anger go and now thought, *It's a good thing I had Maxine and Mac to keep me straight. If they hadn't been around—!*

She'd come perilously close to losing her head over Sturgis, but it'd been the experience of Maxine and the wisdom of McGonigal that had made her realize at last that the man was nothing but an egotist and a womanizer. When she'd confronted him with it, he'd lashed out, telling her that she was just a foolish girl who read too much into things. That had been the end of her infatuation—and of their meetings. She'd felt like the world's biggest fool, but that too had passed. She shook the memories away and began to write again:

> I know you were worried that I was infatuated with Barton Sturgis—I guess I was, but that's now gone forever. He's a fine writer but not a very admirable human being. That may sound judgmental, but I hope I've gained a little discernment since I've been here. There is no way I could ever forget the wisdom and kindness of President Huddleston or the comradeship of Mac McGonigal! Solid gold! And what would I have done without Maxine? I shudder to think! Those three I shall miss when I leave here, and a few of the students. But after being an army girl so long, I've learned how to say goodbye to friends.

Laurie paused and tried to think of some way to avoid hurting her parents. She simply loathed the thought of going back to that forlorn post in Arizona, but she could not let them know that.

> It will be so good to see you all again! I have enough money to pay the railroad fares for me and Star, so I will leave here as soon as the last class is over—that's next Friday. I must run now, but we will have plenty of time to talk when I arrive at the post.

Signing the letter, she sealed it, then rose and went to gaze out the window. The leaves had already turned red and yellow, but not with the flaming colors they'd had a year earlier when she'd first seen them. They looked old and dead, and the sight of them depressed her. She slipped into her riding outfit, pulled on her wool coat, and left the room. The campus seemed deserted, but she knew that most of the students were holed up in the library studying for finals. As she left the house and walked toward the stables she saw Maxine walking out of the academic building and hailed her. "Maxine—I'm going to the post office. Do you want me to mail any letters for you?"

Maxine looked up, startled, then headed toward Laurie. Looking down at the letter that Laurie held, she demanded, "You're going to be stubborn about this, aren't you?" Laurie just nodded, and Maxine said angrily, "It's nutty! My dad would be glad to pay your tuition. You can pay him back after you graduate and go to work."

"I know, Maxine," Laurie smiled. "I wrote and thanked him for his kind offer, but I just can't take it."

Maxine bit her lip with vexation. She'd grown fond of Laurie and had tried every argument she could summon to get her to come back for at least one more year. But she saw that further persuasion was useless, so she shrugged, saying, "I think you're making a big mistake—but I guess I've made my share. Tell you what, I'll meet you in town and buy you the biggest steak at Courtney's."

"All right. Meet you at six. We'll cry all over each other while we eat."

"Right!"

Laurie made her way to the stables, where she found McGonigal sitting on an upturned bucket whittling a stick of red cedar. Laurie watched him peel paper-thin shavings that curled like a pig's tail, then fell into an aromatic heap at his feet. "Mac, why don't you whittle *something*—like a bear or a whistle?" she asked, coming to stand by him. "All I've ever seen you do is make shavings."

McGonigal glanced up at her from under bushy eyebrows, looking much like a terrier. "Faith, and do we always have to be making *something*?" he grunted. "An artist like meself—why the pleasure of the thing, that's where it is!" He let another shaving fall to the ground, then snapped the blade of the knife shut and dropped it into his pocket as he stood up. "A little ride is it?"

"Going to mail a letter, Mac."

Something in the way the girl spoke caught the Irishman's attention and he glanced at her sharply. The past year had been made bright by her presence, and he'd come to understand Laurie better than most. "What's the trouble?" he asked, noting the small lines on each side of her lips, a sure sign that she was worried. "Your parents aren't sick, I hope?"

"Oh no," Laurie answered quickly. She had never mentioned her financial problems to McGonigal, but now she wanted to tell him what she had to do. They'd grown very close through the year, and she knew her leaving would be a loss for the little man. "I've got to go home, Mac. No more money to keep me here."

Her words hit McGonigal hard, and he stood there silently, thinking what a dull place it would be without this spirited girl. The two of them had the bond that good horsemen have, and she'd become an expert rider under his tutelage. She'd been a fine rider when she'd arrived, but he'd made her into an expert. And besides the standard gaits, he'd taught her fancy trick riding—which he'd done himself for years before he was crippled. "Just a bit of fun," he'd told her, but when word of her skill had gotten around, she'd performed often at fairs and for schools in the area. He'd taught her how to go completely under Star's belly while the big gelding was running at full speed by using several straps he'd added to a special saddle. Riding while standing up was easy, but Mac had taught her how to rope and even shoot at a target with his pistol. The two of them had worked out a repertoire of stunts, including one that always brought the crowd to its feet and made the women scream. It consisted of a concealed strap with a snap that Laurie could secretly attach to her belt. Then, riding her horse at full speed, she would suddenly throw herself over backward. The strap caught her when her head was almost on the ground, though it looked to the spectators as if she'd be trampled by Star's pounding hooves.

The two of them had spent long hours working on this, and now McGonigal and Laurie both knew that they would miss those times. "No way out of it?" Mac asked.

"Afraid not. I wish—"

When Laurie broke off abruptly, Mac blinked and said, "You don't want to go? Is that it?"

"No, I really don't," Laurie confessed. "But we all have to do things we don't like."

"That we do, but only if God puts us to it."

"Well, Mac, I've prayed every way I know how, but it's come down to the end. I'm going to town now to buy my ticket and that's all the money I've got. I can't stay here, so I have to go home."

McGonigal shook his head stubbornly. "Maybe God wants you to go home, maybe not. But don't the Book say He'll give us the desires of our heart?"

Laurie was accustomed to Mac's quotations from the Bible. He had one for every occasion, and usually they were apt. But she was weary of struggling with this matter and sighed, "I guess it says that, Mac, but I don't see how it's going to work out this time."

"I'll saddle Star for you," McGonigal said, and she watched as he quickly readied the horse. When she swung into the saddle, he said, "I'll be asking the good Lord to give you what you want."

"Thanks, Mac," she smiled down at him fondly. "You always look out for me." Then she turned Star's head, and as she galloped out of the stable she suddenly fell from the saddle and dropped out of sight. Clinging with one hand to the horn, she was invisible to anyone on one side of the horse, and she cried out, "I'll bring you a paper from town!"

President Huddleston had just stepped out the door of the main building when the big horse thundered by, apparently riderless. Then suddenly Laurie popped into the saddle and waved at him, crying out a farewell. Huddleston stared at her in shock, then a smile softened his stern lips. "This place won't be the same without that girl!" he whispered softly as he watched her ride off at a breakneck pace.

Laurie could not enjoy her ride to town, thinking about being back at the barren post within a week. Actually she was not happy at college either, for she'd come to doubt her dream of becoming a writer. Her disillusionment with that career had begun with Barton Sturgis. From the very first day in class, she had built him up very high. When he proved to be one of the most unworthy men she'd ever known, that had caused doubt to creep in. She'd struggled with this and had finally come to see that a bad man can write a good book—just as a good man can write a bad book.

But it was her own calling to the art of writing that she had come to doubt. She loved to write, but she'd learned that publishers wanted what was selling, not necessarily what was good. Many of her pieces had come back with letters advising her to make them more saleable—which to Laurie meant making them poor writing.

Sturgis had advised her, "Give the crowd what it wants. At least until you make it. Then you can do the things you like and the devil with the mob!"

Unhappy with the thought that she might be wasting her family's very meager resources, Laurie had floundered between her dream of being a writer and the suggestion made by some that she do something that paid better and provided more security. Maxine had said bluntly, "Money makes the world go round, kid. Get the cash!"

Now as Laurie rode to the post office she suddenly felt a relief—of sorts. *At least I won't be wasting Dad's money on something that may never pan out,* she thought. Throwing off the dark mood, she touched Star with her heels and galloped down the main street. When she got to the post office, she was about to step out of the saddle when a voice called her name.

"Hey, Laurie—come on with me and see the show!"

Laurie turned to see Clint Bonner, the blacksmith, passing by, leading a tall gray stallion. "What show, Clint?"

"Why, the Wild West Show. Didn't you read about it in the paper?" He drew up alongside her and shoved his hat back on his head, adding, "I been shoeing horses for Buffalo Bill himself all morning. This is his own personal mount."

"I can't afford it, Clint."

Bonner grinned and shook his head. He was a heavy-shouldered young man with very dark skin and gleaming teeth. He'd always shoed Star, refusing to accept any money. "Don't matter. C'mon, the show ain't until this afternoon, and I'll even introduce you to Colonel Cody and some of his fancy cowboys."

Laurie knew of William Cody's fame and had hoped to meet him someday. Suddenly a desire to see him perform came to Laurie and she said, "All right, Clint, I'll go with you." She pulled Star around, and the two rode toward the outskirts where the show was to be held in an open field.

Clint had seen the show the previous evening and spoke of it in an animated fashion. "Those Indians scare me a little," he confessed. "Supposed to be tame, but I'd hate to meet one of 'em on a dark night!" He gestured as they approached a large gathering of wagons and herds of horses tethered closely together. "There he is—the big man in buckskins—that's Buffalo Bill."

The blacksmith led the gray horse up to the three men who were having some sort of argument. Laurie pulled Star up, remaining back a few feet, and as Cody turned to greet Clint she studied him with interest. She had read about his exploits as a scout, Indian fighter, and hunter for the railroad, but what she hadn't told Clint was that her father had met him while serving under General Sherman. Cody looked much as her father had described him—big man with bold features and a pair of piercing eyes. He had a black mustache and a small goatee, which made him look rather natty, but there was no question, Laurie noted, of his strength and agility.

"Got your horse all shod, Mr. Cody," Clint said, and dismounted to hand the reins to the famous showman. "I built up that left rear shoe, just like you ordered."

"Fine! I do treasure that horse!" Cody's voice was a mellow baritone well suited to carrying over a large arena. He glanced suddenly at Laurie and smiled. "This pretty lady your wife?"

"No, but I wouldn't mind if she was," Clint grinned. "She's a college girl. Miss Laurie Winslow, this is Buffalo Bill Cody."

Cody advanced and put his hand up, smiling. "That's a mighty fine horse you're riding, Miss Laurie."

"Thank you, Mr. Cody." Laurie felt the power in Cody's grip, and when he released her hand, she said, "My father served with you once—under General Sherman."

Cody listened carefully as she related the circumstances, then exclaimed, "Why, certainly! I remember him well—Captain Tom Winslow!" He looked around at his two companions and winked. "This is an army girl, boys. None of your shenanigans, you hear me?" Then he said, "This is Johnny Baker, The Cowboy Kid, and this is Major Frank North. Miss Laurie, get down and I'll introduce you to the performers."

Why he's the biggest flirt I've ever seen! Laurie thought, and it came as a shock to her. But there was no mistaking the way Cody held her arm as he took her around, introducing her to the men who made up his show. *I'll have to tell Dad that Buffalo Bill is a lady killer—or thinks he is!*

Cody waited until last to introduce the Indians who were gathered over to one side of the encampment. He led Laurie up, squeezing her arm and whispering, "Don't be afraid, little lady. They look fierce, but I'm right here beside you!" He lifted his hand and said, "This is a guest, Running Bear. Miss Laurie Winslow. Miss Laurie, Running Bear is a great Sioux war chief."

Running Bear stared at Laurie out of flat black eyes, then said something in his own language. The braves around him laughed and Laurie's face burned. She had been a great friend of Luis Montoya, her father's best scout, and he had taught her a great deal of the Sioux language. Running Bear had made a crude joke about her, and without thinking, she responded in his own language, "Does a great chief of the Sioux speak so to a helpless woman?"

Her words fell like a blow on the Indians, and Running Bear's eyes opened wide with astonishment. He studied Laurie, then said, "The white woman is wise in the ways of the Sioux. How do you come to speak the language of the People?"

Colonel Cody stood staring at Laurie while she explained, his eyes filled with admiration. He himself knew only a few words of the Sioux language, and when Laurie finished, he said, "Now, Miss Laurie, that is *something!* Speak it like one of their own!" He took her arm again and led her to the cook tent, where he sat her at the table, piled her plate high, and told everyone how she'd handled Running Bear.

"What did the varmint say, Miss Laurie?" Johnny Baker demanded. He was a wiry young man barely twenty, and he had the palest blue eyes Laurie had ever seen.

"Something no gentleman would say to a lady," Laurie smiled. "I'm sure *you* would never say such a thing!"

"Don't you believe it," Cody laughed. "He's a real ladies' man, Johnny is." At that moment he caught a smile on Laurie's face as she looked at him, which made him falter. "Well, now, about that fine horse of yours, ever race him?"

"Oh yes," Laurie nodded. "He's pretty fast."

"How about a race?" Cody asked instantly.

"I'm not much for betting."

"Why, no, Miss Laurie," Cody protested. "Just for the fun of it."

Laurie allowed herself to be persuaded, and after the meal, the cowboys all followed Cody and Laurie. The Sioux came also, and Running Bear asked in his own language, "Can your horse win?"

"Bet on him!" Laurie said confidently, and the Indians at once began making bets with the cowboys.

Cody mounted his gray horse and winked at Laurie. "I like to be courteous to women, Miss Laurie, but when I race a hoss, I just plumb have to win!"

"Do your best, Mr. Cody, but I might make you one little wager."

Cody beamed at her. "How much?"

"Not money. If you win, you can take me to dinner with you after the show."

"That will be my pleasure!" Cody beamed.

"But if I win," Laurie went on, "I want you to think seriously about a request. I don't ask for a promise, just that you'll listen carefully."

"Done!" Cody agreed. "We'll race to those trees over there and back again. Johnny, give the signal—"

The two riders sat their horses, and when Johnny yelled, "Go!" they both took off at the same moment. Both horses were fast, but Cody's was somewhat stronger. He led as they reached the trees, and on the return, with the crowd yelling, Cody led by two lengths. When they were a hundred feet away from the finish line, Laurie screamed and threw herself backward. Her cry reached Cody, as did the sudden yells of the cowboys, and when he turned and saw the girl thrown backward, her head only inches away from the razor-sharp edges of Star's hooves, he drew up his big stallion, turning him to make a grab for Star's reins.

As soon as Laurie saw Cody stop and turn his horse, she pulled herself back into the saddle by the strap, dug her heels into Star's sides, and the astonished Cody watched her cross the finish line and turn to wave at him.

A loud cheer went up from the cowboys, and the Sioux were babbling with delight. Cody's face turned red—and then he threw his head back and roared with laughter. He spurred his big gray forward and put his hand out. "You win," he smiled. He looked around and saw the Indians collecting their bets. "You fellows got took as bad as I did." Then he turned to face Laurie. "I never was a welcher, Miss Laurie, but I sure would like to take you to supper after the show. Now, what is it you want me to think about?"

Laurie stared at the showman and said as firmly as she could, "I want to go with the show as a trick rider."

Cody was a hard man to surprise, but shock ran over his tanned face when he heard her request. His mouth opened, but he couldn't seem to find anything to say. Finally he shook his head and said, "Well, by gum—I'll do it!" Admiration shaded his glance, and he smiled, a handsome man, well aware of his success with women. "If you can do a few more tricks like that last one, I'll make a star of you, Laurie Winslow!"

At once she said, "I won't argue about salary, but this will be a *business* agreement and nothing more."

Cody's face fell, for her meaning was unmistakable. But he needed a novel act such as this. Some of his men were fine trick riders—but none were as pretty as this one. She had the nerve and the looks—and he regretfully put other ideas out of his head. He was a showman, this man, and yet he knew when to fold his cards.

"Why, of course!" he said, allowing shock to tinge his voice. "The daughter of my old friend, Captain Tom Winslow? I'll look after you just as though you were my own daughter!" He caught her slight smile but ignored it. "Come now, we'll go over the terms. This will be acceptable with your father, I take it? I can't have you if he doesn't agree."

"He will agree, Mr. Cody," she assured him.

"Fine! But you do understand, these men of mine are the finest in the world, but they're a little rough. Their language—things like that."

"Their language is probably as refined as the troopers in my father's command, and I got along fine with them."

Laurie was happy at this sudden change of events, more so than she'd ever hoped, and her eyes shone with excitement. *I don't have to go home!* she thought. And then she remembered the words of her friend Mac McGonigal: *He'll give you the desires of your heart.*

★   ★   ★   ★

Late that night, McGonigal was rudely awakened by a pounding on the door. Throwing the cover back, he stumbled across the room, stubbing his toe on a box, and then throwing the lock, shouted, "Who's there?"

McGonigal was driven backward as Laurie Winslow came through the door like a small whirlwind. She was babbling something as the door slammed back, leaving Mac standing there in an agony of embarrassment. "Will ye get out of here and let a man get his pants on?" he demanded.

"Oh, forget your pants!" Laurie laughed, but she turned her back while he hastily lit a lamp and found a pair of pants to put on. Whirling around again, the words spilled out of her as she related her adventure. "And I'm leaving with the Wild West Show Saturday, Mac! Isn't it wonderful—and it's the desire of my heart, just like you said! The Lord's done it!"

"I'd not be so quick to blame everything on the good Lord!" Mac snapped sharply. He shook his head dolefully. "These acting fellers—they've got no more morals than an alley cat. You can't go runnin' around the country with the likes of them!"

Laurie's eyes glowed, and she took his arms firmly. "But I'll have a chaperon to look out for me, Mac. He'll see that I'm all right."

"And who might that be?" the old man asked, rubbing his tired eyes.

"You!" Laurie laughed with delight at the shocked expression on the Irishman's face. "You're dying of boredom here, Mac—and Mr. Cody wants you to come with the show. He needs a good man to take care of the horses, and I told him you're the best there is! Oh, Mac, you've got to do it!"

Michael McGonigal was confused. He hated his job, and he loved this young woman as a man loves a daughter. Ever since the first day she had ridden up the lane at Wilson College, she had been the light of his life—and now it seemed that his sun was about to die. He thought of what it would be like to be rid of the stables and to travel with other horsemen—and to be close to Laurie.

He suddenly rubbed his eyes fiercely, muttering, "Got some sleep in me eyes, I reckon—" He turned his back and stared at the wall, then cleared his throat. Finally he faced Laurie and gave her a beautiful smile.

"Well, now, Laurie—I reckon the good Lord is about to give *both* of us the desires of our hearts! Ain't it a wonder, now? Ain't it grand to be a child of the great King?"

Then she fell into his arms, and the two did a happy little dance on the wooden floor. The horse in the stall outside poked his head over the wall and stared toward them wild-eyed, wondering what it all meant.

This was the beginning for Laurie—a new life such as she'd never dreamed. Over the next few months, both Laurie and McGonigal were kept busy learning new skills. But whenever Laurie seemed to face a new challenge, her Irish friend was always there with firm support and good advice.

McGonigal's firm conviction that the Lord always had a hand on all things slowly began to have an effect on Laurie. As she settled into her routine, the years of godly advice that had soaked into her from childhood surfaced. When trials or temptations came, she seemed almost to hear the voice of her father or her mother reading scripture, and she grew to love the Bible in a fresh way.

Laurie had always longed to hear from God in a personal way—such as she had seen in her parent's lives—and as times passed, she spent all her spare hours reading the well-worn Bible her mother had given her that last day.

With the passing of time, a new peace and sense of the presence of God came to rule over her spirit. And it was McGonigal who noticed her new walk with God and summed it up:

"You've grown up in the Lord, Laurie—now we'll see what God has in store for you!"

PART TWO

CODY ROGERS

★ ★ ★ ★

CHAPTER SEVEN

THE WAY OF A WOMAN

★   ★   ★   ★

The best time of the day for Hope Winslow was the early cobwebby hours of the morning—the time when the sun began to light the east, shedding the darkness of the plains. She lay in bed enjoying the coolness, knowing the heat would soon come. As the bedroom began to grow lighter, she turned her head and watched Dan sleep. He always slept on his back and was one of the few people she knew who didn't snore in that position. Lying on her side, she traced his strong features as the light illuminated them. Cautiously she reached over and smoothed the black hair where it had fallen over his forehead, smiling as she thought how much he looked like a little boy as he slept. He always folded his hands over his chest, and she noticed that he was smiling a little, his features relaxed. She liked the way he slept, and now, as the morning dawned, she leaned over and whispered, "Wake up."

Dan Winslow did not come awake like most people—slowly, a little at a time. At once his eyes flew open and he turned his head and looked into her eyes, saying, "Good morning." He unfolded his hands, rolled over on his left side so that he faced her, reached over, and stroked her light brown hair. "How is it," he murmured, a smile turning the corner of his lips up, "that every morning of your life you get more and more beautiful?"

Hope had heard this, or some form of it, practically every morning of their married life, but it never ceased to give her a sense of pleasure. She thought quickly of her first two husbands—the first one so far back that she could barely remember him at times. He had given her Cody, for which she was grateful, but her memories of him were unpleasant ones. He had not been gentle in his lovemaking, but selfish and demanding. Her second husband she put quickly out of her mind, for she had known nothing but cruelty from him. But this man lying by her side was totally different. She had learned what true love was only with Dan Winslow. She had been amazed to find that a man could be so sensitive and so strong at the same time. Stroking his arm now she whispered, "I got a prize when I got you, Dan Winslow. Just think of how many women would like to be in my place!"

He laughed, amused at her thoughts. "What would you do if you found one in your place?"

"Scratch her eyes out!" Hope said, trying to look mean and vicious and failing miserably.

They lay there in the bed holding each other, talking about unimportant things. This early morning interlude had been a time that Dan had also learned to treasure. He had found in Hope Winslow the woman that he had always longed for, and he thanked God every day of his life that he had been blessed with such a wife.

"I guess we better get up," Hope said reluctantly. When Dan reached out and held her, kissing her firmly, she surrendered to his caress for a moment—then she pushed him away, laughing. "Never mind all that, I've got work to do."

Dan lay back, locked his fingers together, and watched her as she began to get dressed. "I think I'll have breakfast in bed today," he pronounced. "You know what I like best, so just bring it in here."

"That'll be the day!" she scoffed. "Get out of that bed, you loafer! I've got half a dozen things for you to do." Dan rolled over reluctantly, got out of bed, and began to get dressed. As he walked over and poured the shaving water into the basin at the washstand and began to work up a lather, he said, "What did you think of that last letter from Tom?"

Hope straightened up from where she was making the bed

and looked at him. "I was sorry to hear that they had decided not to come and go into ranching here. Do you think we should try and urge them to change their mind?"

"I don't think so. You know how Tom is—stubborn as a mule sometimes." He began to brush his face with a rich, creamy lather, then picked up a razor, tested it, and carefully drew it across his cheek. He had a tough beard that was hard to cut, and his eyes watered. "I wish I could swear like I used to over shaving," he said. "It always seemed to help." Then he turned more serious and said, "No, Tom won't leave the army. It's the kind of life he was made for, and I'm just grateful he's got a good wife to share it with him. Not many women could follow a man out on those lonely, miserable army posts."

Hope finished the bed, came over, and sat down to watch him finish shaving. She knew him better than she had thought a woman could know a man. She traced his strong, stark features, admiring the light blue eyes that all Winslow men seemed to have. Something had been bothering her, and she had learned that she could share anything with Dan, so she said, "I'm worried about Cody."

At once, Dan turned to look at her. "I know. I've been worried myself." He drew the razor down and wiped it on the towel across his shoulder, then proceeded to cut another swath. Finally, after a few more painful passes, he was finished. He washed his face, took the clean towel she handed to him, and then turned to answer her. "He's too caught up with Susan, and she's not the kind of girl he needs."

"She's a good girl, I don't think there's any question about that."

"No, I don't think there is. As many men as have been chasing her, I guess she's done fairly well. That sort of thing is liable to turn any girl's head."

"I know. She's so pretty—but I don't think she'll ever make a rancher's wife, and that's all Cody's ever wanted to be." She looked at him and watched as he combed his thick, black hair, then asked, "Do you think you might talk to him about her?"

Dan finished combing his hair, picked up a handkerchief and jammed it into his pocket, then said, "I don't know, Hope. It's a pretty touchy situation. A young fellow like that, he's like all the

96

rest. Like I was." He smiled at the thought of his own past and shook his head. "Nobody could tell me a thing when I was Cody's age."

Hope sighed. "Well, I'm going to fix breakfast now. We'll just have to pray that girl will settle down, because Cody's bound and determined he's going to marry her." She left the room and went to the kitchen, where she found Ozzie Og already stomping around, rattling pans, getting breakfast ready.

"You make more noise cooking than any man I've ever seen," Hope smiled. She walked over, picked up a large bowl, and began mixing biscuits. "I don't know why you don't let me cook breakfast anyhow."

Ozzie Og was a short stumpy man of forty-five, pessimistic as a person can be. Loyal to Dan Winslow and the Circle W, he'd come up the trail with Hope and her family and loved the young woman as if she were his own daughter. "Because I can cook a whole heap better than you can," he stated emphatically. "You can't cook eggs without burning them." He began to complain and fuss, but Hope only smiled at him, and together the two of them put together a huge mountain of food that would satisfy any cowhand.

As soon as the table was readied and the food set out Og went to the bunkhouse to get the hands. They all came trooping in, and soon the large dining room was filled with cheerful talk and the laughter of the men. Hope moved around, filling coffee mugs, and thinking how fortunate she and Dan were to have such a loyal crew. However, she did notice that Cody had not come down for breakfast. It bothered her, but she said nothing.

After the crew had left, Og mentioned Cody's absence. "Well, he got in about three hours ago. I heard him ride in." He looked over the huge pile of dirty dishes on the table and shrugged. "He won't get nothing to eat here." With an armful of dirty dishes he headed for the washbasin. Then he stopped, turned back toward Hope, and added gloomily, "That boy won't be worth nothin' either if he don't stop chasing around after that Susan gal."

"He works hard, Ozzie. You know he does," said Hope, trying to put the best face on it.

"I know that. The trouble is he works just as hard chasing

that girl as he does chasing these cow critters!"

Stomping over to where a calendar was nailed to the wall, he fished a stubby pencil out of his pocket and crossed out the date, muttering, "June 6, 1883." He stared at the calendar as if it had some deep meaning, then turned around and came over to stand beside Hope. "I'm worried about that boy," he admitted finally. "I know you and Dan are, too." He stood there uncertainly, wanting to think of a good word to say, and finally shook his head. "Well," he said, "I guess, like all young fellows, he's gotta eat his peck of dirt, and it looks like that gal is set to provide just that kind of a diet for him."

An hour later, after Og had left to go cut firewood, Cody entered the kitchen. His eyes were red from lack of sleep and he hadn't shaved, but Hope paid no attention. "I saved you some bacon and eggs, Cody," she said. "Sit down and have breakfast."

"Thanks, Mom." Cody sat down and ate hungrily as Hope joined him, drinking a cup of coffee. Finally, noting that he seemed surly and unhappy, she said, "Cody, you're staying out too late. It's not good for you, missing all that sleep, then working hard like you do all day."

"I'm all right," he shrugged, reaching for another piece of bacon.

"No, you're not." Hope took a deep breath and said firmly, "Cody, I've been wanting to talk to you for a long time about Susan. You're seeing too much of her, I think."

A stubborn look came over Cody's face. He was a handsome, tall young man with a wide mouth, straight tawny hair that fell over his forehead, and very dark blue eyes. His build was lean and strong, as a rider had to be to do the hard work he did. But the stubbornness that was in him rose up now and his face grew slightly red. "Don't worry about that, Mom," he muttered.

Hope studied him, knowing instantly that any further mention of the matter would do no good. This tall son of hers had always been an independent young man. He'd ridden up the trail to the ranch doing a man's work by the time he was fifteen, and now, at the age of twenty-one, he was as good with cattle, with a rope, or with a gun, as any rider in the entire valley. He'd grown beyond her control and was now a man, so she said merely, "Be careful, Cody. More men get into trouble over women than over any other thing."

Cody stared at her, but as much as he loved her, this one area of his life he had blocked out. "Don't worry, Mom. I'll be all right, but I've gotta have Susan. You know how much I love her." He got up abruptly and left the house, and as he slammed the door unconsciously, Hope shook her head thinking, *He's headed for trouble and there's nothing I can do about it!*

★ ★ ★ ★

Susan Taylor left her house and soon reached the center of town. Crossing the busy main street, she headed for the short building with the newly painted sign. The *Sentinel* was one of the better small-town newspapers of the territory, and as she entered the door, she always felt a small thrill of pride knowing that she was a part of it.

"About time you got up and came to work." Mason Taylor, her father, was a heavyset man with a batch of thick black hair and sharp black eyes to match. "Susan, I've warned you before about this. This paper can't get itself out."

"I'm sorry, Daddy," Susan said. She came over and turned her large eyes on him, adding, "I'm real sorry. I won't let it happen again."

Mason Taylor knew people very well and was not fooled for one minute by Susan's big eyes, or by her apologetic attitude. "What time did you get in last night?" he demanded. Then without waiting for an answer said, "Never mind, I know what time it was. No time for a young girl to be coming in. From now on you get yourself in earlier, you hear me?"

"Oh, I'll be more careful, Daddy," Susan promised. Then quickly changing the subject she said, "Let me get busy now, and I'll work hard and catch up."

Before he could say another word, she went to work. For the next hour she bustled about the *Sentinel* office. Finally, she sat down at her desk and was going through some papers when she heard a familiar step and looked up.

"Well, how's my best girl today?" Harve Tippitt, a tall, well-built man of about twenty-five, stepped in and came to stand before her. He pulled his hat off, his blond hair falling over his forehead. He had searching blue eyes that were bold and prominent. He smiled broadly, aware that he made a handsome picture. "I didn't keep you out too late last night, did I?"

Susan shushed him, glancing over, for her father was sitting at his desk peering at them over his glasses. "Daddy says I have to be in earlier," she said loud enough for him to hear, "and I think he's right."

Harve Tippitt turned his head so that Taylor couldn't see, and gave her a wink. "Well that's right, a young woman can't be too careful about her reputation." As he stood there talking, Susan thought of all the young women in the county who would give anything to be the center of Harve Tippitt's attention. He was the son of George Tippitt, owner of one of the largest ranches in the county, and about half the town. As she flirted with him, she thought, *Big, handsome, rich, and lots of fun. What more could a girl want out of a man?* But aloud she said, "I can't go out with you tonight, Harve. I need to stay home more."

Harve Tippitt leaned over on the desk, smiled and shook his head. "You can stay home when you're an old lady," he whispered. "There's a dance over at Fairview tomorrow. Be ready at six o'clock." He straightened up and said, "Mr. Taylor, I'm going to borrow your best worker for a dance tomorrow. If it's all right with you, that is."

Taylor well knew that Harve Tippitt's father, George, was one of his best customers, and the most influential man in the county. He said, as amiably as he could, "Have her in early, Harve. She needs to get more sleep."

"I'll have her in early enough to suit everybody," Tippitt assured him. Then he turned and left.

As soon as he was out of the door, Taylor rose and came over to stand beside Susan's desk. "You're flying pretty high, Susan. Which one of those two men you gonna have, him or Cody?"

Susan looked up. She made a pretty sight, her eyes glinting. She had beautiful blue eyes that went well with her blond hair, giving her a dramatic look. When she smiled her lips were soft and curved upward humorously. "I won't even tell *them* that, Daddy. You don't expect a girl to tell everything she knows, do you?"

Taylor shook his head and went away muttering, "You'd better pick one or the other of them or there's gonna be a whale of a fight someday."

His warning had little effect on Susan, and all afternoon as she worked, humming to herself, she thought about the dance at Fairview.

★　★　★　★

The community building that was used for the dances in Fairview had been decorated extensively by the ladies of the town. Brightly colored draperies hung from the ceiling, and the walls liberally caught the bright amber glow that a myriad of lamps cast over the dance floor. As Harve Tippitt entered with Susan on his arm, he looked around the already crowded room and commented with satisfaction, "Well, I don't see Cody here. Maybe he's decided to let the best man win."

Susan smiled up at him and shook her head. "I doubt you'll get rid of Cody that easy," she said. She was wearing a bright red dress, which few young women could wear with such aplomb. Her blond hair was piled up in curls on top of her head, and two small pearl earrings dangled from her ears. She looked beautiful and knew it. "Come on, Harve, let's dance," she said at once.

The two moved to the dance floor, and as the music began Harve commented on her dress and her lovely appearance. He had a certain flare with women, having had much experience. As Susan well knew, he had been in trouble several times, primarily for fighting and drinking. But being the son of George Tippitt, he had never received more than a reprimand. He looked smart in his brown suit with the white shirt setting off his florid complexion. He was entertaining, too, keeping her amused as they twirled round the floor, until suddenly he stopped and a frown crossed his face.

"What is it?" Susan asked. Then looking over toward the door, she saw Cody come in. She concealed a smile, knowing that Harve was terribly jealous. She secretly took pleasure in keeping both men off balance. She had learned this knack of handling men when she was no more than sixteen years old, and had refined it almost to an art. "Why, there's Cody," she said sprightly, and waved at him. "Look, he's coming over. I think he's going to cut in."

She was not wrong, for when Cody came up, he gave Tippitt

a crooked grin, saying, "You don't mind, do you, Harve?" and then turned his attention at once to Susan. Putting his arms out, he moved her away in a sweeping series of turns, laughing as they went. "Old Harve doesn't like to be cut out, does he Susan?"

"You're *awful*, Cody!" she rebuked him. But she was smiling, and the two danced the rest of the dance without incident.

As soon as the dance was over, Tippitt was right at Cody's side, saying, "All right, my turn." Though he was smiling, there was a tenseness around his mouth as he suddenly asked, "Cody, why don't you get a girl of your own?"

"Got one," Cody said. He looked over at Susan and nodded. "You're looking at her. I'm just letting you bring her to this dance because I'm bighearted."

Tippitt took Susan's arm, squeezing her so hard it hurt, and swung her away as the music began. As they danced, she admonished him, "You shouldn't be so short with Cody." Looking at him curiously, she asked, "You two were good friends for a long time, weren't you?"

"When we were kids. Cody's a pretty good hand, but he doesn't move in my circles now." He purposely said this as a reminder of the difference in status between him and Cody. Cody was little more than top hand on his stepfather's ranch, while Harve was heir to a large cattle empire plus various business ventures. "I don't see why you don't tell him to stop coming around, Susan. You and I have fun, don't we?"

"Yes, we do, but Cody's fun, too." Susan had been half waiting for Tippitt to make some sort of comment about a more permanent arrangement, but he did not. *He's a hard man to pen in*, she thought, *but sooner or later, he'll come to heel*. She was not at all a spiteful girl, but she was enjoying being the center of attention of these two eager suitors.

The dance went on without incident until almost eleven. At that time, some of the men had gathered around a table to play the old arm-wrestling game. Sturdy Ben Williams of the Bar X had been the champion for a long time, and he looked around after defeating his last opponent, asking, "Any more takers?"

"Go on, give him a try, Harve," Cody grinned.

Harve was proud of his strength and sat down in front of Williams. "I'll have a try," he agreed. Harve put his whole effort into the match, but Williams was too much and put Tippitt's hand down without any trouble. Williams grinned, "You may have all the money in the world, Harve, but I ain't never been beat at this game."

Tippitt got up, his face red. He was a man who did not like to lose, and he glared at Cody, challenging him, "Have a try yourself, Cody. Let's see what a man you are."

Susan encouraged him, "Go on and do it. If you beat him, I'll let you take me home."

At this, Cody's glance went at once to her face, but a streak of jealousy, almost a rage, ran through Tippitt. "He can't beat Ben," Tippitt stated flatly. "Nobody can."

Cody looked at the husky Williams, sobered, then walked over and took his seat. He extended his hand, and Williams grinned back. "How much you pay me to let you win, Cody? Then you can take that pretty girl home."

Cody shook his head, saying, "Let her rip whenever you're ready, Ben."

Ben smiled a little contemptuously and began exerting the pressure. Almost at once a look of surprise flitted across his face. He was such a powerful man that he had little trouble putting most men's hands down almost at once, but he was having difficulty now, and his lips drew into a fine white line as he threw all of his force into his forearm. Cody's arm was pushed halfway back toward the table, but he lowered his head and threw every ounce of his will into his right arm, bringing the force of Williams' massive power to a slow halt. The two men appeared to be frozen, but everyone saw the power exerted by both. Cody did not seem to be strong enough to hold Williams off, but he had spent a lifetime in the saddle, besides working in the forge doing all the heavy, hard work of a ranch hand. And now he was calling forth every ounce of strength in him to push Williams' hand back.

"Look at that!" a man next to Tippitt whispered. Tippitt looked on in amazement at what he saw. The hands of the two men were moving, and to everyone's surprise, Cody was actually forcing Williams' big arm upright. A murmur went around the room, and a bead of sweat popped out on Williams' face. Gritting his teeth, he tried to stop the pressure, but the steely hand of

Cody Rogers had closed around his hand with a grip he had never experienced, almost paralyzing it. Cody looked up, and a wild fire burned in his eyes as he looked into the eyes of the man opposite him. With a final burst of strength, he slammed Williams' hand down against the table.

At once Ben Williams got up and said with astonishment, "I never knowed you could do that, Cody! Here, you're the top hoss from here on in at arm wrestling."

Cody looked at his own hand that was tingling and his arm that felt almost dead. Then he grinned up at Susan. "Looks like I'm the one to take you home." Turning his gaze back to Harve Tippitt he said, "Too bad, Harve. Go do a little growing up, then maybe you can take her home the next time." He laughed, took Susan by the arm, and swung her out on the dance floor for the last dance.

Harve Tippitt stood there, anger flowing through him. He wanted to fight but knew this was no time for it. Charlie Littleton had come up behind him and now said, "Well, Harve, that's one dance you won't get. Probably one kiss, too." Littleton was a rancher out in the deep hills, rightly suspected of being a rustler. He was the only one who could tease Harve Tippitt, for he had nothing to lose. "Now was that me, I don't think I'd let that yahoo take my girl away."

And then Tippitt's eyes went a little crazy. So wild that Charlie Littleton, for all his toughness, blinked and stepped back. He had seen murder written in a man's face before, and he knew at once that Harve Tippitt was only a step away. "Hey, take it easy, Harve," he said quickly, shaking his head. "She's only another girl." Then seeing that Tippitt was not listening, he turned and walked away.

Staring at the pair on the dance floor, Harve Tippitt muttered under his breath, "We'll see about who takes whose girl. We'll just see about that!"

CHAPTER EIGHT

No Quarter Given

★　★　★　★

When Les Dunbar decided to give up being a puncher for the Circle W and start his own small spread, he received all sorts of fatherly advice, mostly negative, from the crew. Smoky Jacks, upon hearing the news that Dunbar was going to marry Mary White and become a rancher, gave a slight smile and said, "Les, take the advice of one who's like a father to you. Never stray far from a steady paycheck, honor your parents, cherish the little red schoolhouse, speak respectfully of all our great institutions— and don't ever try to run a jackrabbit ranch." The trim rider shook his head sorrowfully, saying, "You're looking at one who busted his back trying, and found out it's harder than it looks."

But young Les Dunbar was a man in love and not to be denied. The affair proceeded and finally, in August, a cabin raising was organized by Dunbar's friends to set the new couple up on their small ranch.

When the day arrived and all the logs had been cut, Dan Winslow proclaimed a holiday, and the whole crew left just after daybreak for the cabin raising. After a steady ride, with a few stops to rest their mounts, they reached the small ranch by ten o'clock. Dismounting, they tied up their horses a ways off from the pile of rough lumber and logs that marked the future house of the young couple. Les Dunbar had picked a long, narrow meadow that lay against a small river, and being practical, he had also found a spot relatively close to the railroads, where he could ship his cattle.

The site was covered with more than one hundred people milling around—most of them from town, but many of them from small ranches and farms nearby. They were drawn not so much by the fact of a marriage as by the need they felt for an occasional cheerful gathering. Families worked hard to eke out a living from the land. The day's labors started early and often went till long after the sun set, especially for those who had stock. Any social event that came along helped ease the strain of it all.

As people arrived the field began to fill up with saddle horses and wagon teams that were soon grazing lazily. The wagons that arrived were filled with families with excited children that greeted one another. As soon as they unloaded the wagons, the men—young and old—gathered in crews with newly sharpened axes to prepare the logs that would soon form the wall of the cabin. Others set about with saw and wedge and froe to rive out the cedar shakes for the roof. One crew set about erecting the fireplace, which, being a matter of some delicacy, had been put in charge of the man who seemed to know most about depth and width necessary to assume a proper "draw."

This was, in effect, a holiday for the settlers and ranchers over which the groom and bride-to-be had little control. The young couple stood to one side, and the bride-to-be whispered to Les, "Let them do it the way they want, Les. After they're gone, you and I can fix it like we want it."

The women wasted no time in getting several cheerful fires burning off to one side. To feed the amount of people who had come to lend a hand would take a better part of the day. Yet in the midst of setting pots over the fires, and keeping an eye on the children that played about, the ladies kept up a continual chatter of friendly conversation, giving them all a chance to catch up on the local news. As for food, each woman took pride in setting out her favorite dishes for all to see. There were all kinds of fruit pies, fresh butter formed in various patterns, sausages, cucumbers in cream and vinegar, and assorted jams. Even some of the men boasted of the game they had been able to hunt and bring to roast.

Shortly before sunset, the last log was set in place and the house was finished. Perspiring men came out with the heavy log ends with which they had beaten down the earth floor, which the bride's mother had insisted on, in preference to puncheons "because the earth is more healthy." The wedding guests proceeded to move in a four-posted cherry wood bed that had traveled two thousand miles overland, homemade chairs and tables, dishes and cooking utensils, a feather mattress with pillows and a patchwork spread, a barrel of sugar and a barrel of flour and sides of cured meats—all the trinkets and accouterments of a home. As the ladies scurried about making the last touches, someone lighted a fire in the finished hearth. In a matter of hours the cabin was looking like a real home. Many of the wedding gifts that were brought were simple furnishings, and after being shown to the couple they were set in place in the cabin.

Just as the last of the dishes were put in the cupboard, and a brush broom tipped against the wall, a man drove up with a wagon and a team. In the wagon were a plow and a harrow. As soon as Mary White saw her father get down and tie his team to the door, she ran to find Les and the minister, who were off somewhere talking.

Cody stood beside Susan Taylor and wished that Harve Tippitt had not been able to come. The two had worked on separate crews, each keeping a careful eye on the other to see that neither of them slipped away to spend time with Susan. Now, as the work was done and the minister stood in the meadow, the two young people before him, Cody leaned down and whispered, "I wish that was you and me."

Susan turned to face him, her eyes bright, but she made no answer. On the other side, Harve, who had heard the words, leveled a hard look at Cody. The crowd spread out in a circle around the young couple, and as the sun dropped west, the hour of water-clear light settled upon the land with its fragrance and its stillness—so complete that the minister's voice resounded all down the meadow. He married them and pronounced his benediction, and then he put his Bible in his rear trouser pocket and stood back while young Les Dunbar, completely oblivious to all those standing around, accepted his wife with a vigorous kiss. The new Mrs. Dunbar was smiling, composed, and then her father said, "Supper. C'mon, we got a-plenty."

Cody moved toward the tables laden with the food and piled his plate high, noticing that Harve had walked up and joined Susan. Smoky Jacks, standing close, murmured with a sly twinkle in his eye, "Better watch out. Looks like ol' Harve is attaching himself to Susan like a barnacle on a ship."

Cody shook his head, "I wish that fellow would find another girl. I'm tired of having him around." Filling two plates, he walked over to where they were talking and said, "Harve, you better get that food before it's all gone."

Harve Tippitt shook his head. "I'll just have some dessert a little later." Then he looked at Susan and said, "I'll be driving you home, won't I, Susan?"

Susan Taylor was in her element. She was a pleasure-loving girl, one of the most sociable young women that Cody had ever seen. She loved parties and gatherings of all kinds, and more than once Cody had wondered how he would keep her entertained when they had their own place, and such festivities were rare.

Susan cocked her head, and with a demure smile said, "You and Cody will have to decide that. I can't ride home with both of you."

"You wanna flip a coin?" Cody asked quickly. "Or maybe have a shooting match, or a horse race even?"

The mention of the horse race stirred a simmering anger in Harve Tippitt, and he shook his head. "I'm not gettin' in any fool contest, Cody. I'm taking Susan home tonight, and that's all there is to it." There was an arrogance in the man as he set his shoulders firmly, fixing his eyes on Cody.

"We'll see about that, Harve," Cody murmured, then turned to Susan and began to talk to her as if Tippitt were not even there.

After the meal was over, a man jumped up with a fiddle on his shoulder and let out a whoop, hollering, "Where's Simon to call for us? Come on now—come on, we've got to dance off these provisions before we go home!"

The stars were brightly glinting in a sharp, black sky, the musicians were shouting, and the sound of the fiddles and the mandolins tuning up was tinkling on the air. One of the men disappeared and came back toward the fire laughing with a keg under his arm. He got a bucket, poured the contents of the keg into it, and walked in the house for a dipper. He came back with a second bucket, and with both buckets and dippers, he made his rounds. "Whiskey or water? Can't dance without sweatin'. Whiskey or water?"

Most of the men declared for the whiskey, but Cody shook his head. He was not a drinking man, disliked the taste of it and even more the effect afterward, so he contented himself with the water. Finally, the fiddler launched into a familiar tune and the caller—a tall, thin man with bright red hair and a prominent Adam's apple—stood up and called out, "Partners, form your sets! We got room for two sets at a time."

"Come on, Susan," Cody said, but found that he had been forestalled, for Harve had stepped around beside him and pulled Susan to her feet and was walking with her toward the opening where the dancers were beginning to form the sets. Cody shook his head in disgust, muttering under his breath, "I've gotta move as fast as that if I'm gonna cut Harve out tonight."

The dancers moved in time to the lively music and the caller sang out, "Form and balance all! Let her go, Jed!" The fiddler sank his bow on the fiddle strings and swung into a reel. The two sets formed, four couples to a set, near the fire. The caller's voice whipped them around; they stepped over the trampled grass of the meadow, out and back. "Oh, take your girls, your pretty little girls," cried the caller while the onlooking spectators clapped to the lively music. "Virginia is a grand old state. Come on, boys, don't be late."

The dance proceeded for over an hour, and soon a contest developed between Cody and Tippitt, as was expected by everyone. They both sought to dance with Susan in every set, and their rivalry became the object of some crude jokes among the ranch hands.

But Dan and Hope were not amused. They danced several times themselves, but Hope remarked, "I don't like the way those two are acting, Dan. Susan ought to put a stop to it."

"Not her," Dan shook his head. "She loves every minute of it."

"Well, she's creating a problem for herself, urging them both on like that. I wish she'd make up her mind so that it was all settled."

She looked up at Dan and shook her head, adding, "There's going to be trouble, I'm afraid, between those two."

Her words proved to be prophetic, for not five minutes later, when Cody reached to take Susan's hand, he found his wrist grasped, and it was pulled aside. Whirling around, he saw that Tippitt was grinning loosely. His eyes were bright with the effect of the liquor, for he had been drinking heavily from the bucket containing the whiskey. "I think this is my dance, Cody," he said. "Go find another girl."

Cody jerked his hand back and stood staring at the larger man. "You're wrong about that, Harve," he said through clenched teeth. "This is *my* dance. You had the last one."

The liquor had loosened Tippitt's temper, and he shook his head, his lips growing into an even broader smile. "Get along, little man. I'm dancing this set." He pulled at Susan, but suddenly Cody reached out and struck his forearm with the edge of his palm. The hard blow numbed Tippitt's arm, and he released the girl's arm at once. But anger laced his voice as he said loudly, "Nobody lays a hand on me, Cody. You know that."

Cody shrugged. "Come on, Susan. Let's get to the dance." He reached out for her, but without warning Harve Tippitt struck out and his hard fist caught Cody high on the forehead, knocking him to the ground.

Susan cried out, "Oh no, Harve!" and her cry attracted the attention of the others, so that a muttered exclamation went up, and the fiddles scraped to a stop.

Cody was not hurt badly and came to his feet like a cat. He moved toward Harve, but Ozzie Og and Smoky Jacks grabbed his arms. "Take it easy," Smoky murmured, although his own eyes were hot with anger. "You can't have a fight here."

But Cody had caught the insolence in Tippitt's eyes and knew that if he let this pass he would never live it down. There was an arrogance in Tippitt that would not be stopped with anything less than a physical beating. "Come on," Cody said, "we'll settle this once and for all."

"That suits me," Tippitt growled. The two suitors turned and walked away and were followed at once by most of the men.

Dan stepped up as the two opponents squared off and said, "You fellows need to cut this out. It won't settle anything."

Cody shook his head, "He's asking for it, and I'm going to give it to him." He held his hands down at his sides and looked at Tippitt carefully. Tippitt was well over six feet and bulky with muscle. He was a strong, powerful man and had a record as a brawler.

Now he looked at Cody, taking in the smaller man's lean form, and sneered, "I propose to stop this foolishness tonight. The loser lets Susan alone. Are you agreed?"

At once Cody nodded, "Fine with me," but he barely got the words out of his mouth before Tippitt threw a thundering right at his jaw. He was caught off guard, not quite ready, but managed to move his head so that the blow merely grazed his cheek. Cody was a fast young man with very quick reflexes. As Tippitt lunged by, he reached out with a quick right and caught the larger man with a hard blow to the body.

Tippitt grunted, but was well covered with muscle, and simply whirled. He held up his hand then, and there was a hatred in his eyes that sobered Cody. *This is not going to be easy*, he thought to himself, and as the larger man came in, he backed away, keeping high on his toes, knowing that his only hope was to stand off and let the bigger man tire himself out. He was aware of the crowd around him watching, some of them crying out to their favorites, but then all of that faded, and his vision centered on the face and the fists of Harve Tippitt.

Tippitt moved forward, flat-footed, throwing punches that he seemed to pull from the ground, any one of which would have ended the fight. Cody caught them on his forearms, slipping them with his fist, but he could not stop them all. One wild right caught him flush in the mouth, and he staggered backward, tasting the warm blood as it ran down his jaw. A cry went up from Tippitt, who rushed forward, intending to end the fight. He threw blow after blow, many of them landing, some on the chest of his opponent, but most of them caught on Cody's forearms.

To all observers, it seemed the fight was going Harve Tippitt's way, but Smoky Jacks leaned over and whispered to Og, "Look at that, Ozzie, Cody's lettin' Tippitt wear himself out. Soon as he runs out of breath, you'll see something."

Og shook his head, saying, "If he don't get beat to death before that happens."

Soon, it became apparent that Tippitt was beginning to tire. His face was flushed with the whiskey and the tremendous efforts he was putting into the fight. With each punch Tippitt threw, Cody noticed his opponent moving slower. Finally, he knew it was time to carry the final punch to Tippitt. When the bigger man drew his hand back to throw another thunderous right, Cody suddenly stopped his backward progress, stepped forward with one quick step, and threw a hard right hand that moved so fast Tippitt did not even see it. It caught him on the nose and brought an excruciating pain that made him blink his eyes. Before he had time to catch his breath, another blow, this time a left, caught him high on the head, splitting the skin over his eyebrow. With those two blows, Harve Tippitt's face suddenly became bloody. He stopped to wipe the blood running out of his eyebrow with his sleeve, and then found he was being pounded by such quick blows that he had no defense. With a roar, he threw himself forward and caught Cody around the body with his huge arms. Driving ahead, he tipped the smaller man over, and they fell to the ground. A yell went up as the two rolled over and over, this time with Harve getting the best of it, using his superior weight to punish Cody.

Cody fought back as best he could, but he knew that if he ever got trapped on the ground, as Harve obviously intended to do, he would be beaten to a pulp. Frantically, he shoved and fought, trying to shake free, but the huge hands of Harve Tippitt were like vises clamped on him. Cody suddenly was trapped as Harve straddled him and lifted his hand to throw a heavy fist into Cody's face. There was a vicious look on Tippitt's features—his eyes mad with the fury that had risen up in him—and he drove his fists down on the helpless man pinned to the earth. The blows caught Cody on the side of the head as he attempted to dodge, and the world exploded into a series of flashing lights. Another blow caught him, this time in the throat, which gagged him. *Got to get him off,* he thought wildly. And when Harve drew back his fist, Cody surged upward with all of his strength, shoving with his heels and driving his fists with a blow that caught

Tippitt in the solar plexus. The air came out of the larger man with a *whuff*, and Cody struck again, managing to shove him off so that he was free.

The two men got to their feet, and somebody shouted, "You fellows ought to stop it." But they ignored him, and once again, it became a contest of Tippitt's strength against Cody's quickness. The two circled each other, marshaling their strength, knowing that the fight could not last much longer. Cody was growing tired himself. Both of them were moving much slower now, having thrown many blows and taken many. Cody had one chance and took it. Leaving his face wide open, he pivoted and threw the hardest right hand he'd ever thrown at the unprotected stomach of Harve Tippitt. Tippitt had raised his hands to protect his face, and the blow caught him, again, right in the solar plexus. He gagged, and bent over slightly, trying to suck the air in, but he could not. He stood there almost helpless as Cody rained blows into his face. Only once did he manage to get a blow in that caught Cody flush in the mouth and drove him backward. But Cody was back at once, driving blow after blow, moving forward, driving the bigger man backward. Finally, Cody landed a hard right on the point of Tippitt's chin that drove him backward. He fell loosely to the ground, his legs kicked spasmodically, and then he seemed to relax like a man going to sleep.

"He done did it!" Ozzie Og cried out. He came over and threw his arm around Cody, shaking him, and holding the younger man up. "You done the necessary, Cody," he cried, his eyes bright with victory. Ozzie Og turned to look at Dan, saying, "Well, he done the necessary, didn't he, Dan?"

But Dan Winslow knew it was not over. He turned and walked away from the crowd, going back to where Hope was standing, her face pale and her hands clinched tightly together. "Well, it's over," he said heavily. Shaking his head, he added, "But not really. Cody whipped Tippitt, but that man will never take a whipping."

"What will happen, Dan?" Hope asked, concern edging her voice. She looked over in the darkness to where some of the punchers were taking Cody to the well to wash his face, all of them hollering and pounding him on the shoulders. "What will happen now?"

"The two agreed that the loser would step aside, but that'll never happen," said Dan. He was unhappy, for he had always had a special fondness for Cody, and he saw nothing but trouble looming up ahead. He was a man who had known trouble himself, and this had the smell of it. He had watched Harve Tippitt grow up, and understood well that even a whipping such as he had endured would not turn him aside; rather it would make him more determined to have his own way. He could not voice any of his concern, however, to Hope, but he knew that she understood most of it in any case.

After Og and Smoky Jacks had gotten Cody cleaned up and put him into a wagon along with Susan, they watched as the couple drove off. Og said, "Well, I reckon that settles it, don't it, Smoky?"

"No, it don't," Jack said thoughtfully. "It don't settle nothin'."

"Don't settle nothin'? Why you heard what Tippitt said, the loser steps aside."

"You're a smarter man than that, Ozzie. You know what kind of a yahoo Tippitt is. He ain't never had nothin' but his own way all of his life. You think he's gonna change now?"

Og glanced at him sharply, then sighed deeply. "I reckon that's right. Sure hate to see it."

"What bothers me," Smoky remarked, his words falling slowly into the night air, "is that Harve Tippitt's done been beat twice. There ain't but one thing left for him now."

Og stared at him for a long moment, then glanced out to where the wagon had disappeared in the darkness. He turned his head over to where Harve Tippitt was getting into the saddle, being helped by some of his friends. "You mean," he said, "it might be a shootin' affair?"

"I've seen men shot over less," Jacks shrugged. Turning to Og, he said, "We'd better keep an eye on Cody. I think he's just about young enough—and in love enough—to do something foolish. So from now on, you and me are appointed his official guardians." The two men stood there for a moment, peering into the darkness. Finally they mounted and rode off, carrying their thoughts with them.

CHAPTER NINE

CODY LOSES OUT

★ ★ ★ ★

Fall came early to Wyoming that year. The searing days of summer were replaced by the cool breezes from the north, and as Cody rode toward the Circle W, a blast of colder air touched his face. He looked up to the hills that would be white with snow in a few weeks. Winter lurked up in those high places like a gray wolf, and would one day come down and touch the grasses of the valley, shriveling them into dry, burned stems.

But this was September, and after the burning summer the cooler air felt good on his face. He rode along the ridge that made a half circle around the southern boundary of the ranch, wondering if there'd be anything left to eat by the time he got there. For the last three days he'd been chasing recalcitrant steers all over the high ground, trying to herd them back down to the lower pastures. Once the winter struck, any cattle left in those high spots could freeze and die before any of the hands could get to them.

His horse, a small gray named Smoky, was moving slowly, for he was weary. Cody leaned over and patted his shoulder, murmuring, "Just another mile, boy, and I'll give you a good supper and a good rubdown." The horse lifted its head, snorted, and picked up the pace, for he knew the ground as well as Cody. The rider smiled, saying, "Know what's waiting for you, don't you, Smoky?" And then he grimaced, for the smile hurt the tender parts of his face—scars left from his fight with Harve Tippitt.

The memory of the fight came to him as he rode along the ridge, and it was not a good memory. He'd driven Susan home, but she'd been cool and reserved, giving him a brief kiss and a short farewell. He'd stared after her as she closed the front door behind her, wondering what a man had to do to please a woman. Then jumping up into the wagon, he had driven the team home at a dangerous gait.

And Tippitt had not given up his pursuit of Susan. Word had come to him more than once that the two had been seen together, usually at church. *I can't whip him again for taking her to church*, Cody thought morosely. He turned Smoky into the last bit of the trail, a long corridor cut through heavy first-growth pines. The silence fell on him, the only sound the sibilant raking of Smoky's hooves across the thick mat of brown needles.

Can't go on like this, he thought. *I'm not good for work—or anything else.* He was a simple young man, liking the basic things. Complications bothered him—and nothing had been more complicated in his life than his pursuit of Susan Taylor. He'd gone out with a few girls, but those times were only lighthearted encounters. Something about Susan—and he could never pin down exactly what it was—drove him to speeds and actions that seemed foolish. Shaking his head in self-disgust, he spoke his thought aloud, "Nothing like a woman to get a man to make a fool of himself. But what's a fellow to do when he's in love? Let Harve Tippitt have her?"

He was still wrestling with this thought after he arrived at the ranch, but he pushed it aside as he cared for Smoky, then walked to the house. It was too early for the hands to be in from the range, but he'd be in time for supper. He entered through the front door, called out, "Mom—?" and started toward the kitchen.

His mother had been peeling potatoes, but at the sound of his voice she stepped out of the kitchen and came to meet him. She was wearing a plain blue dress and her apron. At once Cody saw that she was troubled. "What's the matter? Somebody get sick?"

Hope gave him a stricken look and said, "I've got something to tell you, Cody." She hesitated, then added, "It's not good news."

Cody felt a quick spurt of fear. "Is it Zane or one of the kids? Or is it Dan?"

"No—no, it's not that," Hope said quickly. "Everyone's all right. This is bad news—for you."

Cody could not think what could be disturbing his mother and demanded, "Well, what *is* it, Mom? Tell me, for cryin' out loud!"

Hope brushed a lock of her light hair up over her head and came to stand by him. She was a quiet woman but was obviously disturbed, and her face was drawn tight with concern. "I just got news from town. Something that you should have heard first, Cody."

Cody was mystified. "News from town?" he asked. Pulling off his hat, he ran his hand through his light blond hair, a question in his dark blue eyes. "What kind of news?"

"About Susan—and Harve Tippitt," she said hesitantly.

He stared at her blankly, not understanding what she could mean. Then an idea came to him and he asked tersely, "What about Susan and Harve? Did you hear about them going out together?" He shook his head half angrily, saying, "That's old news. I've heard that already—half a dozen times."

"That's not it."

"What then—what is it?" Cody knew that his mother was not given to devious manners, but something about the way she hesitated caught him. "Come on, let's have it."

Hope reached out and put her hand on Cody's arm. She felt the muscle tense and knew that inside he was wound as tightly as a steel spring. "They're engaged, Cody. Her father came to see you," she said quietly. "He knew you'd be angry and wanted to talk to you first. He said he tried to get Susan to put it off, at least until she'd talked to you, but he couldn't do anything with her, and—"

"And what?" Cody grated out as the news seemed to settle in him heavily. "What else did he say?"

"He—he said he was afraid of what you might do. That there might be trouble between you and Tippitt."

Cody's lips went thin, and he looked down at the floor steadily. His heart seemed to be drumming in his ears as the anger rose in him, but he managed to hold it down, and he finally looked up to meet Hope's eyes. "I can't believe Susan would do it," he said. "I'm going to talk to her."

He turned to leave the room, pulling his hat down on his head, and as he left Hope said, "Cody, go see Susan, but stay away from Harve. I don't want the two of you having more trouble." He waved his hand and looked back but did not answer. Hope stood there at the door, watching as he saddled a fresh horse, swung into the saddle, and drove the animal out of the corral at a fast run. She turned and went back into the house, sat down, and began peeling the potatoes that she had left. "Oh, Lord," she said fervently, "watch over him and keep him safe."

★   ★   ★   ★

"I wanted to tell you, Cody, but I was afraid to," murmured Susan, trying to avert her eyes.

Cody stood looking down at Susan, anger evident in the tense line of his body and in his expression. He had ridden up in front of the Taylor house, had stepped out of the saddle, and had gone at once to knock on the door. Mrs. Taylor had met him, and he saw the fear in her eyes. She had tried to put him off, but he had demanded to see Susan right then. "Mrs. Taylor, I'm going to see Susan, and it might as well be now as some other time." Knowing that it would be no use arguing with him, she reluctantly let him in. And now Cody and Susan were standing in the parlor facing each other.

"I can't believe you're saying this, Susan," Cody said. Reaching out, he took her arms and shook her. "We've made plans. It's all been settled."

Susan shook her head and pressed her lips together firmly for a moment, staring at him. She had not seen this side of Cody, at least in private. Only when he was around Harve Tippitt had he shown this kind of temper, but now he looked so stern that she was almost afraid. But she lifted her head and said, "No, it hasn't been settled, Cody. I've tried to tell you that all along. It's not easy, you know, for a girl to choose the man she's going to marry."

"And you think it's easier for a man?" he demanded.

"I don't know about that. I'm a woman and I can't tell what a man feels." She looked down at his hands that were pressing against her arms and said quietly, "You're hurting me, Cody." He released her at once, and she rubbed her arms, then continued, "I've been worried a long time about us."

"Worried about us? You never mentioned anything about it. What's wrong? Why didn't you come to me before you made this decision?"

"You wouldn't understand, I don't think."

"Understand? What is there to understand? We love each other, and we want to get married."

"No, there's more to it than that," Susan said. For once this carefree girl was tremendously sober. She took two steps to the right, holding her elbows, then turned back to face him. "I thought I loved you, and I guess I always will feel something for you, Cody. But do you know what I've been thinking lately?"

"What?"

"I've been thinking that those stories—and they got married and lived happily ever after—you know how they all end?" She shook her head, almost violently. "They end with a marriage, as if there was nothing that went on afterward. But something does go on, doesn't it?"

"Of course something goes on," he said irritably, not understanding in the least what she was getting at. "After we get married, we go on with life. We have children, we work—that's what goes on."

Susan sighed, her eyes very honest. "I don't think you understand. Men and women, when they're married, have to get along, don't they, Cody? And would you and I get along? That's what I've been worried about."

"Why, we've always gotten along. We've never had any fights."

"That's because we've been courting, and everything's been temporary, but, Cody, you know what I'm like—I like parties, I like fun, I like people, and that's not what our life would be. You're going to be a rancher, and I'm not fitted to be a rancher's wife."

"I thought love was supposed to be a little bit more than what a man did for a living," he said bitterly. He wanted to shake her, to grab her and throw her on a horse, and take her away and force her to marry him.

Carefully she took a step toward him and put her hand on his arm gently. "I could never be happy, isolated like that for weeks at a time. You can see that, can't you, Cody?" she pleaded. She made a pretty picture as she stood there, and her beauty made the grief and disappointment that he felt even sharper. As she began to tell him how she felt, she ended by saying, "I'll never forget you, Cody, but I'd make you miserable. You need a wife who's used to ranching, who'd like it. We'd never be happy together."

Although he knew she was speaking honestly from her heart, he could not hide his bitterness when he spoke. "I suppose Harve Tippitt will make you happy, is that right, Susan?"

Her eyes dropped, and she said quietly, "I don't want to talk about it anymore, Cody. I'm sorry that I've hurt you. I see now that I was wrong, that I should have broken it off a long time ago. You'll have to forgive me."

He stared down at her and knew that it was all over. A black sense of despair seized him. He turned and headed for the door. He heard her crying after him, calling his name, but he ignored it, shoved on his hat, leaped off the porch, and then mounted his horse. As he galloped away, the sound of her calling, "Cody, Cody—" reached him, but he refused to hear. It was like slamming the door on that part of his life, and as he rode along the street a numbness set in on him such as he had never known before. He passed along the main street, more than once answering automatically when somebody called out to him, but he was like a man that had been struck by a bullet in a battle and was severely wounded, still able to move forward, but hard hit.

"Hey, Cody. Cody." A tall, lean cowboy accompanied by one much shorter stepped in front of him, almost being run down by Cody's horse. "Hey, come on. You've been working hard enough. Time for a vacation."

"What's up, Legs?" Cody said, staring down at the two punchers.

He'd known the two a long time. Both of them were punchers for the Diamond H, not far from his own place—Legs Freeman

and Wash Melbourne. The three of them had made a trio growing up together, and usually he was glad to see them, but not
now. However, Wash reached up and slapped him on the leg,
"Come on, you slab-sided galoot, me and Legs got some celebrating to do."

"Celebrating what?"

"Celebrating not punchin' cows," Legs grinned. "We're going
to ride the train over to Murray's Bluff and pick up a herd for the
old man, but in the meanwhile we can get as drunk as we want
to—until the train comes in."

"Yeah, we've been looking for somebody to put us on the
train," Wash grinned. "It wouldn't look good for the Diamond
H's two best cowboys to get left drunk in town while the train
went without us. C'mon now, you've gotta do it."

Cody hesitated, then agreed. "Okay, I'll be your keeper. What
time does that train pull out?"

"Not till eleven o'clock tonight," Melbourne said, "so we got
plenty of time to do our heavy-duty celebrating. Come on, tie
up that horse and let's get at it."

The two punchers bracketed Cody and led him to the Palace
Saloon, where they advanced to the bar and propped their feet
up on the brass rail. "Joe," Legs Freeman called, "we intend to
test the quality of your liquor. You see this fellow here? He's
supposed to put us on the train. If he gets drunk, too, you'll
have to do it. So see that he don't drink too much."

Joe Wells, the bartender, scowled at him. "I ain't no nurse-
maid to cow punchers," he said. "Keep your own selves sober
and on your own train."

The three ordered drinks, and when they came, Cody lifted
his thoughtfully. He did not like to drink, but a recklessness had
come over him after his conversation with Susan. He tried to
shake it off, but the whole situation had left him numb.

"Whooo!" Wash Melbourne said, almost choking. "That'd
take the hair off a cow, wouldn't it now?" His eyes watered at
the power of the drink, and he shuddered, which made the fat
on his body quiver. "I better have another one just to make sure
it's that bad. Set 'em up again, Joe."

"If you don't like my liquor, go somewhere else," Joe grum-
bled, but he filled the glasses again. When he moved away, Free-

man and Melbourne began talking freely. Soon the three moved over to a table, sat down, and drank steadily. After a while, the two punchers began dancing with some of the bar girls, but Cody just sat at a table nursing his drink along.

He was still there an hour later, and by this time Freeman and Melbourne were both fairly drunk. He himself felt a numbness, and the sound of the tinny piano in the saloon seemed muted. He still felt the sharp sting of Susan Taylor's rejection as he had never felt anything in his life. He had hoped that the noise and the activity of the Palace Saloon would give him some peace, but instead he felt restless and dejected. "I'll just have to get so drunk I can't think about it," he muttered under his breath. Pouring another drink, he tossed it off just as his two companions came back, and falling into the chairs, they drank up, then began to tell outrageous lies.

Finally, Legs Freeman asked, "What time is it?" He had an owlish look now as he stared across the table at Cody. "Don't wanna miss our train, you know. You being our keeper and all, you got to watch for that."

Cody pulled out his watch. "It's only ten o'clock," he said. "You've got another hour yet."

"Another hour," Wash glared at him. "By that time, you'll have to carry me to that train."

He was not far wrong, for the two drank liberally, seemingly determined to get so drunk they couldn't walk. Cody, while not matching them drink for drink, was aware that he was drinking too much. But the alcohol did not seem to touch that part of him that was crying out on the inside. It was ten-thirty when he heard a voice say, "Look, there he is."

At the sound of Legs' blurred voice, Cody looked up and saw that Harve Tippitt had entered the Palace and was standing at the bar.

"That's the feller that tried to take your girl, ain't it, Cody?" Wash said with indignation. He was the gentlest of men when sober, but alcohol seemed to turn him mean. This was unfortunate, since he had never won a fight in his life, even sober. But now he said, "I'm going over and whip him myself. You fellers wait here."

Cody reached out, grabbed Wash's belt, and shoved him back

into the chair. "You stay out of this, Wash. It's none of your business."

Wash looked at him with astonishment, and with a slurred tongue said, "Ain't none of my business when somebody steals my buddy's girlfriend? What kinda friend you think I am?"

"All you'll do," Legs said, "is get yourself busted up. Now you set there and hush. We gotta get on that train. Might as well wander down to the station."

Legs and Wash staggered to their feet, laid their money down on the table, and began to navigate toward the door. Cody got up swiftly, too swiftly, for when he was upright, the room seemed to reel. It was then he knew he had had far too much to drink. He put his money on the table and started to follow the two outside, but when he got clear of the tables, Tippitt's voice reached him. "Well, look who's here. How are you doing, Cody?"

Cody looked at Tippitt and saw a triumphant smile on the man's lips. Tippitt's face was still scarred—as was his own, from their fight—but Cody, sick at heart, did not choose to continue the feud. "All right, Harve," he answered. "Gotta take these boys to the train."

Tippitt stepped over and caught his arm. "Wait a minute. You can't go yet. You haven't congratulated me." Tippitt spoke loudly so that the men at the bar standing close heard. Having gotten their attention, Tippitt nodded, keeping his eyes fixed on Cody. "We've always said may the best man win, ain't that right?"

"Whatever you say, Harve."

"Well, the best man has won." Tippitt reached over and poured two glasses full of liquor and handed one of them toward Cody. "I'm asking you to congratulate me, Cody."

"Congratulate you for what?" Wash demanded indignantly. "I ain't heard about you winning no fights."

Tippitt stared at him and said, "You look like you've had too many already, Wash, but I'll tell you what I'm celebrating." He raised his voice even louder so that everyone in the saloon could hear it. "Me and Susan Taylor are gettin' married."

A murmur ran through the saloon, and most of the men fixed their eyes on Cody. They had known of the competition between the two men, but all of them had thought that in the end Cody might win. Joe, the bartender, stepped forward, saying, "You buying for the house, Harve?"

"Why not? Set 'em up." There was a sudden rush toward the bar as Joe, the bartender, filled the glasses, and then Harve turned toward Cody. His lips were twisted with a triumphant smile, and he said, "I'll just ask you to make the toast, Cody."

Cody wanted to smash the man's face in, as a bitter anger ran through him. "I'll drink a toast to her, but not to you, Harve. Here's to the finest girl who ever lived." He hesitated, and then with a sneer on his face said, "And here's to the rotten scoundrel she's marrying."

Silence fell over the saloon, and he drank his drink and turned and threw the glass at the mirror behind the bar. It shattered with a loud, tinkling sound, and Joe cried out, "What did you do that for?"

Tippitt's face went pale, and he said, "You're a sore loser, aren't you?"

Cody felt the anger and the rage rising in him, but he was powerless to stop it. "Tippitt, stay out of my way or you'll be sorry," he warned.

Shaking his head, Tippitt answered, "I'll be here in this town a long time, Cody. I'll come and go as I please, and when I see you, I won't turn the other way. You're just a sorehead anyway."

Cody considered him and said, "Maybe I'd better use my hands on you, Harve—as I did once before."

The reminder of the fight and the outcome of it brought a redness to Tippitt's cheeks as he said, "Keep your hands to yourself."

Cody laughed. "Maybe I'd better take a gun to you, then. You're wearing one, why don't you go for it?"

"Aw, come on, Cody, let's get outta here. You gotta get us to our train," said Wash.

"No, let's see what a big, bad man Harve Tippitt is," Cody said scornfully. "Go on, go for it. This is a good day to die."

The men behind Tippitt scurried to one side and Harve very carefully put the glass down and lifted his hands. "I'm not fighting you. I'm no gunfighter."

"You're not much of anything, are you? Better stay out of my way," Cody said. "I'm gonna let you off this time, but the next time I see you, I might put a bullet right between your eyes."

"Come on, let's go," Legs said urgently. He closed his hand

on Cody's arm and practically dragged him from the saloon. "Are you crazy? You don't want to go to jail for killin' a man like that. He ain't worth it."

Cody was not listening. He was thinking what a fool he'd made out of himself and murmured, "I know. I'm drunk. Not drunk enough or too drunk, I guess. You fellows get to the station by yourself. I'll see you when you get back to town."

The two protested but left, struggling not to trip over themselves as they headed for the train. Cody started for his horse. He mounted up, noticing how slowly he was moving, and then started down the street. He got almost clear of town and then, on impulse, stopped his horse, dismounted, went into a saloon, bought another bottle of whiskey, and headed out of town. By the time he was halfway home, he had consumed most of the whiskey and was still angry. A coyote appeared and he pulled his gun, but missed with two wild shots. By this time, he was swaying in the saddle, so he dismounted, tying his horse to a tree. He sat down, nursing the bottle of whiskey along, going over all the things that had happened. "She shouldn't have done that to me," he said bitterly. Then he thought of Tippitt and said, "If he gives me one word, I'll break his back." Slowly, he consumed the rest of the whiskey sitting there. With the effects of the liquor and the strain of the day, a drowsiness soon came over him. He leaned back against the tree, saying, "Just rest a few minutes, just a few minutes."

He awoke slowly, squinting at the sunlight that fell on his face. His mouth was dry and tasted terrible, and when he sat up he cried out as pain racked his head. He had had only two hangovers in his life and this was the worst. Carefully, he got to his feet, glared down at the whiskey bottle, and shook his head. "I shoulda had more sense," he said solemnly. "Sleeping out all night like a common drunk."

He was stiff and sore from his night on the ground and groaned as he stepped into the saddle. Finally, he settled himself and said to his horse, "Let's go home. I sure hope nobody sees me like this."

He made his way to the ranch, thinking of how he was going to have to put Susan behind him, yet knowing how hard that would be to do. When he rode into the ranch yard, he saw two strange horses tied outside. As he dismounted, Sheriff Rider stepped out from the house, accompanied by his deputy, Del Fanning. His mother and Dan were there, too. He quickly tied his horse and turned as they came up. Managing to grin crookedly, he said, "Don't tell me you came all the way out here to arrest me for being drunk and disorderly."

"No, I've come to arrest you for murder," Sheriff Rider said soberly. He was a tall man with snow white hair, and there was sadness in his eyes. "I have to take your gun, Cody."

Cody stood there, speechless, as the deputy lifted his gun. He shook his head trying to clear the cobwebs, but one glance at his mother showed the agony in her eyes, and he knew this was no joke. Dan Winslow was looking at him, his lips tight and his body tense.

"What are you talking about, Sheriff? I haven't killed anybody."

"Where have you been all night, Cody?" Fanning asked.

"Just a minute. You don't have to answer any questions," Dan said quickly. "We'll get a good lawyer, and he'll do your talking for you."

"Dan, I've been out drunk. Slept all night passed out by the river."

"Anybody see you?" Fanning inquired.

"I don't think so. It was dark. I just woke up about an hour ago." Cody felt cold twinges of fear beginning to close around him. "What's this all about? Who's been killed?"

"Somebody shot Harve Tippitt last night when he was on his way home, Cody."

Suddenly the world seemed to reel, and Cody stared at the sheriff. A silence fell over the yard, and finally Cody said, "Well, it wasn't me. I came straight home."

"You threatened him in the bar," said the deputy. "Twenty witnesses heard you." He held up Cody's gun. "Two shots fired. It was two shots that killed Tippitt. Forty-four caliber—like yours."

"That was just talk. I shot at a coyote!" Cody exclaimed. "If you locked everybody up for threatening somebody, your jail would be full."

"I'm gonna have to take you in, Cody. You'll have a chance

to defend yourself. Come along."

"Let us have a few words with him, Sheriff, before you go," Hope pleaded.

"Of course, Mrs. Winslow. We'll just be out by the horses." When they had mounted and pulled up a few feet away, Hope said at once, "Did you do it, Cody?" Her voice was quiet, but her eyes belied the fear that was gripping her.

"No!" he said instantly. "I got drunk. We had some words in the bar, I got some whiskey, and I got drunk and fell asleep on the trail on the way home, but I didn't shoot him!"

"Go on with the Sheriff. I'm glad to hear you didn't do it," Dan said quietly.

"You believe me?"

"Yes, I do. Whoever shot Tippitt shot him in the back," Dan said. "You might have shot him all right, but it would have been from the front, and you'd have given him a fair chance. I know that much about you."

Cody stared at Dan, then whispered, "What's gonna happen?"

"We'll get the best lawyer there is, and they'll have to prove you did it. It's not enough just to prove you could've done it; can't be circumstantial evidence. Don't worry, we'll fight this thing out."

Hope moved forward, put her arms around Cody's neck, and drew his face down. She kissed him, then when she moved her head back, she said confidently, "God will be with us. We'll beat this thing."

At that moment, Sheriff Rider called out, "I guess we'd better be going, Cody."

Cody moved back, stepped into the saddle, and joined the two men. "I won't put the cuffs on you," said Rider. "You're not dumb enough to run away."

"No, I'm not running away. If I did, I'd be running the rest of my life, wouldn't I?"

Sheriff Rider liked Cody, and he had been shocked when Harve Tippitt had been found ambushed. It had gone against his grain to have to come out and arrest this fine young man. However, he was a man who had seen much death, and he had seen many young men go wrong. Some of them apparently as good-hearted as Cody Rogers. So he said now, "Just keep yourself steady, boy. Your folks will do all they can for you. You'll get a fair trial."

Somehow the words seemed to bring a gloom to Cody. He was still half-stunned and almost unable to believe what the man had said. But as he rode beside the two men going back toward town, he realized that it was not a dream, and that he was faced with the most dreadful moment of his life.

CHAPTER TEN

CODY'S DAY IN COURT

★ ★ ★ ★

The courtroom was packed—as it had been since the first day of the trial of Cody Rogers. The room was not large so extra chairs had been brought in, but the walls were still lined with curious spectators standing and watching the proceedings.

Dan Winslow stared around the room, his eyes hot with anger. "Like a bunch of buzzards!" he muttered. Looking down at Hope he asked, "You all right?"

"Yes." Hope looked up at Dan and tried to smile, but it was not a success. She thought of Cody in the small jail, of the visits she'd made there while waiting for the judge to arrive for the trial. It had been two weeks already, and every day—it seemed to her—Cody grew more morose and bitter. Both she and Dan had visited him often, but nothing they could say seemed to bring any hope to Cody. He had lost weight and there was a sense of fatalism about him that was a shocking contrast to the happy-go-lucky young man they knew.

"Do you think it'll be over today?" she asked Dan.

"I guess so." Dan struggled to find something encouraging to say, but he was troubled. The trial had become a power struggle, for Harve Tippitt was the son of a big rancher—the most powerful man in the county. In addition to his thousands of acres, he owned several businesses in War Paint. He was a man who could not brook interference, and his temper was a fearful thing when stirred—and the death of his son had stirred it. Dan looked across the courtroom where Tippitt sat and thought, *If I ever saw hatred on a man's face, it's right there.* Tippitt was a large man with a paunch, but he was very powerful. His face was florid by nature, and the anger that had built up in him since the death of his son seemed to glow like a furnace.

Dan said quietly, "I tried to talk to Tippitt, to tell him Cody's not a killer."

Hope glanced up at him expectantly, but he shook his head, his lips drawn into a thin line. "No use. He just cussed me out. Nothing's going to make him give up on getting his revenge. He's convinced Cody is guilty, and he's done all he can to see that's the way it comes out."

The jury filed in at that moment, and Hope waited until they were seated before whispering, "But this is a court, Dan. How can Tippitt influence a trial?"

"Look at the jury." Dan swept the jury with his eyes, then added, "They're all town people or big ranchers. Everybody on it owes Tippitt—them or their people."

"But—they won't let that influence their vote!"

"Look at Dayton Prince, Hope. He owns the general store. Since Tippitt owns the bank, he's probably got a note on Prince's business. Or even if he doesn't, anytime he chooses, Tippitt could open another general store and lower the prices until he drove Prince out of business."

Hope stared at Dayton Prince, then shook her head. "I don't believe Dayton would let that influence him. He's a good man, Dan."

"Yes, he is—and the others are good men." Dan struggled, not knowing whether to speak his mind to Hope. Finally he said, "But their lives are at stake—not like Cody's—but all the same, Tippitt can crush any of them like he would a fly."

"I can't believe it, Dan!" said Hope in frustration.

"I don't want to—but it's not only George Tippitt. It's the evidence."

"But it's all circumstantial, Dan." Hope stared at him. "They can't convict a man on that kind of evidence."

Dan nodded, saying, "That's right. We'll just have to hang on and hope that the prosecution doesn't come up with anything new." He saw her lips tremble, and with more confidence than he felt, said, "Don't worry, Hope. It's like you say, all the evidence is circumstantial—" He broke off abruptly and put his hand on Hope's arm, for Cody had just been brought into the courtroom. Two guards flanked him, and he took his seat beside Dave Lyons, the lawyer that Dan had hired to defend him. Lyons bent over and began to speak to Cody, who seemed listless. *I wish Cody would show some fight*, Dan thought. *He looks like a beaten man to the jury.*

At that moment the door behind the raised table opened and one of the jailers said, "All rise," as the judge entered. He was a small man wearing a black suit, and he took his seat at once. Judge Olan Phelps was known as a hard man—some even called him a "hanging judge"—but his conduct of the trial had been, Dan admitted, fair and impartial. He had snow white hair and a pair of level gray eyes, and now he spoke up, "Does the prosecution have any more to present to the court?"

The prosecuting attorney named Cole Lattimore, a tall man with red hair and blue eyes, rose, saying, "Your Honor, the prosecution has a few more testimonies—but with the court's permission, I would like to briefly sum up the case we have built against Cody Rogers."

"Go ahead, but be brief, Mr. Lattimore. You will have opportunity to do most of that in your summation."

"I will be very brief, Your Honor." Lattimore was a good courtroom lawyer. He would have made a fine actor, for he not only knew how to use words, but he also had a dramatic flourish in his actions to match his presentation. He was too clever to go after defendants ferociously, having learned that in most cases this was likely to gain sympathy for the accused. Instead, he methodically brought forth the evidence, lingering over each item, so that he made them seem more important than they actually were. He moved over to stand in front of the jury, nodding at them in a friendly manner as he began to speak.

"I ask the jury to remember three things. One, Cody Rogers has had a grievance against the victim for some time. It's common knowledge that he beat him severely in a fight only a few weeks ago. This is not a new thing, but it has gone on for months.

Second, I ask you to remember that on the night Harve Tippitt was shot in the back, Cody Rogers threatened to shoot him. You have heard the testimony of several witnesses who were present at the Palace Saloon, so there can be no mistake about that."

Cody watched the proceedings, thinking of what a fool he had been. Ever since his arrest he had been in some sort of emotional coma, so that at times he wondered if he was losing his mind. Day after day he had half expected to be released for lack of evidence—but when that had not happened, he had grown bitter. Instead of opening himself to his parents and his lawyer, he had clamped his lips shut and answered only in clipped monosyllables. Now as Lattimore spoke on, putting down line upon line of evidence, Cody thought, *I should have been more of a fighter*. Turning his head, he glanced toward his mother and saw the pain in her eyes. *Fine thing for her to remember—she'll never be able to get this out of her mind.*

Lattimore went on, stressing the enmity that Cody had shown toward Tippitt, never mentioning that the deceased had been just as virulent. He spoke of the third element, the fact that Cody's gun had been fired twice, and that the two slugs taken from the victim were of the same caliber.

"And the accused tells us that he shot at a coyote! And he asks you to believe that he slept on the ground all night instead of going home!" Lattimore spread his hands wide, rolled his eyes, and said dramatically, "Why would a young man sleep on a rock when all he had to do was ride home and sleep on a good bed?"

Finally Judge Phelps interrupted, "Mr. Lattimore, you have been over this ground once already. If you have any new evidence, I suggest you present it—or else I will recognize the defense."

Lattimore never showed the slightest irritation toward the judge and now said quickly, "I apologize, Your Honor."

Dan whispered, "If that's all he's got, we're all right, Hope!"

But then Lattimore said, "The state does have an important witness. I call Pike Simmons to the stand."

A mutter ran around the courtroom, for Pike Simmons was a well-known man in the county. "What's Simmons got to do with this?" Cody whispered to his attorney.

"Don't know," Lyons murmured. He sat up straighter in his chair, his eyes narrow with attention on the man who came from the back of the room to take the single chair that faced the jury. "I don't like it," he muttered.

Simmons, a burly man with a shock of black hair and a pair of muddy brown eyes, put his hand gingerly on the Bible, and when the oath was read, he said, "I do." Simmons owned a small ranch over in the bottoms, but he was better known for his barroom brawls and uncontrolled drinking. Simmons was a fairly sensible man when sober, but when drunk, he lost all reason. He was a wicked fighter and had served a year in the state penitentiary for killing a man in a fight—he had gotten the man down and kicked him to death.

"Mr. Simmons, would you tell the jury your occupation and how long you've been in that position?" said Lattimore.

"Own a ranch over by Cripple Creek. Been there for nine years." He hesitated, then added, "Was gone one year. Got sent to the pen."

"On what charge?" asked the attorney.

"Manslaughter," Simmons shrugged.

"That was four years ago, I believe? And when you were released, you went back to your ranch?"

"That's right."

"No other trouble since then?"

"Naw, nothing to get sent up for. 'Course, I drink sometimes and get too rough in fights."

Lattimore let the witness go on in this manner, and Dave Lyons groaned, "Lattimore's smart! He's taken away the advantage I'd have of showing what a no-good Simmons is!"

Lattimore asked easily, "Mr. Simmons, will you tell the court what you did on the evening of September 4?"

"Went to town for a little fun."

"How is it that you can remember that date?"

"My birthday's on the third," Simmons grinned. "Every year I give myself a birthday party, and I went to town the day before to get all my business done."

"What was your business on that day?"

"Took ten head of stock to Mel Pounders."

"Can you prove that?"

"Got the bill of sale—and I reckon Mel will say as how I was there."

"Yes, we will hear his testimony, too," Lattimore nodded. "Now, tell us, if you will, what your movements were on that evening."

"I drove the critters into the stockyard, and me and Mel settled up."

"What time was that?"

"Oh, 'bout five o'clock, I guess," shrugged Simmons.

"And then what?"

"I went down to the cafe and had supper. And while I was there, Bart Prince came in. He asked me to go play poker, and that's what I done. We went to the Oxbow Bar and played until late."

"Prince will testify that you were there?"

"Him and about ten more," Simmons nodded. "I lost all my money to him, so he ain't likely to forget it."

"Your Honor, these men can be called as witnesses to verify Mr. Simmons' statement." Lattimore grew serious, coming to stand in front of the witness. "And after your game, what did you do?"

"Went home."

"And did you see anything out of the ordinary?"

Simmons looked directly at Cody and nodded. "I seen Cody Rogers on the Old Military Road."

"That's a lie!" Cody leaped to his feet, his face contorted with rage. "I wasn't anywhere near that road that night."

Lyons pulled Cody down, saying, "Be quiet!" Then he addressed the judge. "I apologize, Your Honor. It won't happen again."

The judge nodded. "You may continue, Mr. Simmons."

Simmons was enjoying his moment in court. He grinned loosely at Cody, then continued, "I was on my way home, and when I was 'bout half a mile from the bridge, I seen a rider coming down the road. It was night, 'o course, and I heard the hoofbeats first. Horse was running like the devil! And then this rider came down the road, and I don't reckon he saw me until we was close. The moon was full that night, or I couldn't have saw him. But when he passed me, I saw it was him."

"Can you identify the man you saw?" asked Lattimore.

"There he sets—Cody Rogers," pointed Simmons.

Instant commotion broke out all around the room. The talking was so loud that Judge Phelps pounded his gavel sharply on the table. "Order! Be quiet or I'll clear the court!" He waited until the room was still, then nodded, "You may continue, Mr. Lattimore."

Cody listened as Lattimore led the witness through all the traps that Dave Lyons might lay for him. He was feeling like the time when he'd been kicked in the stomach by a horse. Up until this moment he'd been concerned only with the disgrace of the thing and the unfairness of it all. Never once had he thought he might actually be convicted! Now, however, looking at the faces of the men on the jury, he felt cold and sick, for every face was fixed on Simmons, and they all believed what he was saying!

Finally Lattimore said, "And this spot where you saw the accused, you say it was perhaps half a mile from the bridge over Seven Point River?"

"Yes, not more'n that."

At that point, Lattimore turned to face the jury. "And as you may know, the murdered man was found exactly half a mile from that bridge! So we offer you eyewitness proof that Cody Rogers was not asleep on the road to his own ranch, for that is ten miles to the west of the Old Military Road. No, gentlemen, he was not, for the witness's testimony put him running away from the scene of the crime at the approximate time the victim was killed!" He then turned and faced Dave Lyons, and said defiantly, "Your witness, Mr. Lyons."

Dave Lyons was a good lawyer, but he knew as he rose and faced the jury that unless he could shake Simmons' testimony, Cody had little chance. He spent the next forty-five minutes peppering the burly man with question after question—all to no avail. Simmons never grew flustered, and when Lyons finally was ordered by the judge to stop repeating himself, he became frustrated and angry. He pointed out that all the evidence was circumstantial, and that it would be unjust and unfair to convict a man on such a basis.

When Lyons had finished his cross-examination, Judge Phelps nodded toward the prosecuting attorney. "Mr. Lattimore, we'll have your summation." Lattimore was crafty enough not to say too much, for by the looks on the faces of the jury he knew they were already convinced. He spoke briefly, ending by saying, "I ask that you bring a verdict of first-degree murder against Cody Rogers."

Lyons rose and did his best in his concluding remarks to the jury, but when he sat down, wringing wet with sweat, Cody stared at him. "It's not good, is it, Mr. Lyons?"

"Never try to second-guess a jury, Cody," Lyons said. He sat there as the jury filed out, and when Phelps left for his quarters, Dan and Hope Winslow rushed over to Cody.

"It'll be all right, son," Hope said. "You'll see."

But Dan was staring at Lyons' troubled face and saw that the lawyer was not happy. "What do you think, Dave?" he asked quietly.

Lyons moved his shoulders restlessly, then he ran his hand nervously over his hair. "I don't like it. That fellow Simmons may be lying, but there's no way to shake him."

Cody asked abruptly, "What if the verdict is guilty? What will that mean?"

"We're hoping for better than that," Lyons said quickly. Then when Cody kept his eyes fixed on him, he shook his head. "It won't be hanging, Cody. Not on this kind of evidence."

"How long—in prison?"

"Depends on the judge. He'll set the sentence."

Time crawled on, but to the surprise of the spectators, the jury filed back in less than forty-five minutes. "Is that good or bad?" Dan asked Lyons.

"You never know." Lyons watched the faces of the jury and shook his head. *They're not looking at Cody—a bad sign.*

"Gentlemen of the jury, have you reached a verdict?" Judge Phelps asked as soon as he returned and faced them.

"We have, Your Honor."

"Read it to the court. Prisoner will rise and face the jury."

The voice of Judge Phelps seemed to echo hollowly inside Cody's head. He felt Lyons pulling at his arm, and on legs gone suddenly feeble, he rose to his feet. He fixed his gaze on the face of Milo Fenderman, owner of the blacksmith shop. *He's shod many a horse for me*, Cody thought numbly. *We used to joke about things—and now he won't even look at me.*

The foreman's hands were unsteady as he held a single sheet of paper close to his eyes. "We—we find the defendant guilty of murder—in the second degree."

"So say you all?"

"Yes, Judge."

Judge Phelps sat looking down at the youthful face of the prisoner. He allowed no emotion to show on his face as he pronounced sentence. "You have been found guilty of murder in the second degree. For that offense, Cody Rogers, I sentence you to fifteen years in the state penitentiary."

Hope gasped and whispered, "Oh, God! No!"

Dan put his arm around her. "We'll appeal, Hope. It's not over yet. We've got to keep on believing God."

They both rose and walked to where Cody stood beside Dave Lyons, who was saying, "It won't stand up, Cody."

At that moment Hope rushed to Cody and threw her arms around him, trying to keep back the tears. His body was stiff and unyielding, but she looked up into his face, whispering, "Cody, God will help us!"

Cody stared at her blankly, then his face seemed to freeze. His voice was sharp and bitter as he answered her. "God? Don't ever talk to me about God, because He's not up there!"

The deputy, who had been standing by silently, spoke up, "Sorry, Miz Winslow"—he stepped up and took Cody's arm—"You can visit him any time, ma'am."

As Cody walked out of the courtroom, he kept his back stiffly erect. He was aware that many were watching him, waiting for him to break—but he did not. He refused to show any emotion.

After returning to the jail, the deputy locked him in his cell, then paused, saying, "Bad break, Cody. But I've seen sentences reversed. Just trust the Lord like your ma says."

But Cody only gave him a bleak look, then he turned and walked over to the bunk. He lay down and stared up at the ceiling, and when the deputy looked at his face, he shook his head. "Hate to see you take it this way, Cody." But there was no answer, and the young man did not move as the footsteps of the deputy faded.

CHAPTER ELEVEN

BEHIND THE WALL

★　★　★　★

Shorty Cavanaugh took going back to prison philosophically enough, but then he'd been there twice before. He was one of those unfortunate beings who found life on the inside of walls less confining than life outside. For him a cell was less threatening than the walls of his own mind, and his years in prison had taken all the fear out of the experience. He knew the worst of it—and to Shorty, that was preferable to the horrors he would face on the outside.

But there was a strange sense of compassion in Shorty Cavanaugh, buried deeply enough beneath the toughness of the professional criminal. He understood himself well enough, and had come to accept the world of prison as normal. Still, he had faint memories of his first imprisonment and how terrified he had been.

And now as he looked at the young prisoner who sat across the stage from him, he had a sudden streak of pity. *He's young to be going to the Rock, and that's a fact—no more than twenty-one or twenty-two.* Leaning forward, he ignored the chain that linked his hands and feet, saying, "First time up, I guess." When he got a mere nod, he said cheerfully, "Well, my name's Cavanaugh, but call me Shorty."

"Cody Rogers."

Cavanaugh noted the long pause and knew that fear was gripping the young man. Shorty looked at the hard-faced guard who kept his gun on his right side, where it could not be grabbed by the prisoner, and said, "Got a cigarette, Mr. Danton?" Shorty had discovered the man's name and addressed him very respectfully. As a result the two had been treated more gently than some. Danton stared at the small convict, then reached in his pocket and pulled out a small pouch with the makings. "Hey, thanks a lot," Cavanaugh said. "You're all right, you are."

Danton shrugged, saying only, "Guess you'll be scarce on smokes at the Rock, Shorty."

"Not a bit of it! Plenty of tobacco for a man who knows his way around."

"Well, you should know your way. Third trip, ain't it?"

"And the last," Cavanaugh said. "How about a smoke for the lad here?" Getting an approving nod, he handed the makings toward his fellow prisoner, who shook his head. "Don't smoke? That's good. I like to see a young fellow who don't have no bad habits."

"He's got one bad habit," Danton grinned suddenly. "He's got a habit of shooting men in the back."

Cody turned his head, and there was such violence in his expression that Danton fumbled for his gun.

"Here, now, lad—none of that!" Shorty broke in. "You got to be respectful to Mr. Danton. He's a square one—and you'll be meetin' some who ain't such gentlemen as he is." Then turning to the guard he said, "Don't mind him, sir. He's going for his first jolt, and that grates on a fellow's nerve, you see." Shorty kept the conversation going, and after a time Danton took his watchful gaze off Cody.

The stage rumbled on, and after a stage stop, Danton stared at the pair, saying, "I'm riding on top. Drop out any time you want to, and I'll be glad to save the state the trouble of feeding you." He had a sawed-off shotgun in his hands, and there was no doubt that he'd use it.

"Nothing like that, Mr. Danton," Shorty chirped. Holding up the manacle that was joined to Cody's wrist, he grinned. "Where would we be going all chained up like this? We'll be fine, no trouble, sir."

As soon as Danton climbed to the seat, the driver called out, "Hup—Babe—Job!" and the stage rocked forward as the horses trotted down the dusty road.

"Now that the fat devil is out of the way, we can spread out a little," Shorty said with evident pleasure. "Real swine, ain't he, now?"

Despite himself Cody was amused. "Mr. Danton? I thought he was a real gentleman."

Shorty winked at him, and a crooked smile revealed yellow teeth. "Kept us from gettin' half-starved and in out of the weather. Part of the game, Cody," he assured his companion. Then he studied him and asked, "How long you got at the Rock?"

"Fifteen years."

Shorty caught the look of despair in the young man's eyes, and said quickly, "Aw, now that ain't so bad. You'll come out a young man—maybe with time off, it'll be only ten years."

"I won't stay there that long."

Instantly Shorty leaned forward, hissing, "None of that, boy! It's the shortest way to the lime pit. That's where they put the bodies of them that try to escape."

"I'll get out," Cody gritted his teeth. "Man wants something bad enough, he'll find a way."

"Maybe most things, but not escape from the Rock," said Shorty flatly.

"It's been done, hasn't it?"

"Not that I ever heard." Shorty drew smoke into his lungs, expelled it, and then said, "Lemme tell you the way of it, Cody, then when you get there, you'll see there ain't no sense in hopin'." He spoke quickly, his eyes darting like a bird's. "The prison itself, why it ain't much. Got bars and steel doors, but a man might get out of those. It's what he finds *outside* that's rough."

"What's outside?"

"See, the chief guard's name is Jocko Valentine. He don't like much, but he does like huntin' down prisoners. It's his hobby, like, and he's had quite a few years to sharpen his skill. It's like a game to him, I'd say." He puffed on the cigarette with enjoyment, then added, "Like some men enjoy hunting deer, well, Jocko likes hunting men."

"I'll take my chances when I'm outside."

"That's it, Cody, you won't *have* no chance! If it was just Jocko, I'd say maybe, but he keeps three Apaches, and blamed if they ain't like huntin' dogs! I swear they can *smell* a man farther off than most of us can *see* 'im!"

Cody sat there, rocking with the motion of the stage. His skin was slick with sweat, which the fine dust that boiled into the coach coated with a gray film. He hadn't had a bath for three days, not since Danton had come to pick him up at War Paint. He had slept in fits and snatches and had eaten little. Only one thing was on his mind—even before he got to prison—and that was getting out.

Shorty tried to reason with the young man, but soon saw there was no use. "All right," he sighed finally. "You'll see when you get there. But listen to your old Uncle Shorty, 'cause I been there. Don't give the guards no sass—none of 'em. They don't care no more about us than if we was dogs. One word—even a look like you give Danton—and it'd be the Oven for you."

"The Oven?" asked Cody curiously.

"Yeah, a pit two feet wide, two feet deep, and six feet long. You get in it, and they put a heavy piece of sheet steel over you. You get one canteen of water." A tremor ran through the small prisoner, and his eyes filled with fear. "Temperature gets up to 115, and you lay there cookin' in that pit. Can't roll over—have to face that steel, which gets hot enough to burn your hand."

"You were in it, Shorty?"

"Once—and just for one day." Shorty looked at his hands, which were trembling. He held them clenched tightly together and whispered, "Some men go crazy in there. They kept one feller in it for a week, and he come out raving mad." He pulled himself together and took a deep breath. Expelling it, he shook his head and said earnestly, "Don't get out of line, Cody. You might be a tough young fellow, but they got ways of breaking tough men. They like it when a man tries them out. Kind of breaks the boredom for them, one of them told me once."

"I'll watch it—and, thanks, Shorty."

"Aw, we got to stick together. Wish we was gonna be cell mates, but they never put two new men together. But we'll be seein' lots of each other. I can put you wise to the way things is—make life a lot easier."

By the time the stage reached the prison, it was dusk. Shorty had talked constantly, sharing his wisdom gained by long stays at the Rock, until Danton had climbed back down into the stage. But when Danton had returned, Shorty stopped talking at once.

"Here we are," Danton said finally. He stretched his legs and arms, saying, "I'll be glad to get rid of you two."

"Aw, now I don't feel that way, Mr. Danton," Shorty said cheerfully. "You been the best guard I ever had, and that's no lie."

Danton ignored this and climbed down. "All right, out of there."

Cody got out of the stage awkwardly, handicapped by his chains. One of them caught, and he stumbled and fell, almost pulling Shorty down with him. A rough laugh scored the air, and he was yanked to his feet as if he'd been a child. "Can't even get out of a stage, con?" The man who held him was over six feet four and powerfully built. He wore a white suit with a white planter's hat, and his eyes were hard as bolts. "Come on, con, get up."

"Hello, Captain Valentine," Shorty said, hopping to his feet. "Good to see you again."

The huge man stared at him, and then he snorted. "You again, Cavanaugh? You didn't get enough your last two trips?"

"Well, I'm back, Captain!" Shorty grinned. "Looks like you'll be having me as a permanent guest."

Captain Valentine glared at him, then turned his eyes on Cody. "Name?"

"Cody Rogers."

Instantly a massive hand struck his cheek and almost knocked him down. He caught his balance and remembered Shorty's advice. "Say *sir* when you speak to a guard—any guard!" ordered the captain.

"Yes, sir, Captain. It won't happen again."

Valentine glared at him, and then he seemed to lose interest. Turning to a guard, he said, "Put Cavanaugh in with Taylor—Rogers with Bailey."

Cody stood still as Danton removed the manacles, stuffed them into a bag, then turned and got back on the stage. Even before it pulled out, Cody was prodded with a stick carried by a heavyset guard. "This way, you two."

Cody and Shorty moved obediently toward the large two-story building that loomed before them. Looking around, Cody saw that it was in the middle of one of the most barren and arid spots he'd ever seen. Even in the falling darkness he saw that the desert stretched away beyond the eye's sight. *Guards could spot a man five miles off,* he thought, but when the guard prodded him again, he turned his head and followed Shorty inside the gate. The prison was built around a large square yard, and the guard led them at once to one of the doors. "New prisoners for A, Mulligan," he called out, and there was the sound of a heavy bolt scraping. When the door opened, the guard said, "This little one goes with Taylor, the young one with Bailey."

"Okay," answered Mulligan, stepping aside as they entered.

Two guards stood inside, and one of them said, "Brad, you take them to lockup, will you?" as he slammed the door shut. Both men carried shotguns, which they kept leveled at the two new prisoners.

"You two, up those stairs."

"Ah, I always like the second floor," Shorty remarked. "More air in the night." After walking past a few cells with prisoners curiously staring out, he was ordered to stop. The guard produced a chain full of keys and unlocked the cell, pushing open the steel door. Shorty stepped inside, saying, "Be seeing you, Cody."

"Get down the hall," the guard commanded, giving Cody a shove. When they had walked by what seemed like many cells, the command came, "Stop right there. Turn around and I'll cut you in half!" Cody stood very still as the guard fumbled with the key. Finally the door creaked open and the guard said, "In with you."

Turning, Cody stepped into the cell, and the door swung shut. As the key turned, it grated on Cody's nerves, and he stood there, trembling from fatigue and fear.

"Just get in?" said a voice behind him.

Cody whirled to see by the faint light of a lantern in the hall a man sitting up on his bunk. "Yeah. Name's Cody Rogers."

"Al Bailey." The response was spare, and after a silence, he said, "You missed chow. I got a hunk of bread and some bacon."

Cody discovered he was hungry, but he shook his head. "No, I don't want to be a moocher."

"Sit down," Bailey said and began searching for something. When he came up with a small package, he handed it to Cody. "Go on, eat it."

For a moment, it looked as if he was about to hand it back. Instead, Cody slowly unwrapped it and muttered, "Thanks."

Bailey watched as he devoured the small fragments, gulping them down. Then he said, "Water in the bucket to wash it down." After Cody had drunk freely of the tepid water, he asked, "Been a long trip?"

"Three days."

"First time in for you?" asked Bailey.

"First time," muttered Cody.

Bailey pointed, saying, "Take the bottom bunk. You're bigger than me." He ignored Cody's protest, saying, "You're probably tired, and we'll be rousted out at dawn. Get some sleep."

Cody suddenly discovered that the pressures of the last three days were catching up with him. He sat down on the bunk and pulled his boots off, which seemed to weigh twenty pounds apiece. He lay down with a groan of relief, and sleep came to him so suddenly it was as if he'd been clubbed.

Al Bailey stared at his new cellmate and shook his head.

"Welcome to the Rock, Cody," he murmured softly.

★   ★   ★   ★

"Come along, Rogers—you got visitors."

Cody straightened up with surprise and stared at Captain Valentine. Cody had been building a stone wall for a new addition, and his hands were raw from handling the sharp rocks. "Visitors for me, Captain?"

"Come on, go get cleaned up." Jocko Valentine grinned at Cody wolfishly. "Can't have folks thinking we don't take good care of you men, can we now?"

Cody moved quickly, not forgetting to say, "Thank you, sir." He'd taken the advice of Shorty Cavanaugh and Al Bailey, and had lasted six months inside with no trouble. Early on he'd seen the brutal treatment a couple of prisoners had received for mouthing off at the guards. After that he'd decided to be the most polite convict at the Rock, and ever since, even Valentine had stopped watching him for an escape attempt. Quickly, Cody washed up at the pump, put his shirt on, and then followed Valentine to the south wing. He had been there on cleaning detail, and when Jocko nodded at a door, he entered. Inside he found Dan and his mother seated at a table.

"Here he is," Valentine nodded. "You've got thirty minutes."

Dan and Hope rose, and both were shocked at the sight of Cody, though they tried to conceal it. He had lost weight and was burned a rich copper hue from the blistering sun. His hair was cropped short, and his face was concealed behind a beard.

"Son!" Hope said and moved toward him. She embraced him, and for a moment she feared that he would stand there motionless—and then his arms went around her, and she held him fiercely. The two stood there holding each other, and as Dan watched, a hollow sadness filled his heart.

Finally Hope stepped back, and Dan moved forward to grip Cody's shoulder. It was thin but muscled like whipcord. "Good to see you, son," he said.

Cody stood there, trying to cover the sudden surge of emotion that flooded him. He was so accustomed to keeping things inside that he could not speak or react as he wished. "Well, it's good to see you both. You're looking good."

"Sit down, Cody," Hope said quickly. "We brought you some things to eat, and Captain Valentine said we could give them to you."

And he'll take them away as soon as they're outside the gate. Cody took a piece of cake Hope forced on him and ate it slowly. "That's real good, Mom," he said. "You always were the best cook in the world." Then he said, "Tell me about everything."

For ten minutes he listened as they brought him up to date on what had happened. Finally Dan cleared his throat and said, "Son, my brother Mark came to see us. I wrote him about your trouble, and he came as soon as he could." Dan's eyes were hopeful as he continued, "He's hired a private detective, Cody—a good one."

"What does the detective say?" Cody asked.

"Oh, we don't know him," Hope said. "He wants to remain unknown. But he'll find out the truth about the murder. I'm sure he will."

"That was good of Mark. Thank him for me, will you?" said Cody as he finished eating what they had brought.

Hope felt a sense of despair at the deadness in Cody's voice. *He doesn't believe in anything anymore.* "It'll be all right, Cody, you'll see."

"We've been praying mighty hard for you, and so have all the family. Tom and his bunch, especially. And that girl of theirs, Laurie? She wrote your mother the best letter. You got one, too, didn't you?"

"We don't get much mail," Cody shrugged. "They throw most of the letters away. Don't ever send money, because I'll never see it."

Dan sensed the futility of trying to change Cody in one brief visit, so for the few remaining minutes, he and Hope tried to be as cheerful as they could. When the guard stepped inside and said, "Sorry—time's up, folks," they quickly arose and went to Cody.

Holding him tightly, Hope whispered, "Please—don't give up on God, Cody!"

He didn't answer, but he squeezed her tightly. When he turned to the tall man beside her, he said, "You've always been a real dad to me, Dan—better than any real father I might have had." He hesitated, then added, "Best if you just forget about me," then turned and walked out of the room without looking back.

"He didn't mean that, Hope," Dan said, putting his arm around her. "He's just discouraged. He'll be all right when we get him out of this place." He led her out of the door, and she kept her tears back until they got into the buggy that Dan had rented. She sat straight, the tears running down her face, but she turned to Dan and said quietly, "God will deliver him, Dan. I *know* it!"

But there was no such hope in Cody, and that night when he and Al Bailey talked about the visit, Cody expressed his true feelings. "My folks think they can get me out of here," he said. "But they're wrong. If I ever get out of here, it'll be over the wall."

"You know how that goes," Al said softly.

"Better be killed by Apaches than rot in this place!"

Bailey was silent for a long time, then said, "I feel the same way—and I'm goin' out, Cody!"

At once Cody leaped out of his bunk and stood up, peering into Bailey's face. "Mean it, Al? You're really going to try for it?"

Bailey nodded. "Been making plans for a long time, but never found a man I'd trust till you came along." He sat up, and while his legs dangled over the bunk, he began to speak rapidly. "It'll be tough, but it can be done, Cody. Now, here's the way I've got it figured . . ."

CHAPTER TWELVE

RACE WITH DEATH

★ ★ ★ ★

"It'll never work, Al—we must be crazy!"

Al Bailey turned his light blue eyes on Cody, snapping angrily, "You been hollering for a month to make this break. Now come on and keep your mouth shut!"

The two men had just left the main building, entering the crowded open compound called "The Yard." It was a busy place, filled with men standing in small groups talking, while others walked around getting their exercise. A babbling sound of voices filled the air, and Cody stared around nervously as the two walked steadily on the outer perimeter of the square. Looking up, he saw the guards with shotguns and hunting rifles lining the roof of the building and shook his head in a jerky motion, saying, "Al, it's broad open *daylight*! Those guards can see everything we do!"

"We've been over that a hundred times. Every escape that's ever been tried here took place at *night*. They've gotten careless in the daytime, Cody, but they tighten up as soon as the sun sets. So we'll outfox 'em by taking off when they're not looking for anything."

"They're *always* looking for something," Cody muttered, then shot an embarrassed glance toward his companion. "Sorry, Al," he said apologetically. "I'm being a pain in the neck."

Bailey grinned slightly, shrugging his frail shoulders before asking, "Want to back out, Cody?"

"No—I'm in, Al. Just got a little case of buck fever, I guess." He took two more steps, which brought them to the wall, then wheeled and started toward the other end of the yard. "You got the liquor?" he asked, his eyes running over the guards who lounged on the roof.

"In the infirmary, all doped up."

"You dope it up with that stuff you been stealing?"

"Laudanum. I put enough in there to put an elephant down."

"I don't want an elephant down, just those three Apaches."

Their plan to break out was based on the simple fact that Al Bailey worked in the prison infirmary. Weeks ago when he'd first told Cody about his plan, he'd said, "Cody, we can get outside the walls—but nobody makes it to the train. Can't no man shake them Apaches. So for a long time I been stealing booze and laudanum. What we do is dose the whiskey with the laudanum and get the Indians to drink it. I guarantee they won't be chasing *anybody* for at least twenty-four hours."

It had sounded fine, but now that the actual moment had come, both men were nervous. Both of them understood that it was life or death. "They'll bury us in the Oven till we cook if they take us alive," Bailey reminded Cody. "If they don't kill us first."

"They'll have to kill me," Cody snapped, his jaw tense. "Better be dead than buried in this forsaken hole!" He glanced up at the sun, then said, "It's time, don't you think, Al?"

"Guess so. Let's do it."

Breaking the pattern of their walk Al headed for the door that was open. Inside, the two guards looked up with surprise. "What's wrong with you two? Don't need the exercise?"

"Cody is feeling sick, Mr. Danner," Al said. "Want him to see the doc before he leaves for lunch." The guard nodded languidly, and told the two inmates to make their way to the infirmary. When they got there, Bailey tried the door, which was locked.

"He's gone," Cody sighed with relief. "See if that key will work, Al."

Bailey removed a key from his pocket, inserted it into the lock, then turned it. As the lock made a click, he nodded, "Took me a month to make this key. Come on—" The two men stepped inside, and Bailey quickly moved to a deep cabinet along one wall. Opening the door, he moved bottles and beakers with a clinking sound, then straightened up. "Here it is," he said with relief, holding up a brown bottle holding a quart of liquid. "I was worried that somebody might have found it." Taking the top off, he smelled it, then held the bottle forward. "Smells like booze, don't it, Cody? Laudanum don't have a strong smell."

Cody glanced over his shoulder, then said, "Now, getting the stuff down those Apaches—that's the hard part."

"Won't be hard if we catch them right. They're like all Indians—they love liquor, and it drives them crazy."

"What if they get too rowdy and somebody comes to see about them?"

"Well, that's the risk," Bailey admitted, "but we knew it would be risky. But nobody messes with those Apaches much—except Jocko. The rest of the guards are scared of 'em." He stuck the bottle under his shirt inside his trouser band, then said, "Come on. We don't have much time."

Cody's eyes narrowed, and a sharp thrill ran along his nerves. He'd felt it before, just before a fight or when mounting a wild horse. Danger did that to him—made him think and react faster. Bailey had noted this, and it was for this reason he'd chosen the lean cowboy to join him.

"You got the pass from Jocko?"

"Right here." Diving into his pocket, Al held up a single slip of paper, and a thin smile touched his lips. "Leo and Andretti are pretty sick boys, but they'll be all right."

"How in the world did you manage that?" Cody asked.

"When I heard they was going to take the supply wagon out to the work party, I got some stuff from the infirmary. Gave it to them in some of the whiskey I had stashed. I knew they'd come running to the infirmary, and when they did, I reported to Jocko that his two men were down sick. That was the real hard part, Cody!"

"What if he'd gotten somebody else to drive the wagon?"

"Then we'd have had to wait for another six months," Bailey shrugged. "But I waited until Jocko was real busy. He cussed and raved like it was my fault. Then he said, 'You take the supply wagon, Bailey. You've been loafing too long.' I tried to argue but that made him worse, like it was my fault his men got sick!"

"Well, guess he wasn't wrong—but he didn't tell you to take me, did he?"

"No, he said to take Dick Manti, but he won't have time to check before we're on our way. C'mon, I want to get out of the compound soon as we can."

The two men exited the infirmary and hurried down the hall and made their way to the stable. A guard stared at them, asking, "What you two up to?"

"Captain Valentine told us to take the supply wagon out to the job," Bailey said wearily.

"What happened to Andretti and Leo?"

"Got sick—and Captain blamed me for it!" Bailey complained. "I don't want to get out there with those Indians. They're crazy enough to do anything!"

The guard laughed. "All they can do is scalp you, Bailey. Now, get that team hitched up."

"Somebody's got to get them Indians." The Apaches always accompanied the supply wagon, and the guard grinned. "Don't worry, they'll be at the gate like always. Take them two horses over there."

Quickly the two men hitched the horses to the wagon, then Bailey complained, "Ain't we gonna' get no help loading this wagon?"

"Why don't you take it up with Jocko, Bailey?" the guard sneered. Then he turned sour and with a curse said, "Get the wagon loaded and get on your way."

Bailey and Cody loaded the supplies onto the wagon, then climbed up onto the seat. "You drive, Cody," Al said.

Grabbing the reins, Cody called out to the horses, and the team pulled out of the building into the bright sunlight. When they arrived at the gate, the two guards looked up, and the older one asked, "Where's the regular drivers?"

"Sick," Bailey shrugged. He reached into his shirt pocket and pulled out the pass from Valentine.

The guard took it, stared at it, then handed it back. "Open up, Sid," he said, and the younger guard unbolted the gates and swung them open.

Cody spoke to the horses and they moved through the opening. As soon as they were outside, Cody said, "There they are, Al."

The two men watched as three mounted Indians came riding toward them. They were wild-looking warriors, armed with rifles and six-guns at their belt. They drew up in front of the wagon and stared at the two men. Quickly Bailey said, "Regular men are sick."

The flinty-eyed leader studied him so long that both men grew tense, but then he wheeled his horse and the other two joined him. Two of them took position beside the wagon, and the third led the way.

Cody expelled his breath and whispered, "We made it!" His words, soft as they had been, were caught by one of the Indians, who gave the pair a sharp glance. *Those Indians can hear a caterpillar walk across moss at a mile and a half!* thought Cody as he clamped his lips together.

The road was rough but plainly marked with old wagon ruts, and soon the prison faded from sight. The guards alongside the wagon grew lax as they rode together, speaking their guttural language. The leader looked back from time to time but seemed uninterested.

"Where do we make our play?" Cody asked softly.

"I don't know. Never been out to the work camp. But we got to do it right, Cody. We wait too long, we'll be in sight of the guards. I got out of one of the drivers that the camp was about six miles—but how we gonna know when we've gone three miles?"

"I can make a pretty good guess," Cody nodded. "Getting them savages drunk is the trick. Has to be done right, or they'll get suspicious." The two of them spoke quietly, trying to plan, but there was little to be done. Finally Cody said, "I think we're about halfway there."

"Not a soul in sight," Bailey murmured, studying the horizon. "Look, we got to let them think the whiskey is *their* idea. We can't just invite them to have a drink with us."

"How about we sneak us a drink every now and then—until they catch us?"

"That's it!" Bailey said with relief. He took a deep breath, and reached under his shirt. When he had pulled the whiskey bottle out, he pretended to take a drink, turning his head as a man would who was trying to hide something. "They didn't see me," he said. "You try it."

Cody picked up the bottle, lifted it to his lips, then lowered it. He made his movements furtive and cut his eyes around. "Didn't see me either. Let me try again—"

This time, the trick worked. The leader had turned just in time to see Cody put the bottle back under the seat, and at once the Indian turned his horse and drove him toward the wagon. Pulling the animal up cruelly, he stared at Cody out of obsidian eyes. Pointing at the seat, he held his hand out and uttered a single word, "Give!"

Cody blinked and tried to look guilty, but he had little time. The other two Indians had moved to stop the team, and a quick question drew a brief answer from the leader, who lifted his rifle, training the muzzle on Cody. "Give!" he said coldly.

Cody wiped the sweat off his face and said weakly, "It's just—water."

But the Indian drew the hammer back on the Spencer, and Cody cried out, "No—don't shoot—" Reaching under the seat, he picked up the bottle and handed it carefully over to the Apache.

Bailey cursed and said, "That no good for Indian!"

The Indian ignored him, took the top off, and smelled the contents. Then he smiled for the first time and said something to his fellow guards, who came to him at once. He lifted the bottle and drank deeply, then handed it to one of the other Indians.

Bailey made a show, standing up and saying, "Captain of guards will not like it. Firewater no good for Indians."

One of the Indians, a short pug-nosed man, drew his pistol and sent a shot close to Bailey's head, whereupon Bailey at once fell into the seat. The three Indians all laughed and began to take turns with the whiskey.

The effect of the liquor was almost magical to the white men. They were shocked at how quickly the whiskey hit the Apaches—and then saw that things were getting out of control. The three began arguing over the bottle and soon were shouting at each other.

"Watch yourself, Al," Cody muttered. "They'd just as soon kill us, crazy as they are."

And he was almost right, for soon one of the Indians fell from his horse. He got up staggering, and his eyes grew wild when the other two laughed at him. He pulled his pistol and fired a shot, not to kill, but in anger. The other two laughed and pulled their revolvers and began firing wildly. Cody and Al could only sit there hoping they would be ignored.

But that was not the way of it, for soon all three Indians were on their feet, allowing their horses to drift away. They scuffled with each other and pulled knives, but drunk as they were, they did not kill each other. "Just a few minutes and we're okay," Cody breathed, but at that moment the leader glanced at him. His eyes were wild and staring, and he uttered a wild scream and made for the wagon. He had a Colt in his left hand, but with his right reached up and pulled Cody from the seat. Cody sprawled in the dust, and one of the other Indians ran around the wagon and pulled Bailey down. They were all three screaming and dragged the two men together.

The next ten minutes were the worst Cody had ever known. The Indians were insane—there was no other word for it. They fired shots that missed the two men by inches, and both Cody and Al knew they could be killed at any moment.

When the Indians tired of that, they began to beat the two men, who covered their heads and suffered silently. Most of the blows they caught on their arms, but one brave hit Al in the nose, producing a spurt of crimson blood. The sight of the blood increased their rage, and the Indians threw the men down and began to kick them. They were wearing moccasins instead of boots, which was all that saved the two convicts.

After a few minutes, one of them drew a wicked-looking knife and made jabbing motions at the pair. The other two cheered him on, and more than once the razor-sharp blade caught the flesh of both men, and cut their now-bloody shirts to shreds.

Can't stand much more, Cody gasped silently. *They'll kill us for sure!*

A few seconds later, one of the braves suddenly swayed and fell to the ground, totally unconscious. The other two hooted at him and shared the last of the whiskey. Both of them were weaving and moving very slowly—but were as dangerous as rattle-snakes.

Finally the Apache screamed and fell on Al Bailey. Drawing his knife he held it across the man's throat, and the leader was crying out something.

He's telling him to kill Al! The thought raced through Cody's brain, and he reacted instantly. The chief of the three was standing beside him, not two feet away. His eyes were fixed on the struggling white man and the maniacal Apache, who was intent on slitting the helpless man's throat. Cody, despite the buffeting, had been watching the Indians as they fired their guns and had noted that the leader had fired his rifle most of the time, firing with his Colt only twice. The Colt was in a holster on the Indian's right thigh, and in one motion Cody threw himself forward and snatched at the gun. He knew that if he missed he was a dead man—but he didn't miss!

The Colt came free, and at once Cody leveled it at the Indian who was slicing into Bailey's throat. The slug hit him along the skull, leaving a ragged track, and he crumpled to the ground.

Drunk as he was, the Apache beside Cody whirled and lifted his rifle. Cody saw the muzzle rise and point at his stomach. With his left hand he shoved the muzzle to one side just as the rifle roared. Cody shoved the Colt in the Indian's side and pulled the trigger—but the hammer snapped on a spent shell. Instantly, he lifted the heavy revolver and brought it down on the man's skull even as the Indian got off another wild shot. The Apache fell as if pole-axed, then Cody whirled to look at the third Indian—but all of the noise had not disturbed him, for he lay still on the ground.

"Al—you all right?" asked Cody, breathing heavily.

Bailey was dazed and stared uncomprehendingly at Cody. He'd almost been a dead man, and he was amazed at the way Cody had exploded into action right then. He touched his throat, then stared at the blood on his fingers. Then he managed a weak smile, "I guess so—but it was a close thing, Cody."

"We've got to get out of here," Cody snapped.

"What about them?" Bailey asked, gesturing at the three Indians.

"These two won't die. We'll leave 'em here. Al, if we miss that train, we're dead men!"

After picking up the weapons, they captured the Indian ponies, and then drove the horses from the wagon until they were ready to drop. Avoiding the work camp, they circled around and found the tracks of the railroad just where one of the men had told them. Within minutes, they found the water tank, and Cody said, "We've got a chance, Al!"

Quickly dressing in some of the old work clothes that had been designed for the camp, they huddled behind a clump of sage and waited.

"If they find out we're gone," Al said as they listened for the train, "they'll know where to look for us. Hope the train's not late!"

It wasn't long before they heard the distinctive sound of the train coming out of the east chugging across the desert. When it stopped to take on water and firewood, Cody and Al climbed into a stock car and hid among the steers, which stared at them suspiciously.

Finally the train began to move, and Al gleefully grabbed Cody and hugged him. "We made it! We made it!"

Cody was still cautious, though elated. "We can't stay on this train for long, Al. We need to get off and get us some horses. They'll check this train down the line." He laughed then, his face filled with exultation. "But we made it, Al!"

Bailey looked embarrassed, then said, "Well, you saved my life, Cody. I owe you."

"No, it was you that got us out, Al, so we owe each other." Cody struck the smaller man a friendly blow on the shoulder, then an odd look crossed his face. "Know what I feel bad about?"

"What, Cody?"

"I feel bad that I can't be there to see Jocko's face when he hears how he lost his prisoners!"

The thought struck Bailey as funny as the two of them stood there in the smelly cattle car, and finally they roared with laughter.

The train moved across the desert, passing into foothills and revealing small ranches. That night they slipped off the car and found a small herd of half-wild horses. Cody managed to lasso two of them. "Hate to be a hoss thief," he said regretfully as the two of them mounted and rode away. "But we got no choice, have we, Al?"

The night soon swallowed them up, and they disappeared into the short hills, then began to climb the steeper heights. Once they passed close to a mountain lion and it let out a shrill scream—almost like a woman in terror. But then it turned and padded away, the echo of its cry fading into the stillness of the night.

* * * *

"Can't tell you how grateful Hope and I are, Mark," Dan Winslow said. The two men were sitting at the kitchen table drinking black coffee from large white mugs. Ever since Mark had arrived earlier that morning, Dan had tried to express his gratitude, and now shook his head, adding, "I know how busy you are—"

"You'd do the same for me," Mark broke in. Leaning back in his chair, he looked relaxed, but there was an alert air about him, and he said, "Would have been here earlier, but I wanted Heck to come with me."

"He's a good investigator, you say?" asked Dan.

"Heck Thomas? Best there is." Mark nodded firmly. He sipped his coffee, then added, "I didn't want to be seen with him—and you don't need to either. He'll be around, but you'll never know it—nor will anyone else."

Hope had been taking a cake out of the oven, and now she set it down on the counter and came to stand beside Dan. "I don't understand that, Mark. What can he do?"

"He'll be working undercover, and he may have another man with him. Nobody will connect him with Cody or with you. That way he'll be able to move around unhindered. Heck's the best man in the world for getting information out of people."

Hope put out her hand and rested it on Dan's shoulder. "Does he think he can help?"

Mark shook his head. "You'll never get Heck Thomas to say about that. He keeps his mouth shut tight as a jug until he's got the job done. Most secretive man I ever knew."

"We want to pay him, Mark," Dan insisted.

Mark reached over and slapped the muscular shoulder of his brother. "Don't try it," he grinned. "What's the use of being rich and famous like me if I can't be a big spender. You wouldn't want to bruise my ego, would you?"

"It'd take a pile-driver to do that," Dan smiled. Then he said, "It's going to be hard, just waiting."

"Yes, that's the hardest thing there is," Mark admitted. "But we've all got to do it. Watch and pray, that's our job now—and leave the method up to Heck Thomas."

★　★　★　★

The minute Dan stepped off his horse, Hope knew something was wrong. He tied his horse, and then slowly walked over toward her. There was a tightness to his lips that warned her.

"What is it, Dan?" she asked quietly.

"It's about Cody," Dan said, then hesitated. He'd tried to think of some way to break the news to her in an easy way, but he knew there was no way to do that. "He's broke out of prison, Hope."

"Oh no, Dan!" she gasped.

Dan pulled a single sheet of paper from his pocket and handed it to her. She scanned it, then lifted her face to him. "Why did he do it? We told him about Mark hiring the best detective in the country to find the truth."

"I guess it was pretty rough on him. I've known men who could stand anything except being cooped up. I guess Cody is one of those."

"What will happen now?"

Dan shook his head. "I doubt he'll get in touch with us. What we have to pray is that he doesn't get caught. He'll be listed as armed and dangerous—and a lawman could shoot first."

Hope shook her head, her fine eyes clouded with grief. "But Mark said that Heck Thomas was making some headway. If only he could get proof!"

"If he does, we'll have the story put in all the newspapers in the country, Hope. Maybe Cody will see it and give himself up."

They stood there on the porch, hurting and filled with uncertainty. Finally Dan put his arm around her and turned her toward the house. The two of them moved slowly, almost painfully as they entered the door. "We'll keep on believing God," Hope whispered. She leaned against him, and deep down a cry rose, but she choked it back and grasped his arm tightly.

PART THREE

THE FUGITIVE

★ ★ ★ ★

CHAPTER THIRTEEN

A NEW FRIEND

★ ★ ★ ★

From the moment the two big men had piled into the boxcar, Sam Novak had known that they would be trouble. He himself had scrambled on at a small town twenty miles north and found the boxcar occupied by only one man. He had tried to start up a conversation, but his fellow traveler had been uncommunicative, simply answering in monosyllables. He had finally pulled his coat around him, had lain down on the straw, and had gone to sleep.

The train had clattered over the rails, stopping only once. The door had slid open with a clatter, and two more big men had gotten on and slammed the door behind them. One of them straightened up at once, looked around the car, and saw the two men already there. He said nothing but fixed his glance on Novak, as if trying to figure something out. The other hobo, a tall, lean man with long arms and a thatch of blond beard, plopped down and took a deep breath. "We made it, Deuce," he said. "I thought for a while there our goose was cooked."

"Shut up, Harry." The man who spoke was not as tall as the first, but was very broad and large inside the plaid wool coat that barely met over his burly chest. He glanced again at Novak, then demanded, "Any brakeman been checkin' this car, Bo?"

"Not since I been on," Novak answered briefly.

The man named Deuce nodded, then sat down, his back to the side of the car, and drew his legs up. The two were typical hobos, Novak knew, differing only in that they were bigger and stronger than most. An alarm went off in his head, and he thought, *Sooner or later they'll shake me down—or try to.* He had no illusions about his own ability to withstand two such opponents. He was a lean young man, not over five ten, well built but not massive, as were the two who sat silently staring at him as the train rumbled over a trestle.

The cold December air blew in through every crack in the boxcar, chilling Novak to the bone. He pulled his coat closer about him and yanked his black cap down, folding the flaps over his ears. He had been almost asleep when the train had stopped and the two new passengers climbed on, but now he knew he would have to remain watchful. As he sat there, he made up his mind to get off at the next stop. Casting a glance at the fourth occupant of the boxcar, he wondered if he ought to do something to warn the young man, but he shrugged his shoulders, thinking, *I guess he wouldn't welcome any advice from me.*

Despite the frigid air whistling through the car, Sam Novak's eyes began to grow heavy. He had not slept much for the past two nights and had eaten almost nothing in twenty-four hours. Determined to stay awake, he leaned his head back and fastened his eyes on the pair, studying their features by the first thin rays of dawn that filtered through the slats of the car. They were, he saw, vicious men, feral and sly. He knew then for certain that he would have to stay awake.

But the rhythmic clicking of the wheels over the rails, the swaying of the car, and his lack of sleep caught up with him. Slowly his eyes shut, and twice he snapped his head upright, forcing himself to stay awake. Finally he dropped off into sleep, his chin falling on his chest.

He awakened suddenly to a hand touching him. Without thinking he struck out with all his might and drove the taller of the two men backward. Instantly the one called Harry stood up and came over beside his companion. "You're a butterfingered scoundrel, Deuce," he smirked. "You'll never make a pickpocket." He turned his pale eyes on Novak and said, "All right, Bo, hand it over."

"Hand what over?" Novak challenged, although he knew very well what the pair had in mind.

"Gimme your cash," Harry snapped impatiently. "Come on, snap it up!"

Novak scrambled to his feet, put his back against the wall of the car, and clenched his fists.

Deuce grinned at him, his features blunt and fearsome in the breaking light. "Look at that! Enough to scare a man to death, ain't it?"

The other laughed loudly and said, "I reckon it'll take both of us to get this one, Harry." He stepped forward and his grin dropped from his face. "All right. You can have it either way you want it—easy or hard. But either way, we'll get what you've got in your poke," he said menacingly.

"Yeah. Come on, be smart, Bo," Deuce added carelessly. He slapped one fist into the palm of the other hand, the action making a meaty sound. He repeated it as if he enjoyed the feel of it, and then lifted his right hand. "C'mon, we ain't taking you to no doctor after we stomp you, so let's have it."

Sam Novak knew he was being foolish, but there was a stubborn streak in the young man. He wished desperately that he had a gun or a knife, anything—but he had no weapons at all. Suddenly, he did the only thing he knew. He made a dive, dodging the tall man on the right, and headed for the door, but the instant his hands touched the car door, strong hands like claws grabbed him and yanked him back, sending him sailing across the car.

He slammed into the opposite door, striking his head so hard that for an instant brilliant lights flashed before his eyes. Shaking his head, he scrambled to his feet and held his fists up. Harry snapped, "Come on, Deuce, let's get this over with." He stepped forward, and when Novak threw a blow, he simply blocked it with his left arm and sent a right cross that caught the young man high on the forehead, driving him sideways. It was a disaster for Novak, and only some sort of instinct allowed him to turn and begin to fend off his two aggressors.

The two men made a joke out of it. One of them would hit Novak in the face or the body, and when he heard a gasp he would grab him and throw him across at the other, who would catch him and repeat the action.

"We can keep this up all day, fellow," Harry grinned. "Why don't you be smart now and give us your money?"

Novak's right eye was rapidly closing, and blood was trickling down from a cut over the eyebrow. His mouth was bleeding where his lips had been crushed against his teeth, and his side ached from the pounding he'd taken, but he gave no sign of giving up. Glaring at the two, he shook his head and said, "You're small-time punks!"

"All right," Deuce said, scowling. "Put him down, Harry."

Harry stepped forward to deliver a crushing blow, but at that very instant something gripped his coat near the collar, and he felt himself yanked back bodily. He staggered back against the door, hollering, "Hey, what's going on!"

Deuce wheeled about while Harry caught his balance, and the two of them whirled to stare at the young man who had left his place on the straw and stood facing them. He was wearing a battered hat, and his clothes had seen rough wear. Quickly, Harry took in the form of the man and saw that he was tall, about six feet, but seemed to be slender, although it was hard to tell with the bulky clothes. "You better stay out of this," he warned. "You could get hurt bad."

The eyes that regarded the two from underneath the hat were steady. They were the darkest kind of blue and did not waver. "Let him alone," he said, almost conversationally. "You can get on the other side of the car." Saying this, he moved across, planting himself firmly beside Novak.

Harry cursed, and Deuce shouted, "Get him, Harry." Harry was fairly adept at barroom brawling. He had depended on his burly strength, and now he cocked his massive fist back. But even as he drew it back, the young man snapped a punch at him so fast that Harry had no chance to blink, catching him in the mouth and driving him backward. Deuce yelled and threw a punch, but Novak saw it coming. He didn't attempt to hit the man but kicked with all his might at the kneecap. Instantly, Deuce was on the floor of the car yelling, "You broke my knee!"

Harry came back, his mouth bleeding, but still tough. He threw himself at the interloper, cursing, caught him, and pinioned him to the wall. He raised his hand to slug him in the ear, when suddenly he felt steely hands grasp him behind his neck.

His head was pulled forward just as the young man ducked his head, and Harry felt his nose break. Hearing the sound of the crunch as he took the terrible blow, he turned loose of his adversary. Before he could even move, Sam Novak gave him a taste that he'd dished out to the other man by kicking him in the knee with all his might. He had on hard-toed, short boots, and agony ran through Harry. He did not fall, but when he backed up against the door, his knee felt on fire, and the pain in his mouth and nose was as bad as anything he'd ever felt.

"Had enough?" demanded the stranger. "Or you want your other knee kicked in?"

Deuce got up from the floor of the car, glared at the two, but mumbled, "Come on, Harry—" He hobbled toward the other end of the car, slumped down, and his companion followed him.

Novak watched them, then turned and said quietly, "You saved my bacon that time."

"Glad to help. Are you okay?"

Novak looked at the young man, felt his ribs, and grimaced, "Be a little sore, I guess. Come on down here. I got a blanket we can wrap up in."

The two moved away toward the other end of the car, keeping their eyes on the pair who glared at them as they nursed their wounds. Novak gave his name, and then the other said quietly, "Name's Logan, Jim Logan."

"Just bummin' around, are you, Jim?"

"Yeah, I guess that's it," the young man said. "Looking for work, but it's kinda hard to come by these days. What about you?"

"Oh," Novak said, a smile touching his bruised lip. "I'm just traveling around looking things over. Never been away from home before, and I thought before I did anything serious—like getting married or settling down at a steady job—I better see some of this country."

The broad lips of the tall young man twisted wryly. "Well, you picked a pretty rough side of it for a vacation."

Novak leaned over and picked up his bedroll, pulling the straps off of it. "I got a couple of cans of beans here. No way to heat it, but if you're hungry . . ."

The other man hesitated, struggling with his pride, Novak

saw, so he added quickly, "Here, let me open one of them." He produced a can opener, wrenched the top off of one, and handed it to him. They sat down, and Novak pulled a blanket over both their shoulders, talking all the time to take the sting of charity away from his offering. He talked about the towns he'd seen and several amusing adventures without pausing until Logan had eaten the beans out of the first can. Without missing a word, he opened the second and handed it to him, not even looking.

The train rumbled on, and the two kept the blanket pulled tightly around them. "It feels good, don't it, Jim?" Sam said. "Never knew a blanket could be so welcome."

"I lost my bedroll a way back," Logan said. "It gets kinda cold sleepin' in your clothes under bridges."

Novak glanced at him briefly and after a while said, "You know, I wouldn't mind having a partner, Jim. It's not safe for one man. You think we might stick together for a while, see how it goes?"

He laughed aloud, saying, "You might not be able to stand me. I don't know, but I'd feel a little bit better if I had somebody with me."

His new acquaintance hesitated, chewing on the last of the beans. Then he threw the can across the car where it made a rattling sound. Turning to Novak, he grinned and looked somehow much younger, "I guess if you can put up with me, I can put up with you, Sam. We'll try it anyway."

The two of them sat there. Somehow Novak felt like a decision had been made that was more than casual. His new acquaintance had a hard look about him, as if he'd been ill used, but there was nothing vicious, Novak ascertained. He leaned back, saying, "Nice little town coming up, at least on the map. What do you say we get off there and see if we can scuffle up enough work to buy some grub?"

His new friend did not answer, and Novak looked back to see that he had already closed his eyes and was sleeping soundly.

★　★　★　★

"Well, I guess my plan wasn't so good, was it, Jim?"

Sam Novak was standing at a small bar window looking out,

then he turned and sat down on the lower bunk. "Maybe we should've skipped this town."

"Doesn't make much difference. These towns are all alike," Logan shrugged. "You can get busted just for spittin' on the sidewalk in most of them—as I've found out."

They had dropped off the train at Bent Fork and had not lasted more than an hour before they had been hailed by a long-legged man with a star on his vest. "You two got jobs?" he'd demanded.

"Why, no," Sam had said quickly. "We're looking for work, Sheriff. You know of any jobs?"

"No, but I know you're under arrest for vagrancy. Get going, now."

The two had complained bitterly, but they had been clamped in the jail, tried by a justice of the peace later that day, and had been sentenced to thirty days on the county work gang. After the so-called trial, they were put back in the cell and given an almost inedible meal, after which the jailer—a very fat man called Stump—had put his feet up on the desk and proceeded to take a nap.

Night had fallen now, and Novak said, "I guess I need a little encouragement, Jim. Do you think we'll get out of this thing?"

Logan looked at him in surprise. "Get out of it? Why, no. We'll do thirty days hard, and it'll be hard, too, if I know these counties. They shoot a man just for thinking about running away."

"Oh, I don't reckon so," said Novak, not seeming to be worried. He looked at his companion and saw that he was wrapped in an aura of bitterness. Logan's eyes were cloudy, and his lips were drawn into a straight line as he sat on the other bunk staring blindly at the wall.

For three days they sat in the cell after the trial. Finally Novak looked out the window and said, "Almost eight o'clock."

"What does it matter? We're not going anywhere," complained Logan.

Novak sat down and stared at the fat man, who had stirred from his usual nap and was doing some sort of paperwork. "Watch him," Novak said.

Jim Logan stared with surprise at Novak, then turned to observe the jailer. As he watched, the fat man put his paper and pencil down, got up, and took a heavy coat off of a rack. He struggled into it, pulled a hat down over his head, and left without a word to the prisoners.

"How'd you know he was gonna do that?" Logan asked.

"Because he does it every night. Didn't you know he goes to the saloon down the street and stays for an hour? When he comes back he's always had enough liquor to make him sleep." Novak stood to his feet and said, "Come on, Jim. We're gettin' out of here."

His partner looked at him as if he were crazy. "What are you talking about?" he demanded.

Novak grinned at him, reached inside his pants, and from underneath his belt withdrew what looked to be a long, steel spring. "Key out of here," he said cheerfully, and turning, he reached down and inserted it into the lock. He wiggled it around, his face frozen with effort, and then there was a definite click.

"That's it." Novak pulled the door open and said, "Come on, let's get our stuff and get out of here." He saw the startled look on his companion's face and laughed. "My best friend's father back in Virginia was a locksmith. I hung around his shop a lot when I was a kid."

At once the two hurried out of the cell. "We haven't got long," Novak said, glancing around cautiously. "The eight-fifteen ought to be here in ten minutes." He glanced at the clock on the wall and nodded, "That's about it. Let's find our stuff."

They searched through the desk and through a cabinet on the end and found the few belongings they had. After putting on their coats, Sam picked up his bedroll and said, "We better stay off the street until the last minute. You go take a look out the window."

Seeing it was already dark, Logan went to look. "Can't see a thing," he said, staring out the window.

"Good. You can see if somebody's coming in, though. If they do, we'll have to knock 'em over the head and lock 'em in that cell."

Logan kept a careful watch, and finally he turned to see Novak sitting at the desk going through the contents of the drawer. He felt Logan's gaze and tossed the papers back, saying, "Guess it's time to go. If you see anybody, don't run. It's dark enough that we shouldn't be recognized. We're just a couple of guys going down to the saloon for a drink. We go to the station and head off down the siding. When the train stops, we get on top or find an empty car. Come on."

The two left the jail, and had not gone ten steps before they encountered two men coming right at them. They both pulled their hats down, and as the two men passed, one of them said, "Howdy."

"Hey," Novak grunted. "Cold, ain't it?"

The men did not react, and when they were twenty feet away, Logan suddenly turned and grinned at his friend. "You're a cool one, Sam. I was about ready to slam into those two."

"No need for that. Come on."

They made their way to the station, moved down the siding, and huddled behind two freight cars off on the siding. The train pulled in right on time, and without any difficulty they found an empty boxcar. When the train pulled out, Logan let out a deep breath. He reached over and slapped the younger man on the shoulder, saying, "Well, we're even for the help I gave you, Sam. But I'd still like for us to go double harness for a while."

Sam hesitated, then said, "Suits me, but first look at this." He reached into his pocket, took out a folded paper, and handed it to his young friend. Logan opened it and said, "I can't see anything." Sam reached into his pocket, obtained a match, and struck it on the side of the boxcar. By the wavering, flickering light the words jumped out, *Wanted for murder, Cody Rogers. $5,000 reward. Contact Sheriff Rider, War Paint, Wyoming.*

There was a moment of tension, and Sam Novak wondered if he had done the right thing. Then he said, "You want to tell me about it, Cody?"

Cody felt a warmth rush through him. He knew that five thousand dollars looked as big as the moon to this young man, on the bum as he was, and he said evenly, "You didn't turn me in. You got a hidden bank account somewhere?"

Novak shrugged his shoulders. "Sit down, let's talk about it. How'd you get into this?"

For the next fifteen minutes Cody told his story to Novak, and finally he said, "I'm heading out to Indian Territory."

"Worst thing you could do," Sam said. "You'll get caught sure."

"How do you figure that? Nobody but federal marshals can go in there."

"And every man they see there," Novak nodded, "is an outlaw. They know that, Jim—their job is hunting outlaws. They'd pick you up on suspicion and take you in, then they'd see one of these flyers. You'd be caught sure."

Cody sighed. He was tired, his eyes were gritty, and in a voice edged with weariness, he sighed, "I don't know what to do, Sam."

"I know what to do. Hit the big city."

"What! No, I want to stay away from people."

"Bad idea. Out here where there aren't many people you're real visible. But in some city where there's a bunch of people, who's going to notice one more young fellow like you? Let me tell you how we're going to do it. They don't care much about men wanted in Wyoming back east. We'll go there and get some kind of a job that keeps us on the move. Construction maybe."

He went on talking, and after a while, Cody finally said, "Well, it'll beat what I'm doing now. It might work."

"Okay, we'll do it then," Novak nodded.

Cody stared at him strangely and said, "Somehow, maybe I'll make this up to you, Sam, but I don't know how. I guess I'll be on the run the rest of my life."

The train rattled over a bridge, and then the clattering ceased. The wind whistled by, and the two sat there huddled under the blanket, making plans for the future.

CHAPTER FOURTEEN

BUFFALO BILL TAKES A FALL

★   ★   ★   ★

By the end of her first tour with Bill Cody's Wild West Show, Laurie had learned that show business was not nearly as glamorous as she had anticipated. Show life was the unloading at an empty place. It was the packing up and moving on when you were so tired you could hardly walk. It meant listening all night to the clicking of rails, the wail of the train whistle, the big, dark, unknown country passing by. It was the band playing, horses prancing, people lining the streets of a strange city. Then there was the hot, midday confusion of the grounds, the sweaty canvas men lying in the shade of their wagons, with the steers bawling from the corral, and the cook clanging his skillet with an iron spoon.

Show life, she had learned, was rain drumming on the tent roof while you stood on a bale of straw to change a costume. It was the teamsters lashing the draft horses while the wagon sank hub deep in straw-strewn mud. It was cowboys sitting on a wagon in the sunset, picking their teeth with stems of hay, talking about the outfits back in Texas or Montana. And it was *homesickness*. The aching mind and heart and muscle kindled the desire for a quiet fireside and the circle of lamplight on a checkered tablecloth. It was a homesickness that hurt worse than any physical ailment Laurie had ever had.

She discovered that writing was a panacea for her loneliness, and during the cobwebby hours of the morning, she poured her thoughts into page after page of her journal. She began work on a novel, but the pressures of show business did not allow her the long periods of time necessary for such a task.

One afternoon as the parade began to line up, she swung into the saddle, feeling the high spirits of Star as he pranced sideways, and thought, *I hate so much of this, and yet I would miss it if I were to leave.*

At that moment she glanced down at the spur on her right boot. The ruby sparkled as the sun broke from behind a cloud, and she thought of the day her father had given it to her. A lump rose in her throat, and she swallowed hard at the memory. She never wore it without thinking of him. She wore the jeweled spur only for parades, never when she was performing her stunts. Now the sight of it brought back the memory of her father's face that day when the two of them had stood at the station and said their goodbyes before she left for college. Those days of wanting to be a writer seemed like a distant memory now. Suddenly, the sound of the band striking up stirred her from her reverie, and she hurried to get in place for the parade.

As the parade filed out toward the town, Buffalo Bill rode at the head of the line, doffing his hat to the loud cheers. Finally, in rolled the bandwagon with its six white horses stepping lightly to the strains of "Oh Susanna, Don't You Cry For Me." Not far behind, with a clatter on the stones, came Chief White Eagle and fifteen tawny warriors, and later in the parade Running Bear led his Sioux on their painted ponies. The Mexican vaqueros rode with jangling spurs and buckskin strings bouncing above the bright serapes tied behind their saddles. Their faces were dark under the wide sombreros, and their buckskin jackets were laced with white leather. The street was full of cowboys, long-horned steers, and Indians. The parade ended with a Deadwood Mail Stage, dented with bullets from the desperadoes of the Black Hills, drawn by six black horses.

The parade wound through town and then made its way back to the lot where they were staying. Immediately Laurie dismounted and saw to it that Star was bedded in clean rye straw. She glanced over to where the buffalo were browsing on mounds of dry timothy. Steers grazed over their hay-strewn corral, with a cowboy playing a mouth organ from the top rail. Beyond the cook tent and the bunk tent, opposite the clusters of the tepees of the Indians, rose two A-tents. One of these was for Buffalo Bill Cody and his partner, Nate Salsbury. The other tent was for Laurie and a young woman named Leona Aimes. Leona was a pretty blond woman with a sultry kind of beauty that men admired. She was a trick shot artist and had been with the Wild West Show for only two months. Laurie got along with Leona very well, although there was a wildness in her roommate that troubled her. Leona made trouble among the cowboys of the show, causing them constantly to be caught up in some kind of fist fight. If it were not for the drawing power of her act, Colonel Cody would have let her go long ago.

Or maybe he wouldn't, Laurie thought as she moved toward the flap of the tent. *I wouldn't be surprised but what he's tried to start something with her. He sure tries hard with everything in skirts that I can see.*

Disgust washed over her as she thought of how disappointed and disillusioned she had been to find out that Buffalo Bill was a lecher and a womanizer. He had a wife and children who never traveled with him, and the members of the troop had learned to ignore his escapades with young women.

She walked back to her tent, which she had made as neat and homelike as possible. A pair of curtains framed the opening, and inside were two folding cots, canvas chairs, a steamer table, two wardrobe trunks, a gun trunk for Leona, a collapsible tub, and clean towels on a folding rack. The earth floor was covered by a bright green Axminster rug. Quickly, Laurie changed out of her show outfit, put on a rather plain, tan divided skirt with blouse to match, and grabbing a hat and pulling it over her curls, left to go to town.

She had gotten only as far as the outside perimeter of the showgrounds when she was greeted by Con Groner. "Hey, you going to town, Laurie?"

"I guess so, Con. Wanna come along?"

"Sure, let's let these folks see what a good-looking couple looks like."

He fell into step with her, and Laurie gave him a quick glance.

She was impressed by Groner, who had been a sheriff in the West. He had broken up Doc Middleton's gang, captured six members, and foiled their plot with followers of Jesse James to hold up a Union Pacific train at Garnet Station six miles east of North Platte. He had been a lawman for several years and was also an excellent horseman. The show's publicity, written by Salsbury, credited him with catching ". . . over fifty murderers and more than that number of horse thieves, cattle cutters, burglars, and outlaws."

He was, Laurie discovered, a very lonely man, who at the age of twenty-eight, had never married. Groner was no more than average height, and he had blond hair and light blue eyes. He had been a scout, as had Buffalo Bill Cody, for the army. He was also highly intelligent, Laurie discovered, and commented on it as they walked along.

"Groner, you sure had a way of outfoxing outlaws."

"Well, Miss Laurie," he said, "you gotta be a little smarter than a crook to catch 'em." He grinned at her. "My daddy always told me you had to be a little bit smarter than a mule to train a mule. I guess that's what I was—just a little bit smarter than the crooks."

As they moved along the street, they spoke of the show that was to come and of the dates that had been booked in the future. They spent the better part of an hour browsing in the stores and walking along the streets. Finally they stopped to have the noon meal at a cafe.

As they seated themselves, Groner said, "We get good grub with the show, but I like to shove my feet under a real table every now and then." When the waiter came, they ordered steak and potatoes. As they waited, and all during the meal, the ex-lawman carried on an easy conversation.

"Ought to have a better show than ever next year," Groner said as he put three large spoonfuls of sugar into his black coffee. "From what I hear, Colonel Cody's just about gonna double it."

"I don't know about that," Laurie said. She hesitated, not sure if she should voice her doubts, but then said, "I don't know—I'm pretty tired, and to tell the truth, I'm just not cut out for show business."

He stared at her with his light blue eyes and shook his head abruptly. "Not cut out for it? Why you've got the best act in the whole show, girl," he said. "Certainly you're cut out for it."

"Oh, it's been fun, and I still enjoy a lot of it, but it's confining, too. Nobody knows what hard work it is to keep a show moving, unless they've actually been in one." She saw that her words had disturbed him, and knew instinctively that he was more interested in her than she had supposed. Quickly, she said, "Don't say anything about this, Con. I may change my mind."

"Never you mind, Miss Laurie, I won't say a thing," Con assured her.

Having finished their meal, the two of them rose and sauntered slowly back through the town. They got to the tent only half an hour before the afternoon show.

"I better go get ready," she said.

"All right, Laurie," Con nodded. "I'll saddle Star for you."

"Thank you, Con. That would be nice."

Laurie went at once to her tent to change into her show outfit and found Leona already there, studying her face in the mirror. She looked around and said, "Where have you been, Laurie? In town looking over the crop of men?"

"Oh, Con and I went in for a little while," Laurie shrugged. She began to change, and all the time Leona carried on a conversation, paying little heed to her answers.

When Laurie had her costume on, she stopped and looked at herself in the small mirror. It was only eight inches by ten inches, and she could not see much beyond her hat and the top of her blouse. But Leona looked at her and admired the trim figure in the red divided skirt, the fringed, tan jacket, and the small, narrow-brimmed hat with the low crown that she fastened to her head by a leather string. Sitting down she put on an unusual pair of spurs. They were carefully crafted from silver and a blue stone winked from the twin stones as she slipped them on. They had been a gift from Colonel Cody and she was pleased with them. He'd said, "A star needs a little glitter, Laurie, and these ought to do it."

"These cowboys sure would go for you," she spoke up, "if you'd just give them a chance."

"I haven't got time for that," Laurie smiled.

"What have you got to do that's more important than men?"

Leona grinned rashly and laughed at herself. "Well, you know that about me already, don't you, Laurie?" She straightened up suddenly and said, "There's your cue."

Quickly Laurie ran to the horse lot and mounted Star. Con handed her Star's reins, then turned and opened the flap that led to the arena. Laurie heard the voice of the ringside announcer calling out, ". . . and now, Buffalo Bill Cody and the greatest Wild West stars ever collected!"

There was thunderous applause as Cody went out, took his bow, and made a small speech to the audience. Finally, she heard him say, "Ladies and gentlemen, we present to you the foremost woman trick rider in the world in an exhibition of skill—Miss Laurie Winslow and her wonder horse, Star."

Even as he was saying the last words, Laurie had kicked Star into action. The lively animal hit the track at a dead run and a splattering of applause went up from the crowd. Laurie threw her hand up to acknowledge it, and at once began her routine.

She had worked on this routine constantly since coming with the show, and was now more out of the saddle than on it. Sometimes she would slip off, let her feet hit the ground, and then the momentum would kick her up in the air. She would twist at the top of the arc and come down on the other side. She had learned to do this so easily that she could do it as many as fifteen or twenty times, and with each repetition the applause grew louder. She brought a gasp and a roar from the crowd when she did the fall away, where she fell over backward, her head only inches from the steel-clad hooves. They had never failed to be a hit, and she pulled Star up and had him rear up on his hind legs as she pulled her hat off and waved to the crowd.

As Cody and Salsbury watched, the frontiersman said, "You know, Nate, that was a lucky day for us when we ran onto that young lady. She's pretty and smart, and can she ever ride that hoss of hers!"

"We ought to give her more money, Bill," Salsbury said. This was unusual for him, for he usually kept a tight hand on the purse strings. Catching Cody's look of surprise, he shrugged, saying, "If she quit, it would leave a big gap."

"She won't leave," Bill Cody grinned. "She's got show business in her blood after this tour."

Salsbury suddenly said, "What's that?" He watched as Johnny Baker, the Cowboy Kid, attached a series of balloons at intervals of twenty feet along one side of the track.

Bill grinned at him. "Little trick. Thought it'd add some spice to the act. Watch this, Nate."

Laurie wheeled Star around, galloped him to the end of the track, and wheeled around again. She was not at all certain about how this would turn out, although it had worked well enough in practice. Cody had come to her and asked her to try it, and the two of them had worked hard on the trick. She heard the announcer saying, "And now, an exhibition of exceptional marksmanship and horseback riding. Miss Laurie Winslow!"

As he called out her name, Laurie kicked Star into a violent run. When Star approached the first balloon, she grabbed a special strap that she had added to the saddle far down on the right side. She threw herself down, drawing the pistol from her holster at the same time, so that she was suspended beneath the barrel of the racing horse. The first balloon appeared; she aimed at it, pulled the trigger, and was relieved to see it burst. She passed five more balloons, and a shot exploded each one of them.

When she pulled herself back into her saddle, the crowd was standing up on its feet, applauding wildly. She took her bows and had Star bow down on one front leg, doubling the other up. Then, with a flourish, Laurie turned and galloped out.

As soon as she was out of the tent, she was greeted by Con Groner, who said with admiration, "Well, I never saw that little trick before."

"Oh, it's something Mr. Cody wanted us to do."

Con gave her a strange glance. "I think you'd better walk carefully around Mr. Cody."

Laurie looked at him and nodded. "I know, Con. That's one reason I'm unhappy here."

"That old goat. I ought to bust his head," Groner said grimly, and at that moment looked just about mad enough to do it.

Laurie laughed. "It's all right. I can handle him."

★ ★ ★ ★

The last show had been over for some time, and Laurie had paced restlessly around her tent. Leona had gone to town to celebrate with one of the cowboys, and despite herself, Laurie was glad for the silence. Finally, she came out of the tent, wandered around, and stopped at the Indians' tepees, where she saw Running Bear sitting and staring into a fire. Going over, she said, "Hello, Running Bear."

The Indian looked up, and although he was not a smiling man, a gleam of humor appeared in his eyes. "Ah, my little white Sioux. Sit down."

Laurie sat down by the fire, and as she talked to the stolid Indian who watched her impassively, she felt some of the pressure leave. There was something in Running Bear, a patience that seemed to mold him, that she envied. Finally she asked, "Will you do this forever, Running Bear? Travel around like this with Mr. Cody?"

"No. Not good."

"Why not? You're making money, aren't you?"

"Yes." The answer came reluctantly, and Running Bear shook his head stubbornly. "I miss my land and my people."

"So do I. Maybe it's time for both of us to go home."

The two talked little more, sitting there enjoying the silence. Finally, Laurie got up and made her way back to her tent. She had stepped inside and started to undress when a voice said, "Laurie?"

"Who is it? I'm getting ready for bed."

"It's me—Bill Cody. I need to see you."

Hastily, Laurie pulled a robe on and belted it. "Come in, Mr. Cody." Instantly, she wished she had stepped out to meet him, but stepping outside in her robe didn't appeal to her either. *I've got to get rid of him*, she thought quickly.

"Well, honey, you did fine tonight." Bill's face was glowing with the effect of the drinks he had been having. He was a heavy drinker. Nate Salsbury had made him promise once to cut down to one drink a day, and Bill had solemnly promised, but the one drink grew to be a huge, specially made schooner that would hold at least a quart of whiskey. Bill cut back on the number of glasses, but not on the amount.

"You done real fine. Didn't miss a one."

"It would be hard to miss, shooting bird shot." Laurie

shrugged with a rueful smile. "Somehow that doesn't seem honest."

"Well, a shot's a shot, and maybe you'll get good enough to use bullets, but I don't see any need for it."

He stood there talking, and she could sense the tension in the man. Suddenly he reached out and pulled her toward him. He was a tall man, and handsome, though already beginning to show the excessive use of alcohol. "You are mighty sweet, Laurie," he said huskily, "and the prettiest thing I ever saw."

Laurie began to wrestle with him, but he held her in his strong hands, and only by exerting all of her strength did she manage to twist away from him. "Don't say that to me!" She stepped back and said angrily, "Get out of here. And you might as well know, I'm leaving the show."

Bill Cody stared at her. He was not accustomed to being rebuffed by young women, but her words about leaving seemed to hit him harder than her rejection.

"Why—you can't do that, Laurie! I need you."

"You can get another trick rider," she said.

"Not as pretty as you." He began to reason with her and ended by saying, "Nate told me just tonight we need to offer you more money."

"It's not money. I'm just lonesome."

Colonel Cody had the impulse to offer to console her, but he could not. Instead, he said, "Well, don't make any quick decisions. This idea is good, Laurie. People want to know about the West." He seemed serious for a moment, and a dreamy gaze came into his eyes. "It's more than just money," he insisted. "It's saving something that's going to be lost if we don't do something about it. The West is dying out, and someday"—he waved his hand around—"this will be all there is of it."

Laurie wanted to say, *This isn't the true West. This is just a show*, but she knew better than to argue. Stubbornly she shook her head and said, "I'm not going to argue with you, Mr. Cody. I'll stay one more month, and then you'll have to get somebody else."

Cody argued for a few moments, then she said firmly, "You'll have to go now." He turned and backed out, still begging her.

Laurie discovered her hands were trembling. It was not the

first time he had touched her and tried to kiss her, but she was determined it would be the last. She changed into her night-dress, got into the cot, and pulled the covers up about her. For a while she read from the Bible with the worn, black cover, and then finally she put it down and turned the light down low so that Leona could see when she came back. She lay there silently with her eyes closed, praying for people she knew. Finally, Buffalo Bill came to her mind. "Lord, he is a wicked man. I pray that you would catch his attention, Lord. Let him see that he is ruining himself!" A few minutes later, she drifted off to sleep still praying.

The next day after breakfast she was strolling around when she saw a crowd over at the corral. "What's going on?" she asked Buck Bronson.

Buck Bronson, six feet five and strong as a bull, grinned. "Gonna have a new attraction. We got us a wild, buckin' buffalo."

Laurie moved beside him and saw indeed that there was a huge buffalo. He was walking around, and unlike most buffaloes, which had rather placid looks, there was something wicked about the way he dug his hooves in and shook his head.

"Some of the boys got to saying that they ought to put that critter in a buckin' act. And when Bill heard it, nothin' would do but that's what's gonna happen. Look, there he is now."

Laurie looked in the direction of Buck's gesture and was surprised to see Bill Cody himself walking over to the corral. As she watched, two cowboys on horseback snubbed the buffalo, keeping the pressure on while another slapped a saddle on him. The girth of the animal was so big, they had had to lengthen the girth strap.

When the saddle was in place, Bill said, "Watch, you buckaroos, and see how a real horseman can ride anything with hair!"

He put one foot in the stirrup, the ropes were loosened, and instantly the buffalo began to pitch—not only up and down—but sideways. He had not gone three jumps before Colonel Cody started losing his seat. The distance of his seat from the saddle became greater each time, and finally he came down sideways, and the momentum of the next buck threw him high in the air. He made a complete somersault and landed flat on his back. The buffalo instantly stopped and trotted off to the other end of the corral, looking insulted.

Several of the men jumped off the fence and ran to the colonel, who did not get up right away.

"I think he's hurt, Buck," said Laurie.

"He took a pretty rough fall there. Let's go find out."

There was a lot of talk, and Cody had to be helped to his dressing room. Later, Laurie saw Groner, who told her, "You hear about Colonel Cody?"

"No. Is he all right?"

"Naw, they had to take him to the hospital. Wrenched his back pretty bad."

He shook his head in disbelief, saying, "I'm surprised he didn't break his neck—the old fool getting on a wild critter like that! You can know something about a horse, but nothing about one of them things."

He continued talking, but all Laurie could think of was the prayer that she had made last night, and she wondered, *Lord, is this to catch his attention? It sure is a hard way!* She turned and asked, "Con, will the show go on?"

"Oh, you can't hurt that old codger." Bill Cody was thirty-seven and Groner, twenty-eight, but he had always looked upon Cody as a much older man. He shrugged slightly, saying, "He'll be out there if we have to wheel him out in a wagon. Ain't you found that out about the old man yet? He ain't got much religion, but what he does have—why, it's the show, I guess."

Laurie wandered off, thinking about what Groner had said, and sadly shook her head. *It's a sad thing when all a person has in his life is a show!*

CHAPTER FIFTEEN

THE NET CLOSES

★ ★ ★ ★

The burly foreman of the crew stepped to the edge of the huge hole—at least two hundred feet in diameter—looked down at the men wielding picks and shovels, and shouted, "Quittin' time! Line up at the pay shack if you want your money."

Cody looked up with a grimace and said, "Come on, Sam. I've had all of this I can stand for one day."

Sam Novak was covered, as were Cody and practically everyone else, with the yellow clay that they had been struggling with all day. The cesspool they were digging would be the largest ever built as far as they could discover, and they had been excited and pleased to get a job. But after digging for three weeks in the sticky, almost unyielding clay, they were both sick of it. They climbed wearily out of the hole and lined up in the pay line. When they received their week's wages, they jammed it into their pockets, then turned and walked along the pathway that led to the road. When they reached it, they found it, too, was muddy, for a heavy rain had turned the surface into a sea of mud. The mud made a sucking sound as they pulled their feet clear, and they compromised finally by moving over to the edge. It was not cold, for January of 1885 was mild that year—for which they were both thankful.

As they plodded along, Cody complained, "I don't know

how much more I can dig this blasted clay, Sam." He looked down at his hands and noticed that the entire front of his clothing was coated with the yellow, sticky earth. "I'm used to hard work, but this is different."

Novak grinned at him sharply, his white teeth showing against his muddy face. "Oh, come on, Cody—just think, you'll be able to tell your grandchildren that you helped dig the biggest cesspool in the whole state of Missouri. Now that's something, isn't it?"

As usual, the light-hearted Sam was able to wring a smile from Cody, who, with a frown, said, "Well, that's something, all right. But it wasn't exactly what I had planned for my whole life."

The two of them plodded along the road for half an hour, then turned in to the boardinghouse where they shared a room. It was a relic of a Victorian mansion—the corpse of one would be more accurate. In its heyday, it had gleamed whitely, its proud turrets and gingerbread work one of the marvels of St. Louis. But the town had expanded the other direction, so that now this section had become the dwelling place for the working classes. Entering the house, they made their way to a room up in the attic. It was half-round because a turret formed part of one wall, and it allowed in plenty of sunlight, which pleased them.

"Come on, let's go down and beat that bunch to the tub," Sam said eagerly. Grabbing underwear and fresh clothes, he left the room with Cody right behind him. When they reached the backyard, they walked toward an area closed by a canvas curtain. "I guess we're the first here," Sam said and stuck his head inside. "You here, Jude?"

"Yeah, come on in."

"You go first, Cody—I mean, *Jim*, " he caught himself. "I think you've got more mud on you than I have."

Cody did not argue but stepped inside the enclosure, where the main furniture consisted of a huge, clawfoot, porcelain tub. Over to one side hung a huge, black pot straddling a fire, the water bubbling merrily, and the man called Jude got up and began to fill the tub. As he poured in the last bucket, Cody slipped out of his union suit, shivered in the cold air, and plunged himself into the steaming water. It was almost hot enough to scald, but the next five minutes he sputtered and soaked and lathered as the water turned to a muddy color.

Finally, Sam marched in, saying impatiently, "That's enough, Jim. You don't want to get too clean." Reluctantly, Cody got up, dried off on a towel furnished by the attendant, and then slipped quickly into his clean underwear and clothes. He pulled on his boots and stood close to the fire, waiting till Novak was through, then the two of them paid their quarters and stepped outside. "I'm starving," Novak said. "Let's go get supper."

"Sounds good to me," agreed Cody. The two walked along, keeping as clear of the muddy roads as possible, and twenty minutes later found themselves in the outskirts of St. Louis. The Deluxe Restaurant was no more than a long, narrow rectangle with a portion walled off concealing the kitchen. The large room inside was filled with long tables and straight-back, cane-bottomed chairs in all conditions of disrepair. The two men walked to the back of the building, picked up tin plates, and went through the line for their meals, which was simple enough. One man tossed a chunk of roast beef into the plate, the next man dipped a large dipper full of white beans, and the third dumped a large measure of greens. Holding their plates in one hand, they both picked up a slab of apricot pie from the end of the table, turned, and found places where they sat down.

As usual, Cody waited, for it was a peculiarity of his friend that he always said the blessing. It made no difference to Novak how many or how few were around, and he never asked anyone to join him; he simply bowed his head, muttered a quick prayer, and plunged in and began to eat.

The reaction Sam's prayer aroused amused Cody. Some of the men made fun of him, but Cody noticed that just as many were silent. He knew what they were probably thinking—that their mother or father at home had done the same thing. For Cody it brought back old-time memories of days long ago—painful memories that he tried to put out of his mind. All of these men were wanderers, men without women, without children, having no roots, floating from one job to another. But most of them could think back on a day when they had sat at a table with a family, and when some member had bowed his head and prayed. Cody never commented on it, but he admired Novak for doing such a thing.

They ate slowly, for the food was good, considering the circumstances. The beef was fairly tender, and the vegetables were well cooked and seasoned. Finally, they shoved their tin plates to one side and nodded at the young black girl who moved around filling cups with steaming, black, stout coffee. When she had filled their cups, they sat there slowly eating the pie and taking sips of the hot brew. After enjoying a second cup, Sam finally said, "It's gettin' a little crowded. I guess we ought to give somebody our place."

The two men arose and made their way to the side of the room where there was a large washtub. Depositing their plates and hardware in this, they turned and walked out. When they stepped outside, someone said, "Hey, Novak—" They turned to see a tall, rawboned individual coming out from across the room and they halted until he reached them. "You fellows going to the show?" asked the man.

"Show? You mean a minstrel show of some kind?" Novak asked.

"Naw, this is Buffalo Bill's Wild West Show."

"I don't know, Charlie. Hadn't thought of it," Novak shrugged.

"Well, you better get down there. I went last night, and I'm going back tonight. Best show I ever saw. It's over there in the arena, and they got enough lanterns to light up half of St. Louis. Come on along with me, I'll show you the way."

"How much does it cost?" Cody asked carefully.

"Fifty cents a head."

"Come on, let's do it," Cody said. "I'm tired of that room. Can't stand to sit there again and look at your ugly face, Sam."

"You're on—Jim," he said haltingly. "Maybe we'll join up and get into show business."

The three moved quickly along, and as they advanced along the road that led to the city itself, Cody wondered if the sight of horses would make him homesick.

★   ★   ★   ★

The two men sat squeezed into their seats and watched as Buffalo Bill himself led the grand entry into the arena. He was an arresting figure in a white Stetson, bleached doe-skins, and mirror-finished black boots to the knees. He sat astride Old Charlie, a magnificent half-bred Kentucky stallion, on which, the audience was informed, he had once ridden a hundred miles in nine hours and forty-five minutes.

Behind him, high-stepping to the strains of "The Girl I Left Behind Me," came musicians wearing the uniform of Custer's Regimental Band. Indians rode into the arena in feathers and paint, and scouts followed dressed in buckskin. John Nelson drove the Deadwood coach, then came the Cowboy King, Buck Bronson, ex-sheriff Con Groner, young Johnny Baker, and dozens of others. Vaqueros in black and silver were mounted on swift little mustangs, and cowboys in Stetsons and woolly chaps straddled big American horses.

The procession circled inside the bleachers while the applause swelled and receded and then peaked, threatening to drown out the tubas and flutes. The famous leader swept off his big hat as if to scoop up the noise for later consumption. The applause slid down behind the last rider to exit, and an island of silence fell over the arena.

Buffalo Bill emerged again, announcing, "And now, ladies and gentlemen and my young friends, allow me to give you a slight demonstration of target shooting." From a leather pouch on his saddle horn, he drew a blue glass ball, and with a quick motion launched it underhand into the air. He drew his Colt, cocking it in the same motion, took aim quickly, and fired just as the ball reached the top of its trajectory. It burst, glittering. Polite applause started, only to be lost under more gunfire, as Colonel Cody, now using his left hand, tossed more balls. When the revolver was empty, he holstered it and drew its mate without missing a beat or a target. The glittering of the balls caught the reflection of hundreds of lanterns that hung from poles all over the amphitheater.

"That's not bad shootin'!" Cody exclaimed.

"I guess he's had lots of practice—but look at that!" said Sam. At the moment he spoke, the Deadwood Stage came roaring out of the entrance, and thirty yards behind, rode a group of Indians. The audience rooted wildly for the driver with his exploding whip and powerful lungs as the valiant defender on top of the stage fired blanks at the pursuing band. After the Deadwood

Stage, there was a pageant showing life in an Indian camp, which gave them a chance to rest the eardrums ringing with gunfire. Next came a buffalo hunt with the braves donning robes and horns to infiltrate the herd, then yelping and shrieking and turning the great, dumb beasts with their lances. The earth growled under the drumming hoofs before the Indians turned them over to trained cowboys, who drove them out of the arena toward the corrals.

After their exit, Buffalo Bill appeared again, and the crowd grew quiet. "And now," he said, "we introduce the world's most dramatic trick rider. I give you, ladies and gentlemen, Miss Laurie Winslow—!"

Sam had gasped at the sight of the young woman who came out like an explosion on a beautiful horse. "Look at that," he said. "Ain't she something?" When Cody did not speak, Novak twisted his head and saw that his friend was staring at the trick rider and seemed absolutely stunned. Novak studied him for a moment, then said, "What's the matter, Jim?"

Cody blinked his eyes, shook his head, and said, "Nothing. She—looks like a girl I used to know."

But as Laurie went through her act, Cody's mind flashed back to those days in Wyoming when they had ridden together—this girl dressed in silver and white. The memories were more painful than he could imagine. He stood there watching her move on and off a horse, in perfect rhythm to the hoof beats of the great black gelding. There was a great beauty in her motions, and he swallowed hard as he thought of the times they had shared together—and of the ride they had taken beside the river. The memories inevitably brought other memories of his family and of the ranch and the men he'd been so close to back home. He almost rose and left the arena, but then realized this would look strange to Sam. He kept his seat, applauding automatically when Laurie's act was over.

Sam shook his head with admiration. "I never saw anybody that could ride like that. Look—" he interrupted himself, "looks like we're gonna have another act." The climax of the show recreated Buffalo Bill's desperate dual with Yellow Hand. It was played out in tense pantomime, broken only by grunts and blows, as the star and the formidable Cheyenne from the Snake

River reservation lunged at each other and grappled, their wicked knives slashing. A collective gasp went up when Buffalo Bill pretended to thrust his blade into the Indian's rib cage, and his opponent shouted and buckled. Then Buffalo Bill bent over the body of his vanquished foe, and as he came up with the victim's war bonnet in one hand and what appeared to be his scalp in the other, the band jumped in with a victory song that blew the audience to its feet, applauding and shouting.

As the thundering applause finally died down, the final parade began to file into the arena. Indians and cavalrymen who had died in certain acts resurrected themselves to join their fellow performers. At last Buffalo Bill claimed the grounds alone for a bellowing, "Hail and farewell!" And with a final wave of his hat, he cantered back the way he had entered, accompanied by a brassy salute thrown up by the band.

Cody had kept his eyes fixed on Laurie as she took her place in the grand parade, and then a desire to see her up close overwhelmed him. He didn't mean to speak to her, just to see her. "Come on, Sam. Let's get a closer look at—some of the Indians."

The two men joined the milling crowd, most of whom were leaving the arena. But they left the stream of spectators and pressed their way toward where the cowboys had gathered to speak to some of the onlookers. Cody saw the gleaming white and silver of Laurie's costume as she stood beside a solemn-looking Indian, both of them listening as a man introduced his two small children. He was moving quickly to one side to get a better look at her, when suddenly a hand grasped his arm and pulled him around. Instinctively, he pulled back, jerking his arm free, and faced a rather short, heavyset individual who wore a bowler hat. "Take your hands off me!" Cody said at once.

The broad man reached into his pocket, pulled out something, and held it out in his hand, then said in a gruff tone, "St. Louis Police Department."

Cody stared at the silver badge, then lifted his eyes. His heart began beating faster, but he let none of that show in his face. "Police Department? What's the trouble, Officer?"

"My name's Winfield," the bulky individual said. "Sergeant Winfield. Like to have you come along to the station with me."

Cody allowed anger to show in his face. "What for?"

"Just to have a little talk." But when he saw the resistance on the face of the young man, he reached under his coat and pulled out a snub-nosed pistol. "Don't even think about running for it. You wouldn't get far."

Cody looked at the gun and stared, knowing all was lost. But he bluffed it out anyway. "What are you arresting me for?"

"You're not under arrest," Winfield said. A small crowd had gathered around, and the silence seemed to spread out as they watched the bulky man with the gun. Some thought it was part of the show, but none were quite sure. Winfield did not look like a wild west performer. "I've seen your face on a poster somewhere. A wanted poster," Winfield said. He hesitated, then went on, "I can't remember where. Some place out west. You'll have to come down to the station."

And then he shifted quickly as Sam Novak made a quick move. "Out west?" said Novak. He laughed. "He's never been out west in his whole life, have you, Jim?"

"Not likely," Cody said at once.

"What's your name?"

"Logan. Jim Logan. My friend is right. I've never been out west in my whole life."

"You'll have to come down to the station. We'll settle it there. If I'm wrong," Winfield hesitated and shrugged his bulky shoulders, "I'll buy you a steak dinner as an apology. But if I'm not, I can't let you get away." Then, when Cody tensed up, he tilted the pistol up and said, "Don't try it, son. You can't go anywhere."

At that moment, a voice said, "Jim, where have you been? Colonel Cody is furious!"

Laurie had seen the crowd gathering, had come forward out of curiosity—and had been stunned to recognize Cody! Instantly she had grasped the situation and just as quickly formed a plan.

Winfield looked around at the young woman he had seen a few minutes earlier riding a horse and performing unbelievable tricks. As she came near, he instinctively touched his hat and blinked in surprise, for the woman had gone straight to the young man he had stopped. She had not even looked at the policeman, and her body was stiff with anger as she demanded, "Are you drunk again?"

"Why, no—" Cody managed to stumble, "I ain't had hardly

a drop." His eyes were fixed on Laurie, but he seemed to be caught in some sort of weird performance, in which he himself was also on the outside watching it all. He saw the crowd gathered around the bulky policeman, the beautiful girl in the silver and white riding costume—and himself standing there foolishly. Instantly, he knew that she was out to save him, for though she allowed nothing to show on her face except anger, he realized she was playing a role and inviting him to join her.

Laurie began berating him and was interrupted by Winfield, who said, "Miss, you know this man?"

Laurie wheeled around and appeared to see him for the first time. Her eyes dropped to the gun, then looking up in mock anger, demanded, "Who are you? What are you doing with my brother?"

"Your brother?" answered the officer in surprise.

"Yes. What's he been doing? Are you a policeman?"

"Yes, miss, I am."

Disgust crossed Laurie's face, and she shook her head. "Well, what is it? Was he drunk or bothering some woman again?"

Winfield began to grow uncomfortable. The crowd was growing all the time, and he had received a lecture about false arrest from the chief only the previous week. "Well, miss, I thought he looked like a face I saw on a poster. A wanted man somewhere out in Montana, like that."

Laurie laughed harshly. "That's a joke!" She looked up at Cody and shook her head in disgust. "He's never been farther west than Missouri."

"He's your brother, you say? Does he work for the show?"

"As little as he can," Laurie said in disgust. "He cleans up after the horses—when he's not drunk, that is."

Winfield tried one last strategy. "I thought your name was Winslow, and his name's Logan."

"Winslow is my stage name." She smiled sourly and shrugged. "Who'd come to see a star named Petunia Logan?"

A smile touched the policeman's face, and he reholstered his gun. "Can you get someone to vouch for him? That he works for the show and that he's your brother?"

"'Course I can." She looked up and saw Mac McGonigal. "Mac, tell this officer about this worthless man."

McGonigal had been watching all this carefully and had seen Laurie's quick rescue of the young man. "Sure, Officer, that's her brother all right—but no more like her than a buzzard's like a canary!" He shrugged his shoulders, adding, "I hate for you to go see Colonel Cody because he'd fire this no good, and then Miss Petunia here, she'd have to pay all his bills."

Winfield gave up, saying, "Well, looks like I made a mistake. Sorry."

He turned and left, and Laurie said at once to Cody, "Come on with me!"

Instantly she turned, and Cody followed her through the crowd, which began dispersing, murmuring about what had happened. Mac McGonigal came at once to stand in front of Sam, and with a slight wink of his left eye, said, "Well, you're with Jim Logan, I take it?" And when the young man nodded slowly, he said, "You come along with me while them two gets things sorted out." He turned and limped away, and Novak shrugged his shoulders and followed him.

Cody kept pace with Laurie as she threaded her way through the crowd and led him to the exit. When they got outside and away from the crowd, she turned and he saw her face was very pale. She said somewhat unsteadily, "Come this way."

Cody was breathing in shallow breaths, his nerves tingling. The near tragedy had shaken him, and he knew that he would never have surrendered to the policeman. He would have turned and tried to get away and probably would have died in the attempt. The encounter with his past made him see how vulnerable he was, but he said nothing; he simply walked along beside her.

Reaching her tent, Laurie drew the flap, looked inside, and said with relief, "Nobody here. Come inside." As soon as they were inside, she took a deep breath. Her voice was shaky as she whispered, "Cody, I can't believe it's you!"

Cody stared at her, shaking his head. "You saved my life, Laurie, but you may have gotten yourself in trouble. If that policeman checks, he'll find out that I don't really work for the show."

"Don't worry, we're pulling out tonight. This was the last performance. He'd have to catch up with us and I doubt if he'd do that." Laurie noticed that her hands were trembling, and to hide it she said, "Sit down, Cody." He took the cot indicated, while she sat down on the other. "Tell me about it. Where've you been? What are you doing here tonight?"

Quickly, Cody sketched his history since his escape, ending by saying, "Why, I just came more or less by accident to the show. You could have knocked me over with a feather when I saw you."

Laurie listened hard, then asked urgently, "Cody, have you ever written your folks?"

"No. What good would it do?"

"Why, they're worried sick about you! I write them once in a while. Your mother needs to know where you are."

"What could they do about it?" He hesitated, then shook his head. "Next time you write just tell them to consider me as dead."

"They'll never do that," she said adamantly, shaking her head. She fell silent, and Cody allowed his glance to take in her face. He had forgotten how very black her hair was, how clear her dark eyes, and how smooth her skin. Faintly, he said, "Laurie, you're a star."

A flush touched her cheek, and she laughed shortly. "No! Nothing like that. Buffalo Bill's the star—I'm just a trick rider." And then she got up and took two paces to the left and back again to the right. Several times she changed direction. He sat there and watched her, and finally got up and said, "Well, I guess that policeman's gone."

"Cody, you can't go on like this!"

"I don't have much choice," he shrugged.

"You need to join the show."

If she had suggested he leap over the moon, he could not have been more surprised. "Join the show? How could I do that?"

Laurie had seized on the idea that had flashed across her mind, and at once began speaking rapidly. "It can be done. Don't you see, Cody?" Unconsciously, she reached up and touched his chest. "You'd be moving all the time. Nobody pays any attention to cowboys. Oh, they look on them as actors, sort of, but we'd be moving every two or three days. We're even going to Europe, I understand."

She spoke quickly, convincingly, but at last Cody said, "But I couldn't do anything with a show like this."

"We'll see about that," Laurie said, and a smile touched her lips. "You sit right here. No—you'd better not. I've got my roommate coming in." She thought hard, yet could think of no safer place. "If she comes in, just tell her you're a friend of mine, and I've gone to talk to Mr. Cody about a job. Better not tell her you're my brother. We'll leave that story behind."

"But, Laurie—"

But she had already turned, saying, "You wait right here." Leaving the tent, she quickly made her way back to the arena, where she saw Bill Cody lounging over a table, talking to Nate Salsbury. Moving very close, she said, "Mr. Cody, may I speak with you for a moment?"

Cody looked up, surprised, but said, "Why, of course. Excuse us, will you, Nate?"

At once, Laurie said, "Mr. Cody, I've got a friend that's in trouble."

"Trouble?" the colonel asked, interested. "What kind of trouble?"

Laurie hesitated, then decided the truth, or part of it, was best. "He's in trouble with the law. But, it's all a mistake; he's innocent."

Cody considered her for a moment, then moved to put his arm around her. "Why, Laurie, I can see you're real bothered about this," he said smoothly.

Instantly, she withdrew from his grasp. "Mr. Cody," she said firmly, "you don't need to worry about me. I just need help for my friend."

"What kind of help?" Cody asked, not at all affronted by her refusal. He had expected as much.

"If you could just give him a job taking care of the horses, pulling the tent down, anything. If I could be with him, I think I could help him."

A shrewd look came into Cody's eyes and he stroked his goatee, saying, "Well, I thought you were going to leave the show." He hesitated, thinking hard. "Now if you'd promise to stay with me, I think we might work something out for your friend. But you'd have to promise to stay for at least a year."

Laurie hesitated but knew she had no choice. "Yes. I'll do it."

"All right. What's his name?"

"Jim Logan." She saw interest flicker in Cody's eyes, but was feeling the urgency of the moment. "I'll go tell him, and thank you, Mr. Cody."

"Don't thank me," Cody said with a smile. "I got what I want, and you got what you want. We won't let a little thing about the law bother us, will we now, Laurie?"

Laurie turned at once and went back to the tent. When she stepped inside, she opened her mouth to give Cody the news and discovered that Leona had entered and was talking excitedly to Cody. As always, a new man interested her, and she turned to Laurie, saying, "I've just been talking to Jim, telling him all about what a naughty girl you are."

"Well, you'll have lots of time to talk. Come along, Jim, I've got things to tell you."

As they left the tent, Leona's voice followed them out, "I'll be seeing you, Jim. Don't be a stranger now!"

When they were outside the tent, Laurie turned to him and said, "It's all right. I got you a job working for the show."

"Doing what?" Then he instantly said, "It doesn't matter. It'll be better than what I'm doing now." Suddenly he remembered Sam and said, "What about my friend? He's done a lot for me."

Laurie hesitated, then said, "Oh, there's so many hands working that Mr. Cody never notices how many. We'll get him on somehow too. You'd better go tell him. We'll be leaving on the *Dixie Queen* tomorrow morning, and we still have to work most of the night to get the show loaded."

"We'll go back to our hotel and get our stuff," Cody said. He turned to leave, then swung back to her. "Laurie," he said quietly, "I really don't think you ought to do this. You're putting yourself in danger, and I'd hate to see anything happen to you."

Laurie flushed and looked down, then she lifted her eyes to his. Her soft lips curled upward in a smile and she said, "Maybe you'll do as much for me sometime. You would, wouldn't you, Cody?"

Cody Rogers was feeling a strange stirring inside. He thought it might be the relief from the narrow escape he had, but there was, he knew, more to it than that. He reached his hand out, and she instinctively put hers out for him to take. Her hand, he felt, was strong and firm, and he squeezed it gently, then did something he had never done in his life. He brought it up to his lips, kissed it, and said, "I thank you, Laurie. I'll always be in your debt."

Embarrassed by what he had done, he whirled and dashed out toward the arena, looking for Novak.

Laurie stood stock-still as a rosy flush began on her neck and washed up over her face. She stared after him, then touched her hand gently and said under her breath, "Cody—!"

CHAPTER SIXTEEN

END OF THE DIXIE QUEEN

★   ★   ★   ★

A shudder ran through the *Dixie Queen* as her paddles caught and churned the brown waters of the Mississippi into a froth. As soon as the boat left the shore, most of the show people went wearily to bed. Loading the show had taken most of the night, and everyone needed to catch a few hours sleep. Cody and Sam, however, stood at the stern watching the huge paddles as they cut into the water.

"Well, I'm about as tired as I ever want to be," Sam muttered wearily. "I didn't know show business was so much work!"

"I guess if you're a star you don't have to work so much," Cody grinned. Then he glanced toward the deck that held the staterooms and shook his head. "No, that's not right. Everybody works—even Colonel Cody." He stood there silently, enjoying the roll of the ship as it chugged through the water. "I always liked boats. Planned to run away from home when I was fifteen and go to sea. Never made it though."

Sam straightened his back wearily and groaned, "I guess we better get to bed. I found out we'll be unloading tomorrow at Cairo, Illinois."

"How long will we be there?" Cody asked. He had worked mostly with the horses and had made a good impression on the horse handlers as a whole.

Sam grimaced. "One day—and then we get to do this all over again. Sometimes it makes me wish I hadn't decided to see this here country!"

The two broke off and found their places, which amounted to two bed rolls thrown on some straw down behind the area that held the stock. They went to sleep instantly and only awoke when the hands began groaning and calling to one another a little after sunup. Wearily they got to their feet, brushed the straw out of their hair, and then discovered that breakfast was available. Making their way to one of the dining rooms where the hired hands ate in shifts, they downed a huge breakfast of bacon, eggs, grits, pancakes, and mugs of black coffee. Afterward, they went up on the deck, to the bow this time, and watched the *Dixie Queen* as it forged downriver. As they stood there, one of the cowboys, whose name they couldn't remember, came up. "I'm Con Groner," he said, nodding his head. "Your name's Logan, I hear."

"That's right. Jim Logan." Cody shrugged his shoulders. "All my life, I wished I had a good name, like Duke, or Studs, something better than Jim, and something better than Logan, too."

"Well, a man hasn't got much say about a name—unless he changes it," said Groner as he stood there.

Cody remarked lightly that he was likely to do that someday just to get rid of it, then stood there talking to Groner, who seemed interested in the pair. Sam quickly took over and began describing some of his adventures in the past, and Groner listened patiently. "Where you from, Logan?"

Instantly Cody said, "Grew up in Kansas, flattest place on the face of the earth." He began putting Kansas down, saying, "The best thing would be to dig a hole and make a lake out of it. Then all the dirt next door would be a mountain." Groner smiled briefly, inquired about his family, then moved away.

"A little too curious, ain't he, Cody?"

"Oh, just friendly, I guess," answered Cody, leaning on the rail. The two moved around the ship, fascinated by it, for neither of them had ever been on a large riverboat.

Finally, at noon they pulled into Cairo, and Buffalo Bill appeared, his big voice booming: "All right, let's get this stock unloaded!" He spotted the two and said, "Can't think of your names." When they told him, he nodded and said, "You give a hand with the horses and the buffalo." His eyes were thoughtful as he studied Cody, and he asked, "You making it all right so far?"

"Sure," Cody said quickly. "Been wanting to thank you for the job."

Buffalo Bill grinned, then inquired, "You've known Miss Laurie a long time, I take it?"

"Oh, for a while," Cody shrugged evasively. "Our folks were close to each other."

The bearded showman nodded thoughtfully, then moved away yelling directions to the stock handlers. Cody went to help unload the stock, while Sam was recruited by Johnny Baker to help with the equipment.

"These hosses don't like boats," Buck Bronson complained mournfully. He towered over Cody but seemed friendly enough.

Cody grinned at him. "Well, if they give us any trouble, you can just pick one up and carry him off, Buck. You're big enough to do it."

Bronson laughed heartily and shook his head. "I hope it don't come to that, Logan." Staring across the runway he added, "I guess everybody's out of the way. We can get these hosses and buffalo off now."

Several of the cowboys helped, but others had gone ahead, so they were shorthanded. Cody had been given a small bay named Jack, and it was a pleasure to be in the saddle again. He slapped the horse on the neck, then whispered, "Come on, Jack. We're gonna be real close."

He rode the horse off the gangplank, then stood waiting as the rest of the animals were led out. Some of the horses stepped off steadily. One or two, apparently new at this, were wild-eyed and jittery. When they were all finally disembarked, half of the crew left.

Buck groaned mournfully, "Now them blasted woollies! Sometimes I wish every one of them buffalo would drop dead!" He glanced over at Cody, saying, "Watch yourself, Logan. They either don't cause no trouble at all, or they don't do nothin' else."

Cody, who had never seen a buffalo at close range, was fascinated by the huge animals. They moved forward, prodded by cowboys, and seemed placid enough. Then, as the last of them stepped off, one of them, a huge bull, suddenly snorted fiercely and plunged away.

"Look out! Old Thunder's loose!" somebody cursed. The animal was picking up speed, and without thinking, Cody whipped the lariat from off the saddle and spurred Jack forward, whispering, "Come on, boy—" Before the horse had gone two paces, Cody had made a loop. Two more paces and he flipped the noose in between the front legs of the huge buffalo, then took two quick turns of the lariat around the saddle horn. The buffalo stepped into it, and Cody's horse was yanked forward as the huge bull hit the end. The beast turned one flip and landed heavily on the ground with an audible grunt. Buck went forward at once and threw his rope so the animal was snug by the neck. Con Groner did the same. Cody slipped off his horse and waited to see if his mount was trained to hold. When he discovered he was, he moved forward, removed the loop, and hastily stepped away from the buffalo. "Okay, let him up."

When the animal was up on his feet and had tried the ropes a couple of times, he went along placidly enough. Johnny Baker, who was called the Cowboy Kid, was standing there with Buffalo Bill himself. The two had been talking about the show, apparently, and now Baker said, "That's a pretty neat trick. Seen some good ropers, but nothin' to beat that."

Buffalo Bill nodded in agreement. "Anybody can drop a loop over a critter's head, but to grab one foreleg—" He shook his head and asked suddenly, "Did you do that on purpose, Logan? Or was it just an accident?"

Cody pulled his rope in, made a loop, and said, "I usually catch what I want to."

Buffalo Bill instantly said, "Catch Buck's hat, then." He nodded toward the huge cowboy who had started away, leading Thunder. And at once, almost instantly, the rope snaked out of Cody's hand, forming a very small loop. It closed around the hat, and Cody jerked it off with a flick of his wrist.

"Hey!" Buck shouted. He turned around and saw the owner of the show and Johnny Baker laughing at him.

Cody retrieved the hat, dusted it off, and spurred forward. "The boss wanted me to show off a little. You're not sore, are you, Buck?"

"No. That's a pretty good trick. Maybe you'd better give me a few pointers. But mostly I think I'd rather shoot 'em than put a rope on 'em."

Cody laughed and turned, then heard his name being called. Buffalo Bill gestured to him, and he spurred Jack back to stand beside the two. "You know any tricks with that rope of yours?" said Bill, looking up at the young man.

"A few," Cody shrugged.

"Well," Buffalo Bill said quickly, "we've got to get this show on the road, into Cairo, and set up. But I want to talk to you later. Maybe we can use you in the show."

"All right," Cody said and turned. *Wouldn't it be something*, he thought, *if I turned out to be a star!*

The rest of the day went by like a blur. Cody learned more about how to move the stock around. Timing was everything, and he had to learn when to take them into the arena and when to retrieve them. He even took part in a fake stage robbery as one of the hold-up men with a handkerchief across his nose, firing blank bullets. He enjoyed it tremendously, and when the show was over, he joined in the arduous labor of breaking the show down. It was after three o'clock before they had gotten all the stock and equipment back on the *Dixie Queen*. Sam went to bed at once, but the excitement of the day had awakened Cody. He had the unusual ability of staying up all night and never seemed to miss the sleep—though two nights in a row gave him problems. He walked around the deck, enjoying the silence as the boat slid along the brown water, and was startled when a voice close beside him said, "Hi, Jim."

He turned and saw Leona Aimes in the darkness. She came out of the shadow of the bulkhead to stand beside him, leaning on the rail. "How do you like it?"

"Like it? Like what?"

"Traveling with the show." Then she laughed, a pleasing, musical laugh. "I guess it's nothing more than hard work unless you've got an act."

Cody ordinarily would have said little, but the day had excited him and he began to talk to her. She was a pretty girl, on the verge of beauty. Her best feature was a pair of bold green eyes—which she knew how to use on men effectively. Cody could see them faintly by the glow of the light from the pilot-house. "Maybe I'll be a star," he shrugged with a grin. "Colonel Cody wants me to do a little fancy roping."

Leona leaned closer to him so that her arm pressed against his. She smiled up at him and said, "Can I have your autograph, Mr. Logan?"

He laughed, and for the next ten minutes the two stood there chatting. He soon discovered that she'd had a hard life, and only when she had found her place in the show had she had any kind of security. The talk of her past seemed to trouble her, and she veered the conversation away from it.

Cody said, "I guess it's late. I better get some sleep."

"You can sleep when you're old," she said. "Besides, we won't have to get up till noon tomorrow if we don't want to. We're headed straight for New Orleans, and that'll take a couple of days." She put her hand on his arm and stroked it, the touch of it running through him. "What's the matter? You don't like to talk to me?"

Cody was uncertain of himself. Some women he knew about—but this one was a puzzle. She caught his glance and was pleased to have his attention. She was a woman who had to have the notice of men, and her lips were soft as she smiled up at him. "You're trying to figure me out, aren't you, Jim? Nothing complicated about me—I'm just a woman who intends to have a good time. That's what life's all about, isn't it?"

"Well, I guess there might be a little more to it than that," Cody said wryly. "Like work, doing your job, things like that."

"Time to think about that later," she said. She had a way of looking up at a man and parting her lips slightly. She made an enticing picture and knew it. When she saw the look he gave her, she laughed. "I'm bold, aren't I?" Her grip tightened on his arm, and she demanded softly, "Why is it all right for a man to chase a woman—but not the other way around?"

"Just the way it is, I guess," said Cody, feeling a bit awkward.

"Not with me." She looked up at him again, reached up, and stroked his cheek. "When I like a man, I like him, Jim."

Cody was alarmed and tried to make a joke out of it. "You remember," he smiled, "I've seen you shoot, Leona. I guess if a man got out of line, you'd shoot him."

Leona reached over and pulled him around till he faced her. "Well," she whispered, "we won't know until you try it, will we?"

And without another word, she reached out, put her hands behind his neck, and pulled him down, kissing him firmly. She pressed her body against him, and almost involuntarily his arms went around her, and for a moment the two clung together. Despite her boldness, there was a softness and a freshness about her lips, and yet at the same time he knew that she had her desires even as he had his. Finally, she pulled her head back. An enigmatic smile curved her lips, and her eyes were half-shut. "Wait till we get to New Orleans. I'll show you the town."

She smiled, then turned and left the deck. She went at once to her stateroom, which she shared with Laurie, and began undressing. Laurie was already in bed, reading as usual. "That old friend of yours—Jim Logan?" she said as she slipped out of her clothes and pulled on a pink silk nightgown. "He knows a little something about women."

Abruptly Laurie laid the book down flat and stared across at Leona, who was brushing her hair. "How do you know that?" she demanded a little more loudly than she had planned. Leona turned and looked at her, the corners of her lips turned up in a coy smile. "How would I know? He kissed me. That's the way you tell about a man, isn't it, Laurie?"

When she saw the look on Laurie's face, she laughed, came over, and ruffled her hair. "You're going to be an old maid if you don't wake up, Laurie. There's more to life than riding around on the back of a horse."

She slipped into bed and closed her eyes. The last thing she said before dropping off to sleep was, "I told Logan I'd show him the town when we get to New Orleans. That ought to be interesting . . ."

Laurie sat there, saying nothing. Finally she turned the lamp down, then lay down again, pulling the covers over her head. She was displeased and did not know why she should be so strongly stirred. *I ought to know that Leona is going to try every man she sees*, she thought. But she could not manage to put it out of her mind. Finally, she dozed off to sleep, thinking about the two up on the deck.

* * * *

The next day, Cody noticed that Laurie's manner was stiff, and she seemed to be avoiding him. He and Sam walked around the boat as usual, slept a great deal, had three good meals, and at dusk, after finishing another excellent meal, he came up on the deck. Several men were standing in the bow, so he went to the stern, watching the paddles churn the water into a lusty white froth. He wasn't thinking of anything in particular as he stood there, just enjoying the cold breeze and the sense of being free, when he saw Laurie headed down the deck. He called to her, "Laurie—?"

Laurie glanced up quickly, and he thought for a moment that she would leave. Instead she came to him. "Hello, Jim," she said, then shook her head and frowned. "Hard to call you that."

"A lot safer, though." They stood there for a few moments and finally Cody said, "What's wrong, Laurie? Are you sore at me about something?"

"Why should I be?"

He peered at her as the last rays of light from the sun seemed to melt into the river. "I don't know. I thought I'd done something."

Laurie turned, and he saw the flash of anger in her dark eyes. "If I were you," she said, "I don't think I'd get too close to some of the people in the show."

"What does that mean?" he asked in surprise.

"It means . . . " She stopped and realized what she was about to say and how it would sound. She clamped her lips together, shook her head, and he stood watching her helplessly. "I—I guess it's none of my business, but Leona—well, I've known her for quite a while now, and I ought to warn you that she never sticks with a man."

He suddenly understood that she had seen him on the deck, with the girl. Either that or else Leona had told her about their meeting. Instantly, he said, "That doesn't matter, Laurie. The way I am, I'll never have any long-term relationships with a woman, anyway."

His comment caught her off guard. It displeased her, too, and she turned to leave. He reached out and took her arm. "I know you're just looking out for me, and I appreciate it. But you don't have to worry about that."

They began walking back toward the stern and had almost reached the door leading to the stateroom deck. Suddenly Cody felt that something was dreadfully wrong. He grabbed her arm and held her. "What is it?" she asked, startled.

Cody didn't answer for a moment, then he threw his hand up and pointed. "Look at that light up there. Isn't that another ship?"

Laurie looked up and was shocked to see the vague outlines of another vessel dead ahead. "They're going to hit us!" she cried out. "Is the captain blind?"

Helplessly they stood watching the two ships close on each other. At the last moment, the captain apparently spotted the boat and tried to turn away, but it was too late. The two crafts met with a rending crash, and a jarring so abrupt that if Cody had not caught Laurie with one hand and the railing with the other hand, they would have fallen. The sound of the crashing continued, and the *Dixie Queen* raised up to port from the shock. When it settled down, Cody yelled, "We're gonna sink, Laurie! No boat can take a lick like that!"

Instantly Laurie cried out, "I've got to get to Star!" She wheeled and ran toward the section that held the stock, with Cody following her closely.

Even as they dashed along the deck, wild cries of fear began to pierce the night air. Almost at once the deck was filled with people who came scrambling out to see what the trouble was. The two boats circled each other, the pilots and the crew cursing violently, until finally the two separated as they were dragged downstream by the current.

When they reached the hold where the horses were kept, Laurie started to enter, but Cody pulled her back. "You stay here! I'll get your horse."

He grabbed a rope that lay beside the gate and slipped the lock. As he moved inside, he was driven up against the barrier by a wild-eyed pinto. Pain shot along his back, and he heard Laurie crying out. "Stay back, Laurie!" he yelled. "When I get Star to the gate, open it."

Laurie strained her eyes but could see only the moving

shapes of the terrified horses. Finally a taller form appeared, and she made out Cody on the back of Star. She slipped the bolt, opened the door, and as soon as they were clear, slammed the door and fastened it.

"Can you swim?" Cody asked as he slipped off the horse.

"No. Can you?"

"Not a lick. We'll have to hope this thing comes into shore. If we go down, get in the saddle and guide him to the bank. Never saw a horse that couldn't swim!"

The *Dixie Queen* had been so badly holed that there was no keeping her afloat. The paddles continued to drive her until she went sideways down the broad river. When they came to a turn, Cody said, "Look, we're going to pile up on that sandbar over there!"

As he had guessed, the *Dixie Queen* nosed into the sandbar, which was barely visible in the night by the light of a brilliant moon. Then the whole craft swung sideways and Cody said, "Let's get off of the boat before the current takes her."

They were not the only ones with that idea. Not many of the passengers, and fewer of the show members, could swim, so as Laurie and Cody were leaving the ship, there was a full-scale exodus. The crew lowered the gangplank for the stock, and Laurie and Cody rode their horses down to the sandbar. As soon as he saw that she was safe, he said, "I'll go back and see what can be done with the stock."

"Be careful," she warned. "Remember, you can't swim."

Cody went back and did what he could, but when the animals were loosed, some of them went to the sandbar, and others plunged immediately into the river. A few of them that had managed to land on the sandbar found their way to the woods that lay beyond. Many were swept down the river, and the terrified screams of the horses pulled at Cody's heart.

He helped get as many as he could off the boat, but it was impossible to save all of them. He never forgot that night—nor did anyone else.

When dawn finally broke, they stood shivering on the sandbar, huddled together in the cold, January breeze. They saw the current take the wreck of the *Dixie Queen*, catch her, and swing her out. She floated down a hundred yards, then slowly began to sink.

"There she goes," Buffalo Bill said morosely. He looked old in the gray light of morning and shook his head. "This is worse than an Indian attack, I think."

They waited, and an hour later another steamboat, the *Natchez Belle*, came down and carried them all to the next town. Colonel Cody arranged for as many men as possible to find the few horses that were left and try to round up what was left of the stock. Cody was one of these. He worked hard, along with Con Groner, Buck Bronson, and Cowboy Johnny Baker. Colonel Cody sent a scout back for the stock and his riders, and when they finally pulled into town, Cody stared at the scanty herd. "Is this all?" he groaned.

"That's all we could get, Colonel," Cowboy Johnny said. "They're scattered out in the woods all over the place. What are we gonna do?"

The star and owner stared at the remains of Buffalo Bill's Wild West Show and said, "I wired Nate in New Orleans."

"What did he say?" Groner demanded.

Buffalo Bill shook his head, and his lips curled fiercely. "You know Nate. He said, 'Come on and we'll put on the show in New Orleans.' So"—he looked around wearily—"all we have to do is find a herd of buffalo and new riding stock."

They left that evening on a side-wheeler headed for New Orleans, and as the boat moved downriver, Sam said to Cody, "Well, what do you think of show business now?"

Cody looked at him and, with a broad grin on his face, said, "It's not quite as glamorous as I thought—but it beats being in a jail or a hospital by a huge sight! Come on, Sam, let's get some rest. I got a feeling when we get to New Orleans, that'll be the end of sleeping for a while!"

CHAPTER SEVENTEEN

CODY FINDS A PLACE

★ ★ ★ ★

"Does Jim Logan ever talk much about himself to you, Leona?"

Con Groner had stopped work long enough to have a cup of coffee between acts, coming to sit down beside Leona. His question had come so suddenly that it surprised her, and she looked up at him curiously. "Not much," she shrugged. "But then, I don't talk much about my past to him either. Why do you want to know, Con?"

Groner shrugged carelessly. "Just wondered. I guess most of us in this business don't like to talk much about our past. I sure don't." He sipped the coffee, then murmured quietly, "You've been pretty close to him since we got to New Orleans and put this new show together. You're not gettin' too thick with him I hope, Leona."

Leona's eyes turned hard, and she said, "You jealous, Con? We had our time, but it's over."

"Just a mild warning. He's like all the rest of us cowboys. Not much future. Like to see you do better than some two-bit cattle roper." Hastily, he added, "Not aimed at Logan, of course. Just that we're all pretty much the same in this business." He rose and left without a word, leaving Leona to stare after him.

"I wonder what *that* was all about?" she asked. Sitting there, she thought about the days that had passed since Buffalo Bill Cody's Wild West Show had opened in New Orleans. It had taken a mammoth effort to round up buffalo, stock, and equipment—but somehow Nate Salsbury and Colonel Cody had managed between the two of them. Everyone had worked until they were ready to drop, and at one point Leona had told Laurie that she hoped she never would have to work the hardstock again.

Finally, she rose and left the cook tent, wandering over to the corral. As she had suspected, Cody was there helping to handle the horses that constantly were on the move in and out of the arena. She watched as he was busy, unaware of her, and thought, *Most men with those good looks have more vanity. Jim doesn't know how good-looking he is.* She was a connoisseur of male attractiveness and rested her eyes on the pleasing symmetry in the smoothly rounded shoulders and lean hips of the tall rider as he moved easily among the horses, speaking a word here, quieting them, removing saddles. *He's good with horses,* Leona thought, and a bleak smile touched her lips, *but he sure doesn't care much about women. At least not about this woman.* After the show was over, she found him and smiled up into his face. "Let's go downtown, Jim. I'm bored with this place."

"I'd like to, Leona, but Colonel Cody wanted me to work some with this new stock. Some of them are too feisty and need a little extra breaking. Maybe later."

Leona hesitated, then said, "I've been meaning to ask you something, Jim." A smile came to her lips, and she added, "I just wanted to be sure you'd be around long enough to do what I need."

"What is it, Leona?"

"I need some help with my act," she said. "I want to have someone to help me reload and to throw the balls up for me so I don't have to do two things at once." She looked at him and shrugged, raising her eyebrows, saying, "I know that's not a very glamorous offer, but I really do need somebody. I'd be glad to pay you."

Cody grinned crookedly. "No need of that," he said. "I'll be glad to do what I can."

She was pleased with his response, her face reflecting a genuine satisfaction. "We'll need to practice a little bit. Could you spare some time tonight after supper? We'll come out here, and I'll show you what I need."

"Sure," said Cody.

As soon as she walked off, Sam came ambling up. He had something on his mind, Cody saw. Usually Novak spoke right up, but for some reason he was having difficulty. Finally, Cody said, "Well, spit it out, Sam. You're making a speech to yourself. What is it?"

"Oh, none of my business, really—but I been watching Leona. Don't want to say anything against her, you understand, but she's not what the doctor might recommend for a long-term relationship."

"Been listening to a little gossip, Sam?" Cody asked sharply.

"I guess. But so have you. She seems like a good woman." Sam halted, then said, "No. That's not right. She's *not* a good woman. She's been with every cowboy in the show." Then he stopped again and said, "No, that's not right. Oh, confound it! I'm not really worried about her—it's you I'm thinking about."

"Funny," Cody murmured. He smoothed the mane of a palomino, then turned to face Sam Novak. "Laurie told me the same thing."

"You should listen to her."

"I did listen to her, and I'm listening to you too, Sam." He shook his head almost wearily. "So I'm telling you like I told Laurie. Nothing will ever come of it. I've got no future before me."

Novak looked up quickly, his mouth tightening. "You know as well as I do that Leona's not lookin' for the future. She's one of these that lives for right now."

Cody flushed, for he had thought the same thing. He had a great affection for his friend, but somehow the words had gotten on his nerves. "Why don't you talk to her? If you think she needs religion, just go tell her."

Suddenly Sam smiled. "Why, I've already done that."

Cody stared at him and asked quickly, "What did she say?"

"Told me to mind my own business." Sam grinned widely and said, "I get that answer a lot, though. Sorry, Cody. I didn't mean to butt in, but—well, I think a lot of you. Wouldn't want to see you get shipwrecked." He turned abruptly and walked away. Later that day, Sam spoke with Laurie and told her of his conversation with Cody.

She shook her head, her eyes bright with anger. "He can't see what she is. He's so blind that he doesn't realize that she's like a black widow spider that eats her mates. She's a man-killer, Sam, if I've ever seen one!"

"Well, I've never seen too many of that breed, but in that I guess you'd be right," Novak said. He would have said more, but at that moment McGonigal came ambling up and said, "Laurie, you got a minute?"

Sam nodded, left, and Laurie said abruptly, "What do you think of Leona Aimes, Mac?"

If the question was a surprise to McGonigal, he did not show it. Something flickered in his eyes, but he merely came over and sat down across from Laurie. "I don't think there's much mystery to the woman," he said. He was usually rowdy, but noticing Laurie's mood, he held back his thoughts of Leona. Instead, he looked at her quietly, collecting his thoughts, and said, "You're fond of the boy, aren't you, Laurie?"

"Why—!" Laurie put her hand on her cheek, feeling it burn, and could not read his eyes. "He has problems, Mac. I don't think he needs to compound them by getting mixed up with a woman like that."

"Most men go around looking for a woman like that, at least before they're married," Mac observed. "She's the kind that men want for a fling—but not for a wife. You're not thinking the two are serious?"

"Oh, I don't know." Laurie bit her lower lip, a sign that Mac had learned to recognize long before. "It's none of my business anyway," she snapped.

"You can fool other people, Laurie. You can fool me and you can fool your parents, but don't ever try to fool yourself."

Laurie glanced up at him, startled, and shook her head with a brief smile. "I could never fool you, Mac. You know me too well!"

McGonigal sat there admiring the young woman as always, not only for her clean, good looks, but for her sharp mind and bright spirit. She was a woman of purity, which he also admired, and he longed to say a word that would encourage her. Finally, he sighed, "Well, you and me, Laurie, we'll get God's ear—and we'll talk Him into fixing that young man!"

Laurie stared at him. "Why, you can't talk God into doing something!"

"Who told you that?" McGonigal demanded. Leaning back in his chair he shook his head at her regretfully. "You've been neglecting your Bible, girl! Don't you remember that God told Moses He was going to destroy the Israelites after they made them golden calves? Do you remember that?"

"Why, yes. Of course." When Mac got that look on his face, Laurie knew it was better to listen than argue.

"Now then, do you remember, darlin', what Moses did? Why, he argued with God! All you have to do is read it. Even told God to kill him instead of the others." A fine humor showed on the face of the small Irishman. "And he wasn't the only one. Do you recollect when God told Abraham that he was going to destroy Sodom, and Abraham began to argue? You know, he said, 'Suppose there's a whole bunch of righteous folks in Sodom, would you destroy it?' "

Laurie leaned forward, placing her chin in her palm, listening. "And he kept arguing God down, didn't he?" said Mac. "Until finally he got to if there were ten righteous men?

"You know, Laurie," McGonigal said quietly, "I think Abraham could have saved the whole city if he had just gone a little further. Why, God would have saved that city for one man if Abraham had just had enough gumption to keep on arguing!"

Laurie looked at him, her eyes serious. Her lips were firm as she thought about what he'd said, and she ran her hand across her dark hair. "Maybe there's something to that, Mac. I remember the woman who had a daughter who was sick. You remember, she came to Jesus and asked Him to heal her, and you're right, when He said no, she just asked again. Three times, wasn't it?"

"That's right, darlin', and that just proves to me that God *wants* to be argued with. Why, He's got stones if He wants to throw things, He's got fish if He wants to count up in the billions, but who does He have to *talk* to? Angels and men! I guess He's caught up on His talk with angels—but I noticed He likes mighty well to talk to men. And what a shame it is, we're not quite so anxious to talk to Him!"

216

Laurie bit her lip, then shook her head doubtfully. "Mac, do you remember when Cody first came here? He was in trouble, but I lied to that detective—and so did you and Sam. That wasn't right, was it?"

Mac shook his head, regret in his eyes. "No, it wasn't. I think all three of us were taken off guard."

"Do you think God has forgiven us all?"

"Did you ask Him to?"

"Yes!"

"Then that settles it," Mac said firmly. "First John says if we confess our sins, He is faithful and just to forgive us our sins. Don't let the devil weigh you down with guilt, Laurie. It was wrong, but God always stands ready to take our sins from us. That's what the cross is all about—not just sins in the past—but all our sins."

Laurie rose and smiled ruefully down at the small figure, then put her hand over on his shoulder. "Do you think you'll ever get me raised, Mac?" she asked.

He covered her hand with his own, saying, "You and me, we'll back God into a corner, and He'll have to do something about that young man! We just won't give Him any rest till He does, all right?"

"All right, Mac," agreed Laurie.

★   ★   ★   ★

Later that same afternoon Buffalo Bill and Nate Salsbury were walking through the arena. They had been talking about some dates that they had to meet down the road, when all of a sudden Colonel Cody stopped and said, "Look at that, will you, Nate?"

Salsbury looked over and watched. Standing over to one side of the arena was a young man spinning a rope. At first, he just made a simple loop that circled again and again, and then suddenly it began to rise up and down and around. Neither the colonel nor Salsbury had ever seen a rope obey the will of a roper as that one did. It seemed almost an extension of the man's body. With a mere flick of the wrist, Jim Logan was able to turn the rope in any direction. "He's not bad, is he, Nate?" whispered Colonel Cody.

"Not bad? With a little polish, we could use him in the show. Look at that!"

Cody, unaware of the two men, had gone to a platform that was used sometimes for some of the riding tricks. Clambering up on it, he began to make a circle with his loop, and as the two men watched, the loop got bigger and bigger. Finally, when it was spun out to its full length, Cody stood there with a forty-foot circle spinning around. Then slowly it began to grow smaller until it circled tightly around his body, and with a flourish, he gave it a twist as it rose in the air, then came to rest by his side.

"Logan—!" yelled the colonel.

Cody turned quickly and saw the two men approaching him. Both were smiling, and Buffalo Bill said, "I reckon you're about ready to do an act, aren't you? You got any more tricks like that?"

"I can do a few," admitted Cody.

"All right," Salsbury said with enthusiasm. "Here's what we'll do. We'll introduce you as the lassoing sheriff." His eyes gleamed as he began to spin castles in the air. "You were a sheriff in one of the toughest towns in the West, and you never even carried a gun."

"What did I carry?" Cody asked curiously.

"Why, you carried a rope, and every time anybody gave you any problems, you dropped a loop on 'em and hauled 'em off to jail." Salsbury grinned broadly, and Buffalo Bill was doing the same. Nate elaborated on the scheme. "You're so fast with that rope that you cleaned up Tombstone. Every time a man drew on you, that rope was there to snatch it out of his hand or to rope his arms to his side. You'll be the Roping Sheriff, Jim Logan."

Suddenly, Cody had a picture of himself before thousands of people, but then blinked as he realized the possible danger that could bring. "I—I don't think I could do anything like that, Mr. Cody."

"Of course you can, my boy!" The flamboyant showman waved him off, saying, "Show us what you've got, and we'll put you in the ring. Maybe even tonight."

Cody tried to talk his way out of it, but the two men would not listen. Reluctantly, he showed them all his tricks, and within a few minutes they had worked out a brief routine. Convinced that they had another good act to add to the show, they slapped

Logan on the back and walked out of the arena.

Later, he mentioned it to Sam, who said, "I think that's great!"

"But somebody may recognize me, Sam!"

Sam burst out with a guffaw. "Recognize you? You'll have on a fancy outfit, your hat'll be pulled down over your eyes, and they'll be a hundred feet away, most of them. How are they gonna recognize you?" He continued to talk, and finally Cody was convinced that it might work.

All afternoon he was nervous, but that night most of the other members of the show were caught off guard, because neither Salsbury nor Colonel Cody had mentioned the new act to anyone. But when Colonel Buffalo Bill Cody announced, "And now, the Roping Sheriff of Tombstone, Jim Logan," Cody swallowed hard, rode out into the lights, and for eight minutes, went through his routine. It included roping a gun out of the hand of one of the cowboys, roping four horsemen simultaneously as they rode in a circle, and the finale came when they turned Old Thunder loose, and he roped him by one foreleg, throwing him down again.

When he finished, there was a loud burst of applause, and as he got to the apron of the ring, he saw Colonel Cody. "Well, I don't think you're in danger of being replaced. Not by me, anyhow, Colonel Cody."

"You did fine, my boy, fine! Come on and we'll talk about your salary as a performer . . ."

★　★　★　★

New Orleans was the closest thing to a cosmopolitan city in the United States, with cultures clashing and melding together at the same time. As Sam, Cody, Leona, and Laurie walked through the French Quarter, Leona glanced avidly at some of the posters advertising the delights to be enjoyed inside the buildings. The streets were narrow, and iron balconies overhung even those narrow streets, almost blotting out the skyline. Finally, Leona said, "Let's go in this one," pointing at a particularly lurid poster.

Laurie took one quick look and shook her head. "Not for me," she said.

Cody answered almost as quickly, "I don't think so."

"Are you two afraid of life?" teased Leona.

Cody looked again at the poster, shook his head, and said, "I don't think that's life, Leona."

Leona stared at the pair then glanced at Sam. "What about you?"

Sam scratched his head, then grinned. "Well, I intend to be a preacher one day, and how will I ever be able to describe one of these places of sin if I ain't ever seen one?"

Leona was delighted. She laughed and took his arm, saying, "Come on, Sam. I'll initiate you!"

Cody and Laurie watched them go in, then turned and continued their walk around the French Quarter. Finally, they walked back to the showground and stopped at the door to her tent. "How are things, really, Cody?" she asked quietly.

He looked down at her, the moonlight reflecting in her eyes, accenting the smoothness of her cheeks. "It's better, Laurie. I feel like a man again."

She smiled, and there was a gentleness in her that he liked. He admired, above all things, gentleness in women, having seen it in his mother, and having *not* seen it in Susan. As he thought about his courtship of the girl, he recognized that the mistake of his life would have been to marry her. Those thoughts flashed through his mind, but as he looked down, he was aware that Laurie was watching him carefully.

"Were you thinking of the last time I left you at night like this?" He shook his head. "I kissed your hand, remember that? And I felt like a fool—a Frenchman or something worse!"

Laurie looked at him, her voice barely above a whisper. "It was—sweet of you." She wanted to say more, but somehow she did not know how to frame her thoughts. Perhaps it was because she did not understand the feelings that this young man brought to her. He was a fugitive with no future, everything in his disfavor, and yet to her, there was something about him that was appealing.

There was a quietness in the air, and Cody said with hesitation, "Could I—could I kiss you just on the cheek?"

Laurie took a quick breath and shook her head. "I'm not sure that it would be right, Cody."

"Well, after all, we're cousins aren't we, sort of?"

He looked so boyish that she smiled. There was an innocence about him, despite his past, that she felt certain he would never lose. Some men grew hard and cold, but for all that had happened to Cody, she sensed the warmth and compassion that lay below the surface of what he allowed the world to see. "I—I guess so."

Cody put his hands on her arms, leaned forward, and kissed her cheek. He smelled the jasmine scent that she always used, and her skin was smooth beneath his lips. She turned her face toward him suddenly, her lips available, and without thought, he lowered his head and kissed her. He was shocked at the feelings that rushed through him, and he drew back quickly. "I—I guess being cousins isn't enough," he said. "I'm sorry, I won't do that again, Laurie. Good-night."

He turned and walked away, leaving her in the darkness. She stood there confused, pondering the mixed feelings she had about him. Finally, she went inside and went to bed.

Laurie woke up tired the next morning, having had a restless sleep. After breakfast she saw Sam, who came to her and said ruefully, "I'm glad you didn't go to that show with Leona and me last night! I'm tellin' you, I blushed like a girl!" He smoothed his dark hair and looked down at the ground thinking hard. Finally he looked up and said soberly, "I only stayed for about five minutes—and then I got up and left. It was—well, it was *impure*, I guess you'd say. Even for that few minutes I saw things that I can't get out of my head. Went to bed and when I tried to sleep, they kept coming to me—clear as when I saw them with my eyes!"

"I guess some things a Christian doesn't need to look at, Sam."

"You're sure right about that! And I finally remembered the scripture in Psalms that says, 'I will set no unclean thing before mine eyes.' Never was quite sure what that meant—but I sure do now!" He gave her a rueful grin. "Guess that's the end of my experimenting with sin just to see what it's like."

"I think that's wise, Sam."

The two left the cook tent and began to walk around. They walked outside the arena, savoring the coolness of the air. There was a snap in it, for though the winter was mild, it was still cold.

Finally, Sam said cautiously, "Tell me about your folks."

Laurie raised her eyebrows, surprised, but shrugged her shoulders and began to talk about her home and her parents. Soon, she found herself telling about the whole Winslow clan, those who had wound up in New York, some in the far West, and finally about the original home in Virginia. She stopped suddenly and shook her head with a rueful smile. "You couldn't be interested in all this. I must be boring you."

The ready smile was gone from Sam Novak's face. He looked at her with a strange look and said, "Well, this may come as a shock to you, but I guess I'm gonna break it to you."

"What is it, Sam?" He sounded so serious she was disturbed. "What's wrong?"

"Well, maybe nothing. Only, my father is Thad Novak." He saw something stir in her eyes and nodded. "I think you might remember. He married Patience Winslow."

"Why, she was Sky Winslow's daughter—my father's sister!" she exclaimed. "Sam—" Her eyes shone and she took him by the shoulders. "Is that true?"

He saw she was happy and said with a relieved smile, "It's true enough. I sort of wondered all the time if we were kin, and now we come to find out we're in the same family."

She began to question him, and as they talked he told her how he had had to have one look at the world before he began his career.

"As a preacher?" she asked. "Or are you joking about that?"

"No joke," he said seriously. "I want to see the world and learn about the people. I'll never be a pastor of a big church. It'll always be small, with ordinary people. That's where God has put my heart."

She looked at him and felt the fondness that she had for him grow into something deeper. "Well, it'll be good to have another preacher in the family. We have quite a few in the Winslow clan, as you know."

He laughed and said, "I guess that makes us kissin' cousins, doesn't it?" He leaned over and kissed her cheek and saw her blink in surprise as the memory of what Cody had said the night before came to her.

"Kissing cousins," she said, smiling at him. "That's what we are, Sam." She glanced involuntarily over to the tent where Cody stayed with the rest of the hands, and he interpreted her glance at once.

"He'll come around, and God will provide. You just listen to your kissing cousin!"

Laurie nodded slowly and said, "That's what his mother says, and I'm going to believe it. You and me, his mother, his stepfather, and Mac, we'll all pray for him, and we'll see Cody come through it, won't we?"

The two talked for a long time, and finally Sam left, saying, "I better not steal another kiss. That might not look good for a future minister." It was late, but Laurie walked around for a long time, thinking about her life. Taking out her writing material, she began to put down what was going on inside her. She had learned that putting her thoughts and emotions on paper helped her to think more clearly. She wrote for a time, then ended her entry:

"I shouldn't have let Cody kiss me. He'll think I'm one of those easy girls who kisses every boy she sees! But he seemed so lonely, and I'm not sorry!"

She was confused, but somehow a strange peace had come to her as she thought about the trouble Cody was in. *What a miracle it would take!* And then she remembered what several had said—*Nothing is impossible with God!*

PART FOUR

BUFFALO BILL'S WILD WEST SHOW

★ ★ ★ ★

CHAPTER EIGHTEEN

Sitting Bull

★ ★ ★ ★

One of the reasons for the success of Buffalo Bill's Wild West Show was the ability of Colonel Cody to seek out new acts that would catch the public's attention. One of these attempts that met with the greatest success came when he decided to add Sitting Bull, the conqueror of George Armstrong Custer, to perform in the show.

"Well, he won't actually perform," Colonel Cody said to a reporter who had accompanied him as he went to encourage, or bribe, or hire Sitting Bull to come with the troop.

The reporter, a young man named Jones, stared at Buffalo Bill cynically. "I'm not sure the public will stand for it. I mean, after all, he's the enemy of the United States, isn't he?"

"They'll come out to see him." Buffalo Bill nodded with a stark certainty.

The reporter wrote something in his book, then he asked abruptly, "How do you respond to P.T. Barnum's charge that you stole the idea for the show from him?"

"Barnum is just one of his own freaks to me. He's free to buy a ticket and come in and see for himself."

The two had gotten off the train at Fort Gates, and the reporter, Jones, had been introduced to his first live Indian. He had given the tall warrior a cigar, and the Indian had smoked it with enthusiasm.

"I'll bring you a whole box, Chief," Jones promised airily.

After they had moved away, Colonel Cody said sharply, "Whatever you do, don't forget those cigars. Maybe you didn't mean it, but don't ever promise an Indian anything unless you mean to pay up. Get a box of cigars and charge it to me. Don't forget."

They moved over to the office of the Commander, Colonel Frank Norris, who was not at all in sympathy with Buffalo Bill's proposal. "You understand," Colonel Norris said, "that he's almost sixty. Which, among the Sioux, as you know, is very old, Colonel Cody." He hesitated and grinned. "But he's just about as sharp an operator as you'll find this side of Chicago."

Buffalo Bill nodded and returned the colonel's smile. "I'm aware of that. However, I think I can do the chief some good."

"He's a medicine man, not a chief," Colonel Norris corrected. "If he doesn't want to go, you understand, he can't be made to."

"Oh, I think we'll be able to persuade him," said Cody confidently.

"Maybe." Colonel Norris looked at the showman with a critical eye. "Last year he got an offer telling him he could meet the President, and he didn't get any closer than a New York wax museum. He's a little bit shy of show business right now."

"I understand, but you must understand, too, Colonel, that I know a little about Indians, and I know that breaking a promise to them is unforgivable."

After a little more discussion, Colonel Norris instructed a sergeant to take Cody and the reporter to the chief's. As they crossed the parade ground, Jones looked at the Indians, pulling at his collar uncomfortably. Finally, when they had reached a group of Indians in a cluster he asked, "Who's that squaw with the hat?"

"That's not a squaw," Colonel Cody said. "That's Sitting Bull."

The reporter stopped dead still and blinked his eyes with surprise. He looked closely at the medicine man, whose visions of soldiers falling upside down into the Indian camp had united the Sioux, Cheyenne, and Arapaho Nations, and had led to Custer's massacre nine years earlier. Sitting Bull was small and slight, with hair dangling in graying, unadorned plaits, and he had the puffed eyelids and fallen features of an old Chinese woman.

There was a great deal of ceremony, and, taking his cues, Jones stepped back as Colonel Cody stood before the Indian. Sitting Bull spoke in a guttural tone. "Long Hair Cody is welcome in this house."

The reporter jotted down everything that was said, remembering what Cody had told him about Indians. *They are not in a hurry. They have no clock, and you'll have to be patient.* He learned that lesson well that day, for it was nearly an hour before Colonel Cody broached the subject for his visit. He offered a box that he had brought and said, "These are gifts for the Great Chief." Inside was a great deal of candy. Cody had explained earlier to Jones that candy holds up in the heat, and even if the chief didn't have any teeth he could at least suck on it.

After more negotiations, and having listened carefully to everything the chief said, Colonel Cody said, "We will offer fifty dollars a week and living expenses to the great Sitting Bull if he will agree to tour with the show."

There was a long silence and finally, again, Sitting Bull spoke. "I will join Long Hair Cody's show if he will promise me all the money from selling pictures of me. I will have this in writing." His dark eyes glittered as he nodded, "Words on paper are the only words the white man needs."

Colonel Cody heaved a sigh of relief and assured the chief that there would be no problem. He was aware that the photography concession was one of the Wild West's more lucrative sidelines, and that Nate Salsbury would be furious. But he knew that it would be worth it.

* * * *

Sitting Bull joined the show, making his first appearance in Little Rock, Arkansas. He was accompanied by four of his braves, who were never far away from the short, stubby form of the great medicine man. Con and Laurie watched the crowds who lined up to file by and take a look at the most famous Indian— outside of Pocahantas—who had ever lived.

"He sure don't look like much, does he?" said Con, shaking his head.

Laurie studied the stoic face of Sitting Bull then shrugged. "I suppose not, but looks don't matter all that much, do they Con?"

Later that night, after supper, Laurie changed and was walking through the camp when she saw Sitting Bull and his four bodyguards, as such, sitting outside their tent.

On a whim, Laurie walked over and stood in front of the Indian, saying in the Sioux language, "I welcome the Great Chief Sitting Bull to the show."

A flicker of surprise ran through Sitting Bull's eyes, and a mutter was heard from his four attendants. "How does the white woman speak the language of the People?"

Laurie explained that she had grown up in the West, that her father had been an Indian agent for a while, and was now an officer in the Seventh Cavalry.

Sitting Bull studied her even more carefully. "He was not with Long Hair Custer?"

"No. He was sent by General Custer to be in Reno's group."

The novelty of a young woman speaking the Sioux language fascinated Sitting Bull, and few days passed when he did not manage to have a conversation with her. Then abruptly, he asked her, "You have no husband?"

"No, not yet, Chief."

Sitting Bull shook his head and scowled, "It's bad to waste squaws." He looked around and said, "Tall Antelope—he needs a squaw."

Laurie was not shocked, for she knew the casual ways of the Indian. She smiled at the tall Indian and said to Sitting Bull, "I am honored, but I will not marry for some time, Chief." Laurie was grateful for all that she had learned from Luis Montoya and her father in dealing with the Sioux. Even in turning down an offer of marriage, she answered with great respect, acknowledging the great chief sitting in front of her. She then rose, and started back through the camp toward her tent.

Later, she was invited by Con to go into town to see the sights, and she accompanied him gladly. She had expected, as the days had gone on, to be closer to Cody. But he had thrown himself into his work and seemed oblivious to everything else, so she had accepted the cowboy's offer, and the two had made their way to the center of town. It was not Chicago, or New York, but they enjoyed moving along the main street, looking into the windows. Finally, they came to stand before a furniture store with a display lit by a gas light fixture inside.

"Now that's right pretty, ain't it, Laurie?" Con remarked. He cocked his head to one side and shoved his hat back. His blond hair fell over his forehead. He was, Laurie thought, an intensely attractive man. Not handsome in the ordinary sense of the word, but vital, strong—and there was some sort of magnetism that flowed out of him. Now she looked at him with a smile and said, "You'd have a hard time carrying a room full of furniture around the way we travel."

A strange look flickered into his eyes, and he did not speak of it again until they were sitting in the ornate restaurant at the Arlington Hotel. The waiter took their order, and when it arrived they found the food delicious. Finally, when they were finished, they sat looking at the customers, admiring the heavy, glass chandelier, and enjoying the rich decor surrounding them. And it was then Con said suddenly, "I guess that would be a lot of furniture for a man to carry, wouldn't it?"

"What?" Laurie could not understand the sudden change in conversation and stared at him in bewilderment.

"That furniture back in that store—you said a man couldn't carry that on the Wild West Show."

Laurie answered, "Oh, I did say that. Well, it's true enough, isn't it?"

"True enough, Laurie, but I've been thinking a lot about this show lately." He picked up his coffee cup, and she noticed how large and strong his hands were. They were the hands of an outdoorsman, callused and muscular. He lifted his eyes and spoke almost urgently. "A man can't keep on doing this sort of thing forever—nor a woman either."

"I suppose you're right, Con," Laurie confessed. "It was exciting at first, and I wouldn't have missed it, but it's not for me." She hesitated, leaned back in her chair, and considered the months that had gone by. They seemed almost dreamlike to her now as she thought of them, and yet always, even from the first, there had been a transitory sense about the whole experience. It was as if she had entered into a fairy tale in a book and had become one of the characters. It was exciting to hear the crowds cheer, and to take the ovations that came—but it had no sense of reality. She finally nodded. "You're right, Con. I suppose it's all right for some, like Colonel Cody, but I can't see myself riding around on Star before a bunch of people for the rest of my life."

"You aren't made for this kind of moving around." Con leaned forward and his eyes grew more intense. "I guess I've spent all my life on the move, Laurie. Been a hard life, and there's no way for a man to be a sheriff in the West and stay soft—so I guess I'm a hard man. They say so."

Impulsively, Laurie leaned over and put her hand on his, and he immediately covered it with his free hand. "You did what you had to do, Con. I think you should be proud of what you've done, not ashamed. If it weren't for lawmen and the army—why there'd be no order at all! It's part of the growing up of this country."

"You really mean that, Laurie?"

"Of course I do." She smiled and tried to withdraw her hand, but his two hands closed in on hers, and he fixed her with his light blue eyes. "I'm glad that you've seen that side of me. I wouldn't fool you—there's another side. I've got a temper that's a shame." He shrugged then, adding, "I've learned to keep it under control pretty much now, but when I was a young buck, I was just like a stick of dynamite."

Laurie tugged at her hand but found that he was not willing to release it. "You're holding my hand, Con. Everybody will see it," she said, feeling a little uneasy.

"Let them see." He leaned forward and there was an earnestness in his face. "I want to marry you, Laurie."

Suddenly, his words threw a hush over the rest of the talking in the restaurant—or at least so it seemed to Laurie. Astonished, she stared at him, her mouth half open with the shock of his announcement. She had known that he liked her, but there had never been anything serious—or so she had thought. Now, she struggled for the words, and seeing that she could not speak, Con released her hand and leaned back in his chair. "I know you've never thought of me as a man you might marry."

"I've never thought of *anyone* like that. I guess I've never thought of marriage much, although every girl comes to it. Most of them, anyway."

"You're the finest girl I've ever seen, Laurie," Con said simply. "I care for you, and I'd like to get away from this show business, get a place somewhere out West. Just a small place . . ."

He went on for a while, speaking about a ranch, and when he had finished, Laurie said shakily, "But, Con, that kind of place was what I ran away from. It was an army post, and I felt like I would go crazy there." She went on to relate how earlier she had wanted to be a writer, how she had fled at the first chance to the college, and how she had dreaded going home again when it seemed that was going to be necessary.

"You still think you want to be a writer?" he asked suddenly.

The question caught Laurie off guard, and she said in a halting fashion, "Why—why I can't imagine doing anything else."

"Are you doing any writing now?"

Laurie dropped her eyes and shook her head. "No, to tell the truth, I'm not. All I'm doing is riding Star and going from place to place."

There was a moment's silence, and Con Groner, who was an intuitive man with a pair of very sharp eyes and much experience in watching people, said, "It's Logan, isn't it?"

"Logan?"

"I've seen how you watch him, Laurie. And everybody knows how you two got together. You were friends before, weren't you?"

"We had known each other," Laurie said. "And he was down on his luck. But he'd not think of marriage, and I'm not thinking of it either."

They sat there, and the talk fell away. There was now a strain between the two that Laurie hated. Finally, she rose and said, "I've got to get back, Con." He paid the check, and the two walked out of the hotel and took a carriage back to the showgrounds. When she got out, she turned to face him, and after he'd paid the cab driver and turned to watch her face, she said, "I can't marry you, Con. And it wouldn't be fair of me to give you any hope."

A sudden smile touched the lips of Con Groner, and he said,

"I may not look like much, but I don't give up easy. Oh, you don't have to worry. I won't be pestering you—but I'll be back again someday, and I'll expect a different answer."

★ ★ ★ ★

Con and Laurie were not the only ones who had gone into Little Rock for supper. Cody, after the show, had unsaddled his horse, seen to his grooming, then had picked up a rope and gone back into the arena. For thirty minutes he practiced some of the more difficult tricks that he hoped to add to his act later on. He failed several times on one of the more difficult ones, finally slapped the rope against his thigh, and complained aloud, "Blast it, can't never get that right!"

"You're not swearing, are you, Jim?" He turned quickly to find Leona standing ten feet away, and suddenly he felt foolish.

"Not fair," he said, coiling up his rope. "I don't sneak around and watch you practice and see how many times you miss those little balls."

She laughed and came over and stood close enough for him to smell the perfume she always wore—like honeysuckle. "You don't miss much," she said. "That was a pretty hard one. Think you can manage it?"

"Don't know."

"Well, you can practice some other time." She took his arm and said, "Tonight, you're taking me into Little Rock for an evening out."

She knew how to charm a man, and Cody, tired of the routine and hard work, grinned and said, "I guess you don't give a man much choice, Leona. Let's go do it."

She had been to Little Rock before and showed him a few of the sights. Finally, they had gone to see a production of a play that was given at the Williams Auditorium. It was a production touring company with a famous actress as a star. Cody, who had never seen a performance of this sort, was enthralled. He sat there, caught up with the action, and Leona was amused to see him shifting, and moving, and muttering under his breath, trying to influence the action on the stage. The young star was threatened by a slick-looking villain, and Cody murmured once,

"What's the matter with that girl? Can't she see he's nothing but a snake?"

Leona slapped his arm slightly. "Most women are willing to be fooled by men," she said quietly.

Later on, they went to supper at a rather small cafe with very good food, and he talked with animation about the play all through the meal. Leona sat there, enjoying the meal and his conversation. Finally, she said, "I've never heard you talk so much. Maybe I need to take you to a play every night to keep your spirits up."

Cody blinked with surprise, then shook his head. With a rueful grin, he said, "I guess I just got carried away. I didn't know a play could do a thing like that to a fellow!"

"I could show you a lot of things if you'd crawl out of that shell you're in." Leona leaned forward and said, "You're a strange fellow, Jim. I've never known a man like you."

"Be glad of that," he said brusquely and looked down at the coffee, keeping his eyes away from hers.

"Why do you always put yourself down?" she demanded. She made a lovely picture as she sat there. She had worn a pale green dress that went well with her green eyes, and she had dressed her hair carefully in the newest fashion. There was a sensuous quality in this woman, and she used it almost instinctively. Finally, she said, "Come on, let's go back to the arena."

Leaving the cafe, they made their way across town, and when they got out of the carriage, she said, "It's too early to go to bed. Let's walk."

"All right," said Cody.

They walked around the perimeter of the arena, hearing the snorting of the horses and the nervous movement of the huge buffalo. They passed Sitting Bull, who was taking his nightly stroll, and he stared at them without expression. Finally, she led him to a spot just outside the arena that had been made into a small park. "Look," she said. "There's a bench. I'm tired. Let's sit awhile." She pulled him down beside her, and for some time, they sat there speaking quietly. He spoke of the show and the people in the acts, and for a while she listened, adding a few comments. Then she said, "What do you think of me?"

Cody's head swiveled at once, and he said, "Why do you ask that?"

"I don't know," Leona said in her husky voice. "Most of the time, I know what a man's thinking. But I'm never sure of myself with you."

This was true, and it had piqued her. She was accustomed to controlling men and, in her short life, had learned that this was not a difficult thing for a beautiful woman to do. Very rarely had she met a man who could not be put into a category, and that was why this man fascinated her. She had given him more covert and subtle encouragement than she had ever given any man, yet still he somehow remained distant, in a world of his own.

They were surrounded by a few saplings, and the wind was breathing quietly across the grounds. Suddenly, she reached up and turned toward him, taking his arm. "Don't you ever think of me as anything except a trick shot artist, Jim?"

Cody could not answer for a moment. Some of the lanterns were still on, and by their light, he saw her enormous eyes and felt again the desires that a man knows when he is this close to beauty. "I think of you as a beautiful woman—which you are."

"You've never told me that," said Leona softly.

"Everyone else has. You've heard it enough, I expect."

Something in his words troubled her, and she dropped her eyes, then raised them again. "I've been too free with men. That's what you think."

"Not for me to say," Cody said quickly. "I'm not judging anybody."

From far away came the sound of a train whistle, and she shivered a little, leaning against him. "That's the lonesomest sound in the world, isn't it?"

He looked at her, bending closer, and said, "Why would you say that?"

"I guess because I've heard so many of them, and I've run so far that I just can't stand to think of another train, another town, another—" She almost said *another man*, but she broke off.

"Leona, you don't have to be afraid. You could have a dozen men. Any one of the bachelors in the show would jump at the chance to marry you."

"That's sweet of you, Jim," she said. And then she waited, and there was such a vulnerability, for the first time, in her soft lips, that Cody did not feel intimidated. He leaned forward, thinking, *This is wrong*, but he could not withhold himself. He took her in his arms and held her firmly—there was no holding back, not to this woman. She met him fully, openly, and the kiss he gave was returned with an intensity that shook him from his heels to his crown. He sensed the longings that were in her, and at the same time, there was something of a child that had been lost and was searching for security. He felt that as he let his lips linger on hers, aware of her softness as he held her. Finally, he drew back and said in a husky voice, "You're a sweet girl, Leona. For some man, you've got everything. But I guess I'll never get married."

She rose, and he saw for an instant the tears in her eyes. "Good-night," she said quickly and left him there in the darkness. As she walked away, she realized that the kiss had shaken her in a way that had not come for many years, and a feeling of despair touched her as she made her way toward her tent.

CHAPTER NINETEEN

LITTLE SURE SHOT

★　★　★　★

Laurie never forgot the day that Annie Oakley and Frank Butler joined the show. Buffalo Bill never forgot it either, for though there were many fine performers with his organization, none outshone the tiny young woman who seemed unable to miss any sort of a target with any sort of a gun.

Laurie was first aware of the couple who had entered the arena early that morning after breakfast when Cody said, "That's a nice lookin' couple, isn't it?"

Evidently, the pair saw Cody and Laurie watching them, for they came straight over to them. The man, tall and fine looking, took off his hat, saying, "Do you know where I can find Colonel Cody?"

"I imagine he's with Nate Salsbury. I can take you to him."

The man shook his head. "We'd like to see him out here, if you don't mind asking him to come."

A little mystified, Cody turned and walked away as the man called out, "I'm Frank Butler and this is my wife, Annie."

After Cody disappeared, Butler nodded to Laurie. "Wonderful act you have, Miss Winslow."

Laurie flushed a little, as she always did when she received such praise, then said, "With a horse like Star, almost anyone could be a trick rider."

The young woman called Annie smiled. She was as small and dainty as her husband was tall and well built. "I ride a little," she said, "but I wouldn't ever be able to do the things you do."

Laurie stood there chatting with them, liking the young woman very much, and when she looked up, she said, "There's Colonel Cody."

At once the pair turned to meet him, and the man said, "Colonel Cody, my name's Frank Butler. I'm a trick shot artist, and this is my wife, Annie."

Buffalo Bill slipped off his hat to the diminutive young woman, bowed, and said regretfully, "Well, I do most of the trick shooting myself, me and Johnny. And we've got a young woman named Leona Aimes who's good."

At once Butler said, "My wife shoots, too. I think you ought to see what she can do. She's better than I am, Colonel." After a little convincing, the Colonel agreed to a demonstration, and almost at once, Laurie and the men who had come to watch saw that the youthful woman by his side was far better than Butler himself. Butler hit the target as often as his wife, but she was more certain of herself and took less time in aiming. Annie worked the lever of a rifle and fired as fast as any of them had ever seen, shattering blue glass balls that her husband tossed into the air. And when she had finished, Butler said, "And that's firing real bullets, Colonel, not sand."

This was rather a sore spot with Cody, who sometimes used fine sand in the manner of buckshot. "What else can you do?"

With a grin, the tall man went forty feet away, pulled a cigarette out, and put it between his lips. Annie instantly lifted her rifle and fired, cutting the cigarette off not an inch from her husband's lips. Then Butler held up a dime between his fingers, and she fired again. Finally, he held up a playing card and turned it sideways. "You can't make that shot!" Buffalo Bill exclaimed. But even as he spoke, the rifle exploded and the card was cut in two. Everyone who was watching burst into applause.

"You haven't seen anything yet," Butler called out.

As he spoke, Annie picked up a small hand mirror, held it in front of her with her left hand, and with her rifle barrel resting on her right shoulder, aimed backward. Butler called out, "Are you ready, Annie?"

"Ready," she answered.

He rotated his right hand, feeding out string in an ever-widening circle, the blue glass sphere attached to the other end whistling faster and faster, making a circle ten feet in diameter. When the shrill whir was almost ear shattering, the rifle cracked. The golf-ball-sized globe exploded in a shower of glittering dust. Again, the applause went up, and Buffalo Bill demanded, "Where did you learn to handle a rifle like that?"

"I used to shoot quail on my father's farm in Ohio," Annie smiled prettily. "I never thought it was anything special until they asked me to take part in turkey shoots."

"Tell me, can you shoot from horseback?"

"Yes."

"At dead gallop?"

She nodded and looked him in the eye. She wore her dark hair brushed behind her ears and had a serious expression.

"Annie don't brag," said Butler. "Colonel, she can hit anything from anywhere. Her specialty is splitting a playing card at fifty paces."

Buffalo Bill Cody stared at the young woman and said intently, "Come back to my tent, you two. I think we can work something out."

For the next two weeks, Annie and her husband, Frank, performed, and it was obvious that she was a drawing card for the show. Only rarely did Salsbury put up an individual's name, but he had thousands of flyers printed up now with the name "Annie Oakley, Best Champion Rifle Shot In America."

The pair had their own tent, which they put up next to that of Laurie and Leona's, and in the course of those days, Annie and Laurie became close friends. Leona was jealous of Annie, of course, but did all her complaining to Laurie. Laurie discovered that there was a natural modesty to Annie Oakley, as she liked to be called. "Fame certainly never went to her head," Laurie told Sam one day. "She's the most modest person I ever saw."

One evening after the three o'clock performance was over, Laurie heard a voice calling her. She had been lying down in her tent, resting, and sat up at once and came outside. "Hello, Con," she nodded. "What's going on?"

"Oh, nothing much," he said, shifting his weight. "Could you take a little walk with me?"

At once Laurie was apprehensive. "Why—I don't know, Con. I really have things to do."

He smiled at her crookedly, saying, "You don't lie too well, do you, Laurie?"

She flushed and shook her head. "Not too well." Then she smiled and said, "All right. Just a short one."

The two walked around the perimeter of the corrals, discussing the horses, and Laurie spoke with praise about Annie Oakley.

"She's a fine shot. I never saw a better," Con said.

They finally arrived at a place that had some privacy, located between the corrals where the buffalo and the horses were penned up. Leaning on the fence, Laurie began talking about the horses, pointing out this one and that one. She spoke rather rapidly, for she had an idea of why Con wanted to go for a walk, and finally her fears were realized. "I told you, Laurie, I'd come back," he said. He turned to face her and there was an eager gleam in his eyes. "I don't want to push you, but I'm getting on in years."

"How old are you, Con?" she grinned.

"Well, actually, I'm twenty-eight, but, I mean, look at it this way, Laurie. A lot of fellows, at my age, have found their place. They've got steady jobs, a home, marriage, a family. I've been roaming around since I was sixteen years old, and I'm telling you, it's getting a little tiresome."

"I'm tired myself," admitted Laurie.

Instantly, he said, "Sure you are. You weren't made for this kind of life. Like you said, it's been fun, something to remember, but it's time to make a change."

Laurie said nervously, "Well, I'm only twenty so I guess there's no real rush."

Con shut his mouth abruptly, and a hint of the temper that he had confessed to appeared in his eyes. They grew narrow and his lips tightened into a white line. "I was right, wasn't I? About you and Jim Logan."

"No. You're wrong," Laurie said quickly. "He's just a friend, that's all. Just like you're a friend." She saw, however, that her explanation did not satisfy Groner. He stood there, teetering back and forth. She knew that he longed to express what was in his mind physically. It was what he did best. Whenever he went into action, it was with everything he had, whether it was riding in a horse race or striking the tents; everything he did was with all of his strength. She had never seen him resting, not ever.

Groner bit his lips and shook his head. "I love you, Laurie, and that's all I can say. Maybe you don't love me so much right now, but I can make you happy. There ain't nothin' I wouldn't do for you. If you want a ranch, we'll get one. If you want to go east, we'll go east. I've been everywhere, so it don't matter much to me—as long as I can have a woman like you."

"I'm sorry, Con." Laurie bit the words off nervously. "It's the greatest honor that anyone has ever done me, to ask me to marry them. Every woman appreciates that. But I couldn't make you happy."

"Why couldn't you?" asked Con, trying to control the strain in his voice.

"Because you deserve a woman who will love you just for yourself, and I just haven't fallen in love with you."

"I don't know about all that, Laurie. All the pretty notions about falling in love is pretty much in books."

"Then why could you say you love me?" she countered instantly. And seeing that he was off guard, said, "I can't talk about it anymore, Con. I'm sorry, but I'm telling you that you need to look for another girl. I may not ever marry, certainly not for years."

She turned and walked away, and if she had twisted her head and looked back, she would have seen the anger mixed with disappointment flash out of Con Groner's eyes.

She never regained her composure, not all day long, and everyone noticed it. Finally, Sam said, "Cody, Laurie's got something she can't quite swallow. I've never seen her like this."

"Really? Well, I haven't noticed." He looked over to where Laurie was standing beside Star, after having practiced her ride and her tricks, and said, "Come to think of it, she does look kind of down and out."

"Why don't you go over and talk to her," Sam urged. "You two are old friends, and everybody needs a friend at some time."

"Okay, I'll go and see what I can do."

Cody went over to where Laurie was standing and said cheerfully, "Hi, Laurie. The tricks went well today. I was watching."

"I guess so," she said, tuning and leading Star away toward the corral.

Cody accompanied her, keeping up a cheerful line of talk. He unsaddled for her, and then turned Star into the feedlot. "Let me show you a new trick I've been working on. I've about got it worked out. It'll bring the house down."

"I don't think so. Not right now."

They were walking slowly, and her eyes were on the ground as she spoke. Her voice was so low he had to lean forward to catch it. Taking her arm, he turned around and said, "Come on. Let's go somewhere where we can talk."

"I don't want to talk."

"We need to talk," he insisted. "Is Leona in your tent?"

"No, she went to town." Cody took her arm more firmly and walked toward her tent. Laurie made no resistance, and when they were inside, he turned to face her.

"What's wrong with you, Laurie? You're just not yourself."

"Nothing you could help with," she answered shortly.

"Maybe I could if you'll just tell me what it is."

Laurie could not tell him the real problem. Instead of answering his question, she looked at him and said, "Have you decided to write your parents?"

"No. I've told you I can't do it."

"I got a letter from your mother three days ago. I've been wondering whether to show it to you or not, but now I guess I will." Moving over to the chest beside the foot of her cot, she opened it, took out a letter, and handed it to him. As he read the brief letter, she studied his face, thinking, *Why does he have to be so stubborn? Why can't he give just a little bit?* Then when he was finished, and he handed the letter back, his face frozen in a tense expression, she shook her head. "It's killing her, Cody—and your stepfather, too. I don't think it's right, your not letting them know where you are."

"It wouldn't do any good."

Angered by his response, Laurie snapped at him, "It doesn't mean anything that your mother is praying every day of her life that you'll be all right, that you'll be safe?"

"God doesn't have anything to do with it," Cody shot back

adamantly. He stared at her and shook his head. "I put God out of this thing a long time ago. A man just can't ever depend on God."

"What do you believe in then, Cody?" she demanded.

"A man," he said through clenched teeth, "just has to take what he can get."

A quick anger, almost violent, ran through Laurie. It was only then she realized that if she could be so angry with him, there must be something deeper between them. Refusing to think about it, she said in a shrill voice, "A man takes what he can get? I guess you mean Leona?"

A flush rose to Cody's face, and he stared at her. "Yes. I guess I mean that."

Instantly, Cody regretted his words, for he saw that he had hurt her perhaps worse than if he'd slapped her across the cheek. He opened his mouth to apologize, but she said at once, "I'm going to lie down. Please leave."

He wanted to speak, to tell her that he didn't mean it, for he knew he owed everything to this young woman, but there was something stubborn in him, and he nodded and said, "All right," and left the tent.

★ ★ ★ ★

Annie and Frank returned from their shopping trip, and Butler left at once to work on the props for the next show. Annie went inside and started to change clothes, then paused abruptly. Lifting her head, she listened intently. *That sounds like a woman crying*, she thought. She listened harder, moving over to the side of the tent that bordered that of the two young women, and this time it was unmistakable. Without thinking, Annie left her tent, walked over to the other, and said, "It's me—Annie. Can I come in?"

She waited a moment, and then the flap of the tent opened. Laurie stared at her, then dropped her eyes. "Come in," she said as she turned and sat down on the cot. She looked up at Annie, her eyes bottomless pits of woe, and said, "I'm not very good company right now."

Annie immediately felt a great compassion for this young woman. They had become good friends, and Annie Oakley did not have many good friends. Her whole adult life had been spent traveling. But now she and Laurie had eaten together, worked together, and spent some time alone with each other. That was very precious to Annie, so she sat down beside Laurie, put her arms around her, and said, "You're not the first one to cry. I've done it myself."

"Have you, Annie?" asked Laurie, relieved to have someone to talk to about it.

"Oh yes. Sometimes, before I met Frank, I got so lonely I'd just go off and cry myself to sleep. Then, even after we married, I've had times when I've felt the same."

Laurie looked at her and said, "Tell me about what it's like to love a man, Annie."

Annie was not too shocked, for she had carefully watched the young woman and seen that many of the cowboys played up to her, especially Con Groner. She had also seen that when the cowboy named Jim Logan came anywhere near Laurie, the girl's face became very watchful and oftentimes lighted up. She was too wise to make mention of it, but she began to speak. "Most women," she said, "marry out of desperation. Maybe that's the way it has to be. What else is there for a woman to do in this country? She can either be a schoolteacher, or a nurse, or maybe a servant. Other than that, what choice does she have but to get married?"

"I could never do that," Laurie said, clamping her teeth together. She shook her head, sending her hair sweeping down the back of her neck. "I'd rather be an old maid."

"Let me tell you about Frank and me," Annie said. She told the story of how they had met, and had known from the very beginning, almost, that they were in love. And how she had been young and innocent, and how he had been so gentle with her that marriage, to her, had been a joy. "That's what you need, Laurie. A man like my Frank. One that will love you and cherish you and think of you first."

The two women sat on the cot for a long time. Annie's soft voice was hardly audible, except to the young woman beside her. Finally, Laurie looked up, dashed the tears from her eyes, and attempted a smile. "Thank you, Annie. You're a comfort."

Annie Oakley was not an older woman with years of experience and counsel. She herself looked no more than seventeen, younger than Laurie. And yet, she had managed to drive the sorrow and grief, at least temporarily, out of her friend.

"You'll find a husband. I know you will. Just wait till you're sure you've got the right one."

For a long time after Annie left, Laurie sat on the cot, thinking about the difficulties of life. Finally, she muttered, "It was easier back at the Fort. Then all I had to worry about was a dog named Ugly!"

CHAPTER TWENTY

"YOU LISTEN TO ME PREACH— AND I'LL WATCH YOU SHOOT!"

★ ★ ★ ★

As the Wild West Show of Buffalo Bill Cody made its way to ever larger and larger cities, Annie Oakley became the star of the show. Her shooting of card targets gave rise to the slang term "Annie Oakley" for a pass or a complementary ticket, often punched so that they could be identified while counting receipts. One small card target that she used was about five by two inches in size, with a small picture of Annie at one end, and a one inch, heart-shaped bull's-eye at the other. Such cards, after being hit, were thrown into the audience as souvenirs, and a wild scramble usually took place for the treasured items.

Annie proved her skill in many formal shooting contests. In April, at Dayton, Ohio, she broke nine hundred and forty-three out of one thousand glass balls thrown in the air, using a Stevens .22-caliber rifle. Later that year, at Cincinnati, she broke four thousand, seven hundred and seventy-two out of five thousand glass balls, at fifteen yards rise, with shotguns, in nine hours, loading her own guns.

Annie, somehow, had a way of making friends wherever she went, and one dear friend that she never forgot was Sitting Bull. He had watched Annie often and became very excited over her shooting, shouting, "Watanya cicilia!" thus dubbing her "Little Sure Shot."

More and more acts were added as the crowds grew ever larger, and Buffalo Bill was looking forward with anticipation to the grand opening in Chicago. The huge arena there had been reserved, and Colonel Cody and others expected a record attendance. Sam Novak and Mac McGonigal were talking a week before the show got to Chicago, and as usual whenever the two cronies got together, their talk turned to Cody and Laurie.

Sam was braiding a piece of leather into a lariat, as he had seen the vaqueros do, and finally gave up in disgust. "I think you have to be a Mexican to do this thing," he said. "I'll just use rope."

McGonigal's wizened face grinned at him. "Makes no matter, does it, me boy? You don't catch anything with rope *or* leather."

Sam's face flushed, for his ineptness with a lariat was the joke of the show. No matter how much Cody tried to teach him, he seemed to get worse rather than better. Finally, he said, "Well, maybe I can become a trick shot artist, or a trick rider like Laurie."

At the mention of Laurie's name, McGonigal's countenance darkened. He shook his head sadly. "She ain't herself, that girl. I miss the smiles on her happy face."

Quickly, Sam Novak shot a glance at him, and then looked down at the ground, where he drew a pattern with his boot toe. Then, when he looked up, he said, "I guess you know what's wrong with her, don't you?"

"Know what's wrong with her?" McGonigal snapped, his eyes flashing. "Do I know my own name? Of course I know what's wrong with her! She's got a case of lunacy over that friend of yours."

Sam shook his head sadly. "I guess you're right. I hate to see it."

The two men walked around, looking at the horses, watching some of the actors as they practiced the acts that would be added when they got to Chicago. Finally, McGonigal said, "I've been thinkin' on it, and I've decided there's only one thing that's going to work."

"Well, that's one more thing than I've thought of. What is it?" asked Sam.

"The boy's got to get right with God," McGonigal nodded sagely. "He's going around, down a blind alley, making nothin' of his life, and as long as he's like that, Laurie's not going to have anything."

"Maybe she'll find somebody else."

"I doubt it. She's like a few women I've seen—just a one man woman. I'll tell you, Sam, we've got to do something and I know only one thing that'll work."

"Let's hear it."

"You and me have got to pray that boy will get himself saved. It's going to take somebody besides us to straighten him out. He's got his head all set against it. I know you've talked to him about the Lord Jesus, and so have I. But he's worked up such a case of hardness in that heart of his, I don't think our talk ever gets to him. Somebody will have to get through to him."

Sam agreed, though without much hope, and so the two prayed earnestly, both together and apart, for Cody Rogers. It seemed, however, to do little good, for there was no getting close to the young man as far as talking to him about God was concerned.

But one night, when Sam was sleeping soundly, he suddenly felt someone grabbing and shaking him almost fiercely. He came out of his sleep with a start, and when he opened his mouth to cry out, a hard hand slapped over his lips, shutting them firmly.

"Keep your mouth shut," a voice whispered, and he recognized that it was Mac McGonigal who was holding him. "Now, I'm turning you loose, but don't make a sound."

Sam sputtered as the hand was removed from his mouth. He sat up and saw that only the two of them were awake. "What is it?" he whispered.

McGonigal said, "I've got it, Novak—what to do about that young man."

All the sleep vanished instantly from Sam Novak, and he asked, "What's the idea? You know somebody's got to be able to get to him, and I can't think of—"

"Keep your mouth shut and listen," Mac said fiercely. "Now, who's the greatest preacher in the world?"

Sam blinked, scratched his head, and then said, "Why, Reverend Moody, I suppose. He's the most famous, that's for sure."

"Right! Dwight L. Moody, the greatest evangelist, maybe, that the world's ever seen." McGonigal grew excited. "He's going to be in Chicago when we get there—and we've got to get Cody in to listen to him!"

Sam shook his head. "You'd find it easier to get a buffalo to go down that church aisle than you would Cody. You know that."

"Maybe so, but we've *got* to get him in there. So, that's why I woke you up, Sam. Let's pray right now and ask God to do something to get Cody in that meeting when we get to Chicago."

★　★　★　★

"What's the matter, Laurie?" Annie asked sympathetically. She had seen Laurie get more and more depressed and finally had come to her one morning as Laurie was grooming Star. She stood there, reached out, and stroked the animal's silky side, then gave Laurie a compassionate glance. "You're unhappy and I wish I could help you."

Laurie could not face her for a moment, then finally she turned and with troubled eyes said, "There's only one thing that's going to help me. And that's—" she almost said "Cody," and quickly substituted, "Jim Logan getting right with God. And the only way he can do that is for him to hear the Gospel. And that's what I'm praying for."

Annie continued to stroke Star's silky mane and appeared to be thinking hard. Finally, she said, "Well, I haven't had much chance for church. My family didn't go when I was a girl, and since Frank and I are on the road, it's a little bit hard to get there." She turned suddenly and faced Laurie, asking, "Do you think God answers prayer?"

"I know He does!" answered Laurie.

Annie watched her carefully. She seemed to be trying to look into the very heart of her friend, then said hesitantly, "Well, I don't know. I hope so. I guess Frank and I should go to church more, but I've been watching Sam, and Mac, and you, and I can't help but wish I had thought more about God."

At once, Laurie said, "You ought to, Annie. Can I tell you about the Him?" When the small woman nodded, the two went back to Annie's tent. Frank Butler was gone, and for a long time the two sat down as Laurie gave her testimony, telling her how God had helped her and answered her prayers many times, despite her own limitations and lack of faith. She also told of her father's life, how God had miraculously saved him and her stepmother. "So you see," she said finally, "I know God's there. But, sometimes, Annie, God doesn't answer all at once, and I've asked something so big that I don't know if my faith's big enough."

"What is it?" Annie said.

"Well—" Laurie dropped her eyes and seemed to be struggling with doubt. Then she clamped her jaws together and looked up, saying, "Three of us, Mac, and Sam, and I, are praying that Jim will go to hear the famous preacher, Dwight L. Moody, when we get to Chicago. He's preaching there, and I think if anybody could get through to Jim Logan, Mr. Moody could. He's such a wonderful man and such a great preacher!"

Annie studied her hands, put them together, and clasped them tightly. When she looked up there was a strange smile on her face. "Well, I can't pray, but I can get that young man to go to hear that preacher."

Laurie gasped and thought at first that Annie was joking. "Annie, what do you—"

Annie rose to her feet in a swift motion and said, "You get yourself a new dress to go to church, Laurie. Because you're sure going to have a chance. I guarantee it!"

★　★　★　★

As usual, Buffalo Bill always had time for Annie Oakley. She was the pride of his heart and like one of his own daughters. Not in the least a religious man himself, he admired the strong streak of goodness that ran through Annie Oakley.

"What is it, Missy?" he asked with a warm smile. He had always called her that, and others in the show had adopted the same term.

"I have an idea for getting people out to see the show when we get to Chicago."

Colonel Cody stared at her, then he laughed outright. "Don't tell me you've decided to stop shooting and start in being our advance man? Why," he said jovially, "you get people to come just by being in the show, Missy."

Annie smiled at him, then nodded. "You always say nice things like that, Colonel. But really, I do have an idea. I think you could convince Mr. Salsbury about it, too, and he has such good ideas for bringing people out, I thought for once you could top it."

This was exactly what Buffalo Bill Cody wanted to hear. Although he was the star of the show, he was painfully aware that it was Salsbury who kept the thing moving, who made the plans, wrote the advertisement, and came up with the new ideas. Eagerly, he said, "You just tell me, Missy, and I'll do it."

"All right, here it is. Do you know about the preacher, Mr. Moody?"

"Dwight L. Moody? Sure I do. Everybody's heard of Reverend Moody. Biggest thing that ever hit the country, in the preachin' line, that is. I wish I could get him on a horse and ride him around the arena. Is that your idea?"

Annie laughed. "No. Not quite, but something like that." She sobered and looked at him, saying, "My idea is this, Colonel. You go to Mr. Moody and ask him if the whole show can come and hear him preach. You know—all sit together in the same place."

The colonel looked thunderstruck for one second. Then his eyes lit up and he clapped his hands together. "By thunder!" he exclaimed. "That will do it! It will fill Moody's church up, and it will fill our stands up." He stared at her gleefully and said, "How did you ever think of a thing like that, Missy?"

"Oh, I don't know," she answered demurely. "It just came to me."

★   ★   ★   ★

Dwight L. Moody had been preaching for a week in a huge arena built specifically for his coming. The crowds had numbered in the thousands, and the response had been good, but Dwight L. Moody was never a man to be satisfied. He continually prayed that God would do more and more. Moody was not the typical preacher, especially not the typical evangelist. He was short and overweight, and a beard covered most of his lower face. His only outstanding characteristic was his warm, brown eyes that could seemingly embrace a person or a crowd of ten thousand people. That, and his voice, which was powerful enough to carry over a crowd of thousands. And even more than that, Dwight L. Moody was a specimen of the ministry that America had never witnessed.

Moody had been a shoe clerk in Chicago. He had been converted and had begun at once witnessing for the Lord. At first, he simply went out and gathered a group of ragged boys from the poor section of the city and took them to church. As that developed, he began speaking to them about their souls, and one by one, they were won to Jesus. Finally, he began speaking in very small groups, and it was obvious from the first that there was something about Dwight L. Moody and his message that was unusual.

Perhaps it was that he didn't *sound* like a preacher. "He ain't got no stained-glass voice," one rustic said sarcastically. "He don't puff up like a bull frog and act like he's better than anybody else. No, that Reverend Moody, he just talks to us, so we can understand him." The speaker had ended by shaking his head, "Some preachers, seems like the worst fear they got is that somebody will understand what they're saying."

Moody used simple stories, homey illustrations from the fields, and the fords, and the shops, interwoven with scriptures. And as his admirer had said, he spoke as a man to men, as simply as he possibly could. Moody had told more than one man, "If I could make the Gospel any simpler, I'd do it in a flash."

God had blessed his efforts, so that everywhere he went, in this country or abroad, thousands poured out to hear him, under any circumstances, enduring almost any difficulty to get under the sound of his voice. Within the span of a few years, he had become a phenomenon in the history of the church of America.

* * * *

Dwight L. Moody looked up when his secretary, a young man named Simpson, entered with his eyes wide. "Mr. Moody," he said, almost strangling with excitement. "You've got a visitor that wants to see you."

Moody smiled at the young man, saying, "Well, we have lots of those, Simpson. What's so different about this one?"

"It's Buffalo Bill Cody!" the secretary gasped. "Will you see him, Mr. Moody?"

Moody, like everyone else in America, had heard of Buffalo Bill Cody's Wild West Show. He knew of the man's early life as a frontier scout and of his victorious killing of Yellow Hand, and curiosity got the better of him. Famous people came to see him often, but there was nobody quite like Buffalo Bill Cody. "Of course, Simpson. Show him in."

Moody got to his feet just in time to get around his desk and meet the tall man clothed in fringed buckskin and thigh-high, black boots. Moody was overwhelmed by the presence of Cody, as most people were. "Delighted to see you, Mr. Cody," he said, putting out his hand with a warm smile.

Buffalo Bill had been apprehensive. He had not been on friendly terms with many preachers, having seen quite a few that he did not admire. But the simplicity of this short, rotund figure with the warm, brown eyes, and the openness of manner struck him at once, and he put his hand out, which almost swallowed the other man's. "Reverend Moody," he said, "I'm sorry to disturb you, but—"

"Nonsense, it's not an imposition at all, Colonel Cody. Come over here and sit down and tell me about your show. How have you been doing?"

Cody found himself telling about his early days, about the show, about himself, and he realized suddenly that he had never responded to any man so quickly.

Finally, Moody asked, "Is there something I can do for you, Colonel?"

"Yes, Reverend Moody, there is. You know, I've come up pretty rough, and so have most of the men who are with me in the show. Haven't gone to church like I should. Most of us haven't. So I thought it might be possible that I might bring my whole troop to hear you preach. I know it's hard to get a seat, and some of the men are a little apprehensive. But if we could all sit together, I think they'd all come."

Moody was taken by surprise, but at once said, "Why, nothing easier in the world, Colonel Cody. We'll be delighted to have you come. We'll reserve the front section. How many will you be bringing?"

Shocked at his easy success, Cody talked a few more minutes to Moody, settled the time and the seating, and got up, saying warmly, "I'll be looking forward to hearing you, Mr. Moody. And if you'd be interested in coming to the show, you'll be an honored guest."

"I'd be most happy to come," laughed Moody. "Everyone is talking about your show, how you're trying to preserve some part of our national heritage, and I'm proud of what you're doing."

The words caused Buffalo Bill to pause. He ducked his head, stroked his beard slowly, then nodded. "I'm glad you see that, Reverend Moody. It's more than just a show to me. It's part of America, and I want to do all I can to save it, so that boys and girls, and people all over, can see what it was like in those days."

Moody shook his hand again and said, "You come and listen to me preach—and I'll come and watch you shoot, Colonel!"

CHAPTER TWENTY-ONE

CODY GOES TO CHURCH

★ ★ ★ ★

When Colonel Cody announced that all connected with the show would attend Mr. Moody's church on Thursday evening, the effect was electrifying.

Most of the hands, including all the Indians, denied any intention of going, but Buffalo Bill informed them all that not only would they be terminated, but they would be black-balled with other Wild West Shows. Since there were only about three other shows at the time throughout the country, this brought the reluctant members into line.

On Thursday, they gave their afternoon performance, and immediately, as soon as the last of the trumpets in the band had sounded, and the last customer had made his way out of the arena, Buffalo Bill lifted his booming voice and said, "All right, you Wild West cowboys! Go slick your hair down and put on your silver spurs. We're going to church!" He made his way to Laurie and smiled down at her. "And you wear that pretty silver spur with that big ruby in it. It'll catch that preacher's eye!"

Laurie, her heart palpitating, went at once to her tent, where she found Leona pouting and angry. "I'm not going to any old church service!" she said. "He can't make me go!"

Laurie said quickly, "It won't be so bad, Leona. And I think he's serious about firing anybody who doesn't go." She kept talking until finally Leona's face lost its mulish expression, and she hurried to change her clothes. Laurie put on a riding costume, as Buffalo Bill had insisted, and the sight of the red ruby set in the silver spur made her think of her father as it always did. As soon as she was dressed, she ran out of the tent. She made her way toward the tent that housed the single men, and as she approached, Sam stepped outside. Seeing her, he stood there shaking his head.

"Cody won't go," he said bitterly.

"Oh, Sam! Did you talk to him?"

"Yes, I talked to him, and so did Mac. So did nearly everybody else. He says he won't go, and that's all there is to it. He'll quit first." He kicked at the dirt, sending a clod flying across that scared a pony and made him snort and rear. "Maybe you ought to talk to him. He's over at the corral, I reckon, by now."

"All right, Sam. You pray and I'll talk." Laurie walked rapidly to the corral, where she saw Cody shaking out his rope, preparing to rope one of the ponies. She strode over to him and, without preamble, stated boldly, "Cody, you've *got* to go to church!"

He glared at her and shook his head, his lips drawn in a thin, bitter line. "No, I don't have to go to church. I don't know whose fool idea it was anyhow—the colonel's, I guess. He'd do anything to sell another ticket. That's all it is, just business."

Laurie hesitated, then spoke the truth. "I think you may be right about the colonel—partly anyway. But that doesn't change the fact that Mr. Moody's the foremost preacher in the whole world. Please, Cody," she softened her voice and put her hand on his arm, "come and go with me. I'd feel better if you did."

Cody's eyes lost some of their anger, but he shook his head and muttered, "I'd do nearly anything for you, Laurie—I really would. But something about this seems wrong to me somehow. I haven't made any secret of the fact that I'm not even sure there is a God. And now I'm supposed to dress up and go to church and sing songs and listen to sermons? No, I'll leave the show first!"

Laurie, seeing it was useless, responded quietly, "All right, Cody," then turned and walked away.

He watched her go, and once he lifted his hand as if to call her back. *It wouldn't kill you to go, would it?* he thought. *What kind of hairpin are you? What kind of a man have you gotten to be?* He shook his head, doubt sweeping through him, and somehow his whole future seemed very bleak. As he practiced his roping, he thought suddenly of his parents and immediately knew that what he was doing would be a disappointment to them. But there was a stubborn streak in Cody Rogers that surfaced on occasions, and when it came, nothing short of brute force would change him.

Buck Bronson had been donning his fanciest outfit—including the biggest hat anybody had ever seen, and a silver-plated .44 with a mother-of-pearl handle. "How do I look?" he demanded. McGonigal looked at him with a jaundiced eye. "You look like a mountain with a hat on top," he said to the big man. Then he grinned. "You look fine, Buck. You'll be the envy of every gal's eye in that church."

Buck grinned back and slapped McGonigal with his huge hand, almost driving him to the ground with what he considered a light gesture. "I used to go to them camp meetings—them brush arbor meetings—when I was a youngster. They lasted for a week, two, three, sometimes six weeks, and lots of gals were always there. They'd been kept out in the country. Some of them got religion, and some of them lost some, I reckon." He winked lewdly at Mac, then turned and left the tent, on the way to the entrance where they were all gathering, preparing to go. Glancing over, he saw Laurie standing beside her tent and walked over to her. "Come along, Laurie," he said. "Go to church with a gentleman."

"I—I'm not going, Buck."

Buck Bronson, for all his huge size and tremendous power, had a gentle heart. He saw the tears in Laurie's eyes and at once put his hamlike hand on her shoulder. "Aw, what's wrong, Laurie? Don't cry."

"It's—it's Jim," she said. "I've been hoping so hard he'd go to church. I've been praying, too. But now he says he won't go. He says he'll quit first."

"Why, the colonel says anybody's fired who don't go!"

"Jim's just being stubborn, but I know him, Buck. If he says he won't go, he won't go, no matter how hard I pray."

Buck stared at her, and a light leaped into his mild, blue eyes.

"You say you've been prayin' he'd go?"

"Yes."

"Well, then, I expect you better believe the good Lord will answer your prayers." He squeezed her shoulder, then said, "You get on down to that bunch and go on to church. You may not see me, but we'll be there, and we'll have that young gentleman with us."

"Oh, Buck! Will you talk to him?"

"Course I will! Now, you get on, gal."

Laurie quickly wiped the tears from her eyes and ran to join the group. Con Groner came up at once to stand beside her and asked, "What are you and Buck palaverin' about?"

"Oh, talking about prayer."

"I bet," said Con, grinning. "That man-mountain never prayed in his life. Come on, let's get started."

They got to the arena where Moody was preaching and were greeted instantly by a tall man in a black silk hat who was to be their escort. He came forward, grinning, and shook Colonel Cody's hand. "All right, Colonel. We've got the whole front center section reserved for you and your people. Step right this way."

Laurie followed in the procession that entered into the arena, and as they made their way to the front, applause went up and their leader shook his head, saying, "Mr. Moody won't like that—but I guess you can't blame folks for applauding Buffalo Bill, can you now?"

When they were seated, Laurie found that she was seated just behind Buffalo Bill. At her left was Con Groner, and on her right was Sam, with Mac beside him. McGonigal whispered to Sam, "I don't see him, do you?"

Laurie heard the whisper, and leaned close and said, "He'll be here. Just believe."

★   ★   ★   ★

Buck had arranged a surprise for Cody Rogers. He had gathered six of the Sioux Indians, under the leadership of Running Bear, and explained that Laurie needed help.

Running Bear at once had said, "What she need?"

He listened intently while Buck explained, then a light of humor touched his dark eyes. He spoke something to the six young warriors with him, then turned back to Buck and said, "We go now!"

Buck led the way to the corral, where he saw Cody practicing with his rope. He said in a whisper, "All right, Chief—there he is. Have your men ready."

Cody glanced up and saw the procession coming and blinked in surprise. "What are you doing here, Buck? You're supposed to be in church."

Buck grinned at him and came and stood right beside him. "I'm gonna be in church," he nodded. "But ain't you forgot somethin'?"

Cody stared at him. "What did I forget?"

"You forgot," Buck Bronson grinned broadly, "that you're going too!" And without another word, he reached out and put his mighty arms around Cody and lifted him off the ground. "All right, boys. Get the ropes on him." The Indians immediately tied Cody hand and foot as he kicked and fought. But he was like a child in the arms of the giant, and soon he was all trussed up. He cursed and roared and threatened, but Buck just smiled at him benevolently. "You're gonna enjoy church," he said. "I hear he's a fine preacher. All right, you Injuns—bring him on!"

★　★　★　★

The service had been one such as Laurie had never experienced. She had never been in such a large congregation, and the singing brought her heart to a fever pitch. Thousands of voices rang out, singing the songs she had grown up with. There were several prayers, and finally she had conquered her fear and doubt, saying to Sam, "I believe he'll be here, even though I don't see him."

"Well, that's the faith that moves mountains. Look, here comes Mr. Moody."

Dwight L. Moody, dressed in a plain black suit and looking like anything in the world but the most famous preacher on the globe, had stepped up on the platform and raised his voice. He welcomed the crowd and encouraged them to pray for the sermon. Then he paused and looked down the center of the crowd. "We are especially happy to welcome to our service tonight Colonel William Cody and his Wild West Troop. Colonel Cody, would you stand and greet your brothers and sisters?"

Cody was hardly ever at a loss, but Laurie could see that this was a new experience for him. Nevertheless, he stood, turned around, and lifted his powerful voice that was able to boom across any sort of arena. "Not often do my friends and I have the privilege of attending services. It's hard for men and women on the move such as we are to find a place. But tonight I speak for every man and woman here when I say we are thrilled, happy, and grateful to Reverend Moody for inviting us." He waved his hand, and there was a burst of applause as he sat down.

Moody smiled, noting at the same time some of the deacons were somewhat sour, but he ignored them. "My friends, I would take for my text tonight—"

"Hold on, preacher," came a voice from the back of the auditorium.

Every head turned toward the huge cowboy who was advancing down the aisle. People began standing up to see what sort of procession it was. Most of them gasped when they saw it was a giant wearing a huge hat and a beautifully tooled gun, followed by six Indians, dressed in full regalia. The Indians were carrying something, and they could hear someone shouting in a muffled voice, but they could not see. Finally, the little group reached the front of the auditorium, and Buck Bronson swept off his magnificent hat, bowed to the preacher, and said, "Reverend Moody, I remember once my mamma read me a story about a prodigal son who run away and got himself all in a mess. I never forgot that story, preacher, and tonight I've done all I could to help one of them prodigal sons. Hold him up here, you Injuns."

The Indians suddenly straightened up, and Moody and many of the others saw a young man with his hair messed up and his hands and feet tied together. A shock ran over him, and he demanded, "What is this, sir?"

"Why," Buck said, "it's a prodigal son, Reverend! This here young feller wasn't comin' to church, so we just brung him. Now, you go ahead and preach at him, Brother Moody."

Laurie gasped and said, "Oh no! What have you done, Buck?"

Sitting beside her, Sam's face turned to stone. "Well, that tears it," he muttered. "He'll never listen to anything anybody has to say now."

Dwight L. Moody stood absolutely still. He had been all over the world and had preached to every congregation imaginable—but *never* had a situation like this arisen! Staring down at the young man and noting the bitterness in his eyes, he breathed a quick prayer, asking God what to do.

Cody stood there, humiliated, his face flushed with anger and rage. He had only stopped raving and cursing when they brought him into the building. Now, he looked up at the face of the minister in front of him, high on the platform. His gaze swept around, and he saw Laurie, Sam, and Mac all looking at him with anguish in their eyes. Then he turned back and faced Moody, his jaw set and clinched tight.

Dwight L. Moody felt that God had spoken to him. "I'm afraid, my brother," he said to Buck, "that this is not the way of the Lord. God never forces himself on anybody, and neither do I. Let him go."

"But preacher, he'll run off," answered Buck.

"Let him go, sir." Moody's voice was stern, and Buck at once turned and fumbled with the ropes. They fell away, and Buck stepped back, leaving Cody to look up at the short, rotund form of the preacher.

"No man can be brought to God against his will, my young friend," Moody said very gently. He stopped for a moment, his eyes locking with those of the angry young man in front of him. "You're free to go—but I beg you to stay."

Cody, who had been determined to turn and stomp out of the building, was caught off guard by the obvious gentleness of the man. He could not help but admire the way Moody had responded. Still, he knew he could not stay in that place.

Suddenly, Moody said, "I'm sure many have a feeling for you, as your large brother does here." He hesitated, then said, "Perhaps there's a father or a mother, someone who's been praying for you. Won't you stay for their sake?"

Tears burned Cody's eyes, and he blinked them fiercely away. The reference to his mother cut him like a sword, and he began to tremble. He had never felt so humiliated in his life, yet suddenly he knew what he had to do. "I'll stay," he whispered.

At once Moody said, "Fine! fine! Find yourself a place with your friends." Buck and the six Indians led the way to the aisle,

264

and soon Cody was wedged between the huge form of Buck Bronson and Chief Running Bear on the other side.

"You listen good," Running Bear muttered. "Heap trouble to bring you to church. Don't waste it."

Moody waited until the excitement was over, then said, "I think we should have another prayer." He lifted up his voice and addressed God as simply as if he were speaking to his friend, asking Him to quiet the hearts of the people, to take their mind off what had happened and everything outside, and to think of Jesus.

As soon as he had finished praying, Moody opened a worn Bible and began to speak. "The Gospel is simple. We find it in its simplest form in John 3:16. 'For God so loved the world, that He gave His only begotten son, that whosoever believeth in Him should not perish, but have everlasting life.' " He held the Bible in one hand and began speaking of Jesus. There was no eloquence in his speech—except that of a fiery heart and a zeal that could not be contained. His words were simple, and he began to talk about how man had turned away from God. "Not just some men," he insisted firmly. "*All* men. As Romans tells us, 'All have sinned and come short of the glory of God.'

"The harlot and the murderer may be worse in our eyes than the man or woman who does not commit these sins, but we are all sinners in God's eyes. There is no difference." Then he began to speak about the effect of sin. "The wages of sin," he proclaimed, "is death. Most of you have heard sermons on hell fire, and I would warn you that any man or woman who goes out unprepared to meet God will forever dwell away from God. But, do you know, my dear friends, 'The wages of sin is death.' That word 'death' may not only refer to hell—it may refer to what is going on in some of your hearts right now. Some of you may have nothing but death in your soul even as you sit here."

For the next few minutes, Moody continued to speak on how sin and death did nothing but ruin peoples' lives. Cody sat there with his head dropped, thinking about all that had happened in his own life. When the preacher said, "Life comes from Jesus. He is the one source of life. 'In Him was life and the life was the light of men,' " Cody began to feel something of a battle stir in his heart. Though he sensed the power of Moody's words, a part of him felt a stubborn resistance to all he heard.

On and on the sermon went, though it was not as long as usual. Toward the last, Moody paused and asked with a voice filled with emotion, "What can I tell you about the Gospel? John the Baptist said it all. He saw Jesus one day, and he said, 'Behold the Lamb of God that taketh away the sin of the world.' " Moody's voice trembled slightly, and he cleared his throat. "That is what Jesus Christ does. He takes away the sins of the world and gives life. And I would that every man, and every woman, and every young person under the sound of my voice would know that aside from Him, there is no life, there is no joy."

Moody spoke for a few more moments, and then the service ended with an invitation. Moody invited those who needed prayer to come forward, and then he said a quick benediction.

At once, Buck turned to the young man and said, "Jim, I was wrong to drag you here." Cody looked up into his face and saw tears in the big man's eyes. "My ma was a Christian," said Buck, "and I shoulda listened to her. I wouldn't of led the kind of life I have."

As for Cody, he was stunned. The words of Dwight L. Moody had gone straight to his heart. Every time the name of Jesus was mentioned, he felt that he was being stabbed. There was something in that name, something in those words—"Behold the Lamb of God that taketh away the sin of the world"—that made him want to weep, and he struggled against it, not wanting to expose the tumult in his spirit.

The crowd was moving, and he found himself making his way to the end of the row of seats. He could hardly see, and when he got to the aisle, he heard a voice say, "My dear young friend, may I pray for you?"

Cody looked up and saw Dwight L. Moody standing there at the end of the row, looking at him with a compassionate expression. He said no more, and Cody knew then that this preacher would not beg, nor urge such a thing upon anybody. Cody wanted to run, but somehow feared to do that. Something within him welled up as he thought of his mother, and Laurie, and Sam, and others who had cared for him, and he suddenly bowed his head and shut his eyes. "Go ahead, Reverend."

Moody at once prayed a beautiful prayer. Laurie had come

up to stand close enough to Cody to hear the evangelist as he prayed, and tears flowed down her cheeks. Very simply, Dwight L. Moody prayed that the young man would find peace with God, and that the happiness and joy that come only in the Lord would come to rest in his heart. And he concluded simply, ". . . I ask you, Lord, in the name of Jesus, to put your hand on his life. Amen."

When Cody opened his eyes, Moody was already gone. Cody could bear no more. Choking back a sob, he shoved his way through the crowd and disappeared before Laurie could move.

Sam and Mac came up to stand by her, and the three of them stood, speechless.

"God got him here," Mac said, "and answered our prayers. But now the Word's got to do the work in his heart!"

Laurie stood there, tears running down her face. "Amen!" she whispered—and somehow she knew that Cody Rogers was facing the most trying hour of his life.

CHAPTER TWENTY-TWO

ALL KINDS OF LOVE

★　★　★　★

Laurie had entertained a hope that Cody would go back to hear Mr. Moody preach. However, the days sped by until it was time for the Wild West Show to move on, and he said nothing about it. She spoke to Sam one morning as they were preparing for the afternoon show and found that he had some serious regrets about what had happened.

"I wish Buck hadn't roped him and taken him to that service all trussed up like a turkey." The dark eyes of the young man had a sad look in them, and he suddenly kicked at the dust, sending a cloud of it flying. "Blast it, I know Buck meant well—but I can't think of anything much worse than trying to force a man to get saved!"

Laurie was wearing a brown outfit, consisting of a divided skirt, a white blouse, and a matching jacket. Her hat hung down on her back, suspended by a rawhide thong, and as she moved nervously, the jeweled spur glinted in the morning sunlight and jangled musically. "I know," she murmured quietly, "but Buck was just doing all he knew how. I—I don't guess I've done much better, Sam."

"Well, me neither," Sam muttered with remorse, shoving his hands in his pockets and looking over at Laurie quizzically. "What are we gonna do now?"

"I don't guess there's much of anything we can do, Sam—except just keep on praying."

"I'll sure do that," Sam nodded. "See you later. I'm going over to get a cup of coffee at the cook tent."

A few minutes after he left, Laurie looked up from where she was oiling her saddle and saw Cody as he crossed the lot headed for the corral. She quickly put the gear down, put a top on the bottle of oil, and marched across the lot to intercept him. "Hello, Cody," she said.

Cody turned around and faced her. His face was rather drawn, Laurie thought, and didn't have the usual happy light that made him so approachable. When he spoke, she noticed his words were clipped off a little shorter than usual. "Hello, Laurie." He hesitated, then asked, "Are you about ready to pull out? The show will be leaving tomorrow."

Laurie fell in beside him and the two ambled slowly toward the corral, where she leaned on the gate as he pulled his rope free and began spinning it in small circles.

"I guess so," she sighed, shaking her head. "You know, after a while, every town looks just about like every other town. Chicago looks like New York, and New York looks like Boston."

Cody gave her a quick glance. "Well, I guess London won't look like New York. That's what Colonel Cody is talking about, isn't it? I guess you'd like that." He made the rope rise in the air as if by magic, grow much smaller, and then spread out into a large loop. It flicked out and caught one of the tops of the corral posts, then he flipped it off and began making another loop. "Be lots for you to write about over there, wouldn't there?"

"I guess so. I've always thought I'd like to go see England, but—"

Cody slowly stroked the lariat and found that he was having difficulty even talking to Laurie. Finally, he looked up at her. "You know, Laurie, when I first came to this show, you were real happy. I remember how your eyes always lit up and how you were always laughing."

"Why, I guess I still am."

"No, you're not. You don't hardly ever laugh anymore," he said, and then his jaw clamped tight. "I guess I've been a burden to everybody. Made life miserable for my folks—and now I've come over here and made life about the same for you."

"Oh, Cody," she said quickly, and a warm light touched her eyes. She put her hand on his arm and shook her head. "Don't ever say that! We have our hard times. You have yours and I have mine, but I'm—I'm glad you came." She studied his lean, drawn face, took a deep breath, and asked a question that had been on her lips several times since they'd attended Moody's service in the large auditorium. "Have you—thought about what Mr. Moody said in his sermon?"

Cody dropped his eyes, and then when he lifted them, she saw an almost bottomless despair. "Yes, I have," he almost mumbled.

"You're not worried about hell, are you?"

Cody put his hands together, locked his fingers and squeezed, staring at them. "I guess I'll have to tell you that I am. For a long time after I went to prison, I didn't even want to believe in God. If you don't believe in God or the Bible, you don't have to believe in hell. It's all the same, isn't it?"

"I guess so, Cody," Laurie said softly.

"Well, ever since I heard Mr. Moody preach, it's just like— it's like a big cloud has been hanging over me! I can't sleep right, and I keep hearing what he said over and over again."

"I wish you'd pay attention to what he said about giving your heart to the Lord, Cody," Laurie said timidly. "I know it seems like a big step, but you're miserable the way you are."

"You're right about that."

The two of them stood there, the sun beating down, and Laurie tried her best to make some dent in the wall that Cody had built around himself. But there was a despair in him that she could not overcome. Finally, he nodded curtly and walked away. For a moment, Laurie stood there wondering if her prayers for Cody would ever be answered. Shaking her head sadly, she turned and walked back to her tent.

Later that morning Con came to see her with a determined look in his eye. She knew instantly what he had come for and became very defensive.

"Laurie," Con said evenly, "I've done all I know how to tell you I love you. So I'm gonna ask you one more time to marry me."

Laurie began to tell him again those things that she had already said and saw that the man was deeply hurt. She ended by saying, "Con, it wouldn't be fair to you. You don't want half a woman. Somewhere there's a girl who will love you with her whole heart, and you need to keep on looking for her."

"So, that's your answer." He turned on his heels and stalked away, his back stiff.

McGonigal had been watching the scene from across the room. Now he got up and ambled over to her and sat down beside Laurie. "I guess the boy was after you to marry him again, wasn't he?"

"Oh, Mac, I hate to hurt him, but it would never work."

McGonigal scratched his grizzled head, then shot her a careful look. "I'm glad," he murmured softly, in a voice not like his usual gruff tone at all, "that you don't jump at the first chance that's come along to get married. You don't make a man happy by agreeing to marry him unless you mean to give him everything you've got."

"I know that, Mac, but Con doesn't," sighed Laurie.

"It'll be all right," said Mac. "You stick to your guns."

Later that night at the show, Laurie kept her eyes open, looking for Con. She intended to try and encourage him, but he did not appear. And it was the next morning before Leona brought her the news. She came in from an early breakfast and said, "Did you hear about Con Groner?"

"Hear what, Leona?" asked Laurie, concern in her voice.

"Why, he quit the show," the slender girl said. "I was just talking to Nate Salsbury, and he told me Con came in, asked for his money, and left late yesterday afternoon."

"Did he—did he say why he was leaving?" asked Laurie haltingly.

Leona shrugged carelessly. "No, Nate didn't say, but these cowboys get an itch every now and then. Just have to get out and let off steam, I guess. I expect he'll be back before too long."

Laurie worried about Con, and later that morning, after she had gone through her act several times, she had another talk with Cody. She did not have to approach the subject, for Cody looked at her sharply. "I heard about Con Groner leaving the show," he said.

Laurie merely nodded, saying, "I guess he wanted a change."

Cody was wearing a pair of faded blue jeans with a chambray shirt that matched and his oldest pair of boots. He had been practicing roping the buffalo and was pretty well covered with dust from head to foot. Wiping his forehead with his arm, he gave her an odd look. "You're not telling all of it, are you, Laurie?"

"Why—I don't know what you mean," said Laurie defensively.

"You don't lie too well, Laurie." Cody allowed his eyes to rest on her, then added, "Almost everyone knows how Con's been asking you to marry him. He hasn't made any secret of it. I figure you turned him down."

"Yes, I did."

"Why? He ought to make a pretty good husband."

"I suppose so. But not my husband."

"Why not?"

"Because I don't love him." Laurie lifted her eyes and her lips trembled slightly. "You can understand that. A girl would never marry a man she didn't love, or shouldn't."

"Laurie, I don't know much about love. What makes you so sure about it? You've read too many books, I think sometimes, too many romances."

Laurie at once said, shaking her head, "Oh, Cody, there are all kinds of love. I love my father in one way, and I love my mother in another. They're two different people. Then, of course, I love Mac. Not like I love my father, that's something very special, just for him. Love is tied up with a person, and you can't get away from it."

"What about Sam? What kind of love have you got for him? He says you're kissing cousins."

"That's exactly right, we're cousins. His mother and my father—and your stepfather—are brothers and sister. And Sam is what he is, and I'm what I am, and together, we have a relationship."

Cody stared at her, then his shoulders seemed to sag. "I guess that's right for you, Laurie."

Suddenly, he turned and walked away, leaving her standing helplessly. She wanted to go after him, but she could not think of another thing to say. *Oh, why didn't he ask me how I felt about him,* she thought, *but could I have told him?* She knew that she could not have done it, for she believed that if Cody had any feelings for her, he would have to speak the first word.

★ ★ ★ ★

Sam Novak finished herding the buffalo into the pen, and as the huge, ungainly beasts moved inside in response to his urgings, he shouted, "If I wasn't a preacher, I could cuss! I never saw such contrary critters in all my life! Get on, there!"

"What's the matter, preacher? They botherin' you, them sweet, little woollies?" Buck Bronson had moved in beside him. Towering over Sam, he grinned and said, "Just be glad you don't have to put 'em to bed and tuck 'em in."

Sam glared at him and shook his head. "I won't be sorry to see the last of them," he muttered, then added, "Have you seen Cody?"

"He took off right after the show was over," Buck said. "I think he was going to town. He had a pretty urgent look about him, I'd say." Then a smile broke out on Buck's big face. "You don't reckon he's got a gal stashed away there, do you?"

"I don't think so," Sam murmured. He continued helping with the animals, keeping his eye out for Cody, but he never saw him.

It was after ten that night when Johnny Baker came into the tent that they shared. He looked a little the worse for wear; his hair was messed up, and there was a bruise under his right eye.

"What happened to you, Johnny?" Sam demanded.

"Oh, I had a little disagreement with a feller," he said. He plopped down on the cot and pulled off one boot, explaining, "I went into this saloon, you see, and there was this pretty little red-haired girl over there, so I went over and introduced myself."

He pulled off the other boot, holding it, and grinned at Sam. "But this feller that was with her, he took exception, so he pulled out his gun and pointed it at me. Pulled the trigger, too, but she snapped on empty." He tossed the boots down and started pulling off his shirt. "Well, sir, I tried to reason with him, but he picked up a chair and hit me over the head with it—and that's when the trouble started."

"I hope you learned something from it," Sam Novak said morosely.

"Sure did," Johnny Baker said. He leveled his pale blue eyes on Novak and grinned. "I learned not to ever let a man get the bulge on me. From now on, I'll go in swingin'!" He pulled his pants off, rolled under the blanket, then raised up on one elbow and said, "Hey, did you know Jim was in town having a toot?"

Instantly Novak was all attention. "You saw Logan?"

"See him? Why we hit half the saloons in town together. I tried to get him to come home with me, but he wouldn't hear nothing of it. Says he's gonna bust the town wide open, but I reckon that sheriff there'll stop that. I heard he was a pretty mean one. Lets a fellow get all drunk, then sneaks up and hits him over the head with that special blackjack of his and hauls him off to jail." He closed his eyes wearily, adding, "Then he slaps a big fine on him. Shore hate to see Logan get in a mess like that."

Instantly, Sam leaped to his feet, grabbed his hat, and ran out of the tent. Without hesitation, he saddled a horse he had bought for himself and took off at a gallop. *What could he be thinking!* he thought as he drove the animal hard toward the lights of the town half a mile away. *If he gets picked up, they might find out who he is.*

He had some trouble finding Cody, for there were a dozen saloons in the wide streets. It was in the sixth one that he found him loudly arguing with the bartender.

"Give me another drink, or I'll punch your ugly face in," Cody threatened.

The bartender, a burly man with a shock of black hair, reached under the counter, pulled a club out, and said, "I told you, cowboy, you've had enough. Now you walk out or get carried out."

"Carried out? We'll see who gets carried out," Cody yelled. He would have gone over the bar toward the saloonkeeper, but Sam managed to get to him and jerk him around. Cody's eyes were blurred from the effect of all the whiskey he had consumed. Not recognizing who had spun him around, he took a wild swing that caught Sam high on the forehead. It sent stars flashing in front of his eyes, and Novak was driven backward, flat on his back. He struggled to his feet and grabbed Cody's arm. "Come on, Jim. Let's get out of this place."

Cody blinked his eyes and licked his lips. He was so drunk he had to focus carefully, then he mumbled, "Oh, Sam, I didn't know it was you."

Pushing Cody toward the door he muttered, "Come on," and muscled him out of the saloon.

When they were outside, Cody asked, "What are you doing here, Sam? Did you come into town to get drunk, too?"

"I came to take you back."

"Not going back," Cody said stubbornly, stumbling toward his horse. He also had bought an animal for his own use, and Novak saw that the saddle blanket was tied up into a roll. "I'm leavin'—gettin' out of here," Cody mumbled.

Sam stared at him and shook his head. "Why, you can't do that," argued Novak.

"Why can't I? What good am I doing here?" Cody's mouth was tightly drawn with a bitter line, and his eyes, though glazed, were heavy with anger and doubt. "All I'm doing is messin' up lives, so I'm gettin' out."

Sam tried to reason with him, using every argument he could think of, but Cody simply stood there shaking his head, insisting that he was leaving the show and moving on.

"All right," said Sam finally. "If you're leaving, I'm going with you. Just give me time to go back and get my stuff."

Cody shook his head. "I'm headin' down that road. We'll pass right by the show. You can get your stuff on the way, but, Sam, don't tell anybody."

"I'll have to tell," Sam insisted. "It wouldn't be fair to Colonel Cody just to pull out."

Cody made several attempts to get his foot in the stirrup, then awkwardly pulled himself into the saddle. "All right, tell him anything you want to. Just say I'm gone to the devil." Without another word, he turned his horse around and began moving down the street at a trot. Sam leaped on his own horse, rode up to Cody, and all the way back tried to persuade him to change his mind. When he saw it was hopeless, he said, "Don't go so fast. I'll catch up with you."

"Better hurry it up, then. I want to get out of here."

Sam galloped his horse into the arena and went at once to

Nate Salsbury. He told him what had happened, and Salsbury shook his head sadly. "That's too bad. You go with him, Sam, and bring him back. After he gets over his drunk, he'll feel differently."

"I'll do the best I can—but I can't promise anything," Sam answered. He turned and mounted again and caught up with Cody a quarter of a mile down the road.

"Well, I got my stuff," he said. He determined to be cheerful about the whole thing and began talking about some places they might go, but he received nothing but a stony silence for his efforts. Finally, after riding for several hours, Cody became so sick that he could hardly sit on his horse. Sam gathered the reins of both animals, pulled them over to a grove of trees where he tied them, and then made camp.

Cody spent the next two hours throwing up. He was unaccustomed to liquor in such large quantities, and finally he fell into a fitful sleep. Sam sat there staring into the fire, poking it and watching the sparks fly upward. "Well," he said softly, "the Good Book says man is born to trouble as the sparks fly upward, and I guess that's what Cody's in." He sat there thinking about his friend and praying for a long time.

★ ★ ★ ★

Sam had figured that one drunk might be enough to purge Cody, and that when he sobered up, he'd be willing to go back. But for five days the pair rode along, and every day Cody would stop at a town and buy whiskey, then proceed to drink himself unconscious. Every night he would fall into his blanket in oblivion, leaving Sam to do all the work. He ate almost nothing, and on the fifth day, Sam found a place to camp just outside of a small town. Cody was already bleary-eyed and half-sick. "We've run out of grub," Sam said. "You go on to bed, and I'll go find us something to eat."

"Don't want anything to eat," Cody murmured. But Sam ignored him and rode away from the camp. He was back in half an hour, but discovered Cody was already asleep, tossing fitfully, his legs jerking.

"Don't know how long this can go on," Sam said to himself. "He's gonna kill himself drinking." After cooking a meager supper and eating it, Sam sat there staring at the fire and praying hard for his young friend. Finally, he spread out his bedroll and went to bed.

The next morning, the sunlight fell on Sam's face, awakening him. He blinked like an owl in the sunlight and sat up. He looked across to Cody, and his eyes flew open when he saw Cody was gone. "Cody," he called out, jumping out of his blanket and looking around. Then he saw Cody's horse was gone.

He started scrambling into his boots, when all of a sudden he saw a white sheet of paper weighted down by a rock almost at his feet. Snatching it up, he read the brief note:

> Sam, I'm going to the devil, but there's not any sense your going along with me. Don't try to follow me. You've been a good friend, but there's nothing you or anybody else can do for me. Think of me sometimes. Cody.

Sam immediately threw his gear together, strapped it on his horse, and rode down the highway at a fast clip. Though he searched all day, he could not find a trace of a trail to follow, and he knew that Cody must have cut off the main road. "He could be anywhere," he groaned in despair, and though he asked around at several places at the small towns, no one had seen anyone that fit Cody's description.

Reluctantly, he started back to the town where the Wild West Show was, not knowing anything else to do. It was a long trip back, for his horse grew lame, and Sam became more morose as he went along.

On the third night, he had made camp, telling himself, "I'll have to trade this dumb horse off. The show'll leave before I get back." He was sitting in front of the fire frying bacon in a pan, when suddenly he heard the sound of a horse approaching out of the darkness. He was still a little wary of company and pulled the .44 out of his blankets and held it loosely. Then he called out, "Who's there?"

"Me—Cody."

At once, Sam's heart leaped, and he tossed the gun down and stepped forward eagerly to where the horseman came out of the darkness. "Cody!" he said, grabbing at him as he slid out of the saddle. "Man, am I glad to see you! I thought, for sure, I'd seen the last of you."

Cody looked even more lean and drawn than he had when he left. But by the flickering light of the fire, Sam saw that something was different. Cody's eyes were clear now, and there was a slight smile on his face. "I thought you'd be back to the show by this time, Sam."

"My horse is lame," he said. "Come on, sit down and eat. You look starved."

"Reckon I could take a little nourishment," Cody agreed. He sat by the fire and devoured the plate of food Sam had handed him. Setting it down, he picked up a mug of coffee and sat back and sighed with pleasure. "That's the best supper I ever had in my life, Sam."

"Where have you been, Cody?" Sam asked eagerly. "Are you going back to the show?"

"Well, one thing at a time," Cody said as he gazed across the fire at his friend. He took off his hat and put it down to one side, and his hair fell down over his forehead. "Where have I been? Well, in one sense, I've been twenty miles down that road there." He gave Sam a curious glance, and the corners of his lips turned up. "But I guess I've been at a place you know about."

"Where's that?" asked Sam, trying to figure out why Cody was so different. Only three days before, he was so drunk he could hardly see to ride. Now, Cody sat there with a curious humor flickering in his eyes.

Cody looked down into the fire, picked up a stick, and began poking at it, watching the sparks and listening to the crackle. He paused so long that Sam thought he hadn't heard the question, but finally Cody looked up and said, in a strange, rather tense voice, "I guess you'd have to say I've been with God."

Sam Novak could not have been more shocked if Cody had said he'd been on the planet Venus! Hope leaped up into his eyes, and he demanded excitedly, "Tell me about it. What do you mean you've been with God?"

Cody related how that for hours he had ridden along and still continued to get drunk, but finally he had run out of whiskey. "I woke up one morning," he said quietly, "sick and ready to die—and hoping I would. There was a creek there, and all I could do was crawl over and get a drink of water, trying to wash my face. Well, I sat there for a long time and was real quiet, and I thought about what a mess my life had become. And I thought about you, and Laurie, and my mother and stepfather, and about all the people that have been praying for me. I remembered Reverend Moody's words and his prayer." His voice grew mild as he continued to speak, staring into the fire, "I don't know what brought it on, all I knew was I suddenly was so sick of living, I couldn't go on. I called out to God and asked Him to kill me—and I meant it, too! I think I told God if he didn't do the job, I'd take care of it." He grinned ruefully over at Sam, shaking his head. "I don't know whether I would have done it or not, but as it turned out, I didn't have to."

Sam had been intrigued by the story, and he whispered, "Tell me about it, what did you do?"

"Well, I was in such a hole that I didn't know *what* to do. Finally, after about two hours of wrestling with it, I just kind of gave up, I guess. I'd heard the Gospel enough to know that all you have to do is call on God and ask for His forgiveness. That always seemed odd to me—but that was all I had left, Sam, so that's what I done. I just said, 'Jesus, I've been wrong all my life, but I ask you to come into my life, and if there's anything there you can use, just take it, cause I want to know you.' Sam," he said, "I never would have believed it! But right then, all the doubt, and all the fear, all the anger and bitterness—why they just blew away. And I knew that that couldn't be anybody but God!"

Sam Novak had seen other people come to God in his day, but there was something real special sitting there listening to Cody explain how he had given his life to Jesus. "That's wonderful, Cody." Sam reached over and clapped Cody on the back. "And you turned right around and came back?"

"I figure I needed to tell you and Laurie about it. And Mac, too." He looked over and smiled. "You know, I thought it'd be gone the next morning, but that sense of peace is still there."

"That's the peace of God, Cody. The world doesn't give it, doesn't have it to give, and can *never* take it away."

The two sat there for hours, and never had Sam been so glad to see anyone come out of the darkness and into the light as his friend.

CHAPTER TWENTY-THREE

"I CAN'T DO IT!"

★ ★ ★ ★

"I'm so happy for you, Cody!"

Cody had ridden back with Sam, and the pair caught up with the show. At once Cody had gone to Laurie's tent. Instantly she had seen the change in him, but before she could speak, he said, "Well, you can believe in your prayers, Laurie."

That was when Laurie had exclaimed her gladness and joy, and she insisted that he tell her the whole story. He sat down on Leona's cot across from Laurie. She leaned forward expectantly, her eyes bright, her hands clenched tightly together.

"I don't have to tell you how low I've been, Laurie. And to tell the truth, I don't think a man could get much lower. So, when I rode out of here, I was about as drunk as a man could be, and if Sam hadn't come after me, I expect I'd be sitting in a jail right now." He related the story and ended by saying, ". . . so out there, I just called on God and asked Him to forgive me and change me, and it's all been different ever since."

"You'll have to tell your folks," Laurie said instantly. "They'll be so glad to hear it!"

Cody nodded, then said cheerfully, "You're right about that. Mother's prayed for me ever since I was in the cradle, I guess."

The two sat there, and Laurie basked in the light of the new assurance that now rested on Cody's face. He was different on the outside, and she knew that reflected a change in his heart. Finally, she exclaimed, "We've got to go tell Mac. He's prayed as hard for you as anybody."

"All right. Let's go find him."

They found the grizzled ex-cavalryman lying on his bunk, staring up at the ceiling. At Cody's call, he came off his bed at once, took one look at Cody and a grin broke out on his face. "Well, I see the good Lord finally caught up with you, didn't He, son?"

"That's right," Cody smiled. "And I was never so glad to be caught in my life!" He went on at Mac's insistence and told the whole story again. This time Laurie enjoyed it even more than the first time. Finally, when he finished, Mac nodded firmly. "Well, that's only the first step. A lot more to go, though, before you're really home."

Cody sobered instantly. "Yes. You're right about that, Mac. I don't know what's going to happen, but I know I'm trusting in God." He shrugged, and a rueful look crossed his face. "I've trusted myself, and see where it got me. Now, I'm going to see what God will do!"

The news of Cody's return quickly spread throughout the troupe, and Buffalo Bill himself came by to welcome the young man back. "Well, you ran off and left me in the lurch, young feller, but from what I hear, you done the necessary." He hesitated, then shrugged his wide shoulders. "Not much for church myself, but I'm always glad to see young folks starting out right."

Nate Salsbury came by with a warm smile, hugged Cody's shoulders, and one by one, as they met, Cody was welcomed back. Finally, it was show time, and he said to Sam with a grin, "I've probably forgotten all I know about roping."

He had not, though, and when he went out to perform, he tried several new tricks, all of which worked and had the crowd applauding wildly. When he left the arena, Laurie threw herself toward him. He caught her and held her in amazement, enthralled by the sparkling light in her eyes. "I'm so proud of you, Cody!" she said. "Now let's go write the letter to your mother—no, let's go into town and send a telegraph."

"I guess it better be a letter," Cody said thoughtfully. "I want to say some things that I wouldn't want to be made public."

"Of course," Laurie nodded. "Why don't you go write it, and then you and I will take it to the post office."

Cody went at once to the cook tent, commandeered part of a table off to one side, and sat down and wrote a long letter. It was a difficult letter for him to write, and he would much rather have told it in person. Finally, however, he finished, put it in an envelope, sealed it, and addressed it. Then, rising, he went to find Laurie and nodded, "I've got it all done."

"Uncle Dan and Aunt Hope will be so thrilled!" said Laurie. "Come on, I'm ready."

They turned to go, but before they had made two steps, a voice rang out. "Hold it right there, Rogers."

At the sound of his real name, Cody froze. Then he turned slowly to see Con Groner not ten feet away. The cowboy had a .44 in his hand leveled directly at Cody's heart. "What's wrong with you, Con?" he asked evenly.

"I reckon you already know," Con said, a smirk on his face. His eyes flickered over to Laurie, and he said, "I couldn't let you go on like this, Laurie. This fellow's a murderer, and a convict—and I don't know what else. I saw you falling in love with him, and I knew it wouldn't be right. He couldn't make you happy."

Laurie spoke up at once. "Con, you don't understand. Cody never killed anybody. He was unjustly accused."

"When I was a lawman," Groner said evenly, "I never caught a guilty man. They might be standing over the body with the gun smoking, but they all deny it, every one of them. And I reckon this one's no different."

"You do what you have to do, Con," said Cody.

"I aim to. I've been gone now, lookin' for the flyer on you, and I found it. Here it is." He reached into his pocket, pulled it out, and held it in one hand. "Shot a man in the back, I hear from the authorities up your way. I didn't figure you for that sort, but you never can tell about a man."

Con moved closer, till he was only a few feet away. "I don't have any cuffs, so you just turn around and don't make any funny moves."

Laurie was almost petrified with fear. She cried out, "Con, you can't do this!"

Cody was turning to put his back to Groner, but he saw as

Laurie spoke that the cowboy twisted to face her, so that the gun was pointed at the ground. Instantly, he lunged at Groner, with one hand striking down at the fist that held the gun, knocking it loose with a single blow. Groner cried out shortly, but he had no time to do more, for with his right hand, Cody sent a powerful blow that caught him on the point of the chin, snapping his head back. Groner fell to the ground and lay still.

Cody shook his head, a bitter expression on his lips. "I've got to get away, Laurie."

"Don't do it. You'll be running forever," Laurie pleaded.

"What would you have me do? Go back into that prison? I couldn't stand it, Laurie." He reached out and took her hand. "I'll go back. I'll try to find out who really did the killing I was accused of."

"You'd be recognized immediately," Laurie said.

Cody shook his head stubbornly, and then looked around, his mind racing. They were behind a lot where the horses were kept, and there were no cowboys in sight. Quickly, he ran to the corral, pulled a rope down, and tied Groner's hands behind his back, and then fastened a gag. "I've got to get out of here," he said, his face pale. "There's nothing for me here now. I've got to go."

Laurie hesitated for one brief moment. He saw her face change, and she said abruptly, "I'm going with you."

"Why, Laurie, you can't—"

Laurie shook her head fiercely. Now that she had made up her mind, there was no hesitation in her movements. "I'll get Star, you get your horse. Drag Con over here and tie him to this pole. We don't have long—come on!"

Cody tried to argue, but she was gone at once. He stood there looking down at Con, who was beginning to stir, then, not knowing what else to do, dragged the unconscious man over to a part of the fence and tied him to it. Seeing that Con was slowly coming to, he whirled around and ran to the corral, roped his horse, and saddled him. As he finished tying the cinch, he looked up to see Laurie riding toward him on Star. The sun caught her jeweled spur, and it glittered brightly.

"Ride out slowly," he said. "Nobody will notice us that way."

"All right, Cody," she said. "I'm ready."

The two of them rode slowly around, circling the camp. No one paid any attention to them, and they were a mile away when Laurie exclaimed, "I should have told Mac, and you've got to tell Sam."

"We can't risk going back," Cody said. His lips grew firm and he turned to her. "But you ought to go back, Laurie. You can tell them what happened."

"No." Her voice was adamant, and when she looked at him, her lips were as tight as his. There was a stubbornness in her, and her backbone was straight as she sat in the saddle. Then she put the full force of her large eyes on him and said, "I'm not much for giving up on a man, Mr. Rogers. We Winslows were never known for that!"

Cody grinned and shrugged his shoulders. "Well, I've noticed that about Dan and Tom." They were out of sight of the showground, but he knew the time was short. "It'll make it harder if you come, Laurie. Now they'll be looking for a man and a woman—lots easier to find than just a single rider."

"We'll do what we can," Laurie said simply.

They rode along for a while and finally spurred their horses into a slow gallop. For two hours, they kept them at a good pace, turning off the main road, and finally onto a road that twisted and turned through fresh growth timber. When they stopped to give the horses a few moments to rest and a drink at a small stream, Cody said, "You know, Laurie, I was thinking about something Sam tried to explain to me. About the way God is."

Looking up at him, she asked, "What was that, Cody?"

"Well, he said that we see things in one scene at a time, like we saw yesterday, and then we saw last night, and now we see this morning, then after a while, we'll see night again. You know—in little blocks like that." He shook his head, took his hat off, and wiped his forehead. "But Sam says God's not like that. He says the Bible says that He's the God of yesterday, today, and forever."

"I think that's right." A memory touched her, and her lips softened. "You know, Cody, my dad told me something once that really surprised me. He said, 'God can never be disappointed in you, Laurie.' I was surprised at that, but he went on to say, 'To be disappointed in someone, you have to expect something out of them, and then they have to fail you, and it catches you by surprise. But God is never surprised, because He knows all things that are going to happen.' " She looked at him with a slight smile. "Isn't that strange to think that God knows everything? He knows what's going to happen to us tomorrow."

"That's what Sam said." He patted his horse and looked over at her. "He said it's like a parade. At a certain corner, somebody standing there would see one group pass, another wagon, and then, one by one, they'd all pass. And he'd see them one at a time. But if someone were up in a tall building, he'd not only see that corner, he'd see the beginning of the parade and the end of the parade, all at the same time. Sam said that's what God's like." He arched his back, stretched his arms, then looked over at her. "I think that's hopeful, don't you, Laurie? That we're not alone, and that God knows all about us?"

"Yes, it is, Cody." She had been afraid, but now the fear left and she smiled at him fully. "God will watch out for us. We'll be faithful to Him, and He'll be faithful to help us."

★　★　★　★

Cody stepped off his horse, looked around, and then said wearily, "I guess we're safe enough here, Laurie. I'll make a fire, and you can put the blankets down."

"All right, Cody." Laurie was worn to exhaustion. They had ridden hard for four days, staying off the main roads, always seeking the hill country, the rural regions, and staying away from farmhouses except when it was absolutely necessary. They had seen a few people but had talked to almost no one. Now, as she slipped out of the saddle, the strain of the days on the trail overtook her, and her legs nearly gave way. Then she tightened her lips, shook her head in self-disgust, and began pulling the bedrolls free from the horses.

By the time she had made the beds, Cody had gathered dry wood, kindled a small fire, and gotten out the cooking utensils. "What have we got for supper?" he asked wearily.

Laurie looked at the small supply sack. "One chunk of bacon and two potatoes." She smiled across the fire at him and said, "Would you rather have bacon with potatoes—or potatoes with bacon, Mr. Rogers?"

Cody smiled and shook his head. "We've got to do better than this. We'll have to ride into town and get some supplies."

"I brought enough money, I think, to do us for a while," Laurie said quickly. "Why don't you let me go in and get them?"

He stared at her and shook his head. "A strange woman riding into a small town on a horse like that, dressed like you are. That would be too suspicious. Besides, everybody'll be looking."

Laurie began to speak cheerily as she put the potatoes in the coals to bake and covered them. While they waited, she spoke of her life. As they had sat around the campfire night after night, they had talked about their childhoods till now they knew each other very well. Finally, the food was ready, and she raked the potatoes out, peeled the jackets off, and cut them in two with a knife. The steam rose from the white, meaty inside, and she put one on his plate and the other on hers. "Is the bacon all done?" she asked.

He had been roasting it over the fire and now drew it back carefully and cut it in two, giving her one portion and keeping the other for himself. They ate slowly, knowing there was not enough, but they enjoyed what they had to eat.

After they finished washing down the meager meal with water from the creek, they sat silently, staring into the fire. The night closed in like a cloak about them. There were no stars in the sky, and except for the pale flicker of the yellow flames, there was no light at all.

Cody leaned back against a tree, put his hands behind his head, and stared across the fire. For a long time, the quietness reigned, broken only by the barking of a dog from some farmhouse far off.

Finally, he knew he had to do something. "Laurie," he said, "we can't go on like this. It's no fit life for you."

"I'll be all right, Cody," Laurie said quickly. She got to her feet, picked up two sticks, and added them to the campfire. As she did, he rose and reached over and took her arm. "No, I can't put you through this. It's not right. You're a young woman, beautiful, and you've got everything a man would want."

His words caught at her. He had never said anything like this, and now she turned to face him. The planes of his face were thrown into sharp shadows by the flickering flames, the hollows of his eyes seemed very deep, and his cheeks were angular. She had long thought he was a fine-looking young man, but now she knew that didn't really matter. She whispered, "Do you really think so, Cody? What you just said."

He was taken aback by her question. "Do I think so? Why, I've always thought so," he said. Looking down at her, he could see the black hair, almost as dark as the night itself, as it framed her face. Her black eyes were wide and looked at him intently. He could see that she was tired, but she had not uttered one single complaint. "Most women I know would have quit a long time ago, and I don't know why you don't."

"But did you mean what you said about—about me being beautiful?" asked Laurie hesitantly.

"Why, Laurie, you're the most beautiful woman I've ever seen," he said, surprise in his voice. "I thought you knew that!"

The words seemed to hang in the air, and he saw her face relax. Her face was turned up, and he saw her lips grow soft and tender. Then, somehow, the pressures of the times that they had, the dangers, all seemed to fade, and all he knew was this slim, beautiful woman who stood so close to him. With almost a moan, he reached out and pulled her to him. He held her, his face pressed against hers, as he whispered, "Laurie—Laurie, you don't know how I feel, how I love you."

She was absolutely still in his arms, but then when she drew her head back, he saw tears making silver tracks down her smooth cheeks. Her lips trembled, and she said, "Do you? Do you, Cody?"

"Yes."

"Well—I love you, too," she whispered, and her eyes were blinded by tears. With a gesture completely free and wild, she reached up, pulled his head down, and pressed her lips against his. Her hands tightened around his neck as she clung to him possessively. As for Cody, the touch of her soft figure against his sent riotous emotions along his nerves. Her lips were softer than anything he had ever imagined. He thought as he held her, *I love her so, but I'll never have her.*

Slowly, he pulled his head back, but he held on to her, putting his cheek next to hers and saying, "I've got to go give myself up."

Laurie was very still, but finally she nodded. "I think you do, but first, we've got to go tell your parents."

He held her for a moment, savoring everything about her. The sweet femininity that he had not appreciated, but he now knew was his whole life. Then, as he stepped back and held her arms he said, "We may never have any more than this, Laurie."

"Yes, we will," she said fiercely, throwing her arms around him and holding him close, as if he were a hurt child. "We'll have more than this. God wouldn't let it be otherwise!"

They clung together for a long time, the silence broken only by the horses chomping at the grass and kicking up their hoofs from time to time. Finally, Cody and Laurie moved apart. When they lay down on their blankets, Cody said, "Tomorrow, we'll go home."

Her answer was soft and tremulous, yet there was faith in it, and in her eyes, if only he could have seen it. "Yes, Cody. Home—that's where we'll go."

CHAPTER TWENTY-FOUR

A MATTER OF FAITH

★ ★ ★ ★

Both Laurie and Cody treasured the memories of the days that comprised their journey back to the ranch in Wyoming. They continued to avoid the populated areas, and for days they rode along half-deserted back roads. The weather was perfect; the nights were cool and nice, and the days balmy. Once Cody turned to Laurie with a smile, saying, "You couldn't ask for better weather than this, could you?"

Laurie had glanced at him quickly and wanted to ask if he was worried about the days to come. She thought perhaps that he was storing up the beauty of the countryside, the wonderful weather, against the time when he would be locked up in a gray cell again. But she saw no sign of anxiety in his clear, blue eyes and merely nodded, "It would be nice if we could go on like this forever, wouldn't it, Cody?"

He had smiled at her but had shaken his head. "Yes, but it can't be like that."

By day they rode at an even pace across wide prairies, skirting mountains that lifted up into the sky, as they inched farther toward the northwest, camping every night beside some kind of water. Sometimes it was a flowing river that they had to swim their horses through, but more often, it was a trickling stream that provided music as well as fresh water. Cody had bought a rifle at a small store and used it to bring down enough game for them. Usually, this meant a rabbit, which abounded wherever they rode, but twice he managed to shoot a deer. The second time he had gone out they had made camp early, beside a small brook, and Cody had said, "Bound to be some deer coming down for a drink of water at sundown. You make camp, and I'll go see if I can bring one down."

"All right, Cody," said Laurie as she started to gather wood for a fire.

Cody left, moved up stream until he found deer signs, and found a small grove of scrub oak to conceal himself in. Moving into the cover, he stood there, the rifle cocked but held loosely over his arm, studying the scenery. He enjoyed the sights, including more than one rabbit that came to drink. Finally a family of coons sauntered up, including four small ones, and he enjoyed their antics, thinking, *They look just like bandits with those masks, but they sure do seem to be having fun.* He stood there until late afternoon shadows began to descend, closing like a curtain around him, turning the eastern sky into orange fireworks. The quietness soaked into his spirit, and he could not help but think, *This may be the last.* But he forced the thought out of his mind, as he had for the past two weeks, and now settled himself in to wait. It grew almost dark, and he was ready to give up, when suddenly a big buck with a rack of huge antlers stepped out from the bush across the creek, came to the water, and began to drink. Slowly Cody raised the rifle, centered on the heart of the magnificent animal, and then he hesitated. *One pull of the trigger, and he's gone forever,* he thought. He admired the sleek muscles, the proud look, and the fine, large eyes. He thought about what a miracle it was for God to make such a creature, and was surprised, for he would never have thought this before. He had killed hundreds of deer, and never once had it occurred to him that God had anything to do with it.

He sighed, and the animal immediately threw his head up and bolted. Cody regretfully sent his shot, which caught the buck in midstride and brought him to the ground. Cody ejected the shell, went over, splashed across the creek, and found the animal's eyes already glazed with death. "Too bad," he murmured softly, stroking the rough coat. Then he put the thought out of his mind. Pulling out his sheath knife, he rapidly dressed the animal, and regretfully left most of it, taking only as much as they could use for the next two or three days.

"Cody, you got one!" Laurie said as he walked back into camp with a load of meat in one hand and the rifle in the other.

"Cook this fellow up," Cody grinned. "We'll have a dinner fit for a king tonight. And a queen," he added.

She smiled and flushed slightly at his words, then began stirring the fire up to roast the deer meat.

An hour later, they were sitting before the fire, eating the delicious steaks hungrily. Cody took a bite, chewing it thoughtfully, and said, "I hated to kill this fellow. That's funny isn't it? I must have killed a hundred deer and never once thought about it."

"Why was it hard for you?" Laurie asked. She had eaten her fill and had opened a can of peaches. Dividing it into two portions, she put half of it into a cup and handed it to him. She fished out a golden wedge-shaped slice with her fingers and stuck it into her mouth.

"You greedy girl," Cody laughed. "You're gonna choke! Never saw a kid that went after sweets like you do."

Laurie did almost choke, but when she swallowed, she made a face at him. "I'm not a kid," she said. "And you're just as bad. Now, what about the deer?"

He sat there, enjoying the warm sweetness of the peaches, and explained to her that he had thought how marvelous the deer was.

"There was a poet named Walt Whitman," Laurie said. "He was a nurse for the Union during the Civil War, and he wrote a book called *Leaves of Grass*. Some things," she said, "I never liked about it, but he had one thing in there that I will never forget." She held up her hand and wiggled her thumbs, quoting the poet: "The narrowest hinge in my hand puts to scorn all machinery."

Cody cocked his head, his eyes narrowing as he thought about it. "I don't understand."

Her eyes grew bright, reflecting the firelight, and she said, "Don't you see? People talk about how wonderful it is, a steamboat, for example, a machine that has all that power."

"Well, it is pretty wonderful, isn't it?"

"Not as wonderful as this." She moved her thumb back and forth. "That's a hinge, you see, and how hard do you think it would be for a man to make that? This hand—these fingers— all the human body, he's saying, is a greater marvel than any piece of machinery ever built."

Understanding dawned on Cody, and he nodded. "Why, that's true, isn't it? Any man can get smart enough to make a boiler, or a locomotive, but nobody could ever make a human being. Nobody except God, that is."

"That's what Whitman said. I remember another line." She quoted it slowly, as if savoring the words. "He said, 'A mouse is miracle enough to stagger sextillions of infidels.' " She smiled, then nodded.

She waved her hand toward the fiery stars that glittered overhead. "I don't see how anyone could look at that and not know that someone made it all. They didn't make themselves."

They went on talking, their voices low; sometimes they laughed, and finally, it grew late. Cody got up, walked to the creek and filled the bucket with water, and brought it back to hand it to her. "Wash some of that down," he said. She rose to her feet and took a drink, then handed it back. The moon overhead was round and pale and brilliant, shedding its beams over the two of them. Tossing the can down, he reached out and took her hands. "This trip," he said, "these days together, I'll never forget them, Laurie."

"No. Neither of us will," she whispered. She was acutely aware of his hands, and of his eyes that were fixed on hers. Looking up at him, she said, "We'll tell our grandchildren about it. How that we rode all the way across the country together when we were young."

"They'd be shocked," he said with a smile. "They'll wonder, a man and a woman not married spending all that time together." He suddenly looked at her, aware of the beauty of her face, and the attractiveness of her slim form. "It's another miracle," he said, "that as much as I love you, there's not been one single thing wrong with this trip."

"No," she said. She loosed her hand and put it upon his chest, saying, "You've been wonderful, and no man could have been more thoughtful, under these circumstances. Most men would have tried at least to take some advantage, but you never have."

Cody looked embarrassed and said, "Well, I can't always say my record's been that clean, but with you it's different."

"Cody," she said suddenly, "when we get to your home, I want us to be married."

"Why, that's crazy, Laurie!" Cody stared at her and shook his head, his jawline growing tense as he said, "I'll be going to jail for a long time!"

"I don't care," she said. "I don't believe it in the first place—God is going to do something. But even if you did, for the rest of our lives, you're my husband, and I would never have another man."

The sweetness of her, the gentleness, and the beauty leaped out at him. He reached out and tenderly pulled her close; his hands were gentle as they went around her, and his arms were firm, but not possessive. He held her tightly, as she pressed her face against his chest. They stood that way for a long time, then she lifted her face for his kiss. He kept his lips on hers for a long time, then lifted his head. His voice was husky as he said, "There never was a woman like you, Laurie Winslow!"

Laurie felt a loneliness as he stepped back, and she said in a small voice, "We'd better get to sleep, Cody. I guess we'll get to the ranch in a few days, won't we?"

"I figure two," Cody said. The thought so troubled him that he drew a hand across his face and shook his head. "I'll miss all this," he said.

Laurie said, "All my life, my folks read stories to me out of the Bible, and almost all of them involved somebody in big trouble. I guess all people have their troubles." She looked at him and said quietly, "And I reckon ours are bigger than most right now."

"How do you have faith when everything looks black as midnight?" Cody asked. He was sober as he stood there, his body somewhat tense, as he struggled with the age-old question. "How do you believe God when there's not a thing you can see to make you believe Him?"

"That's what faith is, Cody. It's like it's some dark night—you're riding your horse and you come to a precipice. You have to go on, but the night is so dark," she added, getting carried away with her story. "You know you've got to jump your mount down whatever it is. It might be a canyon a thousand feet deep, and it might be only a dropoff of two feet. But you've got to do it."

"I believe I'd turn around and go the other way," Cody smiled gently. Then the smile disappeared. "But this time there is no other way, is there? So I guess we'll just have to take the jump of faith."

"We will, Cody. And God will answer. You'll see."

★ ★ ★ ★

"Well, there it is. We made it."

The two riders pulled up at the top of the hill and looked down at the Circle W Ranch, which was barely illuminated by the pale gleams of the sun rising over the mountains to the east. They had ridden at an even pace, each hour during the last two days seeming to tick off slowly in their minds, tolling like a warning bell. They had spent the remaining time as best they could—talking, enjoying each other, reveling in the setting—but now that they were here, Cody became glum. "I wish this ranch were another thousand miles up in Canada. But, there it is, and we've got to go in."

"Before we go," Laurie said, "I want you to promise me that you'll marry me, and we'll see this thing through together."

Cody lowered his head. A struggle went on in him and he said, "I'll promise you this. If your parents say it's all right, I'll do it."

Laurie stared at him and nodded. "That's a bargain." She pulled her hat down firmly on her forehead, came up with a smile, and said, "Come on. I can't wait to see their faces when we come riding in."

They rode down the slope and across the pasture and finally, into the yard itself. Just as they rode in, someone stepped out on the porch. "Who is it?"

Cody pulled his horse up and stared at the tall man, saying, "It's me, Dad."

Dan Winslow was hard hit by the greeting. He swallowed hard, then turned and called inside, "Hope—come here quick!"

Then he turned back, his eyes fixed on the pair who were dismounting now and walking toward him. Hope stepped out onto the porch and said, "What is it—" and then she saw Cody and the young woman. At once, her face lost its heaviness, and a smile broke across her lips. She ran across the yard, threw herself into Cody's arms, and held him fiercely, her face pressed against his chest. They stood there holding each other. Dan came up to stand beside them, putting his hand on Cody's shoulder, then turning to face the young woman who was standing off to one side. "Well, don't I get a hug, Laurie? Looks like your favorite uncle deserves that."

Laurie had felt left out of the scene, and immediately she went to the tall man, who put his arms around her, then kissed her firmly on the cheek. There was a moment's silence, then Hope drew back from Cody and tried to laugh. It was not much of a laugh, but it was something. "Come into the house," she said. "You two must be worn out."

"I guess we're all right, Mom," Cody said, following the two as they stepped up on the porch and entered the kitchen.

As they walked through the door, Cody gave Laurie's arm a squeeze. She looked up at him, and he could see the tears gathering in her eyes, but she dashed them away and whispered, "They're so glad to see you, Cody."

"I just started breakfast," Hope said nervously. "I don't know if I can cook or not, I'm so excited to see you. Tell us about your trip while I finish this breakfast."

As Hope moved from the stove to the table, unable to be still, Dan said, "We've been trying to find you ever since you left the Wild West Show."

Cody stared at him. "How did you know about it?"

"Got a wire from Sam Novak. He's a nephew of mine, you know. He told us what happened and said to be on the lookout for you." His light blue eyes fell on Laurie, and he said gently, "That was a hard trip for a woman, Laurie."

"Oh, it wasn't so bad," Laurie murmured.

"Tell us all about it," Hope said. She listened as Cody described their trip across the country, and finally set the food on the table. She sat down, saying, "You ask the blessing, Dan, and let's have a good one."

She was not disappointed, for Dan Winslow blessed the food briefly, then poured out his heart in thanksgiving to God for bringing his son home. When he lifted his eyes, they saw that he was tremendously moved.

They ate a little of the food, for all of them were under too much pressure and tension.

Finally, Cody shoved his plate back and shook his head. "I've got to tell you something," he said. "I'm going to give myself up, no other way."

"And I'm going to marry him," Laurie said defiantly, holding her head up.

"Even though he'll be in prison?" Hope asked quickly.

"Yes."

That single word had so much force in it that Dan and Hope both looked at her more closely. "That's pretty hard, tying yourself to a man who may not get out for years," he said. "You're a young woman, you can get married and have a family of your own."

Cody was surprised at Dan, but he said nothing. Laurie, however, said almost angrily, "I don't care what you say, Uncle Dan. Cody's marrying me and that's all there is to it. I have his promise for that."

"Only if your folks agree," Cody said quickly. "And I don't think they will."

Hope gave Dan a look that neither of the young people understood; then she turned back and, with an eloquent gesture, leaned forward, reached across the table, and captured both of their hands. "Oh, I think Tom and Faith will agree," she said softly.

"I don't see why they would, their daughter marrying a jailbird," said Cody, squeezing his mother's hand. Then he got up and walked to the window, looked out on the sunrise, and turned to face them, his lips drawn in a tight line. "I've given you nothing but grief, and I can't make that up to you, I know. But, I appreciate your standing by us." He hesitated, then said, "I'm going into town. Might as well get this over with."

"Oh, stay awhile," Laurie said. "You don't have to go right now."

Cody shook his head. "It'll just make it worse." He stood

there, a lonely figure illuminated by the light that flooded through the window. He had a youthful face, but the last months had marked it so that he was no longer the happy-go-lucky young man that he had been. There was a seriousness and a forcefulness in him now, Dan and Hope saw, that had not been there before. Suddenly he said, "But I've got one good thing to give you." He glanced at Laurie, who was nodding, and said, "I've found the Lord, and I'm a Christian now."

Dan slapped the table with a heavy hand and cried out, "Glory be to God!" He came to his feet, as did Hope, and the two of them went to him, hugging him.

"You don't have to smother me!" he finally gasped.

Pulling him back to the table they made him sit down and tell the whole story of his conversion, which he did. He spoke freely of Sam Novak, and of Mac McGonigal, and of Laurie, and how they had prayed for him. He told of Moody's meeting and the impact that gentle man had on him the night he had been dragged to church. Dan and Hope laughed at the picture he made of himself, roped and tied up like a Thanksgiving turkey, carried into church in front of thousands of people. "But," he said, "Mr. Moody had a real effect on me, and I never got away from it." He said then, "So no matter if I'm in jail, I know I have God."

Hope had tears in her eyes. She dashed them quickly with the back of her hand and said, "Son, you're not going to jail."

Cody stared at her, thinking he had misunderstood her words. "What do you mean, I'm not going to jail?"

"Tell him, Dan," said Hope.

Dan Winslow brushed his dark hair back, and there was a light in his face as he said, "If you had kept in touch, you could have saved yourself grief. Heck Thomas has been on the job for a long time. Now, he came in a month ago, and he had good news."

"He found out about the real killer?" Cody almost jumped at him.

"He did, and it didn't come as too much of a surprise to me. It was Pike Simmons."

Cody stared at him, then said, *"Pike Simmons!"* He slapped his fist into his palm, saying, "Of course, he had to have been paid to lie about me."

"Well, that's what Thomas found out."

"Why did he do it? Why did he lie about Cody?" Laurie asked breathlessly. Her heart was beating fast, and she held her hand over it as if to quiet it.

"Why, Tippitt paid him to do it, of course. He was so anxious to see his son avenged, and so sure that Cody did it, he made sure of it by hiring Simmons to swear to it in court."

Cody's hands were trembling, and his knees felt weak. "I don't see how Thomas made him change his story."

"Wasn't too hard. Simmons was arrested holding up a bank in Cheyenne. The gang all got caught, and the teller was killed. None of them were hanged, but they all got sentences of twenty-five years without parole. Pike Simmons didn't have a thing to lose."

"What did Mr. Thomas do?"

"Why, he promised Simmons a lump sum, which would be enough to keep him in cigarettes and the few things you can buy in the pen for a long time. It didn't amount to much, but that was all it took. He wasn't afraid of what Tippitt could do to him in the pen."

Cody stared at Dan for a moment, dazed by all of it. Then he asked abruptly, "But *why* did Simmons kill Harve?"

Dan shrugged his broad shoulders. "For the money, of course. He knew Harve had picked up a lot of cash from the bank and was taking it home with him. Simmons got drunk and followed Harve. He told Heck he tried to get Harve to frame a holdup, but when Harve refused, he just killed him out of hand."

Hope said, "How awful!"

"Simmons is an awful man," Dan responded. His eyes narrowed and he added, "Ironic isn't it? Tippitt's father is trying to avenge his son's death, and bribing the actual murderer."

Cody licked his lips. The news had caught him hard. He felt as if he had been hit in the stomach, and lost all ability to talk.

Hope saw his problem, came over, and put her hand on his arm. "It's all true, Cody. If we could have gotten to you, if we had known where you were, we would have told you. But, God has brought you here now."

Dan said, "You'll have to go in and go through the formality.

But, the judge says all we'll have to do is a little paperwork and you'll be a free man."

Suddenly, Laurie said, "No, he won't be free." They all stared at her in surprise, and she moved over closer to Cody and took his arm. "He won't be free. He'll belong to me."

Cody suddenly grinned and took her in his arms. "That's right. But you'll belong to me, too." A great sense of joy swept over him, and the heavy burden that had kept him in a state of doubt suddenly lifted. "It's almost like being saved again," he cried out. And then, ignoring his parents, he kissed Laurie soundly. She clung to him, and then stepped back, her face red with embarrassment.

Hope came to her at once and said, "I couldn't think of a better woman for my boy to have."

Dan stepped forward then for a kiss, saying, "Amen."

Cody said, "I've got to wire Sam, and you've got to get hold of Mac. They'll have to come to the wedding."

"Not so fast," Laurie said. "You'll have to do more courting than that. I'm going home, and you'll have to come there and face my father." An impish light came to her fine, dark eyes, and she said, "He'll be interested about that long trip we made together, alone without a chaperone. I expect he might have a shotgun waiting for you."

Cody blinked in surprise, then came to her and took her hands. "I don't care what he has, as long as I have you, Laurie."

The two were so lost in each other that Dan and Hope caught each other's glance and moved silently outside on the porch.

"They're so happy it almost hurts to look at them, doesn't it, Dan?"

Hope turned, and he took her in his arms. Her voice was muffled as she buried her face against him, saying, "I'm so happy." Then she lifted her eyes to him, and her lips trembled. "God never fails, does He?"

"Never," Dan said, and he looked back toward the house that held the young couple. "He never has, and He never will."